THE Thread THAT Binds THE Bones

NINA KIRIKI HOFFMAN

D0190676

AVON BOOKS • NEW YORK

THE THREAD THAT BINDS THE BONES is an original publication of Avon Books. This work has never before appeared in book form. This work is a novel. Any similarity to actual persons or events is purely coincidental.

AVON BOOKS
A division of
The Hearst Corporation
1350 Avenue of the Americas
New York, New York 10019

Copyright © 1993 by Nina Kiriki Hoffman
Cover illustration by Richard Bober
Published by arrangement with the author
Library of Congress Catalog Card Number: 92-97297
ISBN: 0-380-77253-1

First AvoNova Printing: May 1993

AVONOVA TRADEMARK REG U.S. PAT. OFF. AND IN OTHER COUNTRIES, MARCA REGISTRADA, HECHO EN U.S.A.

Printed in the U.S.A.

RA   10   9   8   7   6   5   4   3   2   1

For Dean and Kris and Kate and Damon,
who urged me to fix it and send it out;
For Matt, who encouraged me to clean it up;
And for Debb, the first reader of my dreams:
thanks for letting me use your shower.

Chapter 1

Tom Renfield kicked the door of the girls' rest room open and pushed the mop bucket in ahead of him, wondering if there would be any new graffiti since he last cleaned there a week ago. The room smelled of disinfectant and used tampons, with a hint of perfume. He flipped on the light switch just inside the door, driving night out the window, and glanced at the high pale ceiling to see if there had been any recent wadded-wet-toilet-paper fights. The kids at Portland, Oregon's Chester Arthur High School rediscovered every year that toilet paper plus water and soap equaled a missile that would stick to the ceiling, sometimes falling on somebody else later, which was a satisfying conclusion, worth double the pleasure of just getting something up and not having it fall down again right away.

No new ammunition hung up there, so he didn't need the ladder tonight. He trundled the mop bucket across the gray linoleum, past the stainless-steel half-moon-shaped sink, with its foot-activated sprinkler that sent out a semicircle of showers onto waiting hands, and past the mirror that still hosted a hundred anxious faces touching themselves up, or watching something other than themselves while they talked. Beyond the cloud of emotional memory he saw himself for an instant, startled as always that he had grown up, and up, and out; though he was twenty-nine, inside him there was still a skinny, blue-eyed, black-

1

haired kid waiting at a train station for an uncertain reception
as some new relative came to pick him up.

He parked the mop bucket under the wall by the window
and went back to fetch the toilet-cleaning tools from his
cart in the hallway, and when he pushed through the door
again, he heard whispers.

—Two more.

—When?

—Soon.

"Where?" he said, then shook his head.

—Two more.

—I'm tired.

—Now and forever.

Working in an ammonia haze, Tom scrubbed out the
sink, and then the toilets, wiping off the seats and leaving
them up. He emptied napkin repositories and trash, re-
stocked toilet paper and paper towels, and tried to ignore
the whispers. For almost twelve years he had kept them
away, but in the last two weeks, he had started hearing
them again, and he couldn't shake them out of his head
anymore the way he had managed to ever since high school
graduation. The headaches had also returned.

And the visions.

Having cleaned everything above ground, he was ready
to mop. He slopped the mop in the water, then put it in
the wringer and pulled the squeeze lever, keeping his eyes
away from the shadow in the corner next to the window.
He started mopping in the furthest stall, then along the
wall, and finally he had to look at the shadow as he approached it. It was a huddled girl, wearing a white sweater
and a plaid circle skirt, her dark hair bouffed up, pushed
back with a plastic headband, and flipped under at the
ends. She looked toward him through harlequin glasses
and held out her wrists, displaying the cuts across them.

—He brought me here to the dance and went home with
her, she whispered. Her face squinched up. —It was the
first time anybody ever asked me out.

"Boy, you teenagers," said Tom. The way her eyes

didn't quite meet his led him to assume this was one of the nonresponsive repeaters, stuck pattern ghosts who just said the same thing over and over, without paying attention to what was going on around them. "Doesn't take much, does it?"

Her eyes widened. She rose, hands clenching into fists—there was no blood, not on her sweater or her skirt, just the red lines across her wrists, like stripes painted on with nail polish—and stamped her foot.

—It's the most important thing I ever did!

"That's sad," he said.

She came and slapped him, momentum carrying her on through him. He shivered, not from a physical sensation of cold, but from the feelings of frustration and longing and anger and hate that animated her still, after all these years. The feelings were a sour-sweet taste on his tongue, a cold blade along his spine, a tingle on the back of his neck.

He spat in the sink, casting out her residue. Years ago he had hugged a ghost, invited her in, and she had melted into him and strengthened him; now she was braided so smoothly inside him that he no longer thought of her as someone separate. She had taught him that most ghosts weren't real people, just clots of strong emotion left behind by violent acts, sometimes even the residue cast off by people still alive. He had learned not to fear ghosts, but he didn't often like them.

When he had started hearing the whispers again, he sought for his internal ghost, wanting to ask her questions about what was going on now, why the whispers had come back, but the only person who answered his call was himself.

He missed her.

The shadow had gone, so he finished mopping.

—They bring more pain.

—Why did we do it.

—Now we can't leave.

—Wish they wouldn't.

"Who?" Tom said at last, as he watched streaks dry in the wet slick he'd laid across the floor. "Where? When?"

—They're sitting on the roof. The Caldecott Building. At dawn, they say.

He looked toward the window. The sky was already lightening in the east. The Caldecott Building stood across the yard, its square roof emerging from the departing night.

He dropped the mop and ran out into the corridor, the sound of his footsteps echoing in the wide dim space. When he had first come to Portland looking for work, he had searched for someplace away from death, despite the twelve-year freedom he'd enjoyed from ghosts and their noises. A high school, he thought; a high school would be fine; a lot of young energy, light thoughts, no whispers. Nobody he had known in high school had died there.

By the time he reached the double doors and unlocked them, the chill winter dawn reached halfway across the sky. The birds were in full voice in distant trees. He was afraid he was too late. As his shoes slapped the asphalt of the yard, he felt a headache building. His vision clouded. The sky looked wood-grained, pale violet striations and knots marking it, though they didn't stay still; they pulsed, in waves, some rising, some falling. The air tasted fragrant as fresh sawdust. His hands felt hot. Running toward the Caldecott Building, he glanced at his hands, saw the shadow waves rising from the ground, through him, slowing at his hands, as if he himself were air and his hands were the only solid. Something in him struggled, his ghost voice, perhaps, trying to speak after years of silence.

—There is a way we can—

He saw two people step up to the edge of the Caldecott Building's roof. Silhouetted against the rising light, veiled by the violet surge of waves, they stood on the parapet for long moments. "No," he said, then tried to yell it, but his voice was too ragged to reach that high. They would go over now and there was nothing he could do. Two more shadows would haunt the yard.

He stopped and clenched his fists. There was an answering ripple in the violet waves. He closed his eyes, trying to ignore the pounding in his head, and realized that his hands gripped something in the air, solid-feeling as wind was when he spread his fingers and let it pass between them. He opened hands and eyes and looked up, and the people, a boy and a girl, taking on features now that the sun was up a little, stepped off the roof, clasping each other's hands, and he reached up and tugged on one of the violet sky skins, stretching it, and it caught them.

His heart beat faster. Sweat sprang out under his arms, on his face and neck. He twitched the sky skin one way, and the people almost slid off it; jerked it back, and they were lying in a billow of it, cradled. He worked it like a stunt kite with sweat-slicked hands until the children dropped to the ground without harm, then released it; it fled upwards, past other waves, and stretched to nothing in the upper air.

Shivering, he stared at the boy and girl. The girl looked pale. The boy came at him. "What'd you do, Mr. Renfield, what'd you do? Why couldn't you leave us alone!" he yelled. His shoulders heaved with each fierce breath he took.

"You've got to think," Tom said. His teeth knocked against each other. Exhaustion lay on him like a heavy blanket. "There are too many ghosts here already. They live on their regrets. Don't do it."

"We *have* thought," said the boy. "We—oh, forget it!" He stamped away, gripping the girl's arm, dragging her toward the student parking lot.

"What happened!" said a voice. Tom turned and saw Betsy, one of the cafeteria workers, coming across the yard toward him. "What happened?"

Wondering how much she had seen, Tom shrugged and turned back toward the Rutherford Building. He had tools to put away before school started. He heard the cafeteria worker's steps following him a moment, but then they stopped. He managed to clean up and leave without running into her again.

* * *

Laura Bolte put the sack of groceries on the front stoop of her Portland apartment building and unlocked her mailbox. An advertising circular, a windowed envelope that she hoped held a check, and another envelope fell out. She caught the circular and the windowed envelope. The third envelope landed on the pale blue stoop. Square, thick, and apricot in the afternoon sun, it had fallen face down.

She hesitated. Something about the size and color reminded her of an afternoon from those childhood years she had cut off and cast adrift. She reached for the envelope, then snatched her hand back, remembering. Mother had asked her to address wedding invitations, since she had the best handwriting among the five children. Most of the envelopes went to the same place, to Southwater Clan down by Klamath Falls, but the head of every family must receive one, with each family member listed on the outside; it was part of the Way, the thread that bound the bones. Consulting the Family Book, Laura wrote and wrote, striving to make each letter of each name beautiful, until her hand shook with weariness.

She stared at the envelope. She wanted to step on it, pass over it and go upstairs, pretending she had never seen it. But that would cause trouble. The envelope had come to this address; therefore somebody in the family knew where she lived, despite her frequent moves. If someone could find her here, someone could find her wherever she ran.

She picked up the envelope, turned it over, and saw her brother Michael's handwriting.

She sighed, tucked the three pieces of mail in her grocery sack, lifted it, and went on into the building.

She had a walk-up on the third floor. She closed the door behind her and stood leaning against it, looking at her living room and wondering what Michael would think if he came here. Below three lace-curtained windows, a white couch held a scattering of small square delft-blue pillows. The round rug was white with a fleecy edge, decorated with a spiral of colored appliqué depicting vines. The coffee table, a brass frame supporting a clear glass top, held three magazines, one with Laura's face half-smiling from the cover.

She took three steps and set the groceries on the table, then picked up the magazine and stared at her own clean features, the wide beige eyes, the generous lips, the spills of curling, streaky blonde hair. She could smile on the cover of a fashion magazine because she trusted that no one at home would ever pick one up. Yet Michael had found her.

She dropped the magazine and collapsed on the couch, hugging a pillow to her stomach. The light seeped out of the day. She listened to a drip in the kitchenette sink, and thought about the frozen vegetables thawing in her grocery bag, and she couldn't find the energy to get up, because getting up would mean opening the envelope, and opening the envelope would mean Family trouble, no matter what was inside. She had made her life from scratch, and done it well; she spent most of her time feeling contented with her work, her friends, her home, her solitude; days went by without her feeling depressed, and she counted that a victory.

At last she sighed. She threw the pillow across the room, where it hit a large framed print, Klimt's *The Kiss*. She rose and took the groceries to the kitchenette, put them all away, and finally took the envelope and sat with it in the breakfast alcove.

Michael had most likely addressed the envelope in the kitchen cavern; he didn't like to sit still, and had no desk in his part of the house. Yet the paper carried no trace of home: cinnamon, incense, wood and candle smoke, roasting meat, dank earth; all the scents had been lost in transit.

She slid her finger under the flap and opened the envelope.

Please grace our union with your presence
Michael Bolte and Alyssa Locke
Will be joined, Powers and Presences permitting
September 24
Purification, September 23
We look forward to your arrival

She tapped the invitation on the table, biting her lip. She had a month to think about it.

Finally she got up and went to the phone. "Zandra?" she said to her agent. "I'm going to need some time off next month."

"What? You never take vacations."

"This is Family stuff."

"You have a family?"

"Boy, do I have a family."

"We've worked together three years, and you never had a family before." Zandra sounded suspicious.

"They just never caught up to me before."

"Is that what all this jumping around was about, all these forwarding addresses? This is why you keep running away from great opportunities for me to make lots of money?"

"Partially."

"And they found you anyway, huh?"

"Yeah. I should have known they would."

"Laura, once you do this family stuff, will you stop hiding out in the sticks and come to New York, where I can get you some really great jobs? I mean, now your family knows where you are, right? So you don't need to hide anymore, right? Or at least you could hide someplace sensible for a change, and do some better stuff than department store catalogs. Cover photographers don't go out there often enough."

"Once I do this family stuff, I don't know what kind of shape I'll be in." Laura blinked, hearing her own words. She laughed, then covered her mouth with her hand. "If I'm in decent shape, I'll think hard about it."

"Which days do you need off?"

Laura told her.

"I'll start apartment hunting, sweetie," said Zandra.

After hanging up the phone, Laura put the wedding invitation on the kitchen corkboard. She stuck the tack through the "o" in Bolte. She wondered if Michael felt it. She hoped so.

Chapter 2

Tom stood at the bar in the Dew-Drop Inn in Arcadia, a small town next to the Columbia River on the Oregon side, and glanced at the door, since it was after four and he had just heard the Greyhound bus pull in next to its one-window ticket outlet in the same building. If anybody got off the bus here, they might need a taxi to somewhere. Tom could use a fare; after ten months as a cab driver in Arcadia he knew that Bert Noone had given him the job out of charity, since there wasn't enough business for one cab, let alone a second. Bert had several interests in town, including real estate (not a very active market) and other, unnamed activities; whatever Bert was up to, he seemed to be able to afford supporting a supernumerary. He owned the garage where the cabs stayed when not in service, and it had a number of unused storage rooms above it. Tom lived in one of them, inconveniencing nobody.

The TV down the bar showed pre-game action, and the rest of the regulars clumped at that end, keeping their distance as they always did. Tom knew them by name and spoke to them in passing, and they were pleasant, but they never encouraged conversation.

That suited Tom, for the most part. He had come to Arcadia to get away from Portland and the people who were interested in him. After the peculiar press coverage of the suicide attempt he had foiled, and the thirty-fourth "make me fly like an angel" joke, he had walked away from his janitor job without picking up his last paycheck. The ease with which he gave his spider plant to his next-door neighbor, said goodbye to his apartment, and packed his duffel bag made him realize he still hadn't found the place he was looking for: home.

Something about Arcadia, a hundred and fifteen miles inland from Portland along the river, had whispered "stop here" to him. A ride had dropped him on the off-ramp. He had walked down into town, wandered into the Dew-Drop Inn, thumped his duffel down beside a table, and ordered a glass of milk. The first person he had met was Bert, who offered him a job without asking any questions except whether he could drive and memorize maps.

"Fella I had before you didn't last very long," said Bert. "It's not such a complicated town, but there are ways and ways of getting lost. You gotta be careful here, Tommy."

Tom memorized maps, then applied for and received a chauffeur's license. He hadn't changed his name since his brief notoriety in Portland, but few people in Arcadia took the *Oregonian,* and of those who did, no one appeared to connect him with the weird but accurate press story.

Tom spent some of his nondriving time in the bar, where Fred, the owner/bartender, let him run a tab. Bert had a half-time dispatcher, Trixie Delarue, who would phone Tom at the bar if anybody wanted a cab. On slow days or when Bert was on duty, Tom worked in exchange for things he needed. He chopped wood, washed dishes, cleaned buildings, repaired fences, weeded gardens.

He hadn't seen any ghosts since arriving in town, and he missed them. The people were kind but impenetrable; ghosts at least would have given him some kind of information. He had made one friend, Eddie, who pumped gas and changed oil at Pops's Garage, but Eddie was a short-termer like Tom, and he disappeared three months after Tom arrived in town.

Once when Tom was unloading produce at the grocery

store, Cleo, the grocer, watched him with such a sad look
on her face, he had asked what was wrong. "Nothing,"
she said. Then she shook her head. "You're a good
worker, Tom, and you seem like a nice fella. We'll be
sorry to see you go."

"But I don't plan to leave."

"People usually don't," she had said, and shrugged.

The Dew-Drop Inn was warm and much more comfortable than his room. It smelled of beer and smoke and
sawdust. It hosted a collection of strange taxidermied creatures—a two-headed lamb, a goat with a single horn, an
albino raccoon—on shelves above eye level. Taxidermy
was a hobby of Fred's son's, Fred had explained. Tom
had learned to ignore the creatures and watch people while
waiting for fares. During the quiet months of almost-
isolation he'd spent in Arcadia, Tom had noticed that the
starch in his shoulders was washing away. He was learning to relax again. It made him wonder what he had really
been feeling in Portland, and Reno, and Los Angeles before that. . . .

The pre-game action and ads ended, and the game began, sparking discussion among the regulars at the other
end of the bar. Tom heard the big door squeak on its
hinges, and turned to see a woman standing there, holding
the door open, autumn light behind her. Sun shone through
the edges of her cloudy light hair and defined her shape,
tall and slender. Tom finished chewing a mouthful of beer
nuts, washed them down with ginger ale, and waited,
wondering if conversation would be called for. The murmur from the other end of the bar stilled. Fred stopped
wiping glassware with the towel over his apron.

The woman stepped inside, letting the door close behind
her, and suddenly she had a face, pale and firm, a high,
domed forehead, slanting eyes and eyebrows, high cheekbones, a slender nose, full lips, and a strong jawline. She
wore a black knit dress with a pattern of hand-sized white
stars on it. It clung to her from neck and wrists to mid-

thigh. She wore black tights and flat black slippers. Tom felt something warm and strange stir inside him.

"Miss Laura," said Fred. His tone surprised Tom. He sounded scared.

"Hello, Mr. Forester. Could you tell me who drives the cab outside?" She sounded scared too.

"I do," said Tom.

"I need a ride—a long ride," she said. "Can you take me out to Chapel Hollow?"

"Miss Laura," said Fred, upset, as Tom grabbed his cap. Tom had seen Chapel Hollow on the map. It was about eighteen miles away.

"Mr. Forester, I need a cab. My car broke down on the highway, and the only way I could get even this far was on the bus. Michael's getting married tomorrow. I have to get home. Right away."

"Miss Laura," said Fred, and sighed. Then he said, "Tommy, could you come here and settle your tab?"

Tom turned and looked at the bartender. He had just paid up two days before, and Fred usually let him go a week between payments. Tom took out his wallet and walked down the bar to where Fred was standing.

"Don't take that Bolte girl all the way out to Chapel Hollow," Fred murmured. "Nothing but trouble out there."

Fred was the closest thing to a friend Tom had in the bar. Tom looked at Fred, who wore an expression midway between pleading and scolding. He glanced in his wallet, found a twenty-dollar bill, and handed it to Fred. "Thanks," Tom said, and headed to the door. As he looked at the woman, he listened to the first whisper directed his way he had heard since arriving in Arcadia.

—Come with me. Though the voice was a whisper, it was compelling and promising.

—Come on home, it said.

Awake, afraid, hopeful, Tom followed the woman outside.

The air had a nip in it—night frost had started the leaves

turning the week before—but even in her city clothes the woman didn't look cold. She was tall, must be around five ten; Tom didn't have to look down very far to meet her eyes. Her hair was the color of dried grass: brown, with streaks of bone and beige. Her eyes were the color of shallow water over sandstone. Her mouth did not smile, but her lips looked soft. She cast a glance at him, then walked down the sidewalk toward a soft-sided silver-gray suitcase with a camel-colored coat and a moss-green beret sitting on top. She stooped to lift the bag by a gray shoulder strap, but he beat her to it. She took her coat and hat, gave him a glimmering of smile, and climbed into the backseat of his cab. He put her suitcase in the trunk, then slipped in behind the steering wheel.

Like everything about Bessie, Cab Number Two, the radio took a moment to warm up. Tom pressed the transmit button and said, "Trixie, are you there? I've got a fare." He waited, but no answer came. Trixie only worked about half the time—when she knew planes were going to land at the tiny municipal airport, and most late afternoons and early evenings. The taxi company phone rang at her house, for those times when someone needed a taxi unexpectedly. Then she would phone, or come down and get Tom out of bed or out of the bar and send him out. She knew he always checked the westbound bus in the morning and the eastbound bus in the afternoon; still, she was usually in the office in the afternoon. He tried reaching her once more, with no luck, then shrugged and clicked the flag on the meter.

Bessie growled at him when he started her. She seemed to want to hibernate; the previous winter, he had had to coax her carefully for each start, and now she was getting sleepy with cold. Tom wallowed the car around and headed south out of town on Highway 21, up away from the river and the green it gave to the south shore and the town. Phone lines and barbed-wire fences kept pace with the taxi along the gray asphalt road. Magpies flew across the sky. Tom wondered what they found to eat in the desert scrub, the low lichen-looking green-gray bushes and the scatter-ings of black pumice rock, dead grass lending a warm brown tone to the country. Brown and black cattle drifted away over the rises.

The old cab ran quietly once she started. Tom watched the woman in the rearview mirror. Just being in a small enclosed place with her set something simmering inside him. The air carried a faint scent of cedar and sagebrush: was it hers? Light lay like milk on the curve of her cheek, the column of her throat, as she stared out toward human-shaped metal hieroglyphs a hundred feet high that carried power lines along the horizon.

—Come with me, something whispered, even though the woman was looking away from him.

With, the whisper had said. It had been so long since he had done anything *with* someone on any level below the surface.

When he turned left on Rivenrock Road, she met his eyes in the mirror. "I don't think I remember you from school," she said. "Not unless you're the Meyers kid and your acne finally cleared up."

There was a Scott Meyers about her age—looked like mid-twenties—who was a cook at the Ring-Necked Pheasant Grill. No acne. Tom said, "No, I'm new."

"Why would anybody move to Arcadia? I couldn't wait to get away."

"It's quiet here."

"You can't have been here long if you think that," she said. "The town runs on talk. They talk about seven generations ago, bring you up to the present, and predict that everything will stay the same in the future. That's why I left. I didn't want to get stuck on the same track as my ancestors and relatives."

"It's quiet here for me," said Tom. "I've only been here ten months. Hardly anybody talks to me yet."

"They probably talk about you, though."

"Not where I can hear. The ones who do talk to me seem to think I'm going to leave at any minute. It's like they don't want to get involved with me because I'm only temporary. I wonder if they'll feel that way after I've been here ten years.''

"Do you want to stay?" she asked, amazed.

—Almost home, the whisper said underneath.

Tom blinked at the woman's reflection, wondering which voice to speak to. At last he said, "I want to be here now. I feel as if something's about to happen." Hearing his own words, he realized that yes, that was the feeling he had had since he walked down the off-ramp from the highway. A feeling that slept, until she opened the door to the bar and stood there framed in light.

"Something *is* about to happen," she said. "My brother Michael is getting married." She hugged herself.

He could only think of soap opera reasons why she should be upset about her brother's getting married. He shifted subjects. "Your family lives out in Chapel Hollow?"

"Yes, for ages and ages."

A creek wandered around a low hill and passed under the road via a culvert. Its passage across the country was marked by a meandering line of willows, silver-gray and dusty after the summer's dry.

He said, "What do they do out there? Ranch? Farm?"

"Not really," she said. In the mirror he watched a slow smile surface. Her eyes caught and contained golden light. "No, that's not true. They do both; not commercially, just to supply the family."

"What do they do? Or shouldn't I ask?"

"You definitely shouldn't ask." But she was still smiling. Suddenly she leaned forward, grasping the back of the front seat. "No one from outside is allowed to ask! I am so tired of rules."

—I am so tired of rules, said the whisper.

"Does that mean you want to talk about it?" Tom asked.

She leaned over the back of the seat and looked at him, smiling, her head very close to his. "I'm glad you didn't grow up around here. If you had you would never talk to me this way. You would never have taken me as a fare, if I gave you a choice about it. What did Mr. Forester say about me?''

Sage and cedar and muted amber; the scent was coming from her. He felt hungry for her. ''He said your last name was Bolte.''

''So it is. Laura Bolte.'' She held out a hand to him.

''Tom Renfield,'' he said. He couldn't shake hands without twisting around and maybe losing control of Bessie, who tended to veer to the right given an ounce of opportunity. He touched Laura's fingers.

''Pleased—you don't know how pleased—to meet you, Mr. Tom Renfield. Oh, I love Outside.''

''Why?''

''Because I get to create myself from scratch. If you had gone to school with me . . . if you had grown up in this town . . . if your parents knew my parents and your grandparents knew my grandparents, you would have so many ideas about me there wouldn't be room for the real me. In fact, that's been my biggest challenge—rooting out what everybody's told me about who I am and how I should act, and trying to find out who I really am.''

''I came to Arcadia to ditch an identity,'' said Tom.

''You're—a Russian spy. An ex-con? A mysterious shy comic-strip writer escaping a rabid public? Naw. A country-western singer.''

''None of those,'' he said. He realized he was easing up on the gas pedal to prolong the time he spent with her. He glanced at her, those tan, lucent eyes so close to his, and saw a dimple in her cheek. So she felt stamped by history and heredity; he wondered if all of her family had her attractiveness. Being near her made him feel as if stars were melting in his chest. ''You're the only fare I've taken to this wedding. Are any of the rest of your family coming?''

''Very few of us ever leave,'' she said, and there was a chill in her voice.

"Who's going to perform the ceremony?"

"My great-uncle Jezra. They're flying him in."

"Your folks have an airstrip?" There was a crop-dusting airstrip a couple miles from town, but he hadn't heard of another aside from the Arcadia Airport.

"You might say that," she said.

He slowed to turn right on Lost Kettle Road. The hills rose steeply around them. The road wandered along an old stream bed. Columnar basalt cliffs reared up to the right, their black blocky faces like ancient architecture unburied by earthquakes. "In spring," said Laura, her voice soft, "a cloud of swallows haunts that cliff. I love those birds."

"I lived in a house that had swallows under the eaves once," Tom said. "I loved them too. I found little blue bits of eggshell on the ground, like pieces of sky."

She looked at him, and this look felt different from her earlier ones. Just then the car hit a pothole in the patched asphalt road, and she grabbed his arm to steady herself. The warmth of her hand came through his yellow wind-breaker.

—Who are you? asked the whisper.

"Stop the car," Laura said, low and urgent.

He pulled over at a wide place in the road, where the weedy verge dipped down to a ditch, then climbed beyond under a scraggled and rusting barbed-wire fence.

"You can let me out here," she said, releasing his arm and sitting back. She clutched her coat and hat and climbed out of the car.

He refused to get out. "We're miles from anyplace, Miss Bolte," he said.

"I'd like my suitcase. If you don't give it to me, I won't pay you."

"Please get back in the car. I don't want your suit-case."

"Tom, give me my suitcase," she said, in a concentrated version of her own voice. The whisper double-tracked her, almost speaking aloud.

He jumped out of the car, marched around to the trunk,

opened it, and got out her suitcase. As she took it from him, he woke up and realized what was going on. "Hey!" he said, closing his fingers over the shoulder strap before she relieved him of the suitcase. "What'd you do to me?"

"Goodbye, Tom Renfield." She tapped his hand and his fingers opened. Shouldering her suitcase, she strode off down Lost Kettle Road. "Go on back to Arcadia," she said over her shoulder.

"I'm not a puppet. And I want my fare."

"Go away!" she said in a harsh voice, the whisper expanding it. He started to walk away, then caught himself. Something warm was working inside him, amazed and amused by the fact that Laura could speak a command and he involuntarily responded to it.

—Funny! said a new whisper. It was a voice he recognized: Hannah, the little girl ghost he had welcomed inside him so long ago and lost. —About time we ran into something like this!

Puzzled and delighted, Tom went back to the cab. The engine caught on the third try. He drove after Laura, raising a thin pall of dust in his wake.

"I'll follow you all the way there. I'll get you all dusty. You might as well ride," he said to her profile as she walked. She smiled a little, then looked away.

"Go back," she said in a normal voice.

"No."

"No one naysays the Boltes," she said, and there was the strength of a thousand repetitions in her voice, and a touch of fear.

"Why won't you let me drive you?"

She got her wallet from her coat pocket and pulled out forty dollars. "Here's your fare. Now leave. I'll make it home from here okay."

"Six more miles, in those thin slippers? What's really the matter, Laura?"

She glanced at him as she walked. After a moment, she said, "I don't want you to get hurt. Everything my family touches gets hurt, and I don't want that to happen to you, Tom. I like you.''

He drove beside her, at her walking pace, for another quarter mile. Then he said, ''I want to go to this party. Nobody in Arcadia ever seems to celebrate anything.''

''Go away,'' she said, and a tear trickled down her cheek.

''No.''

She stopped walking and he braked, letting the engine idle. She stared at him; her lips tightened in a grim line. Then she went around the car and climbed into the front seat, putting her suitcase on the floor. She wiped a tear off her face and stared at him. ''You heard me. You understand, most of my family have a stronger command voice than I do. If you take me all the way to the house, where the heart of our power lies, you endanger yourself. People in my family don't bring home strangers; they bring home slaves. If you come home with me, that's what you can expect to be, Tom. These are the things I'm not supposed to talk to outsiders about. I have a lot of relatives, and they'll be at the Hollow, and they'll be feeling tense— marriage is a very serious business in our family. They'll probably welcome a chance to torture somebody new. Whatever Mr. Forester told you about us is probably true.''

''He didn't say much,'' said Tom. He flexed his hands on the steering wheel and looked at Laura. If what she said was true, why was her whisper giving him promises of Home? She wore a face of despair and resignation.

—Truth? his Hannah part whispered.

—Danger, said Laura's whisper. —Come on!

—Why?

—I need you.

Laura frowned. ''What is it?'' she said.

''Huh?''

''Why are you making faces?''

''Just talking to you underneath.''

''What?'' She gripped his arm. ''Who are you?'' she whispered.

"Me," he said. "Tom." Tom who moved seventeen times between the ages of nine and thirty, he didn't say, either underneath or aloud. Shadow-Tom. Nowhere Tom/Everywhere Tom. Tom who could find his feet in any situation.

"How can you talk underneath?" said Laura. "Are you one of us?"

"What do you mean?"

"How can you talk to me underneath, anyway?" she said in a dazed voice. "I can't talk underneath."

"I noticed you don't seem too connected to what you're saying," he said, and grinned.

—She believes she has no voice, said the whisper. —Tom. We're scared of going home. Please come. Please.

"Oh, please," said Laura in an annoyed voice. Then her eyes widened. "I get it. This is a trick." She leaned against the seat back, her shoulders sagging. "A trick. You're a cousin I've never met. You're going to betray me to the *Arkhos* for talking about forbidden things to strangers, and they'll cut the thread that binds the bone and cast me out unfamilied."

"Laura, I'm not a member of your family. I don't think I've even met any of them. I won't repeat what you say to me to anyone."

She reached out and flicked a thumb and two fingers in front of his face in a complicated gesture. For a second a tiny blue flame danced in the air. "Truth," she murmured, "as you understand it. What could you be, then? I don't trust surfaces. You are too perfect to be real."

"What?" he said, staring at her.

"You are my dream: an Outsider, tall, dark, handsome, friendly. Gifted. And you speak of swallows' eggshells, and look at me with appreciation. Can someone as perfect as you exist? I doubt it. Therefore—I get it—lifeskin. Michael has animated a log and placed it where I would stumble over it and desire it, and when I kiss you, you'll turn back to wood and he'll laugh."

"I don't think so," said Tom, turning the engine off.

They sat in the resulting silence. Crickets chirped from the dried grass beside the road. Tom held out his hand. Laura reached toward him. Her hand hovered, trembling, above his a moment, and in her eyes he saw doubts rise up and fade. She put her hand in his.

Though they waited a moment, he did not turn to wood. He felt the warmth in her palm and fingers. Her thumb stroked his knuckles. She smelled of sage and cedar. He waited, eyes half-closed, a long time, then tugged her closer. She slid down the seat to him, leaning into his embrace as he put his arm around her, her sandy eyes looking up into his, flushing golden. "Are you real?" she whispered, but her other voice whispered. —I know you're real. I want you.

Of all the whispers that he yet had heard, that one was the most charged, colored with all the shades of longing. He looked at her kindling eyes and knew he had never met anyone else he wanted so much to connect with, even though he didn't know her at all. He leaned down just as she tilted her face up, and they kissed.

Crickets cocooned them in sound; the cab's window was open, and the merest breath of breeze touched them, as if blowing into the autumn air from a next-door spring. The warmth in them grew. Her hands crept up to grip his head.

After a little while she relaxed her grip and he lifted his head. She sighed and snuggled against him, her hands sliding down to clasp his windbreaker. She opened sleepy eyes a moment later, and peered up at him, her smile spreading wide. She touched his cheek. "Still warm, still flesh," she said.

"Not everything exists just for your benefit."

"I learned that, Outside. It was a hard lesson, but I felt so much better. It's just that—when I get this close to home, every pebble on the road, every weed, every gnat could be a part of someone's plan, and most of my family's plans hurt somebody."

"Why not reverse it? Bring a pebble of your own." Tom touched his chest.

"No, Tom." She took his hand and kissed the palm. "Whatever—whoever you are, I want you safe."

The faintest sound of gravel grating on gravel, and then the car joggled and tilted. Tom reached out and grabbed the steering wheel. "Bessie?" he asked.

The landscape outside—low cliffs to their right, willows walking beside the stream to their left—dipped, and the seats pressed up on them, then relaxed. They were flying, car and all.

Chapter 3

Soundlessly, the car lifted higher than the treetops and cliffs, then cut straight across country, skimming over the stream as it wandered, over the road as it followed the stream, and over the flatlands, where brown and black cattle grazed on tough scrub and dried grass. Chill air whispered in through the open window. Ahead of them, the horizon was much too far away; a butte thrust up from the gently rolling hills.

Tom gripped the steering wheel with white-knuckled hands, everything in him stilled to a stop while he waited to understand what was happening. A prickling pain flickered behind his eyes.

They were flying. Flying.

He accepted it, and relaxed. The pain in his head intensified from pin pricks to ice picks.

"Damn," said Laura. "You see? Not even near the house, and someone's found us, probably Michael. It's too late for me to send you home, Tom, but I tried."

He managed to smile at her. "You tried," he said, his voice cramped by the pain. "Whatever happens next, I chose to be here for it." Out the window, trees passed silently below. He closed his eyes and the throbbing behind them deepened.

The car flew silently, without motor noise or wings.

As the kids had flown down off the building, when he pulled on the purple sky skins—

Pain dived down into the center of his brain. He gasped, clutched his head, and opened his eyes.

"Tom?" Laura murmured, as he gasped again.

Lavender wood grain streamed across the earth, across the sky. Knots and furls and ripples rose, sank, bumped, kissed, faded. The car rode on a purple wave, and it was being tugged by a twist of copper thread that disappeared into the sky ahead of them. A thin pink thread reached from the same distance, plunged through the car's hood and dashboard, and dove into Laura's chest. She was staring up at him, her eyes flecked with gleaming gold, her palms marked with glowing blue-and-gold spirals.

Tom took quick deep breaths. After that last overwhelming explosion of pain, his head had stopped throbbing. He reached out and touched the pink thread with the tip of his index finger, and felt warmth in his finger, followed by a thickening in his throat: affection. Affection stained by fear.

"What?" Laura said. "What is it?"

He rubbed his eyes hard enough to print purple stars inside his eyelids, then looked at her again. The wood grain, the threads, the glowing bits of Laura had all disappeared and everything looked normal again.

"I just saw—" he said. "I just saw the weirdest—"

"What?"

"Purple, and pink, and threads, and—" He took her hand and looked down into the palm. He touched the center. "Blue and gold."

Her eyes widened. She held her right hand over her left palm, and moved her fingers quickly. A blue and gold symbol flared in the air above her hand, then faded. "Like that?" she said.

"Sort of," he said, and traced the track of a spiral on her palm. "Does this sound crazy?" There were so many things he had learned not to talk about while he was growing up. He had seen layers of past lying transparent across

the present, people and things he could walk through who
didn't react to him. When he mentioned what he saw to
the people he was living with, he usually ended up living
with some other relatives. Learning not to see the things
nobody wanted him to talk about had helped a lot. This
deterioration of his self-imposed blindness bothered him.

Laura could flick her fingers and coax colored flames
out of the air.

"No," said Laura, closing her hand around his. "It
doesn't sound crazy this close to Home."

—Othersight, said her whisper. —Rare, but not unknown.

—Thanks, Tom's Hannah voice replied. Tom slid his
arm around Laura's shoulders, and she shifted to get comfortable. They sat watching the world approaching them
out the front window.

"Have you seen things like that before?" Laura asked
presently. "The colors?"

"Only once, like that. I used to see other things. Mostly
ghosts. I gave it up years ago, but it's been sneaking back
this year."

"And you're not a relative of mine? You're sure?"

—Am I? he asked underneath.

—Nobody we know, answered her whisper, —and we've
met every relative we have, here and at Southwater Clan.
If you're related to us at all you must be from one of the
Lost Tribes, who disappeared almost three hundred years
ago.

"You know I'm not," he said.

"Good," she said, giving him a smile.

Faintly they could hear the brook below, and occasion-
ally the calls of crows. Then the brook noise faded, and
the landscape in front of them changed from scrubby autumn sparseness to legions of dark evergreens. The cool
air smelled of clean pine. The ground dipped down between hills, and the car lowered to maintain a cruising
height a few feet above the highest treetops. At last the
car tilted groundward. Trees rose up around it. Unlike

Arcadia's tamed and well cared for trees, these trees looked tough and sassy.

The car sank and settled on a grassy spot facing the front of a house. Traces of a rutted road wandered off behind the car to disappear into the forest darkness. Before them, the house presented a central white front with a big wooden door set deep into it. On either side of the white section, the house straggled off into the forest in a mix of architectural styles, as if pieces from sixteen different jigsaw puzzles had been put together to form one picture— all the pieces fitting, without making sense. The center piece looked adobe, many storied, flat roofed, thick walled; the next piece on the left swelled from the earth, a mud bubble with trees on the roof and caves for windows. Spike-topped minarets showed through treetops, Persian tile patterns girdling them. What looked like a yellow cottage stood off to the right, smoke puffing from a crooked chimney set in a steep thatched roof, and ruffled gingham curtains showing at the windows. Beyond it loomed a weathered wooden barn, mostly obscured by trees. Something like a hex sign was painted above the barn doors, but it had no circle around it and it reminded Tom of the sign he had seen flaring above Laura's hand.

A man stood between the car and the front door, dressed dark so that he almost blended with the door. The house was so overwhelmingly weird that Tom didn't notice the man until he took a step toward the cab. His short curly hair was the same streaky blond as Laura's. He looked upset. He leaned over and peered in through Tom's open window. "What is this? Laura, are you fetchcasting now, of all times?" he asked.

"Didn't you figure that out when you did the comehither?"

"No, I just grabbed. You were getting too late." He frowned. "Besides, how could *you* fetchcast?"

"Well," she said, shrugging and reaching for her beret. Tom slid his arm from around her and they climbed out of the car. "Hi, Michael," Laura said, and stretched, then reached back for her suitcase and her coat.

Tom worked his shoulders, walked around the car, and took Laura's suitcase from her. Michael came after him. "Thanks for the ride," Tom said. He held out his hand to Michael. "Tom Renfield."

Michael took two steps back, his gray eyes catching fire. "Haven't you even started training?" he asked Laura.

"This is my brother Michael," Laura told Tom. "Michael, Tom is not my fetch. He is my guest. I grant him salt privilege."

Michael breathed loudly through his nose for a moment, then took Tom's hand. "Welcome," he said, gripping Tom's hand and releasing it. "Now, Laura? Why now?"

"*Skaloosh plakna,*" she said. "Anyway, you're the one who snatched the cab. He was going to drop me off and leave."

"You mean he's not even someone you know?" Michael opened and closed the hand he had gripped Tom's with, as if to shed Tom's touch. "Let's put him in the lower caverns and work on him tomorrow."

"No," said Laura. "Guest."

Michael looked at Tom with narrowed eyes, then shrugged.

"When's the wedding?" Tom asked.

"Tomorrow, Powers and Presences willing," said Michael. His shoulders were tight with tension. "Ritual purification starts in less than an hour, and you have to get ready. Were you planning not to come?" he asked his sister.

"I got here as fast as I could. The car broke down this morning and I had to catch the bus, and the cab—"

Michael sighed, irritation coloring it.

"Do you have an extra robe for Tom? He didn't have time to pack," she said.

"Come on," Michael said, turning and leading the way into the house.

Laura paused on the threshold after Michael had crossed

over, her hands in fists, and sketched some signs in the doorway with her thumbs, speaking softly in a language Tom had never heard before. A curtain of green and gold sparkles rippled across the doorway, then parted in the middle, the edges around the split lined with the welcoming orange of campfires on cold nights. "Wow," Laura said, looking back at Tom with a wide grin. She reached for his hand, and drew him through the opening; the curtain widened to accommodate him, then faded. Michael stood in the hall waiting for them, his arms crossed, his eyes wide, his face unreadable.

The front hall was dark and wood paneled, but as they walked, it widened into a mine shaft, timbers supporting scooped-out earth walls and ceiling, a board walkway granting them a path above an inch of chill standing water on the floor. The air smelled dank, edged with mildew. Swirls, spots, starbursts of green light flowed across the ceiling and in some places the walls, once even diving down below the water. At first Tom found it as dim as walking in a spook house at a fair, but then his eyes adjusted. It was still strange, but at least it was visible. Openings into rooms above water level on either side of the hall beckoned. Through doorways Tom saw rooms resembling pictures from various pasts: some like lived-in caves with firepits in the walls, furs on the earthen floors, and dressed stone furniture; others like castle interiors, tapestries hanging everywhere, heavy wooden furniture, and torches or candles in sconces, lit with flames that did not flicker; others held museum-quality artifacts from cultures all over the world, stone statues from Central America, wooden sculptures from Africa, an antique globe the size of a weather balloon, a glass-fronted case full of crystal and ivory figurines, a wall of amulets on red velvet behind glass, a Chinese vase as tall as a child, the lid of an Egyptian sarcophagus.

Michael rushed them, so Tom caught only intriguing glimpses. But he noticed two things: no people, and no electricity.

"You want your old room?" Michael asked Laura.

"All right," she said.

"Is he staying with you?"

She looked up at Tom. Suddenly he felt overwhelmed with the strangeness of the whole chain of events—meeting her, plunging into conversation, talking about things he had never discussed with anyone before, kissing her, flying here, and now her being asked if she wanted to share a room with him. After his mother died, he had learned to enter every relationship warily, watching and thinking and listening a long time before making a move, and even then maintaining distance—except for his relationship with Hannah, of necessity sudden.

Laura stared up at him with tawny, gold-touched eyes. Her arm was warm linked with his, and he had the growing conviction that he never wanted a door to close with her on the other side of it again. He smiled at her.

—Are you ready for this? he asked underneath.

—Are you? she answered, and he sensed a laugh in her voice. "Yes," she said to Michael.

The tunnel swelled out into a wide cold space, the ceiling vanishing up into darkness, pierced by five chips of white daylight. The green light curled and twinkled along the walls, vanishing down other tunnel mouths around the cavern. On the right, stairs chiseled from stone rose along the cavern wall. "Come on," said Michael, grabbing Laura's hand and dashing up the stairs, with Tom trailing after.

They climbed above the cold that pooled in the bottom of the cavern. The hall at the top of the stairs reverted to wood paneling and a more summery temperature. Frosted globes along the walls held moving blue-white light inside. Tom tried to stop and study one, since it looked as if a winged fairy were trapped inside, but Laura pulled him on down the hall.

There were doors along the hall, differing from each other in shape, size, and composition. Michael stopped in front of a standard rectangular wooden door with a crystal knob. Laura grasped the doorknob. "Thanks, Michael," she said. "Remember, Tom needs a robe."

Michael's eyes kindled again. "If you were any kind of a Bolte, you—" he began, then frowned and held his hands out toward Tom. He flicked his fingers. Tom felt the air tighten around him. He looked down at his chest and watched as the colors faded out of everything he wore.

After everything else that had happened, this was minor. He buried his hands in his now-white windbreaker pockets and shrugged.

Laura glared at Michael. Tom could sense the anger surging inside her, then felt it stop and freeze. "Your marriage," she said. "Your Purification. Your choice."

Michael's hands clenched into fists. He stormed down the hall away from them.

Laura turned the knob and led Tom into her room. When the door had closed behind them, Tom set down the suitcase and held his arms out. Laura stepped into his embrace. In this cold house, she was warm and breathing. She smelled clean and wild and alive, savory and enticing. There was strength in her hug, and tenderness.

—Are you all right? her whisper asked.

—Fine. I guess. What about you?

—Things could be a lot worse. I've got you.

"Don't you think we should talk about that?" he said aloud.

"About what?" Laura murmured to his shoulder.

He slid his hand up to stroke her hair. It felt soft and fine and smelled like herbs, with just a hint of flowers. "About having each other. You don't know a thing about me."

"But I *feel* like I—" She looked up at him and frowned. "Nnnn!"

"I know," he said. "I feel the same way. For the first time in my life. Enchantment."

"What?" Her eyes widened. "Oh, no!" She pushed him away, then worked her hands in the air between them. A shimmery pink thread stretched from his chest to hers, and a blue light shone between their foreheads. After a second, both faded. "No," she said. "I don't know what that meant, but I didn't put you under a spell to get you out here."

"I never thought that," he said.

"But that's what people in my family do. They ensorcel people out here and then use them. I thought I didn't have the power to do that. I was glad, too, because I don't want it."

"I came here under my own power."

"There *is* some sort of spell—it showed just now when I did 'things seen and unseen.' But it's something besides fetchcasting." She smiled.

—I know, he said.

—This is right—don't you think? asked her whisper.

—I do, he whispered, and listened to the mental echoes of that.

She smiled and patted his cheek. "Going to be fun finding out just what this is, don't you think?"

"I'm looking forward to it," he said, though the prospect terrified him on one level. He wanted to find out everything about Laura; on the other hand, he had spent so much of his time learning to hide who and what he was. . . . He looked around.

The room was windowless and dim. Laura, noticing his interest, walked to one wall and waved her hand at a bump in the rock that was letting out a night-light's amount of light, and it brightened. On a shelf near the light, frozen crystal horses pranced. The bed wore a fluffy white quilt and had a rose-speckled canopy above it, and the vanity, dresser, and desk were white and spindly, trimmed with gilded handles. An array of thin-necked odd-shaped bottles clustered on the vanity. Laura glanced around, then looked back at Tom, her mouth quirking into a grin.

"How much of this is you?" he asked.

"I chose it all. My dad got it for me. He's probably the nicest person you'll meet out here." She raised her eyebrows.

—How much of this is you? he asked.

—None. We copied it from somebody's house in town. She's been searching for an identity for ages now, looking for one that doesn't connect her to the rest of the family.

"Well, that's a relief," Tom said.

"You're relieved that I chose this?"

"I'm relieved that you copied it from someone else."

"Hey!" she said, angry. "How did you figure that out?"

"You told me."

"What?"

"Underneath."

"I did not—" she began, when the door opened. Michael tossed something white into the room, yelled, "Half an hour! Please, please get ready!" and slammed the door again.

Laura took a deep breath and let it out slowly. "Okay. We have to let this go for now, because part of getting ready for Purification is clearing your mind. Please stop asking me things underneath, though, unless it's an emergency. I'm not ready for it. I don't want to think about it yet. I *know* I can't talk underneath . . . what did I say?"

"I'm sorry I'm confusing you. You told me you copied this from someone in town because you were looking for ways to be different from the rest of your family."

For a moment she stood and stared at him, wide-eyed. Then she took her lower lip between her teeth, and looked down. "All right." She shook her head, looked up. "All right. I'll worry about this later. For now, we have to—" She glanced toward a door that didn't lead back out into the hall. "Well, we have to take a shower. I don't think there's time for two separate showers. Besides, I have to tell you about the cleansing. Ready?"

He wanted very much to ask her underneath how often she took showers with strangers, but he resisted the temptation, instead bending to pick up the white thing Michael had thrown into the room, then following Laura into the bathroom.

Chapter 4

The bathroom was spacious and tiled in white and blue, with white light coming from a bump on the ceiling. The air smelled like lemons, real ones, not the kind in bathroom cleansers. The room looked surprisingly modern compared to everything else he had seen in the house. White towels lay in fluffy stacks on shelves behind the door. The shower, enclosed in frosty glass, was the size of a small elevator.

Laura sat on the toilet and slipped out of her shoes, then stood up to slide her tights down. After stuffing the white robe over a towel rack, Tom took off his jacket and looked at the back, examining what had formerly been black stitched letters spelling out "Bert's Taxis" against a background of taxi yellow. Now the script was white on white and looked classy but unreadable. His T-shirt, red only half an hour ago, was ice white as well. He pulled it off and draped it over another towel rack.

"I forgot my robe," Laura said, and ducked out of the room. Tom sighed and took off his hightops, socks, and jeans, and then she was back, placing her robe on the rack beside his, sliding the knit dress off over her head. Her bra and panties were black, with blue and green flowers on them, and lace. Her face was red. The blush spread across her chest. Tom guessed she didn't do this so often after all.

34

"I will if you will," he said, gripping the elastic of his jockey shorts.

"Right," she said, and they both got out of their underwear. She turned on the water; it rained, steaming gently, from the ceiling of the shower.

"The thing is, we have to start clearing our minds, no matter how hard it is in this situation," she said. "You stare at me and I'll stare at you for a couple minutes, so we can get that over with, okay?"

"Okay," he said.

Her breasts were small, tipped with rosy brown. She had tan lines, but she had tan inside them, too, so she didn't always wear a suit in the sun. Her hair below was the same color as her hair above, and her belly and thighs and upper arms were muscular but soft-edged. Everything about her made him want to touch her.

"Glad you like me," she said.

He looked down at himself, then up at her, and gave her half a smile, half a shrug.

She said, "I like you too. Now I'm going to pretend I'm about ten and have never had any thoughts like this."

Tom closed his eyes and remembered being ten: maximum insecurity, still struggling to figure out what he shouldn't say, do, or notice. It varied from household to household. At ten he had lived with Aunt Hermione, a spinster, who didn't like anybody to talk about anything that had to do with the body. Birds, cats, flowers, and weather were just about the only safe topics. Thinking of begonias, Tom opened his eyes again and followed Laura into the shower.

"Um," she said. "This is stronger in *Ilmonish*, but I don't think it would work for you, so let me translate. Hmm. Okay. Please say this: Powers and Presences, grant us your aid in preparing our thoughts and our bodies for you. Guides and Good-wishers, we now seek our balance for Purification; we make ourselves new."

He focused on the words, and with a little coaching, he memorized them. They circled in his brain, eclipsing his interest in anything else, which helped. By the time he and Laura emerged and rubbed down with fluffy towels, he felt trapped and tranced in the circle of words, his heartbeat slowed, his tension gone.

The robe Michael had left for him resembled a long-sleeved choir robe, covering all of him except his hands and head. He glanced at his now-white hightops, wondering if he should put them on, but Laura shook her head and gripped his hand. Without a word she led him out into the hall, where they joined other white-robed people walking toward the stairs. A thread of chant resembling the one Laura had taught him murmured among them, but other than that they moved in soap-scented silence, bare feet whispering on the stone floor.

Down the stairs they went, and then along a tunnel that eventually led outdoors. Night had fallen, the dark sky hosting hundreds of twinkling autumn stars. The air was cool and so was the ground, but not uncomfortable. Breeze moved the pine needles against one another in the surrounding trees, so that the night whispered of ocean and smelled of evergreen spice. A path lit by globes of golden light led through the grass to a natural amphitheater formed of columns of basalt. People scattered in a circle on the flattened earth in the central arena, and then, when all was calm and silent, the ritual began.

People formed a loose ring, each an arm's length away from the next, except for Michael and a young woman, who stood side by side in the center. White garments shimmered in the gold-globe-speckled darkness as if the people were a company of ghosts. A light fingering breeze brought the odors of grass and dust and dew, pine and woodsmoke. A silver goblet passed from hand to hand, and each person sipped; when Tom received it, he saw what looked like water. When he sipped, he tasted sea.

A very old man with a feathery nimbus of hair called a chant in some language full of hisses, hard consonants, and broad vowels. Even without a translation, Tom could tell it was a summoning. It called to something inside him.

He felt the pounding begin behind his eyes, keeping time to the old man's words. Tom squinched his eyes shut, thinking about all the defenses against expanded vision he had built and shored up these twelve years. He murmured, "I release you and I thank you" three times to his protection. A weight that had bowed his head and hunched his shoulders melted away; he could feel his body straightening, delight and relief sparking through it as he drew in deep breaths and released them.

At last he opened his eyes.

Tall shadowy figures rose from the earth, descended from the sky; some traveled outside the circle of people, others drifted inside, stooping to glance into faces, though the people did not glance back. Globes of light danced around and through these phantoms, and little darting sparks flew everywhere. People chanted, calling responses to lines the old man sang out, and the phantoms paused to listen. They all drew in around Michael and the woman in the center. Many-colored lights bloomed and flickered.

The old man called a question.

A pillar of light descended from the sky, shining on the woman. She stood, patient and calm. Tom squinted. The light sliced through her, then shone from inside her, though her expression never changed; she maintained a serene smile. At last the light faded.

The old man called the question again.

This time the white light from the sky shone on Michael. After a moment he fell to the ground, writhing and gasping. He curled up. Veins stood out on his forehead and tendons ridged his throat. Tom took a step toward him, but one of the phantoms turned and held out a hand to stop him. Michael drew in a breath and held it, struggling, perhaps, to let it out, but choking instead. Before he strangled, a shaft of orange light joined the white light that pinioned him, and he relaxed. Breath moved in and out of him, and the rigidity that had held him captive released him. He struggled to his feet, gasping. He smiled. He held out his hand, and the woman beside him took it.

The old man cried out again, a blessing and a thanksgiving, and suddenly everyone in the circle sang a phrase.
The words repeated, but the melody changed slightly with
each repetition. Tom felt his voice trying to sound with
the others, but he did not know the words or the melody.
His heart hurt. Here at last was a home, a family, united
in something. He didn't know what, but he longed to be
part of it. He felt like a dark silent link in the chain of
singing people.

One of the phantoms, a gaunt old man whose eyes
glowed silver—the same one who had gestured him to stop
earlier—came and touched his arm. Tom felt the brush of
a warm feather.

—If you give me leave, I may aid you, the phantom
whispered.

Tom glanced at Laura beside him. Her gaze was fixed
on the couple in the circle's center, and her mouth was open,
song coming out of it. She didn't react to this strange old
man. Tom looked at the ghost again. He had seen so many
ghosts. Most of them didn't talk to him; of the few who had,
some were intent on their own ends, and others were full of
deep sadness. One or two had helped. Hannah had helped;
he wasn't sure he would have survived without her. Tom
stared into the ghost's face. The ghost was not a repeater; he
was alive in this moment, full of energy. His silver hair
crackled about his head. His face looked harsh and lived in,
the brows craggy above the deep-set silver eyes, the mouth
deeply bracketed, smiling now as if smiles came naturally.

—All right, Tom said.

The phantom walked into him, disappearing. He felt it
shrugging him on like a comfortable coat. It tingled inside
him, shivering like a plucked string, but then the strangeness faded. He opened his mouth and sang with the others.
He still didn't understand the words, but the sense of community was strong: he felt linked to everyone here in a
way he had never felt connected to his own relatives, and
he savored the warmth of it.

As they sang, small lights darted among them like

fireflies, touching, tasting, flitting off. Large, bumbling
globes of light moved about too, and the phantoms, not
all of them shaped like human beings, danced above and
below, sinking into the earth and rising into the sky,
weaving between the people.

A shaft of white light came down from the sky again,
this time touching Tom. The phantom walked out of him
and stood before him, watching, its eyebrows lifted. Tom
looked up, but could not see a source for the light. Then
he could no longer move. A vibration like a very low note
felt through the feet rather than heard moved through him,
sorting and searching him. He felt shaken. At last the sorting stopped, and the light vanished. One just like it shone
down to envelop Laura. Her eyes widened. She stood
quiet, and after a moment the light went away again. There
was so much light and spirit activity Tom was not sure if
he and Laura were the only ones singled out or whether it
was happening all around the circle. A globe of green light
came to him, floated just in front of his face, reached out
soft, nonsolid fingers to touch his cheeks, then slid into
his eyes. He blinked, blinded for a long moment. When
he could see again, he saw a glow surrounding his hands.
His right hand lifted without his volition. Laura's hand
grasped his. A glow haloed their clasped hands. His eyes
met hers; her face had a faint blue glow, and she looked
startled. Her voice faltered in the chant, then returned
stronger. They both faced toward the circle's center, but
he felt as if he could see her still, as if something flowed
back and forth between them. Tom's attendant phantom
slipped back inside him, this time not even tingling, and
Tom became a participant again.

He saw the white light touch down elsewhere in the
circle. It skipped some people and touched others, who
froze until the light left them. He saw light slide over
someone small across the circle and stain night blue, then
flick off. The next moment it lanced down somewhere else.

Presently the little firefly lights winked out. The phantoms vanished or seeped away. Then all light withdrew

except starlight. The old man broke the chant in a natural place, and sang something else. Everyone sang a response and held hands up to the sky; Tom sensed energy leaving, something borrowed being returned. But he did not see the green light that had entered his eyes leave. The old man gave another thanks and blessing, and everyone repeated it. In the ensuing silence, they all left the amphitheater without a word.

Tom touched Laura's hand again, and she gripped his. In the night the back of the house looked like a mountain riddled with tunnel openings, some spilling golden light, many dark, some covered with cloth (light leaking through the weave) or glass. People scattered and disappeared into the house.

Laura waited until everyone else had gone in. Her hand was hot in his. He looked into her face, saw uncertainty. Her hand tightened on his and she led him into a central opening toward light that strengthened as they walked.

Chapter 5

The air tasted of roasted meat and woodsmoke. Yellow light came from a side opening ahead of them. Voices murmured.

Though he had not consciously closed his othersight eyes, everything looked normal to Tom, no ghosts, no purple layers in the air, no threads or lights out of place. He glanced around. Stone walls, stone floor, flickering light ahead, and Laura, beside him, her hand in his. The white robe covered her. Her face looked young and worried.

"What is it?" he murmured.

Her gaze flicked to his face, then away. "Come, please," she said. They turned through the opening and stepped into an enormous cavern. Candles and oil lamps flickered in many niches. To their right, a fire crackled in a fireplace the size of a small garage. Nearby lurked counters, a giant butcher-block table, two huge copper sinks, and woodstoves big enough for a person to sleep in. Herbs, garlic braids, chile ristras, and other drying plants hung from the ceiling in braids and bunches. Pots and pans dangled from pegs in the rock walls, and freestanding cupboards stood against other walls.

To the left was a wide open space; most of the light concentrated there. In the center stood a rectangular stone table with stone benches around it. White-robed people were sitting down at the table. Two robed women, an older one with gray hair and glasses and a middle-aged blonde one, were taking a cauldron off a hook above the fire, and a stocky dark man was filling a tray with crystal cups from one of the cupboards.

Laura led Tom to the table and tugged him down beside her on the end of a bench, then released his hand. He glanced at people around the table. Some were dark, some light. Many had traces of the strange slant-eyed good looks Laura had; in one or two the effect was even stronger, verging on the unearthly. Others had a stocky solidness that squared their faces and gave them gravity. Something about them, though, made it clear that they were all related, maybe just the angle they held their heads, alert and curious as birds.

The cauldron's steam scented the air with mulled cider. The women and the man brought their burdens to the table. Someone else went to get a ladle, returned, and filled cups with fragrant honey-colored liquid.

Michael and the woman he had stood beside during the ritual sat at the head of the table, and the old man who had led the chants sat with them. Cider cups traveled around the table until everyone had one. Tom warmed his hands on his cup. He realized he had not eaten in a long time.

The old man said, "The auguries were good." He broke into a smile.

"Praise be," said one of the cauldron bearers, the blonde woman. Her short hair was streaked with varied shades of blonde, like Laura's and Michael's. Her face was square and solid, but her nose was the same shape as Laura's. She looked at Michael. "You took an awful chance, son," she said. "Why didn't you tell us you weren't ready for this? We could have waited a month for you to prepare."

"Preparation wouldn't help," he said. He glanced at a small white-haired woman down the table from him. Her dark eyes glittered as she stared back, her mouth thin and grim. Michael lowered his gaze and traced a pattern on the table with an index finger. "I'm surprised I got off as easy as I did."

"Mischief saved you. She wants progeny," said the blonde woman. "Alyssa, you have bride's right of refusal, having seen how short Michael falls. Do you wish to exercise that right?"

The woman beside Michael put her hand over his and smiled down at her cup of cider. "No," she said. "I would aid Mischief; there's been little enough of that in my life."

"Then let us toast a wedding," said a man with a thick red mustache, holding his cup aloft.

"A wedding," everyone echoed, raising their cups, then taking swallows of cider.

Tom choked on a clove. Laura patted his back as he coughed.

"Oh, yeah. Now that that's settled, what about him?" Michael asked, pointing at Tom.

Tom stopped coughing, held his hand in front of his mouth, and looked up to see everyone staring at him. Few of the faces looked friendly.

He felt a thrill of apprehension. Laura had warned him. Time to face whatever came next. He sat up straight.

"Daughter, who is this?" asked the blonde woman.

"Tom," said Laura. "I gave him salt privilege."

"Let's be accurate," said the mustached man. "You've given him rites and robes. Where did you get him?"

"In town," said Laura. "He's a cab driver. He drove me out here."

The tiny white-haired woman leaned forward, her small hands crabbed into claws, but before she could say or do anything, the slender blond man beside her said to Laura, "You miserable excuse for a Bolte. You never applied yourself to the disciplines, and now you're polluting an important occasion! Why didn't you just stay gone?"

"Hey, wait a minute!" Michael yelled, and—

"Carroll!" cried the blonde woman, and—

Tom blinked. The room tingled with strange forces.

Othersight returned: he saw hazes of colored lights everywhere. Small bright-hued presences lurked in the shadowed reaches of the ceiling, and each of the people at the
table wore a halo of force. Carroll's was strong and fiery;
the tiny old woman beside him wore a vivid shawl of
green, red, and blue-black lace touched with flickers of
ice blue. Setting down his cup, Tom leaned across the
table, grasped a handful of Carroll's red aura, and tugged
on it, startling a gasp out of the other man.

"What happened?" asked someone.

"Listen, Uncle Carroll, I invited Laura here. Leave her
alone," said Michael.

"Anyone watching the Powers would realize Laura was
guided," said the blonde woman, Laura's mother. "She
and this boy were matched. Didn't you see it? Who are
you?"

"Tom Renfield," said Tom.

"What did you do to Carroll?"

"I don't know, but I can do it again." He stared at
Carroll, whose opalescent green eyes stared back, watch-
ful, not afraid.

"What do you mean, May, matched?" the mustached
man asked Laura's mother.

"They got the wedding test, and neither of them
flinched. And they got glows, Hal."

Everyone talked at once.

"What's a glow?" Tom murmured to Laura.

"Those fireballs," she said, "the ones that came in our
eyes." She seemed upset.

"What does that mean? What does any of this mean?"

"Don't you know?" she asked.

"No. I don't know about any of this."

"But you were singing," she said, *"you knew."* Her
gold-blue halo was stained with sickly yellow.

"A ghost helped me with that. I didn't understand any
of the words."

"A ghost?"

He blew a breath up, ruffling his bangs. "There were a lot of ghosts. I thought—didn't you see them?"

"I saw light," she said.

"There was light, and there were all these ghosts. Some were people, and some were animals and monsters. One came inside me. He knew all the words."

"What?" The sickly yellow in her halo was changing to pink.

"Laura!" said Laura's mother.

Laura turned.

"Laura," said her mother, softer this time, smiling. "Do it."

"But Tom doesn't understand."

"That doesn't matter. The Powers and Presences understand. Do it."

Laura turned to Tom. "Will you marry me?"

Startled, he sat back. "I think we should talk about this in private."

"That's not how we do things around here, Tom."

"You can refuse her," said Laura's mother. "You run the risk of offending the Presences and Powers, though. They have linked you during Purification, and they can be capricious if you ignore them."

"This is all new to me. I don't even understand what we just did."

"Don't pollute our blood, fetch," said Carroll. The tiny white-haired woman beside him gripped his arm, grinning, revealing small pointed teeth. The red in her halo darkened.

"Carroll, you court dismissal from this council," May said.

"You don't have that authority."

Tom felt the plucked-string tingle warm his throat. "No," said someone else's voice coming from his mouth (that had happened with Hannah and felt strangely familiar), "but I do. Get thee gone, descendant, ere I unleash the deep fire on thee."

Carroll's eyes widened. He stood up, stared at Tom a moment, and walked out of the room.

The tingle spread through him. Tom felt very strange, as though he were a passenger in his own body. This expansive a possession had never happened with Hannah. It wasn't uncomfortable; he just didn't know what he was going to do next. Mentally he sat back to await developments.

The ghost studied everyone sitting around the table. They all looked shocked. The ghost smiled at them.

The mustached man cleared his throat. "Uh—Honored Presence?"

"Yes, descendant?"

"Is this . . . *tanganar* a worthy candidate for my daughter's hand?"

Tom felt a deep laugh sweep through him; he couldn't stop chuckling. At last, still gasping, the other used his mouth to say, "Descendant, this too is Mischief's province. Pronounce a binding while I hold sway here; it would be thy worst night's work to let this . . . *tanganar* escape."

Laura paled. Her eyes kindled. "I won't! I won't get bound by deceit! I refuse."

"Thou wilt," said the ghost. "Ancient?"

The old man who had led the chants smiled, his eyes sparkling like aquamarines set in silver.

"In brief, for a favor," said the ghost.

"Do you, Thomas Renfield, take Laura Bolte as your wife?" said the old man.

The ghost opened his mouth.

—Wait a second, Tom thought.

—What? said the ghost.

—Let me.

—Will you say yes?

His Aunt Rosemary, favorite and kindest of all his relatives, had told him, "Never rush into anything—unless into is the direction you want to go." He studied Laura, who believed in ghosts, who made light from nothing,

who had the biggest family he had ever seen, and who
eclipsed everyone he had ever dreamed about.

—Yes. Oh, yes, he thought.

—Very well. The ghost let him own his throat and
mouth.

"Yes. I do," he said.

"Do you, Laura Bolte, take Thomas Renfield as your
husband?"

"I—" She looked at Tom, who nodded. "I do," she
said.

"By my lively antiquity, by Powers and Presences above
and below, by ancestors and descendants, by sun and sky,
by earth and ocean, by all auguries, which read exceeding
well tonight, I pronounce you husband and wife," said
the old man. He smiled.

"Honored," said the mustached man, "are you still
present?"

"Yes," said the ghost.

"Will you tell us the joke now?"

"No." He laughed again, then fled out the soles of
Tom's feet, leaving him in mid-ha, so that he blinked and
closed his mouth and stared around at all these strangers.

Laura looked at him. "Tom, is that you? We're married," she said.

"I know."

"We can unbind it. There are some old forms of unbinding—"

"Laura!" cried her mother. The tiny white-haired
woman across the table leaned forward, cocking her head
and studying Laura. Her black eyes glittered.

"—in the memory books in the library," Laura said.
Her voice was tight. "One has a list of all the unbindings,
from cotton thread up to the Great Unbinding. I know
there's a special unbinding for marriages. I can find it if
you want."

"I don't want. That was my voice saying 'I do.' Do
you want to undo it? I know he didn't give you much
choice."

Laura shook her head. "No. No. You're my Outsider." She grinned up at him. Then she sobered. "We have a lot of things to work out, though."

"You said it. For starters, who are all these people?" Something tapped him on the head, then rang on the stone floor. He looked up, surprised, and saw something else falling, glinting. He reached out and caught it. "Wait a minute. May I have your hand?"

She held out her left hand and he slid a ring onto her third finger. The jewelry was a delicate gold band set with a small lapis lazuli scarab. She stared at her hand, then at the ceiling, and finally at the floor. After a moment's study she reached out, and the ring that had fallen first leapt up onto her palm. She took Tom's left hand and slid the ring onto his third finger. He looked at his ring. It was braided gold and silver, set with a black onyx seal depicting a Roman soldier's head. Laura kissed Tom.

He kissed her back, then looked up at the ceiling. Hazy glows moved about. "Thanks," he said.

"Do things like this happen to you often?" Laura's mother asked.

"No," he said. "This is my first marriage."

She laughed and leaned forward, holding out her hand. "I'm May Bolte, young man, Laura's mother. Welcome to the Family. I didn't mean the marriage part," she continued as he shook her hand. "I meant the lights, the possession by a ghost, rings falling from nowhere."

"No," he said. "No, that doesn't happen every day either."

"Let me see those rings," said a stocky blond man. Laura held out her hand, and he tugged at the ring, which didn't budge.

"Cut it out, Jess!" she said, jerking her hand back.

"All right, all right, just let me look at it, then." He grasped her hand and held it closer, leaning over to scrutinize it, snapping his fingers and producing a small light ball. "Old, very old. I think I read about this in one of the seventeenth-century ship manifests." He grabbed

Tom's hand and studied his ring. "Yes," he said. "These have been missing almost three hundred years."

"This is my oldest brother Jess, the family historian," Laura said to Tom.

"Right," said Tom.

"My father, Hal." She pointed to the mustached man.

"What's a *tanganar?*" Tom asked Hal.

Hal licked his lower lip. "Which Presence did you host, do you know?"

"What?" Tom sat back. "I—I hosted Peregrine." He touched his forehead. "Weird. I didn't know till you asked me, but he left traces. Peregrine Bolte."

"Did he tell you the joke?"

"No, and I notice you're avoiding my question."

"*Tanganar* are the mind-deaf, the ungifted, the powerblind." Hal shifted in his chair. "I take it you are not *tanganar.*"

"Probably not," said Tom.

"There are tests—"

"Stop it, Dad," said Laura. "Tom, this is my Greataunt Agatha Keye, *Arkhos,* and Uncle Christopher and Aunt Hazel Keye, my younger brother Perry and my little sister Astra, and Great-aunt Fayella, who teaches us all the special disciplines—" She pointed to the tiny whitehaired woman across the table, whose eyes were bright as fresh-spilled blood, whose mouth had returned to its grim line. "My brother Michael you met; Alyssa Locke, from Southwater Clan, is his fiancée; Great-uncle Jezra Bolte, who married us; Uncle Ferdinand and Aunt Sarah Keye; Cousin Hilary Locke, Cousin Lucian Seale, Cousin Keziah Bolte, Cousin Meredith Seale—of the other people at Purification, about half came up from Southwater Clan, and a bunch of the others have already put in a hard day and have gone to bed. This isn't a full formal council meeting. You going to remember everybody?"

Laura's parents, Hal and May, were distinct to him already. Hilary was the stocky dark man who had fetched the glasses. Great-aunt Agatha had thick glasses and gray hair, and she had helped May carry the cider cauldron to the table. There was no way he could forget Fayella; she gave him the creeps. Jezra, still beaming, looked older than everyone else. Laura's brothers and sister sorted themselves out in his mind. The others blurred. "Hello," he said.

"Enough chitchat," Great-aunt Agatha said. Her glasses glinted in the candlelight. "You've had the wedding. Now we need the consummation."

"Is that something we have to do in public too?" Tom asked.

"No. The house will let us know when it's happened. Go away, youngsters."

"But—" Perry said.

"You had better not say what I think you're about to say, young man," said May. "I repeat, the Presences matched them, and no one with wisdom would come between them. I don't know if that applies to you, Perry. I don't like to get too optimistic about you children when you've given me so little evidence."

Tom rose, Laura's hand in his. "Good night," he said as Laura stepped over the bench. She led him away, leaving sounds and scent and very breath of the family behind in the lighted kitchen. They held hands as Laura navigated twisted ways to take them back to her room.

Chapter 6

"Whew," said Tom as Laura closed and locked her bedroom door with them safely inside.

"Are you all right?" she asked.

"Actually," he said, and stopped. He looked at the glass horses on the shelf. "Better than all right," he said. "If this is a dream, I don't want to wake up yet. How are you?"

"Scared." She went to the bed and sat down. "Everything's happening so quickly. This is so much like my family, and so far from what I thought was real life. I feel trapped on track again. I don't even know you, Tom."

"Except for a few essentials," said Tom, "like, the Presences and Powers matched us. What does that mean, anyway? I mean, I get it that you call ghosts Presences."

"Ghosts, and other spirits; bodiless beings."

"You people let ghosts boss you around?" He sat down beside her on the bed, held out his hand. She slid hers into it. She smelled of evergreens, and he knew her mouth must still hold the spiced tang of cider; his did.

Her brow furrowed. She stared down at their nested hands. "There are lots of different ways to die. Some go on to some other place, and they don't come back. Those who have worked long and hard for the Family, though, those who care very deeply about our survival, they root in our home ground, and we consult them on major decisions. Except we haven't had a spirit-speaker born for several generations now, not since Scylla the Krifter, and she died about twelve years ago, so now we have to rely on auguries and omens." She frowned at the floor, then looked up. "We can tell what the Powers and Presences want from the way the light treats people, like Michael, tonight—it looked so bad—"

"I didn't understand that."

She stared into his eyes. "He's flawed."

"People have to be perfect?"

"They used to have to be, if they wanted to have children. But . . . our numbers are so few, the fewest they've been in centuries. And the babies . . . they die. Sometimes when they're born. Sometimes they just get sick while they're still young, and nothing we do saves them. We can all heal a little, but we haven't had a strong healer in a long time. Scylla foresaw the weakening of the blood. She consulted with the Powers and Presences in 1936, and the council decided to relax some of the breeding restrictions. They did another loosening of those threads in the fifties. People don't have to be as perfect as they used to. But Michael—" A tear streaked her cheek.

"He almost failed," Tom said. "What would have happened to him if he failed?"

"He would lose his power of generation," she whispered.

After puzzling over this, Tom said, "Sterilization?"

She flicked the fingers of her free hand as if warding off evil.

He sat beside her, listening to his own breathing, wondering who these people he'd tangled himself up with were.

After a little while she said, "I didn't know if I would ever come back to the Hollow. I ran away, six years ago, tried to lose myself so they couldn't find me. Because I knew I would never pass. I'm the weakest of my generation—"

"But you did pass, didn't you?"

Her grin lighted her face. "Yes. Oh, yes. I don't understand it.. And you passed, and you're not even a member of the Family." Then her grin faded. "But see, here we are. We're married! That's not how outsiders would handle it, marry on the day they met. And I've always wanted to be an outsider."

"Why?"

"Because the Family is cruel. It's not just the breeding restrictions. Some of my cousins are just plain mean, and they can do worse things to you than anybody outside."

He put his other hand over hers. "Laura . . . I'm confused about a lot of things. One of them is this talking-underneath thing. Underneath, on the way out here, you said, 'Almost home, almost home.' On top you say you don't like being here. Which part of you is telling the truth?"

"I still don't believe you about talking underneath!" Laura said, frowning ferociously.

—Don't force it. She's not ready to deal with this yet, Laura's buried whisper said.

"Okay, okay," he said. "I guess what I really wonder is, where are we going to live?"

—Not here!

"Not here!" she said.

He smiled. "Okay. Glad to have that settled. I have to tell you that as a husband I don't have much to offer you. I live in a shoebox over Bert's Taxis in Arcadia. You want to move in with me? I couldn't ask you to do that. We could get a bigger place. I could try to make more money."

"You don't use your talents to live on?"

"No. Whatever talents I may have, I've kept them buried for years. Do you use your talents to live on?"

"Such as they are. I'm a model. I don't think I'm very interesting to look at, normally, but when the photographers start snapping, I speak to my spark, and it makes pictures of me exciting. I look good in clothes. I have more calls than I can take. I have plenty of money. Would you move to a city with me?''

"Anyplace but Portland," he said after a moment's thought. "Come to think of it, they've probably forgotten by now, so even Portland might be all right."

"Oh—you're *that* Tom Renfield?"

"You heard?" he asked, astonished.

"Teasing!" She grinned. "Why? What did you do?"

"I don't want to discuss it, especially not this very moment." He looked at her, one side of his mouth smiling. She looked back. Her hand was warm inside his, and her scent had strengthened, carrying an undertone of musk. After a moment, they kissed, and this time when his interest deepened, he did not calm it. Laura held him fiercely, then pushed him away and tugged at his robe until he took it off. She pulled hers off too, and they examined each other with hands as well as eyes.

They slipped under the covers. Laura snapped her fingers and most of the light faded.

"Laura . . . I forgot to ask . . . and it's too late now, but—did we need protection?"

She laughed in the darkness. "We were searched, purified, and matched by Presences and Powers. We don't have anything to worry about."

"Was Aunt Aggie serious when she said the house would let them know when we, uh, consummated?" Tom asked drowsily some time later.

"Aunt Aggie!" said Laura, and burst into gales of giggles. "Aunt Aggie!" She tickled him until he managed to distract her. "Mmm, that feels good!"

"Is the house spying on us?" he asked.

"I don't know. It might have missed the first time. Want to go for 'in no uncertain terms'?"

"Uh-huh."

* * *

Above the bed's canopy, a skylight let in morning light, printing a rectangle on the flower-sprigged material. Tom stood up and pulled the canopy down.

"Mm," said Laura, watching him. Sunlight washed gold into her hair, dazzled gold from her eyes as she looked up at him. He sat down amid the crumpled bedclothes and studied her.

"You are so beautiful," he murmured, and watched her answering smile.

"I think you are too," she said. She sat up and put her arm around him. Her hair brushed his shoulder as she leaned, warm and salty, against him. He slid his arm around her, easing her closer. Yesterday morning he had awakened alone and cold in the little room above Bert's garage, wondering if anything interesting would liven up the day ahead.

He listened to her breathing, slowed his to match. They sat quiet for a while, melting into each other without moving. At last he murmured, "What time is the wedding?"

"Last night?" she asked.

"Not ours. Michael's."

"Oh." She held out her hand, and her watch drifted over from the bedside table to land on her palm. She studied it a second, straightened, said, "Oh, no! We have to shower and get out of here." She slid off the bed.

"What are we supposed to wear?" he asked, following her into the bathroom.

She looked back. Her eyebrows lifted.

"I mean, is this another white robe thing? My other choice is that white taxi-driver outfit. Is that appropriate?"

"Uh," she said, "well . . ." She turned on the water, grinning at him.

"You told me marriage was a serious business in your family," he said.

"Yes, but the hard part's over." They walked into the warm rain, and this time they washed each other.

Afterward he sat on the bed and watched her dress. First, underclothes and silky silver stockings; then she took a pale gray V-necked dress overlaid with silver lace flowers out of her suitcase and slipped into it. Its billowy sleeves ended in frothy ruffles that hid her hands, and its skirt was hemmed with points and corners. She fastened a gray belt with a silver shell buckle at her waist, stepped into a pair of gray high heels with silver bead roses on them, then stood back, arms out, in a classic display pose, and quirked an eyebrow.

"I don't know," he said. "Shadowy."

She glanced down at herself. "Isn't that odd? I knew it was appropriate when I bought it, but I didn't know why. It's not a good color on me, but shadowy is how I feel in this house."

"Guess I might as well wear my own outfit," said Tom, rounding up his T-shirt, jacket, shorts, jeans, socks, and hightops. They were so white they glowed. As he dressed, she brushed her hair, then handed the brush to him. She opened the door of a free-standing closet, revealing a mirror, and they stood side by side, studying themselves and each other.

Her tawny hair and summer skin were at odds with her frost-touched gray dress, and his own coloring—black hair, blue eyes, outdoor tan—was intensified by contrast with the smudgeless white of his clothes. He stood half a head taller than she, and quite a bit broader. He hooked his thumbs through his belt loops and bounced on his hightops. "What do you think?"

"Mm," she said, and tugged at his jacket until he leaned over far enough to kiss her.

He said, "You taste great, but this reminds me. When was the last time you ate?"

"Yesterday morning," she said, putting a hand on her stomach.

"I had some beer nuts right before you arrived in the bar. I'm starving."

"I am too. If we hurry, maybe we can snatch something in the kitchen before the ceremony." As she unlocked and opened the door, though, a gong sounded through the halls.

"Damn! It's the summons." She grabbed his hand and ran.

They arrived in the kitchen. People Tom had not seen the night before were hard at work at the business end of the kitchen. None of them looked up as he and Laura ran in. Laura slipped her hand out of his and darted through a small opening, returned with handfuls of brown bread torn from a larger loaf. She handed him a chunk, then tugged him past the workers to a narrow tunnel which took them out into the morning sunlight. They ate as they ran.

Music sounded from the amphitheater, a fiddle, a harp, a drum; the melody mixed klezmer, Celtic, and gypsy, verging on, then veering away from, the familiar.

"Oh, good, they haven't started yet," said Laura.

People wandered or stopped to cluster and talk near the amphitheater, which sunlight revealed as pillars of dark, lichen-laced rock thrusting up in a ring, shoulder to shoulder, offering many places to sit, descending in height toward the wide flat center, the earthen circle where lights and ghosts had danced the night before. A gap between the pillars closest to the house gave access into the circle. At one end of the central open area stood a dolmen, two squat upright stones capped with a flat horizontal one at about waist-height. On the capstone two wreaths of mingled red roses and white lilies lay, also a clay bowl, a silver goblet, a bone-handled knife, and a small sturdy gong, which Michael was striking.

Michael looked pale and disheveled. Alyssa stood beside him at the altar. Sun crowned her hair with gleaming copper. She looked serene. She wore a simple dress colored the pink of clouds at sunrise, and she carried a single lotus blossom.

Everyone drifted into the circle. The musicians set their instruments down on the pillars and descended to join the others.

Uncle Jezra emerged from the crowd and went to stand behind the flower-decked stone. "Welcome," he said.

"Thank you all for blessing this union with your presence."

Michael and Alyssa joined hands and knelt in front of the altar, their backs to the crowd. Tom closed his eyes a moment, and opened them into Othersight.

In daylight people's own light was harder to see, but he caught glimpses of it where an arm shadowed a side, or a skirt shadowed a lower leg. He looked around, and saw that the phantoms he had seen the night before were present too, faded by daylight like stains washed three times. He turned and studied Laura, who smiled at him. She had a blue edging, but over her stomach the light was greener, closer to the color he saw in his own hand.

He sighed and put his arm around her shoulders. One of the ghosts ventured near them.

Uncle Jezra spoke in that other language, his voice reaching out to touch everyone. As he spoke silvery shimmers came from his mouth, and as people responded, turquoise sparkles rose from their mouths, spinning above the circle, waltzing with the silver in visible harmony. Laura leaned her head against Tom's shoulder, her gaze fixed on Uncle Jezra. Tom watched the colors dance, then looked at the nearby ghost.

—Peregrine? Tom thought.

The ghost nodded. —Thank you for honoring my Family.

—What?

—By accepting this bud from my tree, and granting it communion with your seed.

Laura murmured something, touched her finger to her lips, and gestured, as everyone else was doing. Tom suppressed his confusion.

—Peregrine, please help me.

—By your leave. The ghost walked into him. He blinked again, and listened with ears and mind as Peregrine whispered a running translation while Jezra spoke, and used Tom's lips, tongue, and throat to join in the ceremony.

"By the chain of lives from our past into our future, we

bind ourselves, muscle, blood, bone, and mind, pledging our time and gifts to the betterment of the Family,'' Tom said in concert with everyone else.

"By the air above and the earth below. By the water that runs within us. By the sacred fire." Uncle Jezra clapped and a flame appeared, dancing in the air above the altar. "From the fire we each take sparks, feeding the flames of ourselves. Through the fire we temper and ennoble ourselves. When two flames join together with the assent of the Presences and Powers, we rejoice in the continuation of our line."

Jezra lifted the clay bowl. It had something in it. "Through the goodness of the Powers, we have sustenance. Will all partake?"

The bowl traveled around the circle and each person scooped a double fingerful of the bowl's contents, and tasted. Tom, still ravenous, was ready to reach for a handful, but Peregrine guided him into taking only a little. —It's symbolic of the Starving Time, when all we had to eat was this. There must be enough for all.

It was a gray paste, which tasted like salted oatmeal. —Salt privilege, Peregrine added. —We who share the sacrament of salt agree not to make war on each other.

"By the goodness of the Powers, we have drink. Will all partake?"

The goblet's contents proved to be water, a relief after the salt, but not enough of one.

"We stand here gathered, one people, to join these two children together . . . Will you, Michael Bolte, take Alyssa Locke as your wife?"

"I sure will," he said.

"Will you, Alyssa Locke, take Michael Bolte as your husband?"

"I will," she said, her voice firm but low.

"Then, by my status as eldest, by Powers and Presences above and below, by ancestors and descendants, by earth and sea and sun and sky, by permission and with joyous boldness I do pronounce you husband and wife; may your life together be sweet and long and fruitful and full of gifts. Give me your hands.''

They placed their hands on the capstone. Jezra lifted the little knife and nicked their index fingers. ''Mingle blood as covenant of the closeness you will share; grow greater as two become one,'' he said. Michael and Alyssa pressed their fingers together.

''Now kiss each other, and rise to greet your guests, Alyssa and Michael Bolte.'' He crowned Michael and Alyssa with the lily-and-rose wreaths. They kissed and stood up, turned, and clasped hands, smiling at everyone.

—Well done, Peregrine thought.

—Pretty, Tom thought.

Peregrine snorted mentally.

Laura smiled up at Tom. He thought about kissing her, then remembered he had a guest, which might complicate things. —Are you planning to stay inside me? Tom asked, not sure what to do if the answer was yes.

—Are you inviting me?

—No!

Peregrine laughed out loud in sheer delight, then stepped out of Tom.

''Tom?'' said Laura. ''Are you all right?''

''I'm fine. Temporarily possessed, but he's gone again.'' Peregrine was nearby, but he was looking around at other people now, though still grinning, a dimple scored deep into his cheek. Tom said, ''Is this anything like a regular wedding reception? Will there be food? I'm hungry enough to eat grass.''

''Let me make it easier for you,'' said Carroll from behind them. Tom turned to see Carroll gesturing, spinning red and gold coils through the air, and murmuring small red butterflies that flew with rapid wing flutters at him. Colored coils draped Tom, butterflies landed on him. He felt terribly sick.

Then he was splitting out of his clothes, his body barreling, arms, legs, and face lengthening, self growing hair and hooves and tail, ears stretching and furring, hair sprouting down the back of his suddenly elongated neck.

"Jackass," said Carroll. He smiled and walked away.

After a moment the sickness faded as Tom settled into this new shape. The view had changed. He saw different things with each eye, almost no overlap, but he had become accustomed to adjusting to new views, and after a moment he could sort the grayed landscape enough to see that people looked like *that*, and rocks looked like *this*. Smells and sounds had changed too. The different shades of plant smells had become much more important. He lifted his equine head and looked around.

How amazing to be in something other than a human shape! He had never been able to move his ears before.

Laura laid a warm hand on his shoulders, her fingers tangling in his mane. She was grinding her teeth.

Chapter 7

The scentless pale gray shimmer that approached him from the opposite side took Tom a moment to figure out. It bunched beside him so he could see something above it, and it thought —Tom?

—Peregrine? Tom cocked his head to get a better view. The shimmer remained muddy, not exactly person-shaped except in outline.

—Good, you can still sense me.

Tom shivered the skin of one shoulder, amazed at how it felt to have vibrating skin. His relationship with gravity and the ground had shifted radically. He lifted a front hoof, almost fell off balance, placed it on the ground again.

"Tom, I'm so sorry." Laura's free hand clenched into a fist. "If only I had his powers," she said.

His mouth couldn't smile. He felt a lot of long teeth inside his lips. —Peregrine, is this an abuse of salt privilege?

—Not if he can pass it off as a wedding prank. Don't eat or drink. It makes the form harder to shed.

Tom was glad of the warning. The scent of grass was enticing, curling juicy whispers to his tongue, and his hunger felt bottomless.

"Tom?" Laura said. "I can beg him to change you back . . . is that what you want? Nod if it is."

Tom shook his head. He was too busy exploring. Besides, begging sounded like a bad tactic. —How does one shed a form? he asked.

—It depends upon how careful he was.

The gray blotch that was Peregrine traveled back. Tom moved his head to keep the form in sight. —Hmm, Peregrine said. —What do you see when you look at this with Othersight?

Tom looked back at himself, enjoying the sensation of bending such a long mobile neck. He blinked, hoping that Othersight wouldn't confuse him further, but what it revealed looked familiar: red and gold coils, webbing around him in a loose net. Othersight, apparently, worked on some frequency that didn't respect the donkey's sight limitations; the colors of the net were rich and clear. Now that he could see the net, he could also feel its tension as it clung to him. It was itch-irritating, but it didn't feel very strong. He described it to Peregrine.

—That's interesting, Peregrine said. —I am not gifted with Othersight, except as the dead have it, for seeing other dead things. I can perceive the sensation of someone else's power around you—more like a taste than a vision. That . . . net is all that holds you in this shape. In a good spell built to last, it would taste a lot stronger than it does; so perhaps this *is* just a prank spell, short term, and it will wear off after a moment or two. Still, if you can conjure any manner of altering it . . .

"Tom—damn! I wish I could talk to you. I mean, I wish I could understand you. I don't know what to do!" Laura said.

Tom imagined himself tugging the net loose with phantom hands. As soon as he touched it with a mental finger, it frayed to nothing. He closed his eyes during the disorientation of shapeshifting, then opened them again when he was upright on his hind legs. It was less confusing now because his standard human worldview had returned, with only a faint overlay of Othersight. "It's okay," he said.

Her eyes widened. Then she hugged him. "Did you—oh, never mind!"

"I'm underdressed again," he said. He wasn't sure how his new in-laws viewed nudity. He wasn't that comfortable with it himself, not in front of strangers. Most of the wedding party had left the amphitheater, though some had seen him turn into a jackass and back, and a few were grinning at him as they walked past. "Please don't move away from me," he said, facing Laura and keeping his arm around her shoulder.

"But—" Laura said, laughing a little herself. "I don't know if we can walk back to my room this way."

Michael dashed up. "I'll get Carroll for you, Tom," he said.

Surprised, Tom said, "Thanks. I'd rather have a robe. Laura's dress isn't big enough for both of us."

"Oh!" Michael picked up all the scraps from Tom's former clothing, puzzled over them, frowned up at Tom, bit his lower lip, and managed to spell jockey shorts, a pair of white jeans, shoes, and a shirt out of the remnants. The jeans and underwear seemed fairly normal and even fitted; the shoes had changed from hightops into deck shoes; but the long-sleeved shirt was made of scraps from both the T-shirt and the windbreaker, patchwork fashion. Tom put everything on. He decided he liked it. He grinned. "Thanks! And congratulations."

"You too," said Michael. "You really want me to leave Uncle Carroll alone? I don't think it was fair, his pulling something like that on you, even if it was only a short-term spell. You haven't had time to get used to us yet."

"I appreciate your concern. Michael?"

"Yes?"

"When we were driving here, Laura said your family would enjoy torturing me. And you didn't seem very friendly last night."

"Yeah, but now you're married to us. We don't hurt each other. At least, not permanently. And if anybody's going to tease you, I want to start it, but I can't till tomorrow, because it's First Night for Alyssa and me. But Uncle Carroll . . ."

"Don't worry," said Tom. "I'll get him."

"You will?" Michael squinted at him.

Tom smiled serenely. "Sure. Are there any refreshments at this party?"

"Tanganar will be setting up tables by the kitchen." Michael dashed off.

"Tanganar?" Tom asked Laura. He remembered the definition he had extracted from Laura's father the night before: mind-deaf, ungifted.

"Another reason for us to live far, far away. Fetches. Slaves. What I thought would happen to you. But I don't want to attack a long-established tradition. This is the way my family has done things for as long as I can remember. I've never had enough power to change things."

They walked toward the kitchen. Some of the stragglers stopped to offer congratulations. A little dark-haired girl Laura introduced as Pandora gave them each a white rose. Some of the relatives condescended; some sneered; some seemed happy. Laura named them all.

Aunt Agatha came by and stroked the air in front of Laura's stomach. "Caught one already," she said, beaming as if she hadn't changed expression all night.

"What?" Laura sounded stricken.

"Is that what makes it blue-green there?" Tom asked, touching the air near Laura's stomach.

"Good gracious, boy! Can you *see* it?"

Tom raised his eyebrows.

"I'm *Arkhos,* and even I can't *see* them. I can sense them when I'm close enough." She pointed at him. "You come to me. I'll train you. Good gracious, the boy has Othersight," she muttered as she wandered off.

"Tom."

He looked at Laura.

"We're going to have a baby."

"I thought that might be—your halo is blue and mine's green, but right here there's a green-blue patch . . . is this okay with you? Is this too soon?"

She put her hand on her stomach and frowned. Then

she smiled. "I think—I think it will be okay. It's too soon to tell. But I think we can work with this. And—" She grinned. "It's going to drive the others crazy! Most of us have to work hard and cast a lot of spells to get a baby."

"What?" he said, but the sight of tables laden with food distracted him. Laura seemed equally distracted. They raced to the end of the line, and when their turn came, grabbed plates and loaded them with food—sliced meat, dark and light, though he couldn't tell if it were fowl or beast, only that the steam rising from it promised savor; sliced dark bread spread with butter, redolent of garlic; crescents of melon, slices of yellow cheese and white cheese, fresh oranges and pickled apples, mashed potatoes and tureens of gravy—everything promising joy and restoration.

"Delia?" Laura said to the woman holding a large knife and standing behind the table that bore the meat.

"Welcome home, Miss Laura." The woman looked like a shadow creature, thin and pale, with white hair and great mournful dark eyes. She smiled, though, reminding Tom of Laura's talk about sparks. Someone was home in her head.

"This is my husband Tom."

"Honored, Mr. Tom."

He held out his hand, but Delia looked away with a slight shake of her head. He reached instead for a sliver of meat and put it on his plate.

A man about Laura's age came out of the kitchen tunnel, carrying a tub full of fresh apples. "Chester?" Laura murmured. "Oh, God."

The man saw her and ducked his head, looking away. Laura gripped Tom's arm. Tom led her off to a seat in the amphitheater; once there, he ignored all mysteries and ate. "I'm sorry, but I just can't wait any longer," he said between bites.

"I know." She picked up bits of food and put them down. "After ninth grade, he was in my class. His family moved to Arcadia from out of state. Imagine that. They didn't know us. Barney Vernell tried to explain to him about us, but he just laughed, and pulled my hair, and spat on Michael's shoes, and mouthed off to Jaimie and Meredith. Michael and Jaimie and Meredith were too young to do anything about it at first, and I could never do anything anyway, even though I had passed *plakanesh.* I wonder who brought him here, and when.''

"When did you leave?''

"Almost six years ago, just after I graduated from high school.''

"Chester was—*tanganar,* and now he's out here being a slave? Normal people are *tanganar?* And that means you can steal them?'' Tom asked, putting down the piece of bread he had been eating. His hunger had eased, leaving him room for worry.

"Would you like a demonstration of what else we can do with them?'' said Carroll, materializing before him again.

Peregrine, still close by, said —Tom? If you can do anything to him, you had better act; he has been designated official tester.

"I'm glad you came back, Carroll,'' said Tom. "It saves me the trouble of finding you.'' He took a deep breath. —Please help me, Peregrine.

—You need to craft a casting in your mind—a net, I suppose. Cast it over him, and instruct it to change him how you will.

Tom remembered childhood games of cat's cradle and Jacob's ladder that an aunt had taught him. She had given him a string as if it were the most precious toy in the world, and showed him how many different things a string could make between skilled fingers. He stared down at his hands, imagining his fingers were spiders, capable of casting web into the wind. His hands warmed and his fingers tingled. Silver strands flowed from his fingertips. He held out his hands, aiming his fingers toward Carroll, and twitched, watching as the strands veered and tangled.

—Go to Carroll, he thought, and, as if magnetized, they

shot to Carroll and twined around him, sticking to themselves, weaving together in their appetite for close contact with their target. —Now, thought Tom. —Raven. Raven, as he envisioned a black-winged bird with rainbow-sheened feathers.

Carroll compressed before his eyes, squawking and shrieking, his nose lengthening into a black bill, his skin darkening and sprouting feathers. He vanished inside his clothes for a moment, then tore his way out. The hazel in his eyes had stained black, and his legs and feet were black too. He gave an outraged hoarse caw.

"Come back when you've had enough, and ask me nicely," said Tom. "I'll consider reversing it. Maybe." To his net, he whispered, —Keep him healthy, but don't let him change.

Carroll squawked and flew off into the woods.

Frowning, Tom peeled an orange. He felt shaky and hungry again. He could feel sweat at his hairline, under his arms, and down his spine.

—I just transformed someone into something else, he thought, and didn't believe it. —I mop floors. I drive taxis. I turn people into birds.

He shuddered.

"Did you do that?" Laura asked him.

"What do you think?"

"How did I find you? What were you doing in that bar in Arcadia?" She sounded either afraid or amazed.

"Eating beer nuts, and probably waiting for you."

"Did you ever turn anybody into anything before?" This time he heard an edge of laughter in her voice.

"No." He offered her a section of orange.

She took it. "Then how—"

"Peregrine helped me. The ghost, from last night."

"A Presence? But they only manifest when we call them."

He bit into a section of orange and the sour-sweet tang spread across his tongue. "You people don't see them, is that right?"

"Not since Scylla died. Unless we do a special spell to reveal them."

"They're all around, Laura. I think Peregrine's adopted me. He helped me all morning, even told me what was happening during the wedding."

—You would have managed the unspelling and the casting on your own, Peregrine thought.

—But it would have taken me longer to figure out. And the wedding translation—oh, Peregrine, it was beautiful.

Tom laid a slice of cheese and a slice of meat on a piece of bread and ate it. "Peregrine said I better do something about Carroll, because he was the official tester. Did I pass?"

"The official tester?" Laura said, then smiled. "Yes, I see. Oh, you passed." She smiled even wider, and ate. When she had finished everything on her plate, she said, "I'd like to go back to bed now. Would you?"

"Are we allowed to do that?"

She patted her mouth with a cloth napkin, then laid the napkin gently on her plate. "Carroll is the most powerful shifter in our family. I don't think anybody can stop us doing anything we like."

"Is that the end of the testing?"

"I hope so, but probably not."

"But for now—" He got to his feet, setting his empty plate on top of hers in her lap. Then he picked her up. "Want to be carried across a threshold?"

"Mm, okay. As long as it doesn't signify this is our final resting place, just our first." She kissed his neck. "If I had enough power, I could carry you across a threshold."

He thought of the green sparkling curtain she had cast across the front door that parted for them with the welcome of fire. "I think you already have." Following Laura, he had walked into this house, and into aspects of himself whose existence he had never suspected.

Her hands around the plates, she leaned her head against

his shoulder and closed her eyes. "Okay," she said. "I like the sound of that."

Carrying her, he wandered up to the tunnel leading to the kitchen. It was dark after the sunlight outside. When he reached the kitchen, his eyes hadn't quite adjusted yet. Two people were preparing more food, and two others washed and dried dishes. One of the dishwashers was a hulking long-haired man who turned to accept the dishes from Laura. Tom stared at him. The outline was familiar. As Tom's eyes adjusted, he saw familiar tattoos on the man's arms. "Eddie?" said Tom.

Chapter 8

"Tommy? What are you doing here? Did you get caught too? Don't let her play with you. Get away as fast as you can. They like you for a while, then they put you in the kitchen or scrubbing floors or worse." As Eddie spoke, he turned away and began washing dishes again. "Look. My hands do it whether I want them to or not. It's not my body anymore." He sounded horribly resigned.

Tom set Laura on the floor and looked into her eyes. "Laura, can we fix this?"

"I don't know. I tried not to learn about this, so I don't know how strong the bonds are. It might depend on whose fetch he is. Providing you can do something about this, is it fair to release just one?"

"What if we release them all?" he asked. "How many people does this involve?"

"I don't know. Used to be ten. Eddie, do you know?"

Eddie counted mentally as he washed. "Fourteen," he said at last.

Laura looked at Tom. "If you release them all, everyone will hate you."

"Yes, but we're leaving."

She said, "They'd probably just round them up again. It's easier the second time."

"Don't worry about me, Tommy," said Eddie. "That'll

just get you in deeper and dirtier. Get out of here, and
leave her behind.''

"That's impossible. She's my wife." Tom looked up
at the cavernous ceiling, searching out the house spirits he
had sensed there the night before. Few appeared to be
stirring. Perhaps they slept during the day.

An albino gecko the size of Tom's forearm walked down
the wall a few feet.

"Eyoo! What is that?" asked Laura, grabbing his arm.

"Is it a Presence? It's not exactly bodiless. Does that
makes it a Power?" Tom said. "It's one of the beings that
gave us the rings last night. All sorts of things live on the
ceiling. Uh, Ancient?"

The gecko scuttled further down the wall. The women
preparing food stopped chopping vegetables, and Eddie
and the young brown-haired girl beside him stopped washing and drying dishes. Eddie looked at his hands, then
stared wide-eyed at Tom. The girl gazed down at the dishtowel in her hands. The gecko blinked pale yellow eyes at
Tom and waited.

"Is there a right thing to do?" he asked it.

Its slit pupils flicked wide, then shuttered. "Do as thou
wilt," it said. "We grow strong and powerful because
they live here, but we do not condone their everythings."

—Peregrine?

Tom had the sense that the ghost had been trailing them.
He glanced around, and saw a silver form emerge from
the tunnel to outside.—Do you have any advice?

Peregrine, arms crossed over his chest, studied the
kitchen workers. He frowned. —Any established power
system grows decadent over time, if there is nothing with
the strength or motivation to challenge it, and if it refuses
to challenge itself, he said after a minute. —I can see that
this has happened here. Challenge it. Wreak havoc if you
like, honored one.

Tom looked at the kitchen, which was like no other
place he had ever seen, with an operating system that he
didn't understand. For a moment he listened to his old

instincts, which told him to watch, listen, and stay quiet. Then he said, "Anybody want to leave?"

The girl with the towel clenched her fists, the towel gripped between them like a garrotte. She glanced up at Tom, a neutral expression on her face.

The two silent older women who had been chopping vegetables looked up, terrified, and shook their heads.

"They been here too long," said Eddie. "No spirit left." He held up his arms, clenched his fists, flexed his muscles. Eddie had disappeared from town seven months earlier, without saying good-bye to Tom, or to Pops, who owned the garage where Eddie had worked; Tom hadn't been able to decide if that was characteristic or not. Nobody at the bar had said anything about the disappearance—or had they? Vaguely Tom remembered some remark that hadn't made sense to him at the time.

"I'm ready to leave," Eddie said. "Man! But what if they follow me? Bust me down to cellar boy."

Tom glanced up at the gecko. It opened its mouth in a grin and showed him a pale, spade-shaped tongue. Tom looked at his wedding ring and realized the onyx seal was glowing. He had a sense of forces moving around him, locking into his core. He had turned Carroll into a crow, and that was crazy, but the skills were there, inside him, on this side of the threshold Laura had led him across. He held up his fist, the glowing ring uppermost. "I . . ." he said, stopped, licked his lip. "I can put you under my protection." He shuddered. "Then they can't touch you."

"Really?" asked Eddie.

Tom looked at the gecko, at the tunnel leading outdoors, at Peregrine, who raised an eyebrow, and finally at Eddie. "Yes."

"What's the catch? Why are you so nervous?"

"Because—this is a step I don't want to take. If I start this, I have to continue. It's a commitment to—to taking power—" A memory of his cousin Rafe rose in his mind. Rafe had known how to use power. Tom had lived under the lash of Rafe's subtle blackmail for a while when he was twelve, and the stain had never completely washed away. "I would be taking power over people, and that makes me uncomfortable. But I'll do it if you ask me to."

The girl with the dishtowel stepped forward. She was slender, with blue eyes and feathery brown hair. She was wearing red sneakers and blue jeans and a denim jacket; where the jacket gapped in the front, a tie-dyed Grateful Dead skull crowned with roses showed on her T-shirt. She looked about sixteen. "I'm ready," she said.

Eddie's mouth dropped open and his eyes widened as he stared at her. "Maggie?" he said in a hoarse voice. She shot him a glance, then focused on Tom.

Tom held out his hand to her, lifting his eyebrows.

"Maggie Galloway," she said, putting a slender hand in his. "I ran away from home about three years ago. Got in worse trouble from the guy I ran away with than I was in at home, almost. Mr. Carroll came for me at a rest stop on the gorge, and . . ." Her eyebrows pinched together above the bridge of her nose. "Now I'm ready to get out."

"Tom Renfield. I don't know what this will mean. It might just mean—changing owners."

"It's got to be better than here," she said. "Do it."

Tom looked at Laura. She nodded.

—Peregrine? Is there a procedure?

The ghost hesitated, frowned. —You need to connect her to you so she can call you if she is in trouble.

Tom looked at his ring. The stone still glowed bright silver. He took Maggie's left hand in his right and pressed his seal into her palm. "I release you from all earlier bonds. I shield you from the spinning of others by anyone but myself. By—by Powers past and present, by the good will of the House, by my unknown heritage, I free you to go your own way with only this tie: that you may call me when you need help, and I will come as quickly as I can to aid you." As the words came out of his mouth, he felt heat on his tongue, in his throat. His voice sounded strange to him, formalized, stronger than usual.

He lifted his hand from hers. His hand throbbed with

something not quite pain, and a tiny flower of heat blossomed in his chest. In the center of Maggie's palm there was a still-smoking brand, but its lines were silver, not red. It showed the profile of a Roman soldier. Maggie flexed her fingers, then made a fist over the mark and looked up at Tom, her lips compressed. "All right. Thanks. I'm out of here." She glanced toward the tunnel leading outside. Faintly sounds of music, talk, and laughter came in. The scent of dying leaves drifted in on the warm autumn air, the strange spice of change.

"I'll drive you to town," Tom said to Maggie. "Is that okay, Laura? It changes our immediate plans. But I want to get away. I haven't even called Bert to tell him where his cab is."

"You couldn't; we don't have phones. Anyway, Mr. Forester will have told Mr. Noone you took me out here, and he won't be expecting you back. I'll come with you. Or—" She frowned.

"What?"

"I haven't had a chance to talk with Mom and Dad yet, and I'd like to. Maybe I'll stay one more night. I can get a ride into Arcadia with somebody tomorrow, I expect."

"I'll miss you. Will you be safe?"

"Maybe you should brand me too?" she said. He couldn't tell whether she was joking.

"Ring calls to ring," said the gecko.

"Oh," said Laura, looking at her scarab. "All right. I'll be fine, Tom."

Tom looked at Eddie.

Eddie pointed to a place on his upper arm between the tattoos of a skull and crossbones and a snake coiled around a dagger. "Can you do it here?"

"Sure." Tom repeated the ceremony, felt the same peculiar symphony of heat in hand, heart, and throat. "You have anything to pack?"

"No." Eddie looked down at his sleeveless T-shirt, jeans, and work boots. "This is everything I brought. Let's get out of here while they're all celebrating."

Tom kissed Laura. She held him a long moment, then released him and sighed.

Maggie, Eddie, and Tom ran through the house toward the front, Maggie and Eddie keeping them on track. The side tunnels confused Tom. He glanced behind once, and was not surprised to see that Peregrine was drifting after them.

The taxi was the only car parked in front of the house, and the keys were still in it. The three of them climbed into the front seat. Before starting the car, Tom leaned back. —Peregrine? You coming?

—I may come if you let me into your body as you did before. If you give me permission, I may root in you instead of in this home ground. You are not a branch of my tree, but you have connected with it by blood-tie, so I may do that. I desire this, because then I can help to train you, and the child when it comes.

"We going?" Eddie asked.

"One minute. I'm talking to a ghost."

"Jeeze," said Eddie, shrugging. He went back to staring at the front door of the house as if willing it to stay closed.

Tom thought about Peregrine. He opened his hand and looked at the palm, searching for a clue from his past— the gold heart he had picked up as a child. Hannah had lived in that heart, and the heart had melted into his hand and into his soul. With her inside, he had stopped feeling alone. But he wasn't alone now; he had Laura, and these two people he had just bound to him somehow.

Peregrine had been a friend to him. Peregrine understood what was going on with Laura's family. That would be valuable, now and in the future.

—If you come inside, who gets to talk? Tom asked.

Peregrine laughed. —I would speak only from necessity, or if you gave me permission.

—Would you be able to get out and leave me alone for periods of time?

—I could bide in your possessions, if you have any dear to you.

—Yeah, but would you?

A pause. A chuckle. —Yes, I would.

—All right. I give you leave to root in me.

The ghost came through the car's door and sat down, vanishing into Tom. He felt a faint shivery chill all through him, a brief ache in his bones, and then he felt normal again.

He sat forward and started the car. Maggie, beside him on the seat, let out a relieved sigh and leaned back as they bucketed down the weedy driveway. "They sure don't care about road upkeep," Tom grumbled.

"They almost never use the road," said Eddie. "Hey, what's going on in town, anyway? Pops ever say anything about me? Is he okay?"

"He was really upset when you disappeared," Tom said. "He didn't figure you for the type to run off without a word. But Fred told him—" Tom opened his mouth, then paused, amazed, listening again to what Fred had said, the vague memory he had searched for before: "Fred told him a Chapel Hollow sirene got her claws in you." He hadn't understood it at the time, but now it was starting to make sense. "Pops was sad. He's been advertising for help ever since." Tom had done some work for Pops when nothing else needed his attention.

"Anybody apply?"

"Nobody he was satisfied with. You remember Peter Wetherell, Trailer Court Hank's son? He tried it for a while but Pops said he was always falling asleep, and—well, about six people tried it, but Pops found fault with all of them. Mostly he made do with temps or tried to go it alone. You gonna stay in Arcadia, Eddie?"

"Am I safe there?"

The car plunged over potholes, rocking up and down. Tom said, "I don't know these Boltes very well. I only met them yesterday."

"Places are about equal to them," said Maggie. "They

don't go too far afield unless they're on the warpath, but then nothing stops them."

Eddie stared at her, surprised all over again. "I—I'll go back to Pops, if he'll have me. You staying in Arcadia, Tom?"

"That's up to Laura. Her job's more important than mine, and she works in cities, so probably not. I'm a janitor; I can work almost anywhere."

"*You're* a *janitor?*" Maggie asked. She made a rude noise.

"Driving a cab is my second vocation," said Tom, striving for dignity.

"Where does all this—magic fit in?"

"I don't know." Tom hunched forward, gripping the steering wheel. "Until yesterday, I was almost normal. I didn't need or use any of this. Then, when I came out to the Hollow, it was like going to the Twilight Zone, except . . . Michael grabbed the cab off the road and flew it to the house, and I felt that in some weird way I had come home. All these questions came up, and I had answers for them. They didn't even bother me that much. I rose to it."

"So you're one of them?" Eddie asked.

"Guess so."

A large black bird flew in front of the windshield, squawking. It beat against the glass.

"Oops," said Tom. "Loose end." He pulled the car over to a narrow verge and stopped. "Stay here, guys, okay?" He climbed out of the car and leaned against it, looking at the raven. "What do you want?"

"Turn me back!" It leapt for his face. He waved a hand, reinforcing the gesture with a thought to his net around the raven, and sent the bird spinning away. It recovered, leaping up and down in the dusty road. "Turn me back, you dumb *limpana.*"

"Ask nicely, or forget it." Tom crossed his arms.

"Where are you going with those *tanganar?*"

"They're mine now."

"Give me that girl. She's mine, and I want her back."

"Who is that?" Maggie asked. He heard her close the car door, and glanced back. She stood beside the car.

"Uncle Carroll," Tom told her.

Her eyes widened. Then her eyebrows lowered into a fierce frown, and her hands clenched into fists. "Make a cage around him, Tommy. Maybe I can teach him to sing."

Tom stared at her. Tears of rage shone in her eyes, and she spoke through clenched teeth.

"She speaks!" said the raven, hopping closer. "Give me that girl."

"How big are you now, beast? How big are you now?" The color had washed from her face, leaving her pale, her eyes an intense gray-blue. She stalked toward the raven, her hands opening and closing.

The raven cocked its head, staring at the girl. "Careful," it said. "Remember the last time I was a bird?"

She gasped, her hands pressing against her chest over her heart.

"You agreed to come with me then. Come with me now, Maggie."

Tom heard the golden thread in Carroll's voice, the bait angling for a bite.

"Come home and talk to me," Carroll said. "I never knew you could talk. Did this *akenar* cast a spell on you to give you a voice?"

Maggie glanced at Tom, her breathing ragged and deep. One of her hands floated toward him.

—Use Othersight, Peregrine murmured.

Tom blinked, and saw golden tendrils reaching from the black bird to the girl, twining around her head. Tom reached out and pinched the threads. They tarnished and fell apart instantly. Maggie straightened. Her eyes looked enormous and stormy. "Always had a voice, you stupid *paragar,* but I hid it! There's a part of me you've never had." She took a step toward the raven. "And now I'm big and you're little, and—"

The bird fluttered and dipped and muttered.

—Spellcasting, Peregrine told Tom.

Tom rubbed his hands together, imagining that he spun smooth silver metal between his palms. Heat tingled under the skin of his hands. An almost weightless substance grew around his hands as he rubbed them. Open-handed, he threw what he was crafting toward Maggie, instructing it to form a shield around her. Sweat trickled down his back, under his arms, beaded on his forehead and upper lip. He watched as shimmering silver streamed from him to form a globe around her. An instant later something red spun from the raven and struck the shield, and Tom felt it as if the shield were an extended portion of his skin. The spell felt soft, fibrous, and sticky, but it slid off the shield and melted.

The raven screamed and leapt at Tom again. He closed his hands and opened them, imagining a globe enclosing the bird. Suddenly the raven was trapped in a bubble just big enough for it, stubbing its wings against the sides, pecking with its beak, squawking, its noise muted by its prison. Tom's hands burned with a heat that did not consume them, but hurt anyway.

Maggie picked up the bubble and threw it toward a rock. "Hey!" Tom cried, and reached with something other than flesh to the bubble, which was still connected to him as the shield around Maggie was. He stopped the bubble in mid-air, though Carroll still spun inside. "No, Maggie."

"You don't know what he did to me. How he helped me, took care of me, promised to cherish . . . then . . . how he . . . raped me . . ." Tears streaked down her face. "He uses everyone. He's the worst of the lot. Want him dead."

"I'm not going to help you kill him."

The bird quieted in its globe.

Maggie said, "Do it on my own, then."

"Do you want to tie a knot around the worst thing that's happened to you and drag it with you everywhere you go? Don't do it, Maggie."

"It's not the worst—" she began, frustrated, then asked, "Is that an order—Master?"

"A suggestion," he said. Her smoky eyes troubled him.

She glared at him, then at the bird, suspended in a bubble in the air. She climbed back into the car. Eddie patted her shoulder.

Tom closed the car door, picked the bubble out of the air and walked away into the woods with it. When he reached a clearing, he sat on a log and set the bubble on the ground and waited.

Subdued, the bird stood silent.

Tom twitched his fingers, inviting the bubble to release its captive and return to him. It dissolved. Coolness flowed into his fingers, soothing the heat. The raven hopped away, then returned.

"Why did you hurt Maggie?" Tom asked.

"Hurt her? I rescued her from a brute of a *tanganar*. I asked her if she wanted to come with me, and she said yes. Well, not said, because she never did talk—think of the power in that girl, to keep silent all this time—but she indicated assent. Her choice." The raven cocked its head, studying him.

"Did you rape her?" Tom felt a strong sense of unreality stealing over him. He was asking a bird strange questions, and it was answering them. On the other hand, whether the bird was telling the truth . . . He remembered the blue flame Laura had conjured up in front of his lips. He hadn't learned that yet. He would have to consult with Peregrine.

"Rape?" said the bird. It extended a wing, preened a feather. "What is that? We strove together to summon a descendant. I honored her with the promise of my generation. She defied me, but I still took care of her. She is my favorite. I have always liked her. She is healthy, has food and shelter, everything she needs. And now, a voice—she never told me she could speak. She—I want her back."

"Forget it. She wants to leave, and I've told her I'll protect her."

The bird cocked its head, looked at him out of one eye. After a moment, it said, "It's just as it was when I first met her. She clings to a new protector. See how easy? How tempting?" The bird bobbed its head at him.

Unnerved, Tom sat back. For a moment, he wondered about his motives, but then he remembered what Maggie had said about Carroll using people. He blinked, saw a haze of lavender between himself and the bird. He waved a hand at it, and it dissipated. His mind cleared. Carroll had no stake in giving him real information, and every reason to try and deceive him. Whatever Tom and Maggie worked out, he shouldn't talk to Carroll about it. He changed topics.

"Why have you picked on me since the moment we met?" he asked Carroll.

"You're an outsider, a peasant, not fit to associate with my niece. You are not bound to us in the ways that give us structure. We don't know what you bring us. And Laura, she should have married one of us. She's no prize, but she has breeding potential. You came in and upset everything."

"Not enough women to go around?"

"Not enough women, not enough babies, too many sickly . . . Besides, we needed information about you."

"I know. That first spell you cast on me—was that your best shot?"

"It was only a temporary, but it dissolved faster than it should have. I must have gotten the words wrong. Except I never do that." It cocked its head at him. It flew up to a branch of a nearby tree, then back to the ground. "Will you release me from this spell now?" it said at last, settling in the dust at his feet.

"Tried everything else, have you?"

It stared at him out of one eye.

"Do you promise to leave me alone?"

"*Ashkali.* I couldn't keep a promise like that."

"Promise to leave Maggie and Eddie alone."

"I have no interest in Gwen's fetch."

Tom sighed. "What does that mean?"

"Your boy. I'm not at all interested in your boy. I find Gwen's taste for exotics ridiculous."

"Okay. You won't bother Eddie. Now, tell me you'll leave Maggie alone."

The raven flipped its wings and flew up to a low branch in a nearby tree. After a moment it returned. "I can't leave her alone, because she is not alone; she is with you. This has no meaning."

"Goodbye, Carroll," said Tom, standing up.

"No! No. No one at the Hollow can unspell this. What do you want? Say it again."

"Say you won't bother Maggie."

"I won't bother Maggie," it said, then hissed something.

"Swear by the Powers and Presences," Tom said.

"I do so vow," it said, and bobbed its head.

—Peregrine?

—Yes, Tom.

—Is it safe to release him?

—No. It never will be, especially when he has modified this promise with a whisper; nevertheless, you must release him.

—I could turn him into something else if he bothers us again.

—Next time he will be armed against it. But I suspect you could overcome such armor.

Tom leaned forward, studying Carroll with Othersight. A shadow of his human form crouched above the bird; the bird was wrapped round with silver threads as intricate and beautiful as snowflakes under a magnifying glass. —Silver, Tom thought, and felt the web wake to him. —Silver, let the Carroll shape come back. Relax, so that he no longer feels you, but stay with him wherever he goes. Carroll. Carroll.

The shadow Carroll and the bird melted into one another

within the embrace of silver, and then Carroll stood up, naked and human, and stared at Tom. His hazel eyes looked thoughtful. He pursed his lips, then held out his hand.

—Is that a trick? Tom asked Peregrine.

—I don't know.

Tom shook hands with Carroll. Carroll's hand was cool, his grip strong but not punishing. Tom said, "I assume you can get home from here."

"Yes." Carroll dived up into the air and flew away.

Tom sighed, shoved his hands into his pants pockets, and walked back to the car.

Chapter 9

"Well?" Maggie asked Tom as he climbed back into the driver's seat of the cab. She was sitting in the middle of the front seat; Eddie sat quiet beside the window.

Tom looked at her, wondering who she was, this utter stranger. He closed his eyes a moment, then opened them again and saw her just the way he had before: a girl, hugging herself, one shoulder hunched higher than the other, head bent toward the higher shoulder, her brows drawn together above her nose.

He reached for the key, which was still in the ignition.

"Please," she said. "What did you do with him?"

"I let him go."

Both her shoulders hunched higher. She stared out the front window as he started the car. He saw a single tear travel down her cheek, but she made no sound.

They drove in silence for a while. "He said he rescued you from someone who was hurting you. What did he do to the guy he took you away from?" he asked presently.

"He cast a most magnificent hurtful spell on him," she whispered.

He hesitated, then said gently, "Maggie, I'm not Carroll."

She relaxed, sagging back against the seat. "I know." She touched his arm. "I know. That's what's good about you."

After another silence, he said, "But how could you know that when you said you'd take my protection?"

"Watched you with your wife."

"What?"

"You asked her questions, and listened to her answers. You don't trust her yet, but you do listen."

He stared at her, then back at the road. An utter stranger, full of threat and promise, and she carried his mark in her hand.

They bucketed up out of a dip in the dirt drive and came suddenly upon the patched asphalt of Lost Kettle Road. Tom turned right, then pulled over and glanced back. The lane leading to Chapel Hollow was almost invisible, a dirt trace between trees, underbrush dipping over its edges. "No mailbox," he said.

"They got a p.o. box in town. Mr. Dirk picks up the mail a couple times a week," said Eddie. "He's a lawyer. He makes sure none of the zoning or anything interferes with the Hollow."

"Huh," said Tom, frowning. "Eddie, you were living in Arcadia when I got there. You remember hearing about these people before you ran into Gwen?"

"Nothing real obvious. Pops used to say, 'Beware the women.' I just figured he got burned in his marriage, which he doesn't talk about. Didn't think it had anything to do with me."

"Nobody told me anything about them, although people seemed to expect me to leave when I had no plans to. Maybe they expected the people in the Hollow to take me. I heard some guarded comments that I didn't understand. I never asked what they meant." He put the car back in drive and they headed out. "So what are we going to tell them when we get back? I don't want them to know that I'm—that I'm—" He bit his lower lip.

"Related," Maggie suggested.

"Right," he said, smiling at her. "I mean, I have friends in Arcadia. You get the feeling these Chapel Hollow people are enemies of the Arcadians? Or what?"

"I talked to the other fetches," Eddie said. "Delia's been there the longest, and she sort of feels like they're her family. She came there when she was about sixteen and watched a bunch of them grow up. She's eighty now. Some of them are her pets, in a way. She talked about the Old Days a lot, how the Hollow people had real power then and used it to help townspeople. Chester came to Arcadia when he was a teenager and nobody clued him in that this could happen to him, that those Hollow people could come steal him. He could tell there was something weird between Hollow people and townspeople, but he didn't know what it was. So when Miss Sarah started fetching him, he fell hard. Like I did with Miss Gwen, maybe. Aren't they the foxiest women you've ever seen?"

"I don't know if I've seen those two."

"Trust me." Eddie sucked in a breath. "And every bit as sexy as they look. And much, much meaner."

"Some of the Hollow people are nice," Maggie said. "Jaimie. Meredith."

"Shoot, Maggie!" said Eddie, staring at her again. "I still can't believe you can talk! How did you keep quiet all that time? You could have told *us.*"

"No," she said, shaking her head. "Knew if I had a secret it would keep me strong. Done that before, used a secret as my backbone. If it's a good secret, if it's *my* secret, it gives me power even when I don't feel like I have any. If I told anybody, even Barney, some *Ilmonishti* could make them tell, and then I'd lose my power."

"So how come you stopped keeping it up now?" Eddie asked.

She leaned forward, elbow on knee, chin in hand. "Don't know, just had to," she said. "The time came. Now I got to find another one. Here's one. It's a secret Tom can do stuff like the *Ilmonish.*"

"Yes," said Tom. "I don't know how people in town feel about the Hollow people, but if half of what Laura told me about how normal people get treated out there is true, I imagine they're not too happy. I mean, Fred was scared of Laura when she came into the bar. If he found out about me, I don't know if he'd even let me in there again, and that's where I spend a lot of my time.''

Eddie stroked his chin. "Tommy, I'm starting to remember something. It didn't make sense to me at the time. Mr. Hal came into Fred's bar one day. This was before I knew who he was. You were there, too; we were arguing about movies. We rented *The Hidden* on video the night before, remember? Or was it *The Terminator?* Anyway we were talking and all of a sudden nobody else was, and you turned around and looked at the door, and shushed me, and this guy had walked in. We turned around and there he was, a red-headed guy with a mustache, nothing much, walks to the bar, smiles at Fred, and out comes a glass of Fred's private reserve, no questions asked. Remember?''

Tom frowned. The moment came back to him, the sudden cessation of everybody else's speech, the change in atmosphere he had learned to be alert for, the arrival of the undistinguished man. He remembered surveying the faces of the others in the bar for clues, information about what made this event distinct from others. Raising of eyebrows, thinning lips, shuttering of faces, blanking of expressions: the air whispered "threat." Tom had gestured to shut Eddie up, and Eddie responded even though he wasn't usually sensitive to undercurrents. The man smiled, a kind of wry, don't-take-me-seriously smile, walked to the bar, and said, "Hi, Fred. I was just in town checking about the new seed. Got anything for a dry throat?''

Fred, silent, got out the bottle, poured a shot. The mild man drank it, glancing around the bar, smiling. Heads turned away, eyes not meeting his. Tom ducked his head too when the stranger's gaze came his way. Protective coloration.

"Thanks," said the man after he finished his drink. "Is it . . . thanks, Fred." He had walked out without paying.

"Yeah," Tom said to Eddie, coming out of the memory. He tried superimposing the mild man's face over the face of his new father-in-law, got a match. "I sure don't want it to turn into something like that."

"We're going to have to tell 'em something, though," Eddie said. "I don't think people ever get away from the Hollow."

"If anybody asks me," said Maggie, "don't think I remember much, except catching a ride with you when you were running away from them."

Tom grinned at her. "That's a version I can live with."

"Just come out of the wilderness like idiots?" Eddie said, widening his eyes and letting his face go slack. "I could probably handle that," he added.

"Let's try it, anyway. Maggie, where do you go from here?"

"Don't know."

"Home?"

"Not while my dad's alive," she said in a tight voice.

"Oh." They went a ways, made a left turn onto Rivenrock Road, finally a road with decent pavement. "How old are you?" Tom asked.

"Be sixteen sometime soon. Sort of lost track of time."

"So you should be in school?"

She laughed. It grated, edging toward a sob, but not getting there. "Have to play catch-up. Haven't been to school since seventh grade. Not sure I want to go back."

"What do you want to do? Where do you want to live?"

She looked down at the silver mark in her left palm, then up at him. "Take me," she said, holding out her brand. "I'm yours." She gave him the smile of a much older woman.

Chilled, he said, "Stop it."

She relaxed against the seat back, leaving her palm open, its silver mark still visible. She gave him a young smile. "Give me crash space. Can find some kind of job, dish-washing, waitressing. Don't feel up to long-range planning right now."

"Uh—"

"He doesn't have crash space," Eddie said. "He lives

in this little tiny room over the taxi garage. You can stay with me, Mag. I got a fold-down bed in the living room in my trailer.''

''All right,'' she said, but the smudges under her eyes darkened.

Tom glanced at her. A big pothole jarred the steering wheel out of his hands. For a little while he concentrated on driving. At length he glanced at her again. ''Maggie?''

''What.''

''Why is Eddie scarier than I am?''

She turned away, staring out through the windshield, shrugged. ''Not scared. Just tired.''

''Tired of what?''

She frowned and muttered something.

''What?'' said Tom.

''Screwing around.''

''Did I ever hurt you, Maggie?'' Eddie said, pain in his voice.

''No, not really.''

''You came to my bed. You never said no. I thought we were comforting each other.''

''You were warm. Carroll was cold even when he was in me. You were nice, and he hadn't been nice to me in a long time. But a hug would have been enough.''

''You never told me.''

She closed her eyes. ''Secret was more important,'' she said in a weary voice.

''Eddie, can I stay with you?'' Tom asked. ''Maggie can have my room.''

''All right,'' said Eddie.

Maggie put her hand on Tom's arm. ''Don't want to be alone,'' she said. Her eyes were wide and miserable.

''All right,'' Tom said. ''We can work something out.''

They came to the highway, and drove north in silence. When they reached the outskirts of town, Tom looked at Eddie. ''Where to?''

''Is my trailer still set up in back of Pops's garage?''

''I think so,'' Tom said.

"I—I feel—"

"What?"

"Real people—what's it like to talk to real people? I can't remember."

"Guess we could find out sooner instead of later," said Tom, and he drove to the Dew-Drop Inn. After he parked and turned off the engine, he and Eddie and Maggie looked at each other a minute, and that was when people came out of the bar and pulled open the cab doors.

Chapter 10

Judging from the number of people around the taxi, the bar must be pretty crowded for an early Friday afternoon, Tom thought. Maybe it was lunchtime, or maybe they were having some kind of special meeting. Sam Carson, the city marshal, was present, though he was out of uniform. Bert Noone, Tom's boss, was the first to pull a taxi door open. Young Dr. Alton (as opposed to Old Doc Hardesty); Trailer Court Hank; Ruth the librarian, who only opened the library three days a week; Gus, the guy who manned the desk at the bus station for the few hours a day it was relevant; some guys from Diggers Dumpers Delvers Sand & Gravel; two men from the volunteer fire department; and a few assorted others, including the midday regulars, were present. People came to the Dew-Drop on their lunch breaks; Fred's wife Tizzy was a wizard at making sandwiches and nachos. She whipped up a mean guacamole.

Everybody present was excited.

Bert patted Tom's shoulder. He was grinning.

"Tom! Tom? How'd you—what's that you're wearing?"

"Eddie, you okay?"

"Did you come from the Hollow? How'd you get away?"

"We could use a drink," said Tom as he, Maggie, and Eddie climbed out of the taxi.

"Just a darn minute," said Sam, the city marshal, "how old's the girl? She looks like a minor."

Maggie clung to Tom's arm and stared at Sam.

"Shut up, Sam," said Fred. "You're off duty now. What'll you have, Miss?" He held the door open. Tom, Eddie, and Maggie went into the welcome smoky darkness, and everyone else followed.

Fred slipped through the crowd and went behind the bar, where he turned off the television. Tom helped Maggie onto a stool, then sat beside her. Eddie took the stool to Tom's left.

"Drinks on the house, Miss. What's your preference?" Fred asked Maggie.

Her grip on Tom's arm hadn't loosened. She looked up at Tom's face.

"How about a root beer?" Tom suggested, and she nodded. He added, "I'll take a shot of whatever works fastest."

"Eddie?"

"Bud," said Eddie. "Oh, God. Choice. Oh, God."

Fred poured Maggie's root beer from a can into a beer glass, drew Eddie a beer from the tap, poured Tom a shot of whiskey. "Talk. Please, talk to us, people."

Tom tossed back his shot, coughed, and wiped his mouth on his impossibly white sleeve. Warmth spread through him, thawing some of the stage fright he had been feeling. Here on what he had considered solid ground, he felt unnerved by being the center of attention. In the Hollow it hadn't bothered him that much; somehow he had never convinced himself that the Hollow was real.

"Not used to talking anymore," said Eddie. He held his hands out, palms up, and looked at them. "These are mine, you know? For a long time they weren't."

"You were at Chapel Hollow?" asked somebody.

Eddie drank beer. "Yeah," he said.

"What's it like inside that damned house?"

"How many still alive out there?"

"How the hell did you get away? Never heard of that happening before."

"What in tarnation are you wearing, Tom?" asked Bert.

"These were the only clothes I could find."

"They get you naked out there? What were you doing?"

Somebody wolf-whistled.

"Well, I never thought it of Miss Laura," said Fred. "Miss Gwen or Miss Sarah, even Miss Nerissa or Miss Elspeth, but not Miss Laura."

"It's not what you think," said Tom. He wondered how much Arcadians really knew about Hollow people. "When they turn you into something else, your clothes don't—" He listened to his own voice, his own words, and sighed, wondering what any sane person would make of his remark.

Everyone fell into a meditative silence. Maggie sipped root beer.

"They turn people into things, huh," said a voice, but it didn't sound disbelieving, just resigned.

"But you already knew that, didn't you?" Tom said, trying to locate the speaker.

"Heard of it happening," said Ruth. "My little sister said she saw something like that once."

"What'd they turn you into?" asked someone else.

Tom felt heat in his face, which surprised him. "I'd rather not say."

"We need information," Sam said.

"Ask other questions, then," said Tom.

"Did you see my brother Chester?" asked Rufus, one of the firemen.

"He's alive," said Eddie, "but he's in pretty bad shape. If you let it get to you, you go crazy. I saw that happen to one girl—her name was Moira—she got so upset she was screaming and crying, and finally the Family took her off somewhere. I don't know what happened to her, but I didn't see her again. Chester's pretty close to that edge, I think."

"Sam, when are you going out there and make them give us back our relatives? They're not supposed to take relatives."

Tom remembered Cleo the grocer's sad look as she watched him work, her expectation that he would be gone soon. He thought of all the relatives he had in the world—seemed like there were a lot of them, but since Aunt Rosemary's death, nobody who cared where he was. He had come here looking like a loner.

"I'm not going out there to their home ground and get turned into a cow chip," said Sam. He rubbed his hand over his bristly flattop. "Seems to me that would incapacitate me for my job."

"But it's getting worse. Somebody's got to stop it. They took two guys in one year. That's way over the allotment. And they took Chester, and he was almost a native."

"Well," said Sam, "here we are—we got three of 'em back." He swallowed. "How'd you get away? Did you find a weak spot in their defenses?"

Eddie stared at Tom, and Tom squinted back. Eddie lowered his eyes, drank beer in silence while everyone waited for answers. "It was Miss Laura," said Eddie. "Her coming changed things enough so we could run off. I don't think it'll happen again."

"She's leaving the Hollow tomorrow," said Tom.

"Maybe we could ask her—" Sam said.

"It must be a fluke," said Fred. "Blood's thicker than water. Miss Laura may not like what they do, but she won't turn against her own kin."

"You people just go on living here knowing those Chapel Hollow folks steal people and turn them into slaves?" Tom asked. He looked around. Most people refused to meet his eyes.

"They have rules about that," said someone in a low voice.

"They do things for us," said Syd Loftus, a retired man who spent hours in the Dew-Drop every day. " 'Least, they used to. Way back in settlement days, in 1852, they

rescued a lost wagon train, cured the folks who had chol-
era, helped people build, and that's how Arcadia started.
In the bad flu years in the First World War, Miz Kerensa
came into town and conjured the fever out of people; she
was a fine healer and a great lady. In the Depression they
made the land fruitful so we didn't suffer too much, and
they still do that in trouble years if we go out and ask
right. During the floods of '48 and '62 they held the water
away from the town; some towns disappeared right off the
map in those floods, but we're still here. Last twenty-
thirty years, things have been changing. The young ones
are growing up meaner, and they started taking folks. They
didn't used to do that. Except—can't remember. Something—no. It didn't used to be scary to live here, more
like we had angels over the hill. Spring Pageant used to
have real miracles in it, and around Christmas they'd come
in and we would gift each other and have a big feast. But
lately . . .''

—Fascinating, murmured someone in Tom's head. He
straightened. He had forgotten Peregrine's presence.

—How so? thought Tom.

—I have not observed this twining of two settlements,
tanganar and *Ilmonishti,* before, and I am curious about
its operation.

—Do you have questions?

—Ask about the rules of fetchcasting. When I was alive,
it was a thing only the very ill or the very destitute did.

"What kind of rules do they have about, uh, fetchcasting?'' Tom said.

For a moment silence lay heavy in the bar, but then
someone said, ''Never take people out of their homes.''

''They can't take anybody who says no.''

''Yeah, but they can trick you into saying yes.''

''Take only people who have no relatives. Best of all to
take someone nobody will miss.''

''Lately, anymore, since this last generation started
coming into their powers, it's safer to keep the kids inside
after dark,'' said Trailer Court Hank.

"One of the new rules is they can take people who've been real mean to them, like they deserve to get taken because of bad behavior," said Bert. "Used to be you could talk to Hollow folks straight without worrying about the consequences, but lately it's been getting spookier."

"But in the meantime," said Tom, "you kind of cultivate strangers in the hopes that if the Chapel Hollow people come here looking for fetches, we'll be the ones tapped?"

No one answered him for a long moment. Maggie reached the bottom of her glass of root beer and set the empty on the bar with a gentle click.

"It's not like we planned it," said someone.

"We just don't think about it too hard."

"We don't think about them if we can avoid it."

"If you think about them too much, they can hear you and sometimes they come looking for you."

"Lord," said Sam, "and here we are, a group of people thinking hard about them, talking about them, and harboring refugees, too. And we're breaking the most important rule of all: never talk to outsiders about these things."

Dead silence.

After a moment, Sam said, "How could we forget that one? It's built in." He stared at Tom.

Eddie said, "Face it, we're not exactly outsiders anymore. We been further inside than most of you."

"We knew that without knowing it," said Bert. "The way we know when to shut up even when we don't know somebody new is in the room. Like you said, Sam: built in."

"But we're still talking," Sam said. "It's still an invitation to the Hollow people to come and interfere. Syd, Bert, Fred, you're the oldest; you ever heard of fetches escaping before?"

"No," said Syd. "Not getting clean away. There was that attempt not too long ago . . ."

Fred shook his head. "Nobody's gotten all the way away."

Bert frowned.

Sam said, "Think they'll be mad about this?"

"Yes," said Fred.

"Whose fetches are you?" Bert asked.

"No one's," said Maggie, lifting her chin.

"Sorry," said Bert. "Whose were you?" His voice was gentle.

Eddie, Maggie, and Tom looked at each other. "Mr. Carroll's," said Maggie reluctantly.

"Miss Gwen's," Eddie said.

Tom crossed his arms over his chest and said, "Miss Laura's," feeling peculiar because he was confessing to the indignity of being owned; even though it was not true, it felt demeaning. His appreciation for how Eddie and Maggie must feel increased.

Everyone else in the bar moved away from them, either physically or mentally. "Oh, yes, they'll be mad," said Ruth, with a quaver in her voice.

"Couldn't have picked worse people to defy," said Hank. He frowned. "Except Miss Laura isn't—"

"They'll be on the warpath," said Sam in a low voice.

A moment's considering silence edged past. "You want us to go back, don't you?" Tom said.

"We're free and clear," said Eddie.

"What makes you think that?"

"Is Tommy right?" Eddie asked. "Would you rather we went back to Chapel Hollow?"

Silence stretched and lingered. "No," said Fred at last. "We just don't know how to arm against them."

"There was an almost escape six years ago," said Gus. "A stranger none of us ever met ran across country from the Hollow and ended up at the Henderson sisters' place. They wrote down who he was and where he came from. That's all Luke found when he went out there to deliver mail, a note in the mailbox. Margaret wrote that she saw the Hollow people coming toward them out of the sky, and that's the last we ever heard of them. We figured the Hollow folks took the stranger and the Hendersons off."

"They were there," said Maggie. "The women chopping vegetables in the kitchen, Tom."

"They're still alive? They were old even then," said Dr. Alton.

"Yeah, they're alive," said Eddie, "but they're scared. We offered them a chance to run away with us, but they said no."

"See? They knew better," said Sam. "They knew they'd only hurt whoever helped them, and they couldn't get away without help."

"Hollow people will not be coming after us," said Eddie.

"Excuse me, but I grew up with Miss Gwen and Mr. Carroll," said Dr. Alton, "and I don't think they let go of anything they consider their own."

Tom stood up. "Maybe we'd be better off somewhere else. Fred, I lost my wallet out there. I don't know when I'll be able to settle up."

"You did that yesterday, Tommy, remember?"

"Oh, right," he said, then gave Fred a smile. "You did try to warn me. Thanks. Bert, do I still have a job?"

"Anybody who can drive to hell and come back with fares has a job with me. Thought I'd lost Old Number Two forever."

"How about my room? Okay if I stay there?"

"Sure."

"Thanks, Bert. This is Maggie." He touched Maggie's shoulder. She held out a hand to Bert, who shook it, smiling. "Can I clear out one of the storage rooms and put down a mattress for her someplace? She needs to stay close."

"Sure," said Bert.

"Hell, Tom, that's statutory rape," Sam said. Maggie gave him a look, and he flushed.

"She's sleeping alone," said Tom. "If anybody gives her trouble, they'll answer to me." He glared at everyone. Most of them shrugged.

Maggie stood up, close to Tom's side.

"Wait," said Hank. "You can't leave yet. What are we gonna do if—what makes you so sure they won't follow you?"

Maggie held out her hand, showing her silver brand. "We got a magic mark," she said. Tom buried his hands in his pockets, hiding his ring. "You know they have rules. This means they got to leave us alone."

"Where'd you get that mark?" asked Fred. "Could we get one too?"

Maggie's brow furrowed. She glanced at Tom, and he wondered what he would say if she told them everything. Spelling the whole town wasn't something he felt like doing, especially in his present mood. The town had whispered "almost home" to him, but the people in it had welcomed him because he was being set up. Except for Bert, who seemed genuinely happy to see them. Bert puzzled Tom.

"You can only get the mark if you've been a slave out there," Maggie said. "It isn't prevention; it's a cure. It isn't easy to find. Miss Laura brought it. Been waiting for it a long time."

"Oh," said Fred. He looked at Eddie, who pointed to the mark on his arm, and at Tom, who shrugged.

Eddie downed the last of his beer and stood, thumping his glass down on the bar. "I gotta go find Pops," he said, "see can I get my job back. Thanks for the beer, Fred."

"You're welcome. Listen . . . I mean it. Welcome back to town. I don't think we did that right. We're just too damned scared."

"I guess you got good reason for it," said Eddie. "Come on, Tommy, Maggie."

"See you soon," said Bert, as the three of them left the bar through the door where only yesterday Laura had walked into Tom's life.

Chapter 11

"Want a ride to Pops's?" Tom asked Eddie as the door closed behind them. "Bessie needs gas. One more stop before we go home okay, Maggie?"

"Yes," she said.

"That'd be great," Eddie said. They climbed into the front seat of the cab. "Especially if it turns out he doesn't want me back. I feel like I have a disease. If it turns out like that, Tommy . . ." He stared out the front windshield. "Gonna need to blow this town right away. I don't know how that'll work out, with this mark and everything."

"Neither do I," said Tom. "I'll help you do whatever you have to."

"Thanks."

Maggie slumped against the seat, hugging her knees. She looked at Tom. He put his hand against her cheek, tilting his head to look at her. She closed her eyes and leaned her head against his hand. After a moment he patted her hair and reached for the keys, started the car. "Thanks for not giving anything away, guys," he said.

"It's not going to stay like this," Eddie said as they pulled away from the curb. "What do you think they're going to say when they find out Miss Laura's your wife and not your owner?"

"I don't know. I think everything will change. It already has, even though I thought we could stop it. They're not happy to have us back."

"Except Bert," said Eddie. "But then, Bert's always struck me as a maverick."

Tom pulled in beside the bubble-headed gas pumps at Pops's Garage. "Yeah. Something weird about Bert."

Eddie got out, cleared a transaction off the Supreme pump, and dipped the nozzle into Old Number Two's tank. He started pumping gas.

Pops, brought by the ring of tires on the bell-line, came shuffling out of the shop. "Eddie, Eddie!" he cried, breaking into a slow run. "Eddie! Never thought I'd see you again, son!" Then he was hugging Eddie, almost joggling the gas nozzle right out of the car.

Eddie set the automatic feed cock on the nozzle and embraced the little old man. "Oh, Pops. Music to my ears! You're really glad I'm back?"

"I missed you so much. No one else has your touch with an engine. No one else knows when to laugh at my jokes. No one else made coffee with eggshells in it and acted nice before breakfast. You come back to work for me?"

"Sure did, Pops, if you'll have me. Just got back from the Hollow, though. The people at the Dew-Drop don't think I'm safe to have around."

"Nonsense! Any of those Hollow people come by, I'll talk to Mr. Hal. He studied automobiles in the shop with me while he was a boy. I thought maybe you found the woman of your dreams and wouldn't come back. But no?"

"No, Pops. I found Miss Gwen. Or more like she found me, and I was took. She spent a couple weeks playing with me, and that was dynamite, but then she turned into a dishwasher. I hated it."

"I should have gone out there to see Mr. Hal."

"No, Pops. I'm back now. Glad to be here."

"I kept your trailer clean while you were gone, and ran the Harley once in a while."

"That's great!" Eddie gripped Pops's shoulders and

smiled down at him. "After talking to those people in the bar, I thought maybe I'd never feel like this again. Thanks, Pops."

"You're welcome. Eddie, people say Arcadia is a strange place compared to the rest of the world. I've lived here most of my life and don't know. But from what I've seen on TV, we're like other places one way—we got all different kinds of people living here. No good to see some people acting one way and decide everybody will act the same, okay?"

"Okay," said Eddie.

Pops leaned over and peered in through the cab's window. "Tommy? You the one who got Eddie out of there? Fred said yesterday you took off for the Hollow with Miss Laura."

"We escaped together," Tom said.

"You had the transportation. Come anytime for a free fill-up." Pops topped off the tank, then cleared the pump and hung up the nozzle.

"Thanks, Pops. Thanks."

"You're welcome!"

Pops and Eddie headed back into the gas station, and Tom started the car and drove off, jealous of Eddie's welcome from Pops and grateful for it. Maggie still hugged her knees. Her face was blank.

Tom pulled into Bert's open garage, two blocks from the service station, and turned off the engine. It ticked in the echoing silence. The garage was dark except for a slant of sunfall from the open doors behind them and dim electric light from the glassed-in office against the left wall. Grease spotted the concrete floor, and the air smelled of exhaust and pencil shavings. Tom opened the cab door. "Come on," he said to Maggie, "I'll show you my place." He glanced toward the office, realized somebody was there, and led Maggie that way first. The door stood halfway open. He peered around it and said, "Hi, Trixie."

Trixie the dispatcher sat at a big old desk, a fragrant mug of coffee in front of her, a space heater glowing orange to her left, her Adidas-clad feet up on the desk, and her nose buried in the latest issue of *Scientific American*. At Tom's hail, she dropped the magazine and lunged to her feet. "Tommy?" she cried. She raced to him and hugged him.

Arms crossed over her chest, Maggie leaned against a wall and watched, grinning. Trixie, somewhere in her fifties, was tall, broad-shouldered, and wide-hipped. Her short hair stood out in a henna-red halo around her head. Her clothes were casual, jeans and a cable-knit off-white fisherman's sweater. She stepped back and stared at Tom, her fists on her hips and her elbows jutting out. She smiled, her eyes narrowing with pleasure.

"Bert said one of those Bolte sirenes ran off with you, too. Like a plague, first Eddie, then you. Closer together than usual."

"Eddie came back out with me. So did Maggie. Trixie, this is Maggie. Maggie, this is Trixie. Maggie's going to live upstairs with me. Bert said it was okay."

Trixie turned and studied Maggie. "Good lord!" she said. "It's a child!"

Maggie trembled without understanding why. Suddenly everything in her was shaking. She opened her mouth, and a young child's wordless wail emerged. Trixie took two steps and enveloped her in a hug. "There, baby, there," she said. "You go ahead and yell it all out. Nobody listening but us."

It had been a long time since anybody had considered Maggie a child, not since her mother's death when Maggie was nine. A lifetime. Maggie leaned against Trixie's safe warmth, thinking about her mother, and felt tears rise that she had swallowed for seven years. She put her arms around Trixie and clung to her, sobbing against her soft breast, feeling the warm strength of her embracing arms. In that unfamiliar haven Maggie thought of all the fears and sadness she had smashed down inside her. Something warm rested on her head, and comfort flowed from it like warm water. The brand on her palm tingled. A strange river glowed golden through her thoughts, bringing her comfort and carrying away debris from the past. Hurts rose in her one by one and washed away on a tide of tears.

When she had cried away as many things as she could think of that she wanted to get rid of, she lifted her face from Trixie's now soggy sweater front and looked around. The warmth on her head slipped away; it had been Tom's hand, she discovered. She breathed deeply, smoothing out the sobs until they stopped. She listened to her own breathing in the silence of the early afternoon in the garage. Finally she released Trixie, slid out of her arms, and turned to hug Tom. After a moment he hugged her back. She focused on the embrace, reading the undertones. His hands rested on her back as if that was all they wanted to do, not as if it were a prelude to something else; no arousal pressed against her belly. Warmth, and no desire. She pushed her face hard into his shirt front, smelling woodsmoke and male. She couldn't remember feeling safe with a man before.

After a moment she let go of him and rubbed her eyes. "Sorry," she said to both of them.

"Don't be, child," said Trixie. "Sometimes crying is the best medicine you can give yourself."

"I never cry," Maggie said, hearing the tears in her voice, and the anger. "Crying's for people who are helpless."

"Who told you that?" asked Trixie.

"Learned it from looking around."

"Well, it's not true. You can't always judge by appearances. Crying's a power tool to cleanse the soul, if you use it right. I think you used it right. Do you feel helpless?"

"No," said Maggie, checking inside to find out what she was feeling; she couldn't remember the last time she had done that. "Just feel stupid." She rubbed away a final tear and thought a little longer. "Stupid and kind of light," she said, frowning. She glanced up at Tom.

He smiled at her. She read untangled affection and kindness in his smile, and she felt an aching warmth in her chest. She straightened. Had to watch that. It always hurt when someone could touch your heart. "Stupid and kind of light, and stuffed up, and like I must look silly," she said. "Want to wash my face."

"Come on upstairs. I'll show you our rest room," Tom said.

"Tommy, you can't seriously think the child could live here—and share a bathroom, let alone a bedroom! People will talk ugly."

"She needs company, Trix. She was out at Chapel Hollow three years, and they did their worst." Belatedly, he looked at Maggie to see if it was all right for him to share that information. Maggie hunched her shoulders and waited for Trixie's verdict.

"Oh, you poor child. You come on home with me, sweetie. I've got a little guest room—used to be my daughter's before she moved to Seattle—snug and comfortable. Wouldn't you like that?"

"But Tom is my protector. What could you do if Mr. Carroll comes after me?"

"Mr. Carroll?" said Trixie. Her face lost color. "Oh, child, what could anybody do against Mr. Carroll?"

"I want to stay here," Maggie said. She sniffed and looked at Tom, who went into the office and came back carrying a box of generic tissues, which he offered to her. She took several and blew her nose on one.

"If Mr. Carroll comes here—"

"Call me, Trix," said Tom.

She stared at him. A moment edged past. She blinked and lowered her gaze. "All right," she said to the floor.

Tom took Maggie's hand and led her up the steep narrow stairway.

The upstairs hall was dark and smelled musty and damp. Tom reached up and pulled the chain on a hanging light bulb, which lit to show a bare board floor and stained wood walls. He frowned at the chain, realizing it was too high for Maggie to reach; somewhere there must be an extra piece of string to tie to it.

He opened the door to his room and stood aside so she could enter. The room had a window at the far end, its only good feature. A small radiator lurked below the window. Ancient wallpaper with stripes of small fading flowers covered the walls, unpatterned at points by water and other mysterious stains. Against the left wall stood his bed, a camp cot with a foam pad and some blankets on it. Against the right wall was his dresser, a tall, square-edged, substantial piece of furniture painted pink. He also had a card table and a folding metal chair, and a doorless alcove of a closet where several shirts and pairs of pants hung above a neat line of paired shoes.

Tom studied his room as a stranger might. He scratched his head.

"You *live* here?" asked Maggie.

"I spend most of my time in the bar, or working around town. This is just for sleeping."

"I don't think your wife's going to be very happy with this."

"Neither do I." He took her down the hall to the bathroom. It had two stalls in it, like a public rest room, and no shower. She went to the large sink and peered into the mirror above it. The silvered backing was flecked with tiny whirlpools, as if the glass lay flat over boiling water, but she could still see herself. Her face looked swollen, her eyes puffy, and her cheeks red. She splashed cold water on her face and turned to Tom. "Where do we wash?"

"I take showers at the high school, up the hill. The custodian lets me in after hours. Hmm. High school. Seriously, do you want to go?"

"Are we going to stay here long?"

"Probably not." He listened inside, remembering the whispers that had invited him to town, the breathless waiting for something to arrive. The anticipation was gone. Fulfilled, he decided. —Home? he thought.

—Home goes with you, something answered.

"I don't think we'll stay. This is no place for you or Laura to live."

"Don't want to go to school here if we're leaving right away. Tom . . . guess I think I'm following you. Staying with you. Is that all right?"

He stared at the floor, licked his upper lip. After a moment, he said, "Maggie, I just got married to a woman I only met yesterday." He looked up. "I don't know what she wants. If it was up to me, I'd say yeah, you can come with us. I can't speak for Laura. Anyway, we're having a baby. You know anything about babies?"

"Yes," she said. "Had two little brothers and a little sister, and took care of them most of the time, until I ran away. Wonder if they're okay." She hugged herself and hunched her shoulders. "Shouldn't have left them with Daddy."

He watched the misery twist her face, and said, "Maybe we could—," then had second thoughts. "I can't think about this right now, Maggie. Right now I just want to find you a place to sleep. Maybe we can work on your family later."

"It's not your problem."

"I don't think it's yours either."

She stomped across the floor, went to the window, and turned. A dark silhouette against the light, she said, "They depended on me, and I ran away and left them."

"You're not their mother. Could you have gotten away before this and gone back to them, anyway? Was that your fault?"

"Hitchhiking," she muttered. "Daddy always told me never to hitchhike. Did it once, and look where I ended up. How could he be right about anything?"

Tom went out into the hall and began opening doors. A moment later Maggie joined him. They found closets cluttered with junk—wheel-less bicycle frames, an old baby buggy with a rotting fringed canopy, a stack of snow tires for a very small car, boxes of old books and random papers, stacks of *Life* and *Time* and *National Geographic,* a fleet of foot-pedal sewing machines. The air smelled of dust and rust and damp.

"I don't think any of these other rooms has a window in it," Tom said, when they had looked at all of them. "Maybe we could punch one through a wall. See a room you want?"

She picked the biggest one—about six feet wide and nine feet deep. Every room seemed to be a closet, although a lot of the walls looked like one-layer partitions put up long after the building had been built. Tom and Maggie cleared all the junk out of her room, dumping things in the room across the hall. Tom got out a broom and dustpan and swept the floor, waking ghosts of the dust of ages. He changed the hanging light bulb in the room to a higher watt bulb. "You need a bed," he said. "Where are we going to get a bed? Maybe Eddie has an extra."

"Could sleep on the floor."

"You need blankets and stuff. Let's go talk to Trixie."

Maggie wiped her eyes with grimy hands, leaving dust streaks like bruises. "Tom, I don't even have any other clothes, let alone a bath towel. Feel kinda . . ."

"Yes," he said, when her pause lengthened. "Let's go to the thrift shop. I've got thirty dollars in one of my shoes. We can buy you a few things. What did you wear out at the Hollow?"

"They had a big closet with all sorts of clothes in it, all sizes and fashions. It was creepy, as if generations of— of *tanganar* had lived and died and all that was left was their clothes. We picked whatever we wanted."

Tom studied her Grateful Dead T-shirt, denim jacket, jeans, and red hightops. "Hmm," he said.

"These weren't mine," she said. "Wore mine out, and got too big for them anyway."

"Hmm. We better rinse off before we leave." Tom looked down at his own ghostly white clothes. Not a speck of dust on the fabric, and it almost glowed in the dark. "Michael must have made these clothes self-cleaning."

"Mr. Michael *made* something?"

"From scraps," said Tom.

"How'd you get him to do that?"

"I think he likes me."

She cocked her head and surveyed him. "Guess he might. Weird."

They were scrubbing their hands and faces in the communal sink when Trixie called up the stairs for Tom. He dried his hands on paper towels and headed downstairs, wondering if he had a fare.

Aunt Agatha stood beside Trixie, looking owlish behind her glasses. She had lost what he had come to believe was a perpetual smile.

"Why did you run off?" she asked him before he even stepped off the bottom step.

"What?"

"Why did you run away when I told you to stay? How could you desert your bride? I thought you were a boy with manners. And I told you I wanted you to come to me for training. That wasn't just a suggestion, boy. That was a decision from your *Arkhos*."

Trixie, already pale, lost all color. Her eyes widened.

"Can we talk outside?" Tom asked.

"Why? You worried about Mrs. Delarue? She's fixed to the floor; she won't bother us."

"What? What do you mean, fixed to the floor?"

"It's a tool for difficult negotiations. Mrs. Delarue wasn't giving me any answers until I used it. You stick their feet down—a power of earth, though others can master it—I wonder if you have it?—it takes all the fight out of them, mostly, and the ones who are still feisty after that, you can step out of range. Come on, Tommy, come home."

"I don't belong out there, Aunt Aggie."

She reached out and stroked his aura, her fingers rippling over it. "What's this, what's this?" she demanded, prodding a certain section.

Tom opened his Othersight eyes, and saw that she

touched a silvery place he had not noticed before. He analyzed it. "Oh," he said after a moment. "Peregrine."

"What?" Her eyes widened behind her glasses. She touched the silver again, then brought her fingers up to her nose and sniffed them. "A Presence uprooted itself?" She frowned. "It seems to me I have heard—" She paced away and came back, then turned away again. "Honored Presence—you desert us? Is it right that this boy leave the Hollow?"

—Will you grant me speech? Peregrine asked.

—You going to say yes to her?

—Yes.

—Go.

"Descendant, the homestead might not survive if the boy stayed there." Peregrine's voice, deep and rich, came from Tom's mouth again. Trixie brought her hands up to cover her mouth.

Agatha looked at Tom a long moment. "Oh," she said. "Thank you, Ancient. Farewell." She turned and walked toward the outdoors.

"Aunt Aggie," Tom said.

Agatha stopped. "I hate nicknames," she said over her shoulder.

"Aunt Agatha, will you unglue Trixie's feet?"

She turned around. "What about my niece, anyway? One night, one catch—not that we're not grateful—but is that it?"

"She's coming here in the morning. She wants to spend some time with her parents tonight."

"So she stays lost to us?"

"I don't think she'll be so afraid of coming home anymore."

"Very well." She waved a hand, and Trixie stumbled, her feet free. Tom caught her, but she shrank from him, even as he watched Agatha rise in the air; he blinked back into Othersight and saw pale waves surge up out of the ground and support Agatha into the sky.

"You're one of them," said Trixie, trying to shake his hand off her arm.

"Easiest way to fight 'em," he said. He released her.

She stood, arms crossed over her chest, her face distrustful. Maggie came down the stairs then. She touched Tom's arm. "Glad you didn't go back with her," she said.

"Not a chance—unless Laura needs help."

"Child . . . you knew he was one of them?" Trixie asked.

"That's how we got loose. He helped me and Eddie break away." Maggie stepped back, hands on her hips, arms akimbo, and cocked her head, staring at Trixie.

Trixie frowned. "Miss Laura?" she said to Tom.

"My wife. Last night. Kind of a surprise! I didn't go out there looking for any of this."

"You're a cousin or something, though, right?"

"No."

She squinted at him. "No Bolte features," she said. "How—?"

He shook his head, smiling. "Yeah. Why this town? Why now? I don't know. Maybe it's spirits. That's what my new mother-in-law seems to think."

"That thing Agatha talked to—your other voice—is that a ghost?"

"Yeah. One of theirs, and they're scared of it." He grinned. "They're funny. They're superstitious. They believe everything he says, and I think he's been lying to them about me since last night."

"You been possessed by a Bolte ghost, Tommy?"

"I possess *him.* He's been coaching me on how to handle them. Trix, Maggie and I couldn't find any bedding or even an extra bed. We were just going to the thrift shop to get her some clothes, but I don't know if I can afford bedding, too. You got anything you wouldn't mind loaning us?"

"What?" Trixie shook her head, as if trying to wake up. "You don't understand. You're a Chapel Hollow person now. You walk into the Everything Store, point to what you want, wait while they bag it for you, and walk out. They bring it out to the car, but they never, never do home deliveries.''

"I don't have a credit card."

"Hollow people don't use credit cards. Nobody asks them to pay for anything anymore, and they grant shopkeepers and owners immunity in return. I remember in '52, before Mr. Hal married Miss May, he stole a girl, the Everything Store manager's daughter, but the store manager went out to the Hollow and talked to Mr. Israel, Mr. Hal's father, who was *Arkhos* back then, and Mr. Israel got Mr. Hal to let go of the girl before she had a chance to get spoilt. Mr. Hal was always more of a beguiler than a spoiler, anyway. Girl didn't want to be brought back and wasn't happy till the come-hither spells wore off—took three weeks of misery." Trixie's gaze seemed fixed on one of the rafters down the garage.

"I'm not a Hollow person," Tom said.

"Good as. Just tell 'em. Or wait ten minutes; everybody in town will know Miss Agatha came to visit you and left without you. Could see her flying from the interstate. Crazy old woman, doesn't care what kind of stories she leaves behind."

"They out prospecting for new fetches already?" asked a voice from the garage entrance. Tom turned and saw Sam, still in his civilian clothes.

Chapter 12

Trixie frowned. "Naw. Just visiting the new son-in-law," she told Sam. Tom couldn't tell if her voice held anger or fear.

"Whatcha talking about, woman?"

Trixie hunched a shoulder, glanced at Tom, then away. "Tom married Miss Laura, and Miz Agatha came out to take him back to the Hollow."

"What's he doing still here?" asked Sam.

Trixie looked at Tom again. He had his hands deep in his pockets, and he was standing unnaturally still. He could feel, almost see, new lines of alliance struggling to sort themselves out. He wished there was something he could do to keep Trixie on his side, but he couldn't think of anything. She tilted her head and studied him a second, then said to Sam, "Miz Agatha listened to him and then left."

"No! Miz Agatha *listened* to someone?" Sam gaped, eyes and mouth wide. Then he frowned. "Come on, Trix. Quit screwing around. What did Miz A. want?" He sounded anxious and angry.

Perplexed, Trixie looked at Tom. "What?" Tom said. "*You* tell him."

"Yeah, Tommy," said Sam. "What's your take on this?"

"Same as Trixie's," Tom said.

"You . . . *married* Miss Laura? That's not what you said in the bar. Why'd she marry you? They never marry outside their own kind."

"No, they don't," said Tom, although he didn't know whether they did or not.

"But—" Sam paled, and sweat beaded on his forehead. His jaw clenched, the muscles in his neck tightening, then relaxing. "No," he said, "that doesn't make any sense. Why would you hang around town so long instead of just going out there and roaring it up with the family?"

"I didn't even know they existed."

Sam took a deep breath and let it out. "You a Bolte now, and you meaning to live in town? How do you think folks will feel? No place'll be safe."

Tom sighed. "I'm finding that out. We'll leave."

"But—wait a sec. You got Eddie and the girl away? That mark is yours?"

Tom raised his eyebrows, surprised at Sam's insight.

"You could stay here and protect us."

"That's not my job. That's your job."

"I could deputize you—get you on salary if you like. Hell, you wouldn't need money. Whole town would let you sleep and eat free, and Miss Laura too. You stay on—give us all a brand, maybe?"

"Makes you mine," said Tom.

Sam stared at Maggie. She had her arms crossed over her chest, and a defiant expression on her face. Sam's eyes widened. "You said," he began, focusing on Tom again, "you said no one touches her."

"Sure did."

"You gonna be a fleshmonger like the worst of them?"

"No. This child's my daughter now—" He felt a strange golden twist inside, realized that this definition completed a search, label, and understand sequence that had been running ever since he met Maggie. He sighed with relief. "But I don't think I want to adopt the rest of you."

Sam shivered. "Listen," he said after a moment. "I know I haven't always been nice to you. But that's not anybody else's fault. Exempt me, if you want. But the rest of 'em—''

"They're adults, they can leave if they like. They're the ones who decided to live here."

"You are one cold bastard."

"Could be." Tom glanced at the clock on the office wall. It was twenty minutes to five. It must have taken them a while to do all the shifting around upstairs. "Thrift store's going to close soon. Maggie and I have to get going."

"So sorry, your greatness," said Sam, his face bitter.

Tom flicked his eyebrows twice and held the passenger door of Bessie open for Maggie, then went around to climb into the driver's seat. "Trixie, you okay?" he asked out the cab's open window.

She hesitated, then said, "I'm coming with you," and climbed in next to Maggie. "Nobody's going to need a taxi this afternoon. I bet you don't know anything about shopping for a girl. And we can stop at my place afterward and find her a bed. . . . Tom? I could put you all up, you know."

Tom started the cab, looked at Sam, then backed away, raising dust. "You sure, Trixie?"

"Yes. You and Laura could have the boys' room and Maggie could stay in my daughter's room. I bet I even have some hand-me-downs Maggie could wear."

"It sounds great. But what if we get visitors? Mag says distance means nothing to them."

Trixie didn't answer until they had pulled into the thrift store parking lot and Tom turned off the engine. "Tommy," she said, "could you really deal with them? I haven't seen you *do* anything."

"He turned Mr. Carroll into a crow," said Maggie.

"You did?" Trixie asked.

Tom pulled the key out of the ignition. "Peregrine says he'll be harder to deal with next time. I caught him by surprise."

"You turned him into a crow?" Trixie asked.

Tom offered her a smile.

"Wish you'd left him like that," Maggie muttered.

"I know you do," said Tom. He stared at the steering wheel, then looked at her. "I'm not that type of person. I can't just go off and leave him—" But he had left his spell-net around Carroll. Wasn't that the same thing? Tom frowned. It didn't feel the same as trapping and abandoning someone in a foreign form. He would have to work on his ethics while he was learning everything else.

"How could you turn someone into something?" Trixie asked. "Have you ever done it before?"

"No. Peregrine helped me."

"All the time, you could have been turning people into things, and you didn't even know it?"

Tom sat back and thought. He had started seeing and hearing ghosts when he was about ten, and that had confused him—too much going on, nobody else paying attention—and messed up his school work even more than all the moves, though the moves and the ghosts were connected somehow. Hannah had helped him calm his vision so he could focus on what he needed to see when it was important. He had refined that technique into full ghost-blindness, and then, a year ago, he had lost the power to make the visions go away. He had never had any feeling that he could affect what he was seeing, not until that morning at Chester Arthur High when he had grabbed the sky skins and pulled them taut to catch the kids. Now, since he had accepted his vision, he could open Othersight or shut it off whenever he wanted to, which was wonderful. He looked at Trixie. "I don't think I could have turned people into things until today. I had to see someone else do it first. Carroll turned me into an animal, and I learned from that. But now . . ." The nets. The sky skins. They were connected somehow. If he took some time and played with them, he knew he would learn new things. Peregrine probably had vast knowledge to which he had access. Possibilities yawned wide, waiting to swallow him. He shook his shoulders.

"But now?" Trixie prompted.

"Now I don't know what next. Let's go shopping."

The thrift store was run by a local service club. It was full of *Reader's Digest*ed books, stacks of old *National Geographic*s, broken toys, paint-peeling furniture, nearly unwearable clothes from the sixties and early seventies, thick stiff record albums bearing nicks and scratches and a variety of animal hair, dolls with missing or electrified hair, bent and tarnished silverware, and the scent indigenous to attics and garages. "Yuck," said Maggie, paging through dresses with loud flower patterns or overgrown paisleys, sleeves that belled at the elbows or wrists, and hemlines that stopped at nothing.

Tom went to the boys' rack. He found two plaid flannel shirts whose pearly cowboy snaps were mostly missing or presumed dead, but he held the shirts up to Maggie just the same.

"They're ugly," she said.

"They're warm," he said.

She took off her Levi's jacket and tried the shirts on over her T-shirt. The sleeves didn't reach her wrists on the blue-black-and-red plaid one, but the green-black-and-yellow fit her. She stroked the worn plaid. "Soft," she said. She looked up at Tom and nodded.

Trixie found her a red sweatshirt with elastic at the cuffs and hem that still stretched. Tom came up with a pair of bib overalls, and Trixie located some black leather girls' shoes with straps that fit Maggie's feet without pinching. For herself, Maggie found a pink cashmere sweater. She showed it to Tom, holding it up to her chest and waiting, mute, while he looked at it.

His smile started small, then widened. "Yes, Maggie. Yes. I think . . . I think Laura makes good money. We can take you shopping someplace real."

"Can make my own money," Maggie said. Her hands lowered, the sweater a pink rag dangling from the right one.

"I didn't mean it that way." He sat on a ratty sofa so

he could look at her with level eyes. "I just thought—this is fun. It'd be more fun with more money. I've never shopped for anybody but me before. That's all."

She sighed. "Guess I'm scared to trust anybody who wants to do me favors. Had to trust you before—nothing to lose. It hurts more when it means more."

"Yeah."

"Closing in five minutes," said the woman behind the counter, ringing a crystal bell.

Maggie held out the sweater. "Can we afford this?" Its tag read seven dollars.

Tom put the flannel shirt back on a hanger and hung it on the rack again. "Sure. With that you don't need this. Let's go. We can go to Everything and More for socks and underwear, but that'll have to wait till tomorrow."

Trixie showed them another find: a flannel nightgown, its tiny print of carousels almost washed and worn to ghosts. They took their collection of clothes to the counter, and the old woman snipped off the tags and lined them up next to the ancient hand-cranked adding machine. She studied the tags through her bifocals, then looked over her glasses at Tom. "Marshal said a Bolte boy was heading over here. That you?"

"No," said Tom.

She added the numbers up. "Nineteen dollars," she said, and smiled when Tom handed her a twenty.

"Let's go to my house and see what we can find," said Trixie as Tom started the cab. The woman closed the store behind them.

"Hope it's something to eat," Maggie murmured.

"Oh dear. How long since you ate?" asked Trixie.

"Had some wedding food this morning . . . usually get decent meal breaks with good food. They like us to keep our strength up. Miz Blythe is very strict about that. She always watches out for our health, so we can do more work and take more punishment."

"They have this down to a science?" said Tom.

"It's a tradition." Maggie gave him an unhappy smile. "Decades of practice."

"Tom, you eaten lately?" asked Trixie.

"I had a big breakfast, but I could eat again now."

"I have the fixings for grilled cheese sandwiches," Trixie said as Tom pulled up to her house, a two-story Victorian with lots of gray exterior and white gingerbread. All the windows downstairs had lace curtains. Trixie led Maggie and Tom up across the porch and inside.

The air inside was warm and dry, electric heated, and smelled a little like burnt toast. As they crossed the threshold a German shepherd-mix dog jumped up, put its paws on Trixie's shoulders and greeted her with kisses. *"Down, Dasher,"* she said, pushing the dog away and stepping on his back toes. "My son Abel named him after one of Santa's reindeer. He thought that would make it stay Christmas all year. He's not nearly so optimistic anymore."

Dasher yelped and licked Maggie's face, then leaped at Tom, dancing around and barking.

—You could send him to sleep, Peregrine said. —The simplest spellcasting of all, and no bad consequences.

—I'll keep it in mind. For now I'd rather act normal. I don't want to upset Trixie.

Tom held out his hand to Dasher, who licked it.

"Push the dog aside and follow me," said Trixie, leading the way down the hall to a swinging door under the staircase that opened into the kitchen, a room papered in pale yellow and white.

Maggie, carrying a large paper bag with her new clothing in it, looked around wide-eyed. The kitchen was modern and clean, though the air carried the scent of hours-ago coffee. The door they entered through led them into a central food-preparing space framed by three walls and a counter with hanging cabinets above it. Beyond the counter was a dining nook, where a round white Formica-topped table stood firmly rooted atop a square cupboard, with five white metal folding chairs around it, and several more in their dormant state against the wall beside the back door.

Maggie blinked. A tear ran down her cheek. Tom touched her shoulder. She looked up at him. "It's just like my mom's kitchen," she said. "The one she always wanted. Daddy gave it to her, a piece at a time, until it looked like this. She was so happy with it. It was like she could go in the kitchen and walk out of the world. She cooked a lot. I . . . wanted a place I could walk out of the world like that, and then ended up in the Hollow kitchen. Seemed like revenge or something meaner. Had to do everything the old way—heat water over a fire to get it warm enough to wash dishes, boil eggs, cook soup; cut wood for the fireplace and the stoves; sharpen knives on whetstones; and scour the pots out with pumice."

"They don't have electricity?" Trixie asked.

"They don't need it. They have fetches."

"Not even electric lights?"

"They can snap their fingers and make lights. At least, some of them can. Something. Something in the teachings, about light. . . . Heard the younger ones telling a rhyme Miss Fayella taught 'em. *Plakaneshti sirilka, koosh kaneshki porilka.*"

"This means something?" asked Trixie.

Maggie frowned, staring at the floor. "It's a riddle. She was always full of riddles, some of them real mean. This one is kind of—don't know how to tell you the words one for one. Sort of like, 'In changing time, the heavier the light, the lighter the darkness.' "

—Close, thought Peregrine. —She is perceptive. It's a corruption of a proverb. The original reads, "Those who receive a great portion of light in changing time carry a heavy gift." This one means, "The one who receives a great portion of light in changing time has a great power of darkness." I have been asleep too long, Tommy.

Maggie continued, "There's something about it—remember watching Mr. Michael tease Mr. Perry. Mr. Michael'd snap up a light and stick it on Mr. Perry, and Mr. Perry couldn't put it out or control it or even make one of his own. Mr. Michael kept telling Mr. Perry he'd end up just like Miss Laura—wingless, he called it, not quite *tanganar,* but not quite gifted, either. Mr. Perry was so scared. He had nightmares about it. He woke up screaming that Arcadia children were throwing rocks at him and he couldn't stop them.'' She went to the kitchen sink as she talked and washed her hands.

"Imagine them having us for a nightmare," said Trixie. "I always thought it was the other way around."

"Well, Mr. Perry grew out of it," Maggie said. She shivered. Tom patted her shoulder.

Trixie went to the refrigerator and got out bread, cheese, and butter. "Food. You'll feel better." She turned on a gas burner, got out a big Silverstone skillet, and threw some butter in it. The kitchen smelled like somebody's home as the butter melted.

Tom glanced at Trixie as she sliced cheese. He got down cups and took milk from the fridge, poured it, and gave a cup to Maggie. Maggie accepted it, but looked doubtfully at Trixie. "Is this okay?" she asked before sipping.

"Make yourself to home," said Trixie. She smiled, then frowned at Tom. "You knew I felt that way, did you?"

"Felt. Not words. But I should have asked you."

"Yes," she said. She flipped two sandwiches in the pan, one for Tom, one for Maggie, then looked at him. "Okay. You can get yourself what you want. But let me show you where things are first, okay?"

"All right." He gave her a cup of milk, then put the carton back in the fridge. Maggie drank.

"Plates are up there," Trixie said, pointing to the cupboard Tom had gotten the cups out of. Tom got down plates and Trixie put the golden-brown sandwiches on them. He grinned, raised his eyebrows, and glanced toward a drawer. "Right," said Trixie, "the silver's in that drawer."

He got out knives and forks and took the sandwiches to

the table. Maggie carried the milk cups over to the table
and they all sat down.

"Thanks," said Maggie. She wolfed her sandwich
without benefit of fork, juggling the bread to keep its heat
from burning her fingers. Trixie sipped milk and watched
her. "Yum," Maggie said when she had finished.

"More?"

"Yes, please."

"How much more?"

Maggie looked at her for a long minute. "Two?"

Trixie got up and made two more sandwiches for Maggie. Tom ate. Dasher flopped down on the floor and stared
dolefully at Tom's sandwich as it disappeared inside him.

"This is nice," Maggie said as Trixie set more food in
front of her. "Thanks. Thanks. This is so normal." She
held up half a sandwich and just stared at it; she blinked
twice and looked at Trixie. Her eyes were bright. "It feels
so safe. Like maybe my stomach can relax."

"Good," said Trixie. She leaned back, folded her
hands over her stomach, and surveyed her kitchen, her
guests, her dog. She looked happy. "It's so strange having you here, Tom. Never thought I'd feel safe with a
Bolte in my kitchen. Is this what normal people Outside
feel like? Nothing outside going to hurt me, nothing inside going to hurt me, sun's gonna shine in my back door
today?"

"I wonder," Tom said. He remembered eating strange
meals with his Aunt Rosemary, sixteen years earlier, the
two of them sitting in her kitchen together. Sometimes
she made fussy things like stuffed grape leaves; other
times she made him pickle and peanut-butter sandwiches,
or handed him a bowl of dry sugar cereal; it depended
on how much wine she had had that day. He had adored
her. She sat with him as he ate. She smoked cigarettes
and sipped red wine and talked about the religious prac-
tices of the ancient Babylonians or the discovery of per-
spective in art. She had read a lot of odd books. When
his cousin Rafe was away, he and his aunt spent precious

time together. But she died after he had lived with her two years, and he moved on to some other relative's. "I never knew anybody who was normal. Did you, Maggie?"

"Had one great next-door neighbor. Used to tell me good things, strong things. She gave me my first important secret for strength. Don't think she was normal. Everything else—never felt safe anywhere else, really." Sandwiches inside her, Maggie leaned back. She studied her palm, stroked the silver brand. "Guess this is as close as I've come."

A knock sounded at the front door, sending Dasher into torrents of barks and leaps. Trixie jumped up. "Now, who—?" She went to find out.

Presently she returned, with Bert in tow. "Is it true what Sam said about you?" Bert asked. "He's talking to everybody at the Dew-Drop. You a Bolte by marriage now, Tommy?"

"Yep. I didn't want to announce it at the bar. Didn't want everybody to look at me funny, but I guess I can't stop that now."

Bert reached into his back pocket and fished out his wallet. He peered into the currency compartment, then slid two fingers in and retrieved a fragile, yellowing piece of newspaper. "This about you, Tommy?" he asked, handing the folded leaf of paper to Tom. "Always thought it was."

Tom teased the paper open and faced the story from the Portland paper he had run away from:

TEENS FALL OFF SIX-STORY BUILDING, LAND SAFELY

"They flew like angels," said Betsy Willard, Chester Arthur High School cafeteria worker. Willard arrived early for work Wednesday morning. She claimed she saw a male and a female student step off the roof of the Caldecott Building.

At first, said Willard, the teenagers fell. She screamed. "I thought they were going to die," she said.

The girl's mother found a suicide note on the kitchen table of her home when she got up Wednesday morning. She declined to make the contents public, but said the girl and boy had signed a pact to kill themselves together.

"They started falling. Then they flew," said Willard, "or walked on air."

Willard said she saw the school custodian, Thomas Renfield, watching the event from below, reaching out and moving his hands. When the teens landed safely after their six-story descent, the boy berated the custodian, according to Willard.

"It seemed like [the boy] blamed Tommy for making him fly," said Willard. "I was too far away to hear the words. I know this sounds crazy, but the kids are still alive, and they're not happy about it."

Willard consented to a breathalyzer test directly after she reported the incident. The results were negative.

"I believe [the teenagers] fully intended to kill themselves," said Police Investigator Terence Mitchell, who questioned the teenagers after Willard reported the incident. "[The girl] said she was prepared to die. [The boy] said next time they'd do it right, where no one could see them and stop them. Neither of them could explain why their attempt failed, but [the boy] blamed it on the janitor."

Mitchell said a lock on the back door of the Caldecott Building showed signs of tampering, as did the lock on the door to the roof staircase. "Kids aren't allowed on the roof," said Mitchell. "It's for maintenance access only."

Both teenagers have been remanded to the custody of their parents under the condition that they and their families receive intensive counseling.

Renfield could not be reached for comment.

"Where the hell did you get this, Bert?" Tom asked.

"I like keeping track of things."

"How long have you known, boss?" Tom asked. Trixie leaned over his shoulder and took the clipping.

"I've had the clipping since it came out. Before you came to town. Didn't know it was you until a couple weeks after I hired you. I knew the name was the same, but I didn't know if you'd come from Portland until that night we were in the bar watching the Blazers game, and you said it was better live."

"And you never said anything."

"Your business, Tommy." Bert grinned. "I had my hopes."

"Like what?"

"I figured, if you went out to the Hollow, you might surprise 'em. Spike their guns. Yesterday, though, after Fred told me you'd left with Miss Laura, I started feeling awful. I wasn't sure if you would make it. I should have told you . . ."

"But you couldn't, could you? If what Sam said about having a built-in censor was true."

"I could have gotten around that, if I had really tried. I thought it was too soon after Eddie for there to be any action, though. Wrong. Things have been building up for the last while till they're getting nigh intolerable. Time for a change. I'm very glad you made it back." He frowned. "Things are shifting around here in town, though. Your marriage isn't secret anymore, and people aren't going to feel safe with you."

"You don't think I'll get any more fares?"

"Right."

Tom fished the car keys out of his pocket, held them out to Bert. "It was nice while it lasted. Thanks for giving me the chance. I'm not sure how much longer we'll be in town anyway, Bert. As soon as Laura gets back, we'll probably leave."

"No." Bert pushed the keys back. "Keep the cab. Use it for a car. And please don't leave yet, Tommy. I'll give you some other job if you want. Clerk at the Overnighter, if you like—strangers won't be bothered by your status. We need you here until the next event."

"The Overnighter Inn is *yours*, Bert?" Trixie asked.

"Mm," said Bert. Distress crinkled the outer corners of his eyes, the skin above the bridge of his nose. "Didn't mean to let that slip. Don't tell, Trixie, okay?"

"But how could that be? I thought Dale Holloway owned it."

"It looks that way, doesn't it? Tommy?"

"Boss, I don't get this. What do you mean, the next event?"

"I don't know what it will be, but there's bound to be repercussions. You set things in motion by bringing Maggie and Eddie out. Things are coming to a head. Please stay."

Tom stared at Bert, whose brown eyes looked dead serious. It wasn't a mood Tom had seen Bert in before. "I don't know. It will depend on Laura," Tom said at last.

"Before you take off, give me a chance to talk with her. Can you at least promise me that?"

Tom thought. Bert had been unfailingly kind to him, and more than generous. Bert was one of the best things about Arcadia. "I'll do what I can," Tom said.

"Good," said Bert, his face falling back into lines of good cheer. He shook his head. "Can't get over that damned angel suit, Tommy."

Tom looked down at himself. The clothes were still spotless, though he felt a little gritty and sour inside them.

They didn't absorb sweat at all. "Pretty wild, huh? Maybe I ought to change. All my clothes are back at the garage, though."

"Could you fly over and pick 'em up?" Bert asked, his tone mild. Tom narrowed his eyes and studied Bert, who buried his hands in his yellow windbreaker pockets and waited, then smiled.

"Testing?" Tom asked.

"Curious," said Bert. "I've seen a lot of the Hollow folks in action; can't help wondering how you measure up. Kind of an important question at this stage."

"Can you fly?" Maggie asked Tom.

"Did you make these kids fly?" asked Trixie, waving the scrap of newsprint.

"I've never flown except in planes. I'm not sure what I did to those kids. Grabbed a piece of sky, used it like a safety net. Not exactly flying. That story chased me out of town. That's how I ended up here. Kids always coming after me, saying, 'Fly me, fly me.' "

"Could you—could you fly *me?*" Maggie asked. She stood up, pushing her chair away from the table.

"I—" Tom's wedding ring burned on his finger. He looked at it. It was glowing like a spark of sun. "I have to go!"

" 'Ring calls to ring'?" asked Maggie.

"Yes. Laura must need me."

"Take Number Two," said Bert.

"I'm afraid I have to move faster than that."

—Peregrine? How does a person travel quickly without modern technology?

—Will you grant me the use of your abilities?

—They're yours.

He felt Peregrine seep into his mind, and waited. It was different from the previous possessions, more intimate to have Peregrine twining so closely among his thoughts instead of just occupying his body. Then he had the sense that Peregrine moved deeper down to regions Tom had not yet explored.

—Oh, Peregrine murmured.

"Oh, wonderful!" He flexed his hands, grinned an un-Tom-like grin, and sent out a silver seek-strand along the connection between the rings.

Chapter 13

Silver strands spun out and cocooned him in light; they came from the ends of his fingers, which Peregrine moved, using unknown muscles and spinnerets to form the threads. Where the silver touched his bare skin, he felt it, a kiss of breeze, a sleeping breath: faint and pleasurable, an invisible caress, a beckoning. Where skin touched silver, it resonated, matching harmonies with the strands. He could feel the silver's invitation exciting his clothes into matching frequencies, and then his body being drawn into the song. Trixie's kitchen disappeared into blackness. Wrapped in silver, he was a vibrating shadow traveling through a lightless night.

Then color washed across surfaces around him, first deep brown, then overlays of ochre and yellow, finally touches of green and blue; and sound started again, a trickle of water in the distance, arguing voices closer to him. He stared at his hands, pleased and surprised that they were hand-shaped. The rest of his body looked normal as well. He tried breathing, and tasted stew and woodsmoke. He rubbed his eyes and looked around.

He was in the kitchen at Chapel Hollow. Though he could smell the simmer of meat and vegetables cooking, and the undertone of cave, the walls didn't have solid weight: they looked like lacework traceries of red, orange, and gold that reminded him of plastic overlays in anatomy

130

books depicting the circulatory system in human bodies. He could see between the light lines into caverns and tunnels beyond, darknesses embraced by the curling smoke of stone skeletons. Glancing up, he saw constellations of living light. Over in the food-preparation part of the kitchen, webs of dim lavender and baby blue light shifted about. Nearer were three glowing webs, two reddish-orange and one blue and yellow and half-swallowed by the wall's copper embrace. He shook his head, confused, uncertain whether this was a side effect of the method of travel, or even whether Peregrine were still in charge.

He blinked, hoping maybe Othersight would help, and then his vision settled into normal. Where he had seen a yellow and blue web, Laura stood, her eyes wide and angry. She was partly entombed in the kitchen wall, which had grown out over her forearms and calves. Facing her were twin ruddy-haired boys of about seventeen.

Tom glanced toward the business end of the kitchen. The Henderson sisters were chopping vegetables—still, or again?—and keeping their gaze on their work. He focused on Laura. "Is there a point to this?" he asked.

The twins noticed him. "Hey!"

"Get out of here."

"This is a test."

"She has to solve it herself, or she gets cast out, thread cut, and her name gets stricken from the Family tree."

"Oh?" —Peregrine, is there any truth to this?

—The wall test is legitimate, but it is supposed to be held prior to the wedding. It is immaterial now. Powers greater than I have matched and approved you, and there is no longer any question of your or Laura's abilities.

Tom walked over to the wall and put his hands flat on it. He felt anger simmering inside him, but he smiled up at the Presences or Powers on the ceiling. The wall was almost liquid beneath his hands, plastic, flowing, telling his hands that it was used to being shifted and shaped, indeed, longed for it as muscles longed for massage, and would respond to suggestion. He glanced at the twins, then at Laura. "Laura, would you like some help? Is there etiquette to cover this? Since we're married, doesn't that make us one person?"

"Yes," said Laura. "And I, the person, am coming out of this wall."

Tom let energy from his hands sink into the wall and speak with it. The rock shifted away from Laura, freeing her. Rubbing her wrists, she stepped away from the wall, walked over to Tom, and put her arms around him. "I, the person," she said, after hugging him, "am going to turn Alex and Arthur into toads."

Tom looked down at her, dismayed, but she was serious. He spun silver nets, flung them over the twins, and whispered, "Toad. Toad," to the nets. It was getting easier; he felt only a fraction of the fatigue he had felt while spinning his first net.

"I, the person, am not going to make a habit of this, am I?" he asked her as Alex and Arthur collapsed into small warty toads with golden eyes. As they changed, he saw an odd flickering around them, as if their original shapes were still present, but not quite. He blinked and the vision went away. The toads' pale throats thrummed, expanding and contracting. Arthur hopped closer to the wall. Alex's tongue shot out, captured a fly, and vanished back into his mouth.

Laura stooped, her hands fisted on her knees, and studied the toads. A contented smile started at her mouth and reached her eyes. Her dimple flashed. She watched Arthur eat a moth. She gave a long, happy sigh, then glanced up at Tom. "No," she said. "I, the person, don't need to do this often. Once we're away from here, I don't expect to need it at all. But I love this. Okay. Enough."

Tom relaxed his nets, but left them in place, as he had with Carroll. Alex and Arthur turned back into themselves. Both gasped and began hawking and spitting. Alex doubled over.

"What's the matter?" Tom asked, taking two steps toward them.

"They ate bugs," said Laura. She grinned.

"Toads generally do."

"See how trapped their minds are? They should feel they've just had nice crispy hors d'oeuvres, but they choose to get upset."

"How would you feel?"

"I learned to like whatever I happened to eat," she said. "Flexibility was one talent I actually had. It kept me sane . . . if you could call it that."

"Oh," said Tom. He looked into her sandy eyes, saw strange depths there, unsettling evidence of a rocky past. She waited.

"Did you get a chance to spend some time with your parents yet?" he said at last.

She reached for his hand. "Not really. The celebration's just winding down. Come with me?"

"All right."

The way they took through the tunnels this time was different, twisting deeper into the underground. Beyond the kitchen, they walked through one enormous cavern where a sheet of dark water lay, shimmers from witchlight in that windless place reflected sparks on its surface. A drop fell from a stalactite, making a plink that shivered beautiful concentric ripples in the surface of the water, sending the green sparks dancing. The air was cool and smelled faintly of some buried spice, a rock version of cinnamon.

Tom and Laura followed a flat path through the cavern between upthrusts and downshoots of sepia and sand-colored stone. Beyond the spiky, beautiful formations, Tom saw light trails leading to other rooms, other galleries, some edged with stone fangs, some with gardens of stone flowers. Distances held mysteries. And everywhere there were the firefly stars of strange small presences, hidden in coves and crannies in ceilings, wall, and floor. Tom took one look in Othersight, then blinked out of it. The colored haloes were strange and intricate, in shades of light he hadn't seen before, and they were distracting.

On the other side of the cavern they followed a short dry tunnel that sloped upward, ending in open air above a vista that showed green pasture, home to black and white spotted cows and a few Appaloosa horses, and fringed by forest. The first strongest stars showed as the sky stained darker blue. Tom wondered if he and Laura had somehow walked to another state; this was not the high desert south of Arcadia. Laura stopped a moment, drawing in deep breaths. Tom drew in air too, tasting clean, cool sky spiced with pine and earth and grass.

They walked along a broad ledge to the right, toward the forest, and came to another cave entrance, with a tanned cowhide stretched across it. Flickering light shone faintly through the skin, and muted voices spoke beyond it.

"Hoy," Laura said.

"Come in, come in." Hal pulled the doorskin aside, showing a narrow tunnel that opened out to light and warmth and beauty: tapestried walls, Persian rugs overlapping each other on the floor, a wide bed buried under all sizes and shapes of embroidered cushions, most of them earth colors. Knobs of rock between tapestries glowed red, giving off heat, and votive candles in myriad colored and clear glasses sat in shallow niches all over. A samovar steamed against the far wall, adding the comforting odor of English tea to the scents of melting wax and sandalwood incense. May sat on a square-edged red velvet couch.

"Oh," said Hal, looking at Tom, "welcome."

"Thanks."

"May has questions for you."

"This is Laura's visit," Tom said. "We're leaving soon, and we probably won't be back in the near future." He glanced at Laura, wondering if he should have left after rescuing her from the wall. He could not fathom her expression. It hit him again how fast everything had happened. He knew nothing about her, and she seemed to be his future. "She said she wanted to talk with you," he said.

"All right," said Hal.

"Come in. Sit down. Have some tea," May said.

They walked in and Hal pegged the curtain shut behind them.

"Sit down," said Hal, gesturing toward the bed. Laura and Tom sat among the cushions, and Hal sat on the couch beside May. Tom watched teacups complete with saucers float to the samovar's spigot, pause long enough to fill, and come toward him through the air. He caught the first one, and Laura caught the second. The cups were fragile porcelain, pure white; the saucers were about the size of his palm.

"Sugar? Cream? Lemon?" asked May. "You still take cream and sugar, Laura?"

"Yes," Laura said, and set cup and saucer on her knee so she could catch the tea tray as it flew to her.

"Tom? May I call you Tom?" May asked.

"Sure."

"You're taking all this very well, you know. With *tanganar* we either have to enchant them into believing it's all normal, or let them scream a lot the first few days. Are you from a branch of our family?"

"I don't think so. I never knew who my father was, though. Which method do you favor, May, screaming or enchanting?"

"I would rather we didn't fetchcast at all; we didn't do it when I was young, not the way the younger members are doing it these days. But if they must fetchcast, I prefer the screaming. Much better if people have their own minds. Hal is a good enchanter, though—he can pick just the smallest piece of a mind to change, without disrupting anything else—it's a lot quieter and less distressing than screaming."

"I heard Mr. Hal was more of a beguiler than a spoiler," Tom said. "I heard a lot of things in town people never talked about before. You were right, Laura. The town runs on talk. Mr. Hal, did you really work on cars at Pops's Garage?''

"Yes. Pops! I'd forgotten that." Hal looked at his hands, then up at Tom. "There's thin blood in my line," he said. "Before my *plakanesh*, I wasn't sure what would become of me. I thought I'd better have a trade in case I didn't come into power. Pops was terrific. He didn't think poison of me or edge away. Straightforward."

"Did you know that Eddie was his adopted son?"

"Eddie?" Hal frowned. "Who's Eddie?"

"Gwen's fetch," said May.

"Oh." Hal stood up. "Well, she can't keep him. Pops must be getting old now. We can't take his son away. Gwen is so—careless."

"It's already taken care of, Daddy," Laura said. She offered the tea tray to Tom, who declined. She set it on the floor.

"Are you sure? Gwen's tenacious."

"I'm sure," said Laura. "Besides, what could you do to her? Dance to her measure, that's all."

"I could do something," Hal said. "I think I could enlist some of the others; I'm not the only one who's tired of her tactics. You'd help me, wouldn't you, May?"

"I suppose, if I had to," she said, smiling at him. "Apparently I don't. Did you do something about this, Tom?"

"Yes. I took two of them with me when I left."

"Whose was the other?"

"Carroll's."

May stared at him, her face troubled. "No small steps for you, are there?"

"I don't think your family appreciates small steps."

"True." May looked at Laura. "Oh, dear," she said. "I was so happy for you, Laura. Presences blessing a union for you—I wasn't sure I would ever see that. I thought you were wise to leave when you did. But now . . ."

Laura leaned against Tom and smiled. "Don't worry, Ma. I'm happy." Tom put his arm around her shoulders.

"But—still wingless?"

"I've always been wingless," she said. "Ma, are you and Daddy going to spend the rest of your lives here in the Hollow?"

"Is Outside so much better?"

"For me it is."

"Which reminds me," said Tom, thinking about the differences between Outside and Inside. "What about that wall test, anyway? What was it supposed to accomplish? Are there more of those?"

"It's an old test of breeding—" Laura began.

"Wall test?" asked Hal. "What wall test?"

"—Breeding suitability," Laura said. "It used to be everybody who wanted to get married was tested by earth, air, fire, and water, and if they failed, there was some ritual to render them barren."

"Nobody's done the Elements Tests in more than thirty years," said Hal. "Did someone try to wall test you, Laura?"

"The A-twins," she said.

"Great-aunt Scylla declared all such testing void in the fifties," May said. "The blood's too thin to survive it. Those brats! The only test we still do before weddings is Purification."

"Did we cheat on the wall test?" asked Tom.

"No, not really," Laura said. "Two people can act as one. The twins couldn't have moved rock like that if they were apart from one another. What right did they have to test *me*? Only might right, which is the way it works around here a lot of the time. Tom, I'm so glad we're married."

"Might makes us right?"

Laura sighed. "It may not reflect well on me, but I like feeling right for the first time in my life."

"Laura, please explain," said May in a no-nonsense voice. "Alex and Arthur took it upon themselves to test you?"

"In the kitchen wall."

"And you didn't call us?"

"I've never been good at summoning, any more than I was good at other disciplines. I called Tom." She looked at her ring. "He came and let me out, and he turned the twins into toads for me."

After a moment's silence, Hal said to Tom, "This was why the Presence was laughing last night? You have as much potential as the others in our immediate family?"

—Peregrine?

—One of the reasons, yes.

"Yep," said Tom.

"So we don't have to worry about you anymore, Laura," said May.

"I don't think so."

"Well. Welcome to our family, Tom. Thrice welcome." May nodded to him. "Laura is the best of her generation."

"I know."

May smiled. "Of course. Laura, where have you been the past six years? Couldn't you drop us a note?"

"Make Luke come all the way out here to deliver a letter, knowing the way Sarah's been watching him since we were in high school? No, thanks. I didn't think you cared."

"That's not fair."

Laura stared at her mother.

May sat quiet, meeting her daughter's eyes. At last, May said, "I do care, and so does your father. If you had made an effort to keep in touch, we would have told you what was going on. But you—disappeared. You didn't send us an address or any way of getting in touch with you. A lot of things have been happening here, Laura."

"I noticed Annis and Jaimie were missing. Where are they?"

Silence.

"Annis's fetch got her with child," said Hal.

"She asked for Purification and a sanctioned marriage, but Christopher refused to even consider it." May sat a moment staring at the rug nearest the couch, then looked up. "Annis is his favorite daughter. Annis and Jaimie thought Chris was just being ornery, but I think he was dreadfully afraid Annis and the fetch would fail the tests of the Presences and Powers."

"Who's the fetch?" Laura asked.

May rubbed her forehead. "It's a terrible name. Bernie?"

"Barney Vernell," Hal said.

"A wavering, ghostly little man with glasses."

"I know Barney," said Laura. "I remember: he wrote her poems in seventh grade. I thought that was so sad, because they could never—but they have . . ."

"I don't understand the attraction," May said in a meditative voice. "He has straw hair, pale skin, invisibility—who could notice him? I didn't, until this thing with Annis."

"What happened?"

"They ran away—the three of them—and took a lot of the good spirit out of the house."

"Jaimie went with them?"

May frowned at the rug. "Yes. She claimed she'd rather die single than marry anybody in the Family."

"Where are they now? Did they have the baby?"

"We don't know. Agatha had Zenobia and Meredith krift in search of them, but they could find no trace. I don't think any of us realized how well Jaimie learned the disciplines. She has them shielded completely, or perhaps they're on another continent."

"I think they're near," said Hal. "I thought I sensed their traces during the ceremony today."

"When did they leave?"

"Almost three months ago. We could have told you all this if we had known where you were," May said.

"You could have figured it out if you were really interested."

"I tried," said Hal. "You blend right in. You're invisible in a city—you were in a city, weren't you?"

"Good guess." She didn't sound very friendly. "Michael found me."

May sighed. "Michael's more powerful than we are; you must have realized that by now. Do you think we would have let him pester you the way he did while you were growing up if we could have stopped him?"

"Oh," said Laura, her eyes widening.

"Your mother could probably have passed the breeding tests, but I wouldn't have," Hal said. "Scylla dropped them just in time for our wedding. Presences blessed us with five children. . . . Thank the Powers Michael survived Purification. He has the most promise, but the warping on him—so dangerous, but we couldn't seem to counter it. I don't know where he got it. I don't think we're responsible, any more than Chris and Hazel are responsible for how Gwen and Sarah are. Your mother and I have talked this over and we don't know what to think. I'm sorry, Laura."

"There's something about this generation," said May in a troubled voice. "Either the blood is weak or the character's warped. I thank the Powers that brought you and Tom together, Laura. I confess I have often wished I could turn the twins into toads myself."

"Tom turned Carroll into a crow this morning," said Laura.

"What?" said Hal.

"Carroll turned Tom into a jackass first, but he undid that and turned Carroll into a crow."

"We should have stayed for cake," said May.

"We wanted to celebrate alone with each other," Hal said. "Two children successfully linked—a lovely feeling. We left right after the ceremony."

"What did Carroll think of all this?" May asked.

"I don't know," said Tom. "I released him later. He shook hands with me. I've been puzzled about that."

"Acknowledgment of equality," May said. "How unlike Carroll."

"Peregrine wasn't sure if it was a trick or not."

"Peregrine? The Presence? Is it still around? Normally

they only manifest during special rituals, when we summon them,'' said May.

"That's what you think.''

"Oh? You have other information?''

"This place is hip-deep in—in Presences. They just don't use visible light very much.'' Tom glanced around the room, wondering if there were any spirits there. He didn't see any. Suddenly he remembered being eleven and living with one of his relatives. He saw the phantom of his aunt's first husband. It came to breakfast and read a phantom newspaper. Her second husband made orange juice, then sat in the same place as the phantom. The first time Tom saw it happen, he waited for some outcry, which never came; after that he accepted it as normal, until the phantom started telling him how it had died. His nightmares after that, his sleepwalking and sleeptalking had frightened his aunt so much she asked that he be moved somewhere else. Counseling had quieted the dreams, buried the memories until now. "Peregrine . . .'' He held out his hands, palms up, fingers outspread. "Peregrine came inside me. He's training me.''

Hal and May looked at each other. "Have you heard of something like that?'' he asked her.

"In 1792. Rupert Locke,'' she said, "honored by the Presence of Lucian Bolte, who died in 1615.'' She looked down at her hands, which rested on her thighs, then glanced sideways at Tom. "Rupert set a lot of precedents, overturned traditions, disturbed everybody, and generally did the Family a world of good.''

"Am I being set up as a piece of history? I'm not sure I like that.''

—It won't happen against your will, Peregrine assured him.

"You probably don't have to like it,'' said May. "It will just happen. But enough of that. I still have no idea what my daughter's done since she left us, or what your future plans may be. I don't even know what my new son-in-law does—unless you really drive a taxi, which strikes me as highly improbable."

"I'm really a janitor," said Tom. In his late teens, he had been overpowered by a desire to be woodwork, totally anonymous, to disappear, and being a janitor had seemed the perfect way to realize this desire. He had apprenticed himself, learned the trade, and practiced it without looking back for almost twelve years, until he ran away from Portland. "There wasn't any steady work open for that in Arcadia, so I became a cab driver instead. Laura's a model."

"What?" Hal looked surprised.

"I'm going to be modeling maternity clothes soon," she said.

May opened her mouth, closed it. Slowly her right hand rose, nested in her left. "We didn't do any of the fertility rituals," she said.

"Oh, well," said Laura, her voice rising on the first word, cresting on the second without coming down very far. She shrugged. She smiled.

"You'll stay here until after the baby's born, won't you? So we can krift, gift, seal, welcome it?"

"No way," said Laura, as Tom said, "Not a chance."

"Why not?" asked Hal.

Tom looked at Laura, waited for her to speak. "The air here is cold and poisoned," she said.

"Think what shapechangers could do to an embryo," said Tom.

"Babies are sacred," May said, her voice indicating, "This is law."

"Alex and Arthur locked Laura in a wall. What if they had decided to do the render-you-barren thing? What if it had worked? I don't trust you people any more than I would a nest of rattlers," said Tom.

"But—oh. Well, I guess you have reason," said Hal. He frowned. "The twins wouldn't have done it if they had known, though."

"I think we'll be better off elsewhere. I want to get training, too," Tom said.

"In what?" asked Laura.

"Career training. I'm not sure what field. I think I should make more money now. Also midwifery, parenting—I'm not sure this is the best place for that. And—I told Maggie she could come with us, Laura, if it was all right with you."

She stared at him for the space of four heartbeats, then her eyelids lowered halfway. She focused on the floor.

"What do you think?"

"I guess . . . I guess I feel a little upset. I thought we'd share decisions like that."

"I think we should. I didn't tell her it was absolutely for sure. She's helped with kids before. She doesn't have to live with us; we could get her a place nearby. She's so scared to be alone . . . she lived here three years, and Carroll used her. I told her she was my daughter."

Laura put her hand to her temple like someone in a headache commercial. Then she said, "Oh, well." She gave Tom half a smile.

"I think we better stick together," he said.

"Right!"

"If this doesn't work, we can change it."

"Right."

"We don't even know each other."

"You are so right." She looked up and touched his face, then glanced at her parents. "We only met a day ago, and here we are—you, me, Maggie, and baby—a family."

There was an unaccustomed resonance to the word "family" whenever the Hollow people used it that puzzled and pleased Tom. He thought of his cousin Rafe, a ruthless businessman somewhere in Seattle, a family tie Tom had been pleased to sever.

"Are you ready to go home?" he asked Laura.

"Yes." She stood, went to her parents and hugged them. "I expect Tom could do air mail, if I explain it to him properly; we could save Luke the trip. I'll give you my agent's phone number. She always knows where to find me. You could phone from town. You *do* get into town once in a while, don't you?''

"We can if we want to," said Hal.

"All right." She went to the table the samovar stood on, opened a drawer, and got out a pencil and paper. She scribbled a number and her name and handed the paper to her mother. She waited a moment, regarding her parents. A smile surfaced. "I love you," she said. "Sometimes I really hate this place and our family, but I love you."

"We love you too," said May.

"Best of our children," Hal finished.

Laura sniffled and returned to Tom, who put his arms around her. He sent out his silver thread, snagged Laura's suitcase and coat from her room, and carried her and luggage and himself back across the darkness, following the thread he had left during his earlier voyage.

They arrived, blinking, in Trixie's warm, lighted kitchen, where Maggie, Bert, and Trixie were playing cards and drinking coffee. Dasher lifted his nose from his paws, blinked his yellow eyes, moaned, and went back to sleep.

Chapter 14

"Hi," said Tom. The kitchen smelled of coffee. A drip pot sat, half full, over a low flame on the stove.

"Welcome back," Bert said. "Does a straight beat a flush?"

"I'd have to look it up. Laura, this is Bert and Trixie—Maggie you met this morning. Trixie offered us a guest room, since my place isn't big enough."

Laura smiled. "Hi," she said, then lost her smile in confusion. "Did she—did you—?" She eased out of Tom's arms and walked to the kitchen table. "Bert? I know I've seen you before, and"—she turned to Trixie—"aren't you the lady from Tyke's Pharmacy? Mrs. Delarue?"

"Call me Trixie, dear. I sold the pharmacy when my husband died, five years ago. I work part time at Bert's Taxis now. May I call you Laura?"

"Oh, yes, please. Mrs.—Trixie? Is it really all right for us to stay here?"

"Sure."

After a brief hesitation, Laura asked in a very small voice, "Did Tom put a binding on you?"

"What'd I tell you, Tommy? Nothing's normal for these people," Trixie said.

"Oh, be fair," said Tom. "She knows what normal is; she just doesn't expect to find it this close to home. Laura, these are our friends."

145

"Yes," she said. "Is that possible? How do you do it?"

"Why don't you sit down, dear?" Trixie asked. "Are you hungry? Would you like milk or coffee?"

"I—no, I—" Laura took a chair and sat down.

"Tommy, potato chips are in the cupboard over the fridge. There are bowls in the cupboard below and to the right of the sink."

Tom grinned and fetched potato chips and a bowl. "Once you've told me, I can know this stuff for next time, right?"

"Yes."

"Why don't we just pretend you've told me the whole kitchen?"

She sighed. "All right. But you don't know where the linens are yet."

"I don't even know which room we've got yet." He wrestled the bag of potato chips open, dumped chips into the salad bowl, got a glass of milk, and came to sit next to Laura.

"I find that reassuring." Trixie reached out her hand, and Tom slid the bowl across the table to her.

"Who's winning?" he asked.

"Maggie," said Bert.

"Making my own money," Maggie said.

"Starting with what?"

"You didn't pick up your change at the thrift store." She beamed at him. "You can have it back now." She pushed a stack of poker chips toward him.

"Okay. Laura, you ever play poker?"

"Mm. I watched once. A shoot got rained out and we holed up in a coffee shop. I sat at the table with wardrobe and makeup. They lost a lot of money to each other."

He gave her half his stack of chips. "Can we play?"

Trixie put her cards face down on the table. "Wait just a minute, Tommy. Let Miss—let Laura breathe."

Laura drew a deep breath, let it out, and smiled. "Oh, thank you. I do have questions. Maybe stupid questions."

"Go ahead," said Trixie.

"Tom and I"—she glanced over her shoulder at her suitcase and coat, sitting on the floor by the wall—"and my suitcase just came out of the air."

"Same way he left," Bert said.

"You were in trouble, Miss Laura," said Maggie.

"But that—that seems natural to you?"

"You're in Arcadia, M—Laura," said Trixie. "We've seen Hollow people do all kinds of things not common to normal humanity."

"Yes," said Laura. "But I've never seen Arcadians act like you."

"Tommy isn't a proper Bolte, nor, pardon me, are you, Miss Laura," said Bert.

"You're right. You're right!" She leaned back and hugged herself, smiling. "So, if I were to get myself a glass of milk, you wouldn't be upset?"

"Try us," said Trixie.

Laura frowned toward the kitchen. A cupboard door opened, and a glass sailed down to land on the counter; the fridge door popped wide; the gallon jug of milk floated out, poured a portion of its contents into the glass, then righted and capped itself, returning to its place in the cold. The full glass flew to Laura's outstretched hand. She looked at the others, eyebrows lifted.

"Can you snap lights?" asked Maggie.

Laura sipped milk, set the glass down, and snapped her fingers. Bright beachball-sized globes of yellow light materialized in the air above her hands.

"Could you do that before you left?" Maggie asked.

"A little." Laura flexed her hands and the lights winked out. "Why?"

"Heard Mr. Michael talking about you some. He called you wingless. Mr. Perry said the same thing."

Laura nodded. "I am wingless."

"Thought wingless had to do with snapping lights."

Laura's eyes narrowed. "Isn't that funny! You're right, it's one of the earliest tests. I completely forgot."

"What kind of trouble were you in when Tom went to you?"

"Wall test," said Laura.

"Never heard of it," said Maggie.

"I was locked in a wall, supposed to figure my way out. But I never trained my spark to do work like that, or mastered the disciplines. I just longed for Tom to come, and he came."

"Is a wall test a talent test?" Maggie asked.

"N-no; maybe. It's for something else, but maybe it boils down to the same thing."

Maggie hunched forward a little. "What makes you think you're wingless, Miss Laura?"

"It's just something I know, like my eyes are brown, my hair is blonde."

"Think it's just something they told you." Maggie leaned forward, her blue eyes wide and intense. "Bet you could learn."

Laura shook her head. "I don't want to."

"Why not?"

Laura gripped the edge of the table. "Because look where it leads you. Look what those—winged people do. You know that better than anyone, Miss Galloway."

"But they don't *have* to act that way. Tom doesn't. Some of them are much worse than others. Miss Jaimie was nice, and Miss Annis, and then look at Miss Sarah and Miss Gwen, their own sisters, worst of the lot. Miss Alyssa, she came up a week before the wedding, she's terrific."

"Who's Alyssa?" asked Bert. "Came up from where?"

"Some kind of Locke cousin," Maggie said.

"She didn't come through school like other Hollow people," said Bert.

Maggie said, "Different branch. She came from the Southwater Clan."

"Klamath Falls," Laura agreed.

"How many batches of you are there?" Trixie asked.

"Not very many," said Laura. "Some few people scattered in Europe, not living in separate enclaves as we do—''

—That was the way of it in my time, Peregrine muttered to Tom. —We *Ilmonish* lived among others, having our secret grounds for ritual, but otherwise taking on the seeming of those around us. Never have I seen such a separation, a separate nation, as the one here. I came as a Presence to this country with the family's snow-crystal, and was earthed in the old way when settlement was certain; ever since, I have awakened only for ritual observances and updwellings. I have never had the opportunity to study this new system until now, and it puzzles me.

''—whom we know about because of Cyrus Locke, a traveler and a krifter, who found us once in living memory, and left us hints of others elsewhere, but no solid information; and there is Southwater Clan, a holding like Chapel Hollow, only their customs are a little different,'' Laura went on. ''My brother Jess talks about lost tribes. He has old charts of family trees, and lists. He wants to search out the missing ones. But he's not very gifted either, and he hasn't been able to interest anybody powerful in helping him krift.''

''This Southwater Clan,'' Trixie said, ''I never heard of it before.''

''Stands to reason, though,'' said Bert. ''They need other people to marry. Never did meet Ferdie's wife, but I know he's got one.''

''Aunt Gemma,'' said Laura, nodding.

Maggie said, ''And now there's the new batch Miss Jaimie and Miss Annis are starting since they ran off.''

''Ran off?'' said Trixie. ''What'd they do with Barney?''

''They took him with,'' Maggie said. ''Miss him! Played dumb the whole time I was there, but Barney was nice to me anyway. He talked to me. He was the one who explained who everybody in the family was, how they were related to each other. He drew me a family tree. He told me who to watch out for. But that came too late. Mr. Carroll got me first.''

"I can't understand how they came to fetchcast for Barney," said Laura. "He was always so careful not to offend any of us."

"He went too far the other way," Maggie said. "He and Miss Annis—he came out to the Hollow willingly. When he found out what was happening out there, he didn't like it a bit, but too late."

"Anybody heard from them since they ran away?" Tom asked.

"Nary a word," said Trixie. "I didn't even know for sure Barney went to the Hollow until now. Everybody suspected it, but nobody had solid evidence."

Bert shifted in his chair. "I gave Barney and Jaimie a fifty-pound sack of rice yesterday," he said after a moment.

"Bert!" cried Trixie.

"They didn't want anybody to know they were still around."

"Some of the family swore horrible swears when those women left," said Maggie. "They were like brood mares. Family wanted 'em breeding."

"They've still got Gwen and Sarah," Laura said.

"I dread the day one of those Locke sirenes goes broody," said Trixie. "They'll hatch out your true vipers."

Laura glanced down at her stomach, then at Tom. He smiled at her, slid his hand close to hers under the table. She took it. Their fingers tangled. After a moment, Laura looked at Bert. "Any chance you can tell me where Barney and my cousins are? I'd like to see them before Tom and I leave."

"I'll tell 'em you're looking for 'em," he said. "How soon you planning to leave? I talked to Tom about sticking around for a little while, and I wanted to talk to you about that too—hoping you would."

"You want us here?" Laura said, surprised.

''Way I see it, Tom's the stick that stirred the hornet's nest. I'd rather have the hornets focus on him than the rest of us, though I'll help out any way I can. Will you stay on for a little while?''

''Tom?'' Laura said.

''It's all right with me.''

''Miss Galloway?'' said Laura.

''You got to stop calling me that, Miss Laura.''

''I will if you will.''

''Will what?''

''Stop with the misses.''

''What?'' Maggie stared at her, then blinked. ''Oh,'' she said. ''Didn't talk in the Hollow, but I heard it every day for three years, Miss Laura. Not safe to leave a Miss or Mister off—saw people get cuffed a couple times for talking disrespectful about people, and the people weren't even there, just listening in somehow. Mr. Michael made some of 'em bite their tongues every time they forgot a title.''

''That's awful!'' Laura's eyes darkened. ''Tom says he's adopted you. So I guess I have too. You have to learn to call me something . . .''

''Ma?'' suggested Maggie, her eyes bright.

''Sis?'' Laura said.

''Laura,'' said Trixie. ''Laura. Laura. I have to practice that. Seems unnatural.''

''Laura,'' Bert said. ''Please pass the potato chips, Laura.''

The potato chips were in front of Trixie, nowhere near Laura. She hesitated. Then the bowl slid across the table, detouring around cards and poker chips, and stopped in front of Bert. He grinned. ''Thanks,'' he said, munching. Then he sobered. ''Will you stay in town for a little while, Laura?''

''Yes,'' she said.

Maggie said, ''Tom? You never answered my question. Could you fly a bowl of potato chips? Could you fly me?''

''I don't know.''

"Could we try? Always wanted to fly."

Tom glanced toward the window. Outside, night had fallen hours earlier. "Tomorrow," he said, "if I don't have to work. Tonight let's play poker, okay?"

"All right."

"Let's divvy the pot and start a new hand," said Trixie, collecting cards.

"What are the rules to this game again?" Laura asked.

Trixie yawned into the back of her hand as she led them upstairs. She had already shown Maggie to her room and gotten her thrift store and attic clothes stowed away. She clicked on the light in the boys' bedroom, revealing twin beds with Corvettes all over their red bedspreads, brown scuffed furniture, and several model airplanes hanging from fishing line tacked to the ceiling.

Tom moved past her into the room, setting Laura's suitcase down near a battered dresser. "Do you mind if we rearrange the furniture?"

"Not if you do it silently."

"I think I can handle that."

"Fine. Make yourselves to home. Good night."

"Thanks for everything," Laura murmured as Trixie stood back and let her past.

"You're welcome."

As the door closed behind Trixie, Tom walked to Laura and held her.

"Our first home away from home," she whispered. Curtains closed and lights went out.

Tom didn't move any furniture that night.

When he woke, he could tell from her breathing that she was already awake, though she had her back to him. In the narrow single bed they had slept curled against each other, and waking to her warmth delighted him. He stroked her shoulder, letting his Othersight open, and saw a golden glow at their contact points, a color so rich and fine he felt he would like to drink it. She turned in his arms. "Do you think she was right?" she asked.

"Who?"

"Maggie."

"What?" He thought back. "Possibly." He gently released her and sat up. —Peregrine? You awake?

—Yes.

Tom rubbed his eyes. —I forgot all about you last night.

—A reasonable adjustment to our relationship, in my opinion, student.

—Good. You know how they test for power in the Hollow?

—A simple matter. The child was right; ask Laura to snap the biggest lights she can. It's a method of measuring how much oil one has in the lamp.

—I've never snapped lights.

—No need.

"Laura? Peregrine says if you want to measure your power, snap the biggest lights you can."

She sat up and pushed back the cover. She snapped her fingers, and small glowing lights appeared, flickered, and faded.

"Do that again."

She snapped, and this time the glows were dimmer than fireflies.

"You're not trying," he said.

"I am!" She frowned with effort and snapped faint wet flickers. She looked at Tom and shrugged.

"Last night you did much brighter ones. Own your power if you want. Let it be inside you, let it come out." His voice was deepening into Peregrine's. "What you're doing—obstructing yourself—takes more effort than relaxing and doing it correctly." —Grant me, Peregrine thought.

—Go ahead.

Peregrine leaned forward and stroked the insides of Laura's forearms with his thumbs, strong smooth strokes from her elbows to her wrists. "Feel the channel open," he said, his voice rich and hypnotic. "Feel the power flow.

Let it flow. Relax. Relax.'' Gradually his touch lightened until it was almost the brush of a breeze. Heat glowed from her arms. ''Now. Snap,'' he said.

She snapped her fingers, and two small suns shone in the room. They were glaring white, as intense as movie lights.

''Oh,'' she cried in a stricken voice. She hid her eyes behind her arm.

''Don't lie to yourself any more, descendant,'' said Peregrine, gently pulling her arm down. ''Look at your own light.''

She blinked and narrowed her eyes, stared into the little suns. ''No,'' she said, ''it's a lie. You did this. You're only pretending I did it.''

''Stop deceiving yourself.''

She sat with shoulders slumped, even her hair looking limp. She took a deep breath, waited a moment, then exhaled. ''All right.'' She held out her hands to the lights. They lowered and rested on her palms, brightened until all the details washed out of the room, then seeped back into her.

''I feel it,'' she said. ''There's a humming in me . . .'' She turned to him. ''Tom. Be Tom now. Not ancestor.''

He closed his eyes and felt Peregrine sink back into his bones. ''Sorry,'' he said.

''Yes,'' she said. ''I didn't marry *him*.''

He held out his hands to her, and she put her hands in his. ''I didn't ask you about that, either. I'm sorry, Damn!''

''This married business takes getting used to. Look, I'm glad he's there. He helped you when you needed him. I just feel—it's very odd to be sitting in bed with a naked stranger. I don't want that to happen again until I know him better, and maybe not even then. Besides, what about—?'' She looked at their clasped hands, turned hers palms up.

''The light,'' he said. ''Is it all right that this happened?''

"I don't know. I don't know how I feel about this."
She got up and walked to the window, parted the curtains.
The sky was lightening but overcast. She opened the window and looked out. "I feel—" He saw the light around her flare. "I feel dangerous. I'm scared of myself. What if I—?"

"What?"

"What if I *do* start mistreating people? It's what I know."

He got up and joined her at the window. Air so cold it smelled sharp came in. The view showed the cut between the southern hills where the highway lifted out of the gorge and headed across the state toward California. There was a school yard below on the other side of the street, empty in the predawn light, and lining the street stood trees starting to drop their leaves, holding naked arms up to the sky. A scattering of houses stood between Trixie's house and the eastern hills. A dog trotted by on the road below. Tom sensed a strange undertone of music in the hushed landscape, an anticipation of sunrise.

"You can lock it all up again if you want," he said. "Or you can watch how you use it, every time you use it. Wouldn't you like to play with it before you lock it up, though?"

"No," she said. "Then I'd never want to give it up. Show me how to damp it down again."

—Peregrine?

—She has built structures to contain and deny her power all these years, and doubtless those structures are still in place. I just opened their gates. Help her close them again.

Tom held Laura's face between his hands. "You've got walls in here. He opened the gates in them somehow; all you have to do is close them again. Can you imagine?"

She closed her eyes, and he studied her face in repose: golden domed forehead under strands of pale silky hair, brows fine and light, the swell of her lidded eyes, strong high cheekbones, straight narrow nose, tender rose lips slightly parted to reveal the bottom edges of her upper teeth. She had a firm rounded chin. She smelled like wild plants and musk. He looked at her and loved her as he felt the working of her mind between his hands.

She frowned, her brows drawing down a little. "All right. I think I've got it."

With Othersight he saw the strong glow fading around her, leaving a fainter blue aura than she had had when he first met her. "I don't feel good, Tom." She sagged, clutching her stomach.

He gripped her shoulders, looked at his hands with Othersight. The golden glow of contact was gone. Her skin had lost a rosy glow he hadn't even noticed until now that it had vanished. "You shut down *everything*. Open one of the gates a little. You're used to having a little of your spark out where you can play with it."

"Yes." She closed her eyes again. A moment later her aura strengthened, blossomed in faint pink, blue, and gold. She took deep breaths and smiled at him. "All right. I'll keep the little attraction powers. I'm used to them. Feels much better."

"Good." He put his arms around her as they gazed out over the winterleaning landscape. Puddles in the street below had iced over in the night. He suddenly realized the air coming in the window was freezing; Laura had goosebumps all over. "Come back to bed," he said, reaching around her to shut the window.

They crawled back under the covers and shared warmth.

"Trix? What are Trix?" asked Laura, turning the cartoon-colored cereal box over as Maggie got down bowls. It was still early morning. Dasher danced around, staring at anything foodlike with large soulful eyes and making an obstacle of himself. Trixie had not come downstairs yet. Laura was wearing a long-sleeved purple corduroy jumpsuit; she had twisted her hair into a thick cord and pinned it in a coil at the back of her neck. Maggie had on her new overalls, her Grateful Dead T-shirt, and her denim jacket. Tom, wearing his white outfit again, examined the contents of the refrigerator.

"Taste 'em and see," said Maggie. She took the box from Laura and poured two bowlsful of pink, orange, and yellow cereal. Laura, eyebrows up, accepted one. Maggie got milk and spoons and led the way to the table. She poured milk over Laura's cereal.

"Thanks." Laura held her hands above the cereal a moment, whispered a phrase in *Ilmonish,* then took a bite. "Ooh. Weird!"

"Normal American family stuff," said Maggie. She sat down with her own bowl and watched milk sog the little multicolored balls. She sighed and smiled. "Yep. We used to have these for breakfast—times when Dad gave Mom enough money. It was something to look forward to in a day full of potential disaster."

"This?"

Maggie ate a bite and smiled. "Crazy, huh?"

Tom set up the drip coffee pot, put the kettle on to heat water, and made toast.

"Before I headed out here, I told my agent I'd be gone a week," Laura said. "She nearly fainted. I never take vacations. Maggie, I don't know about this stuff. Wait a second." She ate three more bites. "It grows on you. What do you think, Tom? How long will Bert's little while last? I need to get back to Zandra with a revised itinerary. I don't want her lining up jobs for which I'm not there. Nothing can destroy a rep faster than missing appointments."

"I don't think we can be specific," Tom said. "Maybe you could ask her to hold your calls? Where are we going back to, anyway?"

"Well . . ." She grinned. "I *do* live in Portland. Can you stand it?"

"Yeah. I'll change my name. Tom Bolte. Hmm. I wonder if Bert will give me references."

"Your spark could help you get a job."

"But I don't—I—" He looked down at the butter knife in his hand. Earlier, he had been saddened by how easily she pushed her power away, denying herself access to her full potential. Hadn't he always done the same? Until he went to the Hollow, his power had been dormant, waking only in emergencies, and afterwards he buried the memories as deep as he could.

Now his power was alive, and not about to sleep anytime soon. Using it to get a job smacked of cheating to him; but using it to *do* a job—he would have to figure out the right job.

He finished buttering the toast and poured hot water over the coffee grounds.

Trixie wandered into the kitchen as Tom located the dog kibble in a lower cupboard and filled Dasher's dish with it. She headed straight for the coffee pot. She looked more subdued than Tom was used to seeing her, wearing jeans and a fringed brown, white, and black alpaca poncho with llamas marching across it and several holes in it where threads had come unknitted. Her red hair lay flat against her head, not brushed out into full frizz as he'd always seen it at the garage. "Hi, kids," she said as she poured coffee in a mug and downed some.

Someone knocked at the back door. They all looked at each other. Maggie got up and opened the door.

A young woman, her dark curly hair pulled back into a ponytail, her face pale with chill, stood on the back stoop. She wore a baggy green sweatshirt and black jeans, which concealed her body but apparently didn't keep her warm. She had her hands buried in her pockets.

"Miss Jaimie," said Maggie faintly.

"Hi." Jaimie looked around the room, spotted Laura. A smile flickered on her face.

"Jaimie." Laura got up and came to the door. She opened her arms and hugged her cousin.

"Bert said you got yourself a husband and were staying with Mrs. Delarue."

"Yes," said Laura. She glanced at Trixie. "Can she come in?"

"What? Oh, sure, sure," said Trixie, still fuzzy from lack of caffeine.

"Thanks," said Jaimie.

Laura led Jaimie inside, and Maggie shut the door. "Here's my husband, Tom."

"Pleased to meet you, Jaimie," he said, coming around the end of the counter to face her. She had a square chin like May's, but her features tended toward the other side of the family's, slanting dark brows, tilted green eyes like Carroll's, and a generous mouth. Not sure of Hollow customs, Tom didn't extend his hand.

"Me too," she said. She held out her hand, and he took it. "You—know anything about our family, or did you just meet Laura . . . Outside?"

"I know a lot about your family," he said. "I've been to the Hollow and back. Did Annis have her baby okay?"

Jaimie's brows rose. She glanced at Laura. "Mom didn't know," Laura said. "I mean, she knew Annis was expecting, but she didn't know anything since you left."

"Well—the birth part went all right. He's a gorgeous little boy. We hardly had to spell for him at all, and he came out perfect." Her gaze roved the walls, then fixed on Laura again. "We haven't tested him yet."

"Maybe you don't have to. You're not planning to go back to the Hollow, are you?"

"I'd like to," said Jaimie. "I miss the people more than I ever imagined I would."

"Mom said Annis and Barney didn't get married. I don't know how the Presences would react to the whole thing. Did you do any krifting?"

Jaimie hesitated. "You know, Astra and Annis and I were talking in the cavern three years ago before Birth Day, and suddenly we had auguries. Very clear. They pointed Annis toward Barney in no uncertain terms. We never questioned, but we didn't consult anybody else, either. We went out and got him. I told Daddy the Powers and Presences would probably sanction Annis and Barney, but he didn't believe me.''

"Hmm," said Laura.

Tom felt Peregrine restless within him, sending little spurts of self down Tom's arms toward his hands, then retracting them.

"Presences matched us," Laura said.

Jaimie grinned. "So you finally did something by the rules, cuz?" She turned to Tom. "Which branch of Family are you from? Got any good-looking brothers? How come I've never met you before?"

"Nobody's ever met me until now." Then he grinned, thinking that was ridiculous. He'd met more than his share of people in the world, but it had taken him thirty years to find these strangely kindred spirits.

"Coffee, Miss Jaimie?" said Trixie, finally emerging from sleep. "Would you like to have a seat?"

"Thanks, Mrs. Delarue. That'd be great."

"You can call me Trixie if you like."

Jaimie sat down and looked up. "Thank you," she said again, her eyes wide.

"Have you had breakfast yet?"

"We had granola and milk."

"Well, if you're still hungry, help yourself to whatever you see." Trixie brought her own mug of coffee and one for Jaimie to the table and sat down.

Tom carried the plate of toast to the table. It was still warm, steaming with that special smell of browned and buttered wheat. He wondered about that. He had finished buttering it at least fifteen minutes earlier; it should have congealed into an unappetizing mess by now.
—Peregrine?

—Heat is a fine friend.

—Yes, but . . .

—What?

—You did it. I didn't.

—Not true. One of your underground systems accomplished this.

—?

—The eyes that watch everything, even when you do not know they are open. You have a webwork of such systems beyond any other I have seen.

Tom's hand shook a little as he set the plate on the table.

Maggie walked over and sat at her place at the table. The milk in her cereal bowl was pink.

Jaimie smiled at Tom and took a slice of toast, then frowned at Maggie. "You look familiar," she said. She cocked her head. "You're from the Hollow too. The voiceless one. Carroll's favorite—" Her eyes widened. "How on earth did you get away?"

"I took her," said Tom.

Jaimie sat back. "Did you cover your tracks? Carroll will fight! Oh, Lord, he could be here any minute. He might find me! I thought it would be safe—" Her face, which had warmed with the kitchen's heat, went pale again, and she set her toast down and twisted the hem of her sweatshirt.

Laura turned to her and gripped her wrists. "Calm down, Jaimie. Tom bested Carroll once already. We're not afraid."

"But if he should find Annis—imagine what he'd do if he thought we had a *tanganar* baby! He'd purge—we dread the thought—Annis hasn't been well enough for us to run any farther, otherwise we'd be far away by now."

"Annis is sick? Can we bring Doc Hardesty out?" Laura asked.

"Not that kind of sick." Jaimie slipped from Laura's grip, stood and paced. "It's something about souls—I don't remember all the birth lore we had, but there's twined souls, remember? Something about that in the lessons, but Annis and I can't remember it."

"Twined souls?" asked Tom. Peregrine unfurled tendrils all through him.

—Wait! Tom said.

—This is important, Tom. The child must be tested and

classified—sealed, if possible. Twined souls is a common malady any competent midwife could cure.

—Are you a midwife?

—No! Women's work, women's mysteries.

—I don't care about testing or classifying the child, Tom thought, —but if the woman is sick—where can we get a midwife for her?

—The Hollow. Now let me take over; I must see this child.

—No. Don't scare Jaimie.

—Honored! Peregrine's cry was full of anguish.

"Tom?" Laura touched his hand.

"Are you a midwife?" Tom asked, his voice fluctuating between his own pitch and Peregrine's deeper one.

"No," Laura said. "What's going on?"

"He wants to see the child," Tom said.

"Who?" asked Jaimie.

"Tom's got a Presence inside him."

"What? Whose? I've never heard of anything like that."

"Mom and Dad say there's precedent. What does Peregrine want with the baby, Tom?"

"Test, classify, seal. I don't know what any of that means. He said any midwife can cure twined souls, but you'd have to go back to the Hollow for a midwife."

Jaimie stopped pacing. "Come," she said. "Come home with me. Annis has been so worried about little Rupert. She doesn't feel right without the proper rituals. You can give us those, can't you?"

"Yes," said an unknown part of Tom. He shook his head, frowning. "Yes," said Peregrine.

Tom glanced at Maggie. She looked frightened. He held out his hand to her, and she took it, moving closer to him.

"You want to bring her? Oh, I suppose we can use help," said Jaimie. "Please come now, before Carroll—"

Laura looked at Trixie. "Yes, what if he *does* come? Maybe you should come with us."

Trixie groaned. She got a huge brown mug shaped like

a barrel and filled it with fresh coffee. "All right. Hollow business! Oh, dear. Hope Bert doesn't need me."

"How do we get there?" Tom asked.

"How many of you fly?" asked Jaimie.

Chapter 15

Tom, Maggie, Laura, and Trixie looked at each other, then back at Jaimie.

"Oh, dear," she said. "I can manage myself, and one other person, but that's—and we have to be sure not to leave any tracks."

"How about we drive as far as we can, and worry about flying from there?" Tom asked.

Jaimie looked dubious, but at last she nodded. They all piled into Old Number Two, and Tom followed Jaimie's tentative directions: east on the interstate along the gorge for a while; Old Number Two could make fifty-five miles an hour, with a great deal of ratcheting, but cruised more comfortably at fifty. They turned off at a rest stop ten miles east of Arcadia. Jaimie eyed the full daylight around them and sighed.

"I can do invisible, too, but I'm not sure I can do it enough to cover this whole group. What are we going to do?" she asked.

—Peregrine?

—If you give me leave, I can accomplish everything. You have much power in reserve. I hope you'll let me do what's necessary for the infant when we arrive.

—What did she mean, purging the *tanganar*?

—When a child is flawed . . .

—What do you consider a flaw? No way I'm going to let you kill a baby.

—Agreed. If the child is *tanganar,* I will leave it alone. If the child is of our blood, will you let me treat it as we treat our own?

—Does it harm the baby?

—No.

—All right.

Peregrine spread through him even more completely than before. Tom concentrated, relinquishing control of arms, legs, fingers, toes, torso, neck; difficult and strange to do, after building the strength to hang onto control all these years, to contain the fear and anger without outward sign of its existence, to drive the sight away, to stifle the words that might get him in trouble. At each surrender, Peregrine whispered, —Is all well? Are you prepared for this? Remember that I will listen to your wishes and cede it all back to you in an instant. Is all well?

Conscious of Peregrine's regard, the warmth the ghost felt for him, Tom let go, and found himself at last inside his head, looking through his eyes, aware that his body acted without his being in charge of it or even being able to anticipate its next move. Peregrine flexed his hands, staring down at the fingers.

"Tom?" Laura asked.

He gave her a distant smile. "No."

"Peregrine," she said.

"By your leave."

"The Presence?" asked Jaimie, her tone uneasy.

"Yes, descendant. You lead. I'll bring these others." He held out his hands. Laura took one, Trixie the other.

Maggie, forlorn, stood small before him, glancing up with wide eyes, then away. Peregrine, who considered her a young and probably untrained fetch, frowned a moment, wishing Tom had not cluttered them up with these non-essential people. Then he relented. "Climb on my back, daughter," he said, stooping. She ducked around Laura and got on his back, winding her legs around his waist and gripping his shoulders with her hands. By far the best solution, he decided; an almost even distribution of weight. He struggled to rise. The women helped him.

Jaimie glanced around the rest stop, made sure no one else was there to see them, shielded from the road as they were by the rest rooms, and then she rose in the air. Peregrine cast veils of no-see over himself and his passengers. Gripping Trixie's and Laura's hands firmly, he thought himself onto a lifter and tugged the women aloft, following Jaimie's traces up into the sky. Maggie gasped as they rose. She leaned against his back, putting her arms around his neck, and looked over his shoulder. "Oh, yes," she murmured in his right ear, her tone composed of pure joy.

Jaimie waited, almost invisible, above them, leaving only the faintest thread of glisten for him to follow. When he reached her height, she shot across the river.

"Oh, no; oh, no; oh, no," Trixie said as he copied Jaimie's speed. "Tom, I'm going to be sick. This isn't one little bit like *Superman*."

"Close your eyes," he said, strengthening the spell around her so the wind of their passage didn't touch her.

"No, no. Put me down this minute! I don't care about Carroll, I don't care about getting wet, just don't—"

"Go to sleep," he said, and her frightened voice cut off; she hung from his hand, limp weight. He strengthened the protection spell again to help support her. Maggie's hands fisted on his chest; he felt her arms tighten, and her legs. He glanced sideways at her face, and recognized the I-am-not-present look she wore, a common fetch expression down through the ages. He felt a pang. This was Tom's adopted daughter, however worthless she might appear, and it behooved him to take care of her. "She'll be fine," he said.

Her eyes darted to look at him and then away.

"You didn't ask Trixie," Laura said. "You told her."

He heard the accusation in her voice, but he did not respond immediately. He was doing a job in the most expedient way possible—a job she could have helped with, if only she would master her own power. But she cast it away. His comfort lay in knowing he would help care for her child, surely the most interesting child born to the family in a great while. He glanced at Laura. "I'm sorry," he said.

Jaimie slanted down out of the sky, heading for a clump of evergreen and maple trees in a small valley. No recent roads led over the surrounding grass-furred hills; a small creek descended the north slope and disappeared among the trees. As Peregrine followed Jaimie down, a dilapidated, weather-silvered house showed between the trees. A few narrow trails flattened the grass near the house.

They touched ground on beaten earth facing the front porch. Peregrine let go of Laura and turned to catch Trixie as the spell gently released her. Maggie loosened her grip on him and dropped to the ground, then took several steps away. He understood her putting space between them. To his surprise, he felt a small shock of sorrow.

"Trixie? You may wake now," he said, supporting her by gripping her shoulders.

She blinked and woke. "Oh? We're there?" She looked around, shook herself back into her muscles and bones. "Better. Much better. What happened?"

"I slept you."

She glared at him. "That's very Bolte."

"Yes. I am not Tom. I am the ancestor."

"Oh, that's right. All right."

He let go of her.

"You're not staying, are you?" she said.

He felt the heat flash in his head, and knew that his eyes were once again his weapons. She took two steps back, putting her hands up to guard her face. He straightened, shook his head, drew a breath. "No. You are right. I have had my life in the flesh. But I must see this child. Family business. It is an imperative."

"I understand," she whispered, lowering her hands.

He held her gaze a moment, smiled a very little, and

took a step toward Jaimie, who looked frightened of him. But she nodded and led the way across the porch.

"Laura," said a voice as Jaimie opened the door. "Maggie! Trix? And who are you?"

"Barney," Laura said, hugging a slight, spectacled man in baggy rust-brown slacks and a white shirt with rolled-up sleeves. After a moment's hesitation, he returned her hug.

"But what are all you people doing here?" he asked when they released each other. "Maggie? Is this an invasion?"

"This is Laura's husband, Barn," Jaimie said, waving toward Tom, "but he's not, really—he's got a Presence inside him, and it'll do right for Rupert, it says."

"What?" Barney frowned. "Can you cure Annis? Come upstairs."

Inside, the house was clean but sparsely furnished. The stairs were polished wood, bare of carpet. As they clattered up, a baby's awakening wail sounded, then melted into a healthy, angry cry. Barney gathered speed and darted into a small room on the right. He returned with a tiny baby. "Wet," said Barney.

Peregrine reached out, but Barney shook his head. "Wait'll I change him. Annis is in there." He pointed toward an open door across the landing from the baby's room, and they crossed the threshold into the master bedroom.

Annis was a slender mound under a sheet, her silk blonde hair spread out around her head on the pillow, her closed eyes smudged with purple, her cheeks sunken. She had the strong bones of the stockier side of the family, but looked far too gaunt for her size. She opened her eyes.

"Annis!" Laura murmured.

Peregrine strode forward and sketched air signs above Annis with his thumb, watching as they flared red-orange. He looked toward the hall, licked his upper lip, snapped his hand open and shut above Annis as though sprinkling earth or seeds. A cloud of cobwebby threads appeared like the gray wrappings of a caught fly, trapping Annis and twisting into a single fiber that led out the door.

"Oh dear," said Laura.

"Yuck!" said Jaimie. The webs faded from sight.

"Twined souls, yes," Peregrine said.

"And you can't fix that?" Jaimie asked.

"I am not a midwife."

"She needs help!"

"Yes. I can summon help, if one of you will agree to host a Presence—"

"What?" said Jaimie.

"She will need a focus to work through. Or would you rather I summoned—" He stopped to think. He had manifested for the traditional ceremonies, Birth Day, the season changes, each rite of passage, but he could not recall a living midwife at the Hollow in this time frame, only an old, old woman who had healing skills and was training one of the youngest. "Miranda?"

"I'll do it," said Barney, coming in from the hall. He set quiet Rupert on the bed beside Annis. "If it'll help, I'll do it."

"For the proper flow of energies, it should be a woman," Peregrine said.

Maggie came to him, holding out her hands.

"It's dangerous, Mag," Laura said. "Especially for you or Trixie."

Maggie looked at her, eyebrows up. Her muteness had returned full force.

"It can burn out your insides if you're not careful," said Laura, "if you're not connected to our family somehow. You need *sitva* in your bones. Or it can hook into you and refuse to leave. I'll do it. It should be safe for me."

Maggie looked up at Peregrine. He felt a strange thrill that she came to him, trusting, as if he were Tom. "I'll protect you," he said.

She reached out to him.

"Turn around, daughter; let me hold your arms."

She turned her back and he knelt behind her, first holding her head between his hands, setting up safeguards in her mind that said, "I welcome you this far and no farther; for this length of time and no longer; for this task and not much more; and you misuse me at your peril. If there is any sign that your presence harms me, you will leave at once."

As he armored her mind, he felt trembling in her thoughts, fear like black spikes, excitement like dancing blue-green shimmers. He set up the safeguards in Maggie's head, then slid his forearms beneath hers, crooked at the elbows, and turned his hands palm up beneath hers. Her palms kissed his and they twined fingers. He sent out a seeking thread, blessing Tom's power reservoir, and touched the Presence of Ianthe, once, a death away, his daughter, now earthed at the Hollow, and invited her to wake and work. "Only for a very little while," he told her, "and in a very limited way."

"For Family?" she asked.

"For Family."

She sighed. Like many of the others, she was happy to sleep the deep sleep, offering up her interest in consciousness and only waking when invoked by descendants she no longer knew. "Very well," she said.

He led her back. "Precious child," he whispered to Maggie, as Ianthe's red-gold presence passed through him and flowed into Maggie through her hands, up her arms. He felt her tremble in his embrace. He strengthened her fortress of self.

"Don't trouble thyself," Ianthe said, her voice light and floating. "Just let me work." She lifted her hands from his and looked around the room at the others. "What a confusing present! What manner of garb is this?" she asked, grasping a pinch of denim. "Never mind." Her hands worked a fluid dance above the bed, revealing again the tangle of gray webbing that bound mother and child together. She clicked her tongue. "All of you, remove yourselves! Happen this goody and I have work to do."

"I'm not leaving," said Barney.

"Wife, dismiss thy husband."

Annis opened weary eyes, looked into Ianthe's. "Go ahead, Barney. Everybody. I think she knows."

Laura went to the door. She stood on the threshold and looked back as Trixie, Jaimie, and Barney passed her.

"May I stay?" Tom managed to ask, taking back his voice.

"Who art thou?"

"Soon to be a father, and needing skills," said Tom.

"And my father resides in thee?" she asked.

Tom stared at her. How strange to see such a commanding presence inside Maggie, as if the flickery person she sometimes was had wakened to full awareness of her own power.

"Yes," said Tom.

"Go away. This much I vow, that when thou hast need of me, I will return to aid thee. These mysteries are not proper for a man to witness."

Unhappy, Tom retreated into himself, letting Peregrine have control again. Peregrine kissed Maggie's forehead and left, taking Laura's hand as he passed her and closing the bedroom door behind them.

They converged in the kitchen. Laura and Jaimie sat down at the gate-leg table, but Trixie pounced on Peregrine as he entered, and Barney paced, beyond.

"Is that safe for little Maggie?" Trixie asked.

"Safe as spells can make it. Ianthe did not want to be waking; she'll stay no longer than she must."

He felt the suppressed anger behind her face; his words did not quiet it. He wondered where it came from and why. A moment later he shook off that concern and went to Barney. Touching the smaller man's shoulder, Peregrine interrupted the pace-pattern.

"What?" said Barney. He glared.

"My daughter will have done with your wife soon, and then we must test and classify the child. It will help me to know more about you first."

"Like what? My political convictions? My IQ? My street address?"

"No," said Peregrine. He tried to invoke Tom's Othersight, but it wouldn't operate for him. He asked for Tom's help, and saw Barney's aura: a dim turquoise shimmer, with flares of lavender. "May I see your dominant hand, please?"

Barney paced away. "Laura, you married to this jerk?"

"No," she said. "You haven't really met Tom yet. This is a Presence."

"A Presence! Jaimie and Annis keep talking about these Presences as if they were gods. 'If only the Presences bless the union, we have nothing to fear.' Well, goddamn it, I don't think we should have to fear anything anyway. Why can't we just be happy? And what's so wonderful about you?" He whirled and stomped up to Peregrine.

"If I bless and sanction you, the Family will have to condone your union with Annis."

Barney stomped away again. He turned and leaned back against the steel sink. "What if you don't?"

"You are no worse off than you were before. I will not reveal your whereabouts; the Family will have to find and fight you themselves. But I put it to you that Jaimie is homesick, and that I am the least hidebound of Presences. Methuselah would have blasted you to ash by now, and your child with you."

Barney's face went red. He breathed loudly for a moment, then calmed himself. Stiffly he approached Peregrine and held out his right hand.

Peregrine bent his head to study the lines in Barney's palm. He traced a symbol in the palm with his thumb, watched as it flared blue. He let go of Barney's hand then and traced a symbol on Barney's forehead. Its top half flamed yellow, and its bottom half burned blue. "As I thought," said Peregrine. "There are traces of our blood in you."

"What?"

"The men of my family have always been . . ." He paused, smiled, raised his shoulders in a short shrug. "This will weigh in the balance for you. The blood at Chapel Hollow is thinning. They can no longer afford to be purists.''

"Would you bless our wedding?'' Barney said after a moment. "She's so worried about that.''

"Ianthe will know; the child will speak for or against it. But *tanganar* souls rarely twine; Annis's malady is, in a way, auspicious.''

The kitchen door opened and Ianthe came in, followed by a restored Annis, carrying Rupert. Barney ran to her, but she frowned, and he stopped before he touched her.

"Tea,'' said Ianthe.

Jaimie jumped up and got out a teapot and a tea strainer. She filled a kettle at the sink and carried it toward the stove, but Ianthe intercepted her; the stove was not even lit. "Now,'' said Ianthe, holding the kettle in both hands. An instant later the kettle whistled, steam shooting out.

"What kind?'' asked Jaimie.

"Mint.''

Jaimie fumbled a box of tea from a cupboard, managed to fill the strainer and hook it to the rim of the pot. Ianthe touched the pot to heat it, then poured water in.

"Are you all right?'' Barney asked Annis.

"I feel great,'' she said. Peregrine held out his hands for Rupert and she came and handed the baby to him. "Ancient, you honor us.''

They were the first welcoming words he had heard in this house, and they felt strange to him after the anger and suspicion all the others had directed at him, and the fear. "Descendant, you bless our Family,'' he said.

Ianthe brought Annis and Peregrine tea in small cups, carrying one for herself. Peregrine took Rupert to the table, seating himself in Jaimie's now-vacant chair. Ianthe gave Laura a look. Laura stood up, yielding her chair.

Ianthe sat across from Peregrine. "It is a strong soul,'' she said, looking at Rupert as Peregrine laid him gently on the table and opened the blanket he was wrapped in. "The birthing of it laid her low.''

Rupert kicked and smiled between them. Peregrine
sipped tea, then traced a series of signs in the air above
Rupert's stomach. They flared deep gold and pale blue.
"Ahh," he said. "He will be a fire power. I ask you,
father and mother of this child: is it your will he be sealed
to the Families of Bolte, Locke, Seale, and Keye?"

"Yes, oh, yes," said Annis, her voice light with relief.

"What does it mean?" asked Barney.

"We bless and sanction you; you may marry without
fear—"

"Are they not married?" asked Ianthe, her eyes hot and
wide.

"Hush, daughter; a strange age has passed since thou
and I walked the world. Marry without fear. Take the
Locke name for the child. If any naysay you, invoke us.
I am Peregrine Bolte; this is Ianthe Bolte. I am thirteenth
generation and she is fourteenth. Now, father—is it thy
will thy child be sealed to the Family?"

Barney looked at Annis. "Yes," he said.

Peregrine sketched a sign on Rupert's forehead. "In the
name Locke we summon a spark for thee, fire for thy
thoughts." A brief flash of gold.

Ianthe sketched a sign above Rupert's chest. "In the
name Locke we summon air for thee to breathe," she said,
and gold flashed again.

Peregrine opened the baby's diaper and traced a sign
over his genitals, murmuring. "In the name Locke we
summon water to cleanse and keep thee, to flow through
thee." A flicker of gold.

Ianthe traced signs on the soles of Rupert's feet. "In
the name Locke we summon earth for thee to walk upon."
Two little golden glows.

"We gift thee with clarity and strength," said Peregrine. He touched Rupert's forehead.

"We gift thee with love and knowledge," Ianthe said,
touching Rupert's chest.

"Wisdom to choose the right," said Peregrine, tapping
the baby's right hand.

"Power to shield thyself from harm," said Ianthe tapping his left hand.

Peregrine and Ianthe looked at each other a long moment. Time for the electives. "Curiosity," said Peregrine, laying his hand on the top of the baby's head.

Ianthe put her hand flat on Rupert's chest. "Tolerance," she said.

Ianthe and Peregrine sighed and smiled. "Done," said Peregrine.

"I go now," said Ianthe, and faded away. The self-assured tilt to her shoulders, the glow in her eyes went with her, leaving Maggie a diminished person in her wake. But a moment later, Maggie straightened and smiled. She retaped Rupert's diaper. "Thanks," she said to Peregrine. "I liked that! I wanted to find out what it felt like to be boss."

"So I surmised."

"Sure you did, Pa!" She reached across the table and touched his nose. "Tell me another."

He grinned, amazed at her joking, surprised at the delight it waked inside him. She reminded him of Ianthe, whose real features he could no longer recall. The feeling of being father to her—a strange love he had never properly expressed while he had lived—pervaded him. Rupert kicked and cooed on the table before him, and he reached out and smoothed the baby's downy hair, seeing him for the first time. He was a long, thin baby with slender hands and feet, and wide dark eyes, brown like his father's.

Annis came and gathered up the baby. "Thank you, Ancient," she said, her eyes bright. "And thank you, Maggie." She smiled at Maggie, then looked puzzled.

"You are welcome, descendant. Joy in the offspring." Peregrine nested one hand in the other. Jaimie and Laura echoed the gesture; Maggie did too, after a moment, and Trixie and Barney copied her. Annis laughed, cradling Rupert. For the first time the kitchen seemed full of light.

"Will you pronounce vows to wed us, honored?" asked Annis.

Peregrine lifted a hand, then shook his head. "Look to your man, Annis."

She glanced at Barney. He offered her a tentative smile, then came to her and hugged her, baby and all. "What is it?" she asked him. "Don't you want to marry me?"

"Not this way. Not here. Father Wolfe—"

Annis looked over Barney's shoulder at Peregrine.

"My blessings, descendant," he said. "Now I, too, shall go." He let himself sink deep into Tom's marrow, satisfied with everything he had accomplished for the good of the Family.

Tom rubbed his eyes. Then he looked for Trixie, who saw him and relaxed, her shoulders unhunching. He stood and offered his chair to Laura, who shook her head but came to stand beside him. He looked at Maggie.

"I like him!" she said.

"I'm glad. He likes you too. He doesn't usually like people. Thanks, Mag."

"Yeah—thanks, Mag," said Barney, releasing Annis and his child. "Maggie? Maggie, you can talk."

"Yes," she said. "Glad you got away, Barney."

"Did *you?* How did you? What are you doing here?"

"Tom stole me. He stole Laura and Peregrine too. And Eddie. He'll probably leave the Hollow empty before he's through."

"You're—Tom?" Barney asked Tom.

"Mm."

"Well . . . welcome to our home," said Barney. "I— damn—I should have thanked that Presence. I wasn't thinking too clearly. Can you thank him for me? Thanks for helping Annis and Rupert?"

"All right," said Tom. He felt very odd. He had been present on some level throughout Peregrine's actions, without knowing in advance what they would be, or being able to affect them. For the last hour he had felt as if he were watching his friends on a small screen TV with the sound turned low. Now here he was, in a kitchen full of almost-strangers. "Laura?"

"Yes?"

"Would you like some time alone with your cousins?"

She seemed surprised, but after a moment, she nodded. Tom looked at Trixie. She gave him a small smile, a very tired one; he took Maggie's hand and they went out the back door, with Trixie following. "What would you like most?" he asked them.

"A nap," said Trixie.

"Inside the house or out?"

"A bed would be nice," she said.

Tom glanced at the house, wondering about the rooms upstairs. "Oh, they can't object to that!" he said. "Can you stand a short flight?"

"Yeah, I guess so."

He licked his upper lip, concentrating, trying to remember how Peregrine had flown, and Agatha. It was like surfing on waves that rose from the earth—lifters, Peregrine called them, without being able to see them—but it also involved nets. He put his arms around Trixie, which startled her, stepped on a rising wave, and lifted them both up until they hovered outside a second-story window, looking into a room they hadn't seen before. "Probably Jaimie's," Tom said, staring at a neatly made white bed.

"Heaven," said Trixie.

The window was open. Tom helped her in through it, then stood, nonplussed, on air, wondering how one got down off a nonexistent wave that seemed intent on traveling outward. At his thought, the wave lowered itself like an obedient elephant and set him on the ground near Maggie.

"So you can fly," she said.

"I'm not really sure about it. Peregrine could teach me. Is that what you want?"

"Not yet. Let's get away from here."

Chapter 16

Maggie strode off, choosing one of the narrow trails that led deeper in among the trees, and Tom followed. The morning sun had chased the frost out of all the exposed places, but under the trees the white lace still lingered on the carpet of dead leaves. The air in the shadows was chilly, tainted with the breath of winter.

After a few minutes' walk they came to a place where half-bare trees cast what shadows they could over a wide spot in the creek. Maple leaves flared yellow and red; some lay on the water, swaying gently in a loose tapestry against the rocks at the pond's lower end. Maggie shivered. She had come out without her jacket. Tom noticed how little he felt the cold. He wondered if that was something Michael had built into his clothes with the stain resistance, or whether this was another case of heat being a friend.

Maggie sat on a damp licheny fallen log, one touched by sun. Tom sat next to her. "Liked—hosting Ianthe," she said. "She untangled all those webs on Miss Annis and the baby, she cut just the right cords—with light beams that came out of my fingers! She made heat come out of my hands and it didn't burn me. She just wanted that kettle to get warm and it did. Wish she was inside me all the time."

"I think that's dangerous, though. Laura said she could burn out your insides."

She peeked sideways at him through brown hair. "Don't care. I'd like to die from that. Wouldn't mind at all. Especially if I could go home, and then if Dad laid a hand on me—heat! If Carroll came for me, and I could do what he could . . . don't know what I'd do, but . . ." She frowned and tucked her hair behind her ear, staring at the ground. "Ask Pa Peregrine if he can call Ianthe back. Bet *she* could make me fly."

Tom heaved a deep sigh. —Peregrine?

—Yes, honored? He sounded sleepy.

—Maggie wants to host Ianthe as I host you. Is that dangerous?

—? Oh! Peregrine woke with a rush. —Yes, Tommy. For one thing, Ianthe, unlike me, has no wish for half-life. For another, Maggie has no *sitva* in her bones. If she hosted Ianthe for a prolonged period of time, her body would destroy itself. I refuse to wish that on one I . . . consider my daughter.

"He says it would kill you," said Tom to Maggie, "and he won't do that. He loves you."

"Oh . . . how . . ." She looked at him and a tear spilled down her cheek. "How could anyone—"

He gathered her into his lap and held her. At first she was all knees and elbows; her face was hot and wet, and she snarled as he hugged her. Then she relaxed.

Tom let Peregrine share the embrace. Peregrine felt awkward at first, but he reached up and stroked Maggie's hair. She stiffened at his touch, then gradually relaxed. For a long time all they heard was their own breathing—Maggie's interrupted by occasional sniffles.

"Pa Perry?" she whispered.

"Yes, daughter," said Peregrine.

"Can you teach me to fly?"

He closed his eyes, trying to figure out a way a *tanganar* could fly. He thought through Family history, recalling all sorts of games played with *tanganar*, willing and unwilling, cruel and kind. Never had anyone enabled a *tanganar* to fly. "I can think of no way, child. Ask Tom. His mind is less cluttered with notions of impossibility. I am starting to fear that if I train him too well, he will lose some of his abilities."

"But I don't really know how to fly," Tom said, startling himself. Both voices were his, though Peregrine spoke in a lower range.

"However you imagine it will probably work," said Peregrine. "You have immense power reserves, and unknown connections and structures in your house of self. You need only choose a shape for the power's expression and perhaps it will cut itself to your last."

Maggie stirred. Tom opened his eyes and looked at her. "It just seems weird, you telling yourself things," she said. "You don't know what's in your own head, do you?"

"Not until I talk to myself."

She pushed her way free of his embrace. "Tell me about flying," she said, standing on a carpet of fallen leaves.

"These waves pulse up out of the earth. You step on one and it lifts you up. After that, though, you have to cast nets or hooks to pull you where you want to go. I guess you could fly as fast as you wanted if you could think that fast. Faster than flying: it would be easier for me just to pull us back to Trixie's house through the sideways place right now than to fly us across the river again."

"But you'd miss the view, and the freedom. Want to be up there where nobody could touch me and just look down on it all."

He stood up and took her hand. "Okay," he said. He frowned, and blinked into Othersight. Then he touched her forehead. "Look, now. Do you see waves? There's a gray one, like a whale, coming up out of the earth. Then another one inside, lavender, rising up like a bubble, spreading, growing; and others, can you see? Up into the air, then they swoop away . . ." Waves rose, faint but unceasing.

She squinted past his hand, her eyes moving back and forth. He glanced from the shimmery waves to her.

"I can't—I don't see them," she said. She pushed his hand away from her forehead. "I can't see them! You're making all this up, aren't you?"

"Here's one right under us." He let it lift him as it grew and domed. It carried him up until he was level with the upper canopy of the trees. "Wait," he whispered to the wave, and it tensed beneath him and stopped expanding. He could feel its longing to spend itself across the sky, but it waited. "You see it, then you imagine it lifts you. There's one under you right now."

She jumped. She clenched her hands into fists and grabbed a breath. "Lift me, lift me," she chanted, but her feet stayed flat on the earth.

"Down," Tom muttered to the wave he stood on, and it lowered him. "Thanks," he said, and the wave spilled up through him and thinned to nothing in the open air.

Maggie glared at him. "Can't you just cast a spell and make me fly?"

Perplexed, Tom mulled it over. Could there be some way of throwing a net over her that would respond to her wishes? Carroll hadn't needed instructions on how to fly when he had been turned into a crow. On the other hand, it wasn't the first time he had been a bird, from what he had said to Maggie. "If I turned you into a bird—" Tom said to Maggie.

Her eyes looked into distance. She frowned after a moment, then said, "Want to fly like Peter Pan. We flew, Jaimie flew. People can fly, I know they can."

Maybe it had to do with vision. He could manipulate a sky skin once he saw it. He had been able to dissolve Carroll's net over him once he saw it. Though other people at the Hollow operated without Othersight, he knew Othersight gave him an edge. Maybe he could give Maggie Othersight. "I don't know if this will work, but I've got an idea," he said. "Want to try something?"

"Yeah! Ready for a change."

He stood a moment, ordering his thoughts, then cast a tiny net toward the spot between her eyebrows, and requested that the net grant her the same extra sense he had, the ability to shape what she saw, and to shut off her second sight when she wanted.

"Ouch!" she said. She scratched at her forehead and ground her teeth. "Ouch! It's like a toothache."

"Try to relax." He caught her hands.

"Ouch, ouch, ouch!" Her fingers tensed, clenched, released. He could feel the muscles in her hands pulling tight and tense. Her breathing speeded and jerked.

Tom realized his net was trying to close around something that wasn't there—was scrabbling in her brain in search of a missing organ. "Stop!" he said to it, and it slackened and dissolved. "Maggie? Are you okay?"

She breathed like a panting animal, fast and shallow. He let go of her hands, and she put them to her forehead, pressing as if trying to push something through her skin and skull.

Alarmed, Tom opened Othersight and looked at Maggie. Her green and lavender aura had a dark, bruised spot where her fingers pressed her forehead. —Peregrine! What have I done?

—Care, said a woeful Peregrine. —With great care, you can mend it.

Tom knelt in front of Maggie, gripped her shoulders. He tensed, then sent out the smallest tendrils he could imagine, stroking her damaged aura, coaxing it into reweaving itself. His awareness focused down on the project completely, watching as each microfilament healed and wove itself in among the others, with him offering raw materials somehow to replace those that were damaged; the threads he presented were silver, but they stained lavender or green as soon as Maggie's aura accepted them.

He had just gotten to the point where the bruise was gone, overlaid with Maggie's colors—but how fragile the whole looked, now that he had seen its building, how thin the individual threads, how delicate the fabric—when something touched his shoulder, startling him out of trance. "What! No! Not now!" he cried, muscles that had been locked loosening, spilling him out of his crouch.

"Tom!"

The air was chilling sweat on his face; his body inside the impermeable clothes was awash, and he could smell his own odor, strong as it was after a whole day's hard labor under a summer sun. His hands hurt, still locked into the curved grip he had had on Maggie's shoulders. His arms and legs shook with fatigue, and sweat dripped from his eyebrows into his eyes. With great effort he worked himself awake, to realize that the sun had moved and Laura was standing over him. Maggie stood earth still, unblinking.

"What is it? What's wrong?" Laura asked. "Maggie! Are you all right?" She snapped her fingers in front of Maggie's face three times.

Maggie woke. "Oh, God," she said. She rubbed her forehead with the first two fingers of her left hand. "What happened?"

Tom put his hands on the ground, forcing the fingers to open, and sat up. "I tried to cast the spell you wanted, but it worked wrong. Can you think straight, Maggie?" His voice was hoarse.

"Got a terrible headache," she said.

"But your mind, it's all there, isn't it?"

"Huh?" She stopped rubbing her forehead and stared at him, then closed her eyes a moment. "Think so," she said.

"Bless the Powers and Presences," he said, and heard Peregrine speaking in his voice.

She began rubbing her shoulders. "Ow." She opened her jacket and peered under her overall straps and T-shirt. "How'd that happen?"

"What is it?" Laura asked.

Maggie peeked at her other shoulder, then wrapped her jacket tight around her. "Bruises," she said, her face going blank.

Tom looked at his hands. "I did it. I'm sorry. I didn't realize—"

"What happened?" Laura asked as Maggie iced over.

"She wanted to fly. I thought if she could see what I see, she could—but she doesn't have the right equipment. Oh, Maggie, I hurt you in your head."

"I remember," she said in a small voice.

"Peregrine helped me fix it, but I guess I squeezed your shoulders." His fingers were still stiff and aching. "Oh, Lord. Hate me if you have to. I'm just so glad we could undo the harm."

Laura went to Maggie. "May I touch you?" she said.

"Why?" Maggie asked.

"I don't have many of the Bolte gifts, but I have a small healing spark."

Maggie shrugged. Laura placed her long-fingered hands on Maggie's shoulders and began to sing. The sounds spoke of warmth and comfort without using any words Tom knew. He hugged himself, trying to let the sound soothe away his misery, knowing he had hurt Maggie when she trusted him most: he had used both magic and physical strength on her, neither in ways she needed. The more he thought about it, the less he liked himself. Why hadn't he stopped to consider? How could he take such a chance with powers he'd only known for two days? How could he practice on a child when he'd never even experimented on other things? Just because everything else had come easy didn't mean . . .

—Stop wallowing, said Peregrine, in a stern but kind mental voice, —and think about our daughter.

He opened his eyes, realizing that he was sitting there hugging himself, knees drawn up, in the posture closest to invisible, the one he had used in tense situations when he was a child. Laura sang. Tom blinked, saw a strong golden force cloaking her hands, flowing into Maggie's shoulders. Laura stroked Maggie's head, her hands spreading light wherever they touched. Maggie frowned. Her eyes were bright. She swallowed.

—You can creep up to her and beg forgiveness, but who will that serve, you or her?

He expelled breath, let his arms down. "I don't know what I'm doing yet," he said to Maggie.

"I know." Maggie worked her shoulders, turned her head. Laura lifted her hands. "Much, much better. Thank you, Miss Laura," said Maggie.

"Quit calling me that," Laura said, poking her in the back.

"Ma! Thanks, Ma." Maggie went to Tom. "Listen, Tommy. Worse things have happened to me—much worse things, and they took a lot longer to stop hurting."

"I didn't ever want to hurt you, Maggie."

"Know that. After thinking about it, I figured that out. You're not my real father."

He looked blindly up at her.

"Stop it," she said, angry. "You got to listen to me. You're not my real father, you're nothing like him, hear? But if you're gonna be my father, you got to think. You can't give me everything I want. You don't even have to try. Sometimes what I want isn't good for me. You're older. You're supposed to know this stuff."

"Not that much older."

"So maybe you don't know it!" She lifted her hands, shook them in the air. "So maybe next time I hurt you without meaning it. People always hurt people. So don't worry about it anymore, okay? Want some lunch!"

"More like dinner," said Laura. Maggie and Tom glanced around, noting the shift in shadows and sunlight.

"You've been gone a long time," Laura said. "I had to track you down with my ring."

Tom got his trembling legs and arms under control and managed to rise to his feet. He wiped his forehead with his sleeve. It didn't help.

"Do they have any food in the house?" Maggie asked, looking worried.

"Barney started cooking rice in chicken broth half an

hour ago. They have cheese and bread and butter and coffee. Tom? You all right?''

"Just tired."

"Lean on me."

Tom looked at Laura. She wore a jean jacket over her purple jumpsuit, and she looked as fresh as a mannequin in a store display.

"I need a shower really bad," he said.

"It'll have to wait." She came to him and pulled his lax arm around her shoulders. "Come on," she said. She held her hand out to Maggie, and they stumbled back to the house together.

When Laura opened the back door, a gust of warm air came out, carrying the welcome scents of woodsmoke and chicken broth. Laura settled Tom on a chair and handed him a ragged end of a loaf of bread and a hunk of butter on a plate and a knife. Tom ate bread and butter and felt the trembling ease. He took pleasure in eating, recognizing he was restoring himself, fueling up his power systems; he watched his aura strengthening around him.

"Phew," said Trixie, waving her hand in front of her face, "you stink, Tom. Eat in the corner. What have you been doing?"

"Working," he said. "And unless this house has a shower, you're going to have to stand me on the flight back across the river, Trix."

"Just put me to sleep. I'll go quietly. What kind of work? I've seen you working at all sorts of things, but never this hard."

Laura brought him a plate of steaming rice.

"Never mind," Tom said. He thanked Laura and watched Annis nurse the baby until Barney's glare made him lower his eyes. He grinned.

"Laura says you're moving to Portland," Jaimie said to Tom. "Now that we're almost legitimate, we might follow you out there. It would be nice to move to a place where we already know some people. I've lived all my life with people I know. I don't like to think about facing a world full of strangers.''

"Thought you wanted to go home, Miss Jaimie," said Maggie.

"*Sirella*. You can talk—I keep forgetting. Who cured you?''

"I was never really sick," she said. "At least not that way.''

"It was all a lie? You're an amazing kid, you know that? I don't really want to go back to the Hollow right now. I just hated feeling like I was exiled forever. Now, if I really want to, I can go see my parents . . . my sisters . . . not very likely, but possible. You're moving to Portland with Tom and Laura?''

"Yes," said Maggie. "Starting over. My third time, I think." She stared at her hands, which lay relaxed beside her half-empty plate.

"How did you find this house?" Tom asked after a moment's silence. Everyone was eating more slowly. Outside, the chill afternoon was darkening into an even colder evening; in the kitchen, fire purred and crackled in the stove, and someone had made glows, or summoned them, he was not sure how one got them, and hung them about the room so the table was lit with soft, everywhere golden light.

"I heard about the house from Bert," said Barney. "Old Man Morrison used to live out here. He was a hermit, kind of the recluse of Klickitat County. He grew up in Arcadia; Bert knew him from a long time ago, before he rusticated on the wrong side of the river. He died a couple years back. Never heard what became of the house, but Bert suggested we check it out. We came here right after we ran away, and it was all dust and chipmunks. So we figured it was safe to move in. There's an owl in the attic. Jaimie made friends with it. She did most of the fixing up.''

"You helped, Barn," said Jaimie.

"Yeah, but I can't ask dust to dance itself out the doors,

or seal the leaks with patches made of air, or ask the wood to split itself into logs and kindling like you can.''

"You've got a lot of other skills,'' Jaimie said.

"And I,'' Annis said, "I just lay there being sick and a burden.''

"You had a baby!'' Jaimie said, shocked. "That's the most important job of all.''

Annis looked at Rupert, who lay in a nest of blankets in a laundry basket on the floor. "Maybe,'' she said, and managed a faint smile. "I'm tired. I'm going up to bed.''

"You haven't finished your supper,'' said Barney.

"I'm not hungry,'' she said, stooping to lift Rupert. "Good night, everybody. Thank you for coming. I hope you'll stop by again before you leave for the city.'' She headed for the kitchen door.

"Descendant,'' said Peregrine.

Annis stopped on the threshold and looked back.

"What troubles you?''

Her eyes were bright. "You honor me with your presence and aid, Ancient. Please don't worry. I'll be fine tomorrow.''

"What's the matter, honey?'' asked Barney.

"Just tired. It's been a long day. Thanks, Ancient.'' She left.

Barney jumped up. "Excuse me,'' he said, and ran after Annis.

"What's going on?'' Trixie asked. "You—Presence— you explain it, why don't you?''

"She is tired,'' said Peregrine.

"No kidding. What can we do?''

"Nothing, just now,'' he said, "except, perhaps, go home.'' He turned to Jaimie. "Descendant?''

Jaimie eyed him and waited.

"You give me hope for your generation. You are accomplished, and I joy in you. I foresee troubles coming. I want you to call on me if you need help.''

She nodded. "How?''

Peregrine looked at Maggie, who studied her palm, then

held it out for Jaimie to see. "He gave me a mark to summon him with," she said, her face pale.

"You are sealed to him?" Jaimie looked upset.

"Is that what it is, Pa?"

"Yes, child."

Jaimie bit her lip. "No offense, Ancient, but I don't want that."

"Your choice. I will listen for the silver calling, then, as best I can while cloaked in this flesh and *sitva*. My name is Peregrine Bolte, and I am a power of air. Thomas, my host, can persuade more than one element; we have not found his limits yet."

"Thanks," said Jaimie. She frowned. "Ancient, I don't really remember my training in the calling."

"There is something lax in the Family teacher if you can't remember such basic training. You have learned flight and unsee, trace and housewifery; you were an apt pupil—?"

Her cheeks colored. "Well, I . . . but Fayella never seemed to care if I learned anything, or Annis, or Laura, even. We didn't have the . . ."

"You did," Laura said, after Jaimie let the silence stretch a moment. "You used to be an avid disciple of the dark. You were the little teacher's pet."

Jaimie shrugged. "Yeah, well . . . I kind of changed my mind about that direction, and then she didn't care about me anymore. She liked Sarah and Gwen and Marie more. The people who excelled in the dark disciplines, the ones who obeyed her. I think she was scared of Michael, so she tried to keep him ignorant. She left the rest of us to fend for ourselves."

"No wonder the blood is thinning. Without proper tending and teaching, you are all grown up crippled." He looked at Laura. Her jaw firmed and she glared at him. "That is fine, if you are content with it. But it does not advance the Family for its members to weaken themselves."

"Everything must be in service to the Family, huh?" asked Laura.

"Forgive me, descendant; it is my long-term project, the only reason any Presence stays in the Hollow after we return our flesh to the earth. Those of us who don't care about the Family go . . . elsewhere after death."

"So you're in Tom because you think it'll advance the Family?"

"Yes," said Peregrine. "Do you object?"

"I want you to be Tom," she said.

"But I—" he said, in Peregrine's low voice. "But I—" he said in Tom's higher, lighter voice. "Okay," he said.

"But Laura," said Jaimie, "he was going to teach me the silver calling."

"Oh, you do it like this," Laura said, her tone annoyed. She looked around the room, rummaged in a couple drawers, and came up with a tarnished fork. She pushed plates and cups aside to make an open space on the table. "Find a piece of silver—real silver's better. Sketch a circle with it, and these signs at the cardinal points, and this one in the center. The one that's your element, focus on that a little while you're drawing it, so it engages your powerflow. Then you concentrate on the Presence you want, and chant. Oh, something stupid like, 'Peregrine, I summon thee; come to me, to me, to me.' "

Tom felt Peregrine rise in him, almost breaking free of his nets along Tom's bones, floating free of his body. A silvery aura smoked up out of his own green one and took the shape of a tall, sunken-cheeked man, haggard and beak-nosed, his hair long and straight. His eyes twinkled, belying the worry lines on his forehead and the deep brackets that framed his mouth. He took on the appearance of weight and matter. "What do you wish, descendant?" he said, and this time his voice came from the air, unconnected with Tom and unhindered by Tom's natural timbre.

"What?" said Laura. She looked up, saw his phantom form, and paled.

"Child—have you summoned me in vain?" His tone sounded threatening.

Laura and Trixie stared. Jaimie covered her mouth with her left hand. Maggie grinned.

"I was just teaching her the basic summons," Laura said. "That was necessary, wasn't it?"

He smiled. "Next time use a false tool, and a false name," he said. "If you have no special needs, I'll leave you now."

"Wait a minute," said Laura. "Jaimie, did you learn that summoning from the demo?"

Jaimie looked at the symbols on the kitchen table, scratched by a fork tine. "I think I can remember it," she said.

"You've got the symbols down, right?"

"Uh—"

"Look." Laura traced the outline of one symbol. "Those strokes, in that order. That is air. Here's water— see the waves? Fire, and earth here. Get them in that order. In the center, finally, here's ether. This comes from the chapter of the text on things seen and unseen. Do you remember *any* of this?"

"No," said Jaimie. "How come you do?"

"Because—I thought if I only learned it right, maybe it would work and I could get Michael. But I was always afraid to actually try anything." She stood tapping the fork in the palm of her hand, looking down at her scratches on the table top. "Hmm. And that one worked. Peregrine!"

"Yes, descendant."

"Did I do that right, or were you just humoring me?"

"You have the hand of a master, descendant. You executed it perfectly."

"Oh, no. I remember all of Fayella's teachings, including the dark disciplines."

Jaimie said, "Does this mean you *aren't* wingless?"

Laura touched her lips with an index finger; her eyes looked vague and unfocused. "Hmm. Maybe not. Okay,

ancestor." She looked up at him, offered a small smile.
"Thanks for coming."

"You're welcome." Peregrine's seeming faded; Tom
felt him settling back inside, flaring a little here and there,
then sleeping. Tom wondered if the manifestation had tired
the Presence.

Maggie started clearing the table.

"Oh, Maggie, you don't have to—" Laura said. She
picked up some dishes and took them over to the counter
by the sink.

"Everybody shares the work in our house," said Jaimie, grabbing two cups.

"I'm going to sit this one out," Trixie said, leaning
back in her chair. "There's not enough dishes for everybody."

Maggie filled the dishpan, frowning because there was
no hot water in the single pump. She looked at Jaimie.

"I'll do that part," Jaimie said. She held her hands out
over the water, narrowed her eyes, and stood very still,
moving only her fingers. After a moment, steam rose from
the water. Maggie dumped some soap in the water and
stirred it. Tom found a towel and they all worked—Maggie
washed, Jaimie rinsed, Laura dried, and Tom put away.

Barney came back just as they finished.

"Well?" Jaimie asked him, as she pulled the plug.

"I don't know. She's feeling left out and depressed and
useless. Sis, what can we do?"

Jaimie said, "Just know she feels that way, I guess.
Don't talk in front of her like she's not here."

Trixie stood up. "Listen. It's been an interesting visit,
but I've got to get home now. I ran off without even leaving Bert a note. He's probably waiting for us and wondering where we are. What if he needed us? He hasn't got
silver calling or any of that stuff."

"Yes," said Laura. "You're all sanctioned now; you
can come to town any time you like."

"I've got to see Father Wolfe," Barney said. "We'll

set a wedding date as soon as possible, and invite you all. Good night.''

''Can you make it back okay?'' asked Jaimie.

''Yes,'' Tom said.

When they stepped out onto the porch, cold attacked them. Maggie hugged herself, shivering. Trixie stepped back toward the front door. ''Wait,'' said Tom. He thought of fleecy nets wrapping them round in warmth, and they both straightened.

''Oh,'' said Maggie, looking at her feet. The porch was already white with frost, but her new warmth melted dark rings around her shoes, black holes eating outward.

Tom looked at Laura to see if she needed warmth. She shook her head and smiled.

He stooped so Maggie could climb on his back. ''Sleep, Trix?'' he asked.

''That'd be best,'' she said.

He locked arms with her and with Laura. He cast a net of sleep over Trixie, then spun out nets of unsee the way Peregrine and Jaimie had that morning, let a big whale-shaped wave lift them skyward, and used silver threads to pull them back to the place where they had left the taxi that morning.

They drove home without incident. The heater in Old Number Two didn't work very well, but the cold didn't bother them.

Trixie unlocked the back door and flicked on the kitchen lights. ''I wonder if Bert stopped by or left a note,'' she said. ''He's got a key. Anybody want cocoa?''

Dasher howled, a rising note that suddenly choked. Trixie screamed and staggered back. A hairy man with slanted glowing green eyes rose up on his hind legs, his furred hands still closing off the dog's throat. He smiled, revealing pointed dog teeth. ''Where have you been?'' he asked, his voice a slurred growl. ''I've been waiting nearly all day.''

Maggie's hands bit down on Tom's arm.

Chapter 17

Tom touched Maggie's hands, then pried them off his arm and slipped forward, pressing Trixie's shoulder as he passed her. "Let go of the dog," he said. Laura came to stand beside him.

The werewolvish man released Dasher, who yipped and ran to Trixie, cowering behind her.

"Do you recognize this guy?" Tom asked Laura.

She frowned and studied the visitor.

—Sense your own traces, Peregrine suggested. Tom glanced down, using Othersight, and saw the slenderest of threads reaching from his hands to the man: one of the first nets he had ever cast.

"Oh," he said. "Carroll. What do you want?"

Carroll looked at Maggie, his eyes wide and burning. She cringed, edging toward the back door. Then she stopped. Straightening, her shoulders lifted, she walked forward with Ianthe's confidence, each footstep sounding loud and firm. She stepped in front of Tom and leaned against him, pulling his arm around her. She tilted her head. She glared at Carroll.

"No," Tom told Carroll. "What about your promise to me?"

"For a day it bound me, as I agreed. But now it is a new day. As for respecting the home place, this is not her home," Carroll stood taller, staring at Maggie. "Her home is with me."

"No," Tom said again.

"Without her . . ." Carroll turned away, a frown furrowing his brow, then shook his head. *"Faskish* the rules. I'll take the fat one, then," he said. He stalked forward and seized Trixie's arm, grinning like a hungry man who's just seen supper. She tried to break free. He growled at her.

"No!" said Tom.

"You've got two. What can you want with another? Give her to me and I'll go away and leave you alone. Maybe for a long time."

"She's not mine—"

"Then you can hardly object. Come." Carroll stared into Trixie's eyes.

"No," said Trixie. She slapped his face, but he didn't flinch. "No," she said, twisting her arm in his grip. She raised her free hand again. He growled and muttered and her arm stopped in midair; her whole body stilled, as though frozen in a photograph.

"Why are you doing this?" Tom asked, reaching to pull Carroll's hand off Trixie's arm. Carroll spun and snapped at Tom's hand, almost closing those pointed teeth on him, snarling.

—Don't let him bite you! said Peregrine.

—Is he rabid? Is it contagious? I thought he just picked that form.

—There could be several reasons for him to choose it. But any kind of bite has power. Don't take risks with this.

"I need a fetch," said Carroll. "I want Maggie. I miss her, and she's mine. But if you won't let me take her, I guess I'll just go out and find some other little girl." He laughed and edged for the door.

Laura went to Trixie, tugging on her upraised arm. It didn't budge.

"Someone about eleven," said Carroll, grasping the doorknob and twisting it. "Someone I can train myself."

"Wait," said Maggie. "Don't. I—"

"You won't," Tom said to her. "Don't give yourself up to stop him from doing something else wrong."

"If she comes with me of her own free will, nephew, you cannot stop her."

"She's sealed to me. She bears my mark. Why are you doing this? What's wrong with you that you need it?"

"Nothing's wrong with me. Ask what's wrong with yourself, O great hope. Why do you cling to your scruples as if they were your bones, when all they are are bars? All the world is 'I want.' You will be finding that out, now that you're awake. 'I want.' There's no reason to settle for anything less."

"What happens when my wants clash with yours?"

"I win," said Carroll. He laughed again and opened the door. "I'll find a little pretty girl—prettier than this one—younger and tenderer, someone who'll scream for me."

Tom shifted into Othersight and saw the thick red net wound around Trixie. Laura's hands glowed golden as she tried to melt the net, but her light spilled off without effect. Tom saw his own silver net still hazing around Carroll. He pulled it tight, stopping Carroll before he could step over the threshold.

Tom reached out a mental finger to touch the black net around Trixie; it melted. She let out a great whoosh of air and relaxed.

" 'I want,' is it? I want you to stop this," Tom said to Carroll, and he thought change at his in-law.

—What are you doing? Peregrine asked, alarmed.

—Shh.

Tom still felt shaky after his failure with Maggie that afternoon, but, whatever *sitva* was, he knew now it made a difference in people's elasticity, and he knew Carroll had it. He felt himself shifting into an adrenaline high, energy rising to meet whatever demands he was about to make. He told his net to engage with Carroll's systems and consult them at each step to make sure Carroll stayed safe, to stop if the change was harmful. He prayed to the new pantheon he had glimpsed at the Hollow, wondering how far their influence spread from the home place, and whether they would help him if they heard him. He prayed to his own internalized ghost, Hannah, for aid and understanding. He remembered: without any training, he had turned a man into a bird. He had more experience now. "Become what you victimize," he whispered, "become what you most desire."

Carroll keened and twisted, danced and collapsed inward, cloaked in a cloud of light and mist. Swords of silver light sliced at him, whittling without creating waste. When the air cleared, a young naked girl stood by the door, her hand on the knob. She had a tumble of shoulder-length blonde curls and a pale pure body, clean as though she had been sculpted from soap. Her face twisted. She glanced down at herself, touched the little nipples on her chest, looked up at Tom with tear-blurred eyes, and ran out the door into the night.

"Wait!" Trixie cried, and ran after her.

"What have you done?" Laura asked in a hushed voice.

"I don't know. I'm not sure," said Tom. "I don't know how he's going to respond to that, but I feel like it will prevent him from going out and grabbing some other child."

"He's a shifter," Maggie said. "He likes changing shape. That might not make any difference to him."

Tom took her shoulders and turned her to face him. "Was it a mistake?" he asked. In his mind, an echo of Carroll's words sounded: "All the world is 'I want.' " He had wanted something, and he had taken it, without asking. Taking power over people. A chill whispered up his spine while he waited for Maggie's verdict.

"Don't know," Maggie said. "Don't know, Tom. Just because he looks like that doesn't mean he's harmless."

"It may not change anything," Tom said. Except me, he thought.

—Can it—*breed?* asked Peregrine.

—What?

—Can it? I couldn't tell. I couldn't understand your actions. You made adjustments I have never seen before. Is it viable? If you could handle the fine details of such a transformation . . .

Tom waited, but Peregrine didn't continue. —What? Tom asked at last.

—You could . . . make Maggie fly. You could accomplish almost anything if you took the time to think it through. You must be careful.

—I remember.

Being careful not to hurt someone was one aspect of it, and learning how to deal with so much power ethically was another. Tom wasn't sure Peregrine was the right person to discuss ethics with, since some of his attitudes were antiquated.

"Tom?" Laura said.

He focused on her. She had a lot of ideas about the uses of power. Maybe later they could talk—

"Trixie went after him. Her."

"Oh. Oh, God." He turned and ran out the door, Maggie and Laura following him.

They didn't have to search far. The girl's pale skin was a blotch under a shedding maple tree beyond the driveway, and Trixie's voice a low murmur in the darkness. They ran toward it.

"I'm cold," said a light treble voice.

"I have clothes in the house. Please come back. You'll be safe."

"No," said the girl. "No! He's there." She curled her arms around her body.

"I'm here," Tom said.

The girl tried to run away, but Trixie grasped her shoulder, restraining her easily. "Please," cried Carroll.

"He won't do anything else to you. My word on that," said Trixie.

"But you're *tanganar*—how can you control *Ilmonishti*? Let me go, please let me—"

"You can't go running around jay naked in the middle of the night, child. It's already freezing. Come back or I'll carry you back."

"No!" she cried, struggling and kicking.

Trixie picked her up and carried her. "Tommy, you're not about to do anything else to this child, are you?"

"Depends on what she does."

"I can't do anything," said Carroll, lying limp at last over Trixie's shoulder. "You stupid *akenar!* I'm too young! You mean you didn't inflict this form on me with that in mind?"

"Huh?"

Laura said, "Oh, Tom, it's—she looks about nine; if that's her age, she won't come into her powers for another three or four years."

"But—years?" He had thought of this transformation as a temporary thing, to solve an immediate problem. If Carroll couldn't fight back . . . if Carroll couldn't menace anybody for a few years . . . and yet, who was he to dictate what Carroll could and couldn't do? Tom felt too tired to think through the implications. One night, at least, wouldn't hurt, would it?

They followed Trixie up to the house and into the kitchen.

She put Carroll down. "Stay here. I'm going up to the attic," she said. "You know everyone here, I think?"

"Don't leave me alone with them!"

"Tommy won't hurt you," Trixie said, but Carroll clung to her arm, staring with wide green eyes—at Maggie.

Tom looked at his adopted daughter. Her eyes blazed. Her nostrils were pinched, her face pale. He couldn't tell if the corners of her mouth aimed at a smile or a frown.

Carroll hid behind Trixie.

"Oh, no you don't, you beast," Maggie said, and she swooped forward. "Waited a long time for this." She ducked around Trixie and grabbed Carroll's arm, then rained fierce undirected blows on her.

Carroll hunched over, trying to guard her face with her free arm.

"Stop them," Trixie yelled at Tom, reaching into the flurry without managing to grasp either combatant. Carroll tried to hit Maggie back, without much success. She whimpered. Dasher jumped up and down and barked. Maggie was screaming; Carroll wailed, then screamed and snatched at Maggie's hair. Laura started forward, stopped, held her hand out, pulled it back, finally put both hands over her ears as the uproar escalated.

Tom stood paralyzed, his mouth open, his hands reaching toward them.

—You could stop it with a word, Peregrine told him.

—I can't figure out whether that's the right thing to do. I don't know if this is helping Maggie or . . .

After what seemed like a long time, the fight slowed. Maggie's rage had spent itself; she stopped pummeling Carroll and drew back, staring at her fists—the skin had split on her knuckles, and her hands were swollen. She had a cut on her cheek and a black eye, and a button had ripped off one of her overall straps.

Carroll looked like blood-spattered marble painted with patches of dust. Her nose bled, and bruises rose all over her body, as if some dark flying thing inside her translucence smeared wing dust on the inner surface of her skin. She was crying, a high mindless wail.

Trixie gathered Carroll up into a hug. Exhausted, Carroll laid her head on Trixie's shoulder, put arms around her, and cried and cried. "There, there," Trixie murmured. "You were right, sweetheart, I'm sorry I didn't listen, I'm so sorry—"

"You put her down," Maggie said. "Don't you hug her! Don't you touch her. Leave her be."

"How could you? How could you attack someone small and defenseless?" asked Trixie.

"I learned it from her!"

Trixie's hand stopped stroking Carroll's back.

"I learned it from every man I ever met, starting with my dad!" Maggie yelled.

"So you pass it on?"

Maggie waved her hands, clenched them into battered fists. "Oh, God!" She turned toward Tom, then faced Trixie again. "No! I'm not passing it on. I've giving it back. Put her down. She doesn't deserve any more comfort than I had three years ago after he . . . raped me."

Carroll's arms tightened around Trixie's neck. She buried her face in Trixie's shoulder, not even coming up for air.

Maggie cried, "How can you hug him? Heard people talking out at the Hollow, Chester and Barney, about what he was like in town—everybody scared of him—not because he's some helpless little kid, because he hurt people and broke things—now you're feeling sorry for him 'cause he looks so little, but it's just a way for him to trick you—" Maggie's face was red. Tears spilled down her cheeks as she spoke.

Trixie blinked. She thought about everything she knew about Carroll Bolte, everything she had heard and seen. She knew almost no good about him (a baby saved from drowning, an ailing cat healed, but he had done those things when he was very young); he was more destructive than any three other Hollow people, and he did things with more malicious ill will. He had been in the same class in school as her older boy Ray, and she remembered the day her younger boy Abel had had to lead Ray home because Carroll had struck Ray with temporary blindness for looking at a teacher they both had a crush on.

Trixie stooped so that Carroll's feet touched the ground. She tugged at the girl's arms. Carroll held her tighter, lifting her face only enough to whisper, "Please."

"Come on," Trixie said, gently loosening Carroll's arms from around her neck and pushing her to arm's length, then stooping, hands on thighs, to stare into drowned green eyes, remembering the sharp-cheeked, angle-jawed Carroll of years ago, the slender sneaky kid who loved to walk into her husband Tyke's pharmacy, open six candy bars, take a bite of each, throw them on the floor, stamp on them, and leave. Most of the people from the Hollow didn't pay for anything, at least not with money. In her girlhood Trixie had seen other kinds of payments, but lately, not even charms and blessings were offered; Carroll had never paid.

He had looked nothing like this child with the cut lip, the abrasion on her right cheek, the blood drying on her upper lip—yet the longer Trixie looked, the more she remembered. The eyes were the same, and the line of the jaw. The full lower lip, the cleft in the chin, all details softened by gender.

Still, Trixie remembered her first thought on seeing Maggie the day before. Good lord, it's a child! A little hurt child. Didn't that take precedence over everything else?

Maybe Maggie was right. Maybe it didn't. With an effort, Trixie suppressed her comforting instincts, and kept her hands on her thighs.

Carroll rubbed her eyes, then stared up at Trixie, holding out her hands. "Please," she said. "You're so warm and soft and . . . comfortable."

"I'm your electric blanket?" Trixie straightened. Carroll only came up to her elbows.

"No," said Carroll. "No. You feel strong like the earth." She shivered.

"I don't understand," Trixie said. "Does any of this mean anything to you, Mr. Carroll?"

"What?"

"What if you were yourself right now, and Tommy wasn't here? What would you do?"

Carroll hugged herself and looked at Trixie, then Maggie, then Laura. Her gaze fixed on Trixie again. "I would take you away, and you would love me like you just did. Maybe every day."

Trixie felt strangely touched. "What about Maggie and Laura?"

"I would take Maggie back and teach her new things I haven't even thought of yet."

Maggie went white and took two steps toward Carroll, stopping when Tom laid a restraining hand on her shoulder.

"And Laura should have married Augustus or Forrest or Piron," Carroll said. "They need breeders."

"Marry one of them yourself," said Laura.

Carroll jerked as if slapped. She held her hands away from her body and looked down at herself; then she covered her face with her hands. "No," she whispered. She squinched her eyes shut and touched her genitals. After assuring herself of the changes there, she opened her eyes. She ran to Tom and pulled on his shirt. "Let me out! Let me out of here right now. Please!"

"Not tonight," said Tom.

Carroll looked at Maggie, then at the back door. "When?" she asked in a high voice.

"Maybe never."

"Then—" She ran for the back door again, but Trixie caught her before she opened it. Carroll fought like a fury, biting, kicking, and scratching. "I might as well be dead!" she screamed. Trixie caught her hands, held both small wrists in one hand, and carried her away upstairs.

Tom touched Maggie's shoulder. "This is weird. Did that help at all?" he asked.

"I don't know, Tom. I thought . . ."

"Yeah. You can never tell if anybody's learning anything. We'll just have to wait, I guess."

"What, exactly, did you do to him?" Laura asked. "Everything it looked like?"

"I think so," said Tom.

"You're scary!"

"Oh, please not." The chill returned.

"Nobody does that one. They do everything else, but they don't—change the deepest part of a person's identity."

"Is that the deepest part?" Tom asked.

They stared at each other.

Maggie went to the sink and turned on warm water, then thrust her bruised hands into the stream.

"Maggie, let me help," said Laura, breaking out of her and Tom's trance.

"That wouldn't be fair, unless you helped Carroll too, and I don't want you to. Want her to feel it all, so I guess I get to, too." She dipped some of the warm water up in cupped hands and splashed it on her face. "Ow. Ouch. Guess she got me there. Didn't realize."

Laura went to her and touched the cut on her cheek. "No. You don't need to suffer."

"Stop it!" Maggie pushed her hand away. "Don't want to hurt anybody and not feel it myself. That's how he went on and on for years."

"All right," Laura said. She gave a small trembly smile. "Can I hug you?"

Maggie frowned. She turned off the water. She stepped closer to Laura, keeping her hands at her sides. Laura embraced her, and after a long moment she relaxed enough to lay her head on Laura's shoulder.

Presently Trixie returned, having changed her blood-stained black T-shirt for a blouse. She led a scrubbed and subdued Carroll with her; Carroll wore a faded pair of boy's pajamas, the stretchy polyester type, patterned after Spiderman's blue and red long johns. "Are you hungry?" Trixie asked her.

"Yes," said Carroll. She sighed. "I hurt all over. I hate this hair. Can you cut it off?"

"Later. What do you want to eat?"

She glanced down at her stomach, looking puzzled, then up at Trixie, her eyebrows raised. *"Sangany,"* she said.

"What?" asked Trixie.

"It's sort of like oatmeal," Laura said. "She can have those Trix things I had this morning."

"You have food named after you?" Carroll asked Trixie.

"No," said Trixie, laughing.

Maggie stirred, and Laura released her.

"I got your eye," Carroll said, cheering up. "How come she didn't heal you yet? Is that another discipline you failed at, Laura?"

"I'd like you to remember your size and your power, Carroll," said Laura. "You keep baiting me and I may take a swing at you myself."

"What? You, Saint Laura, the perfect imitation *tanganar?* Strike a helpless infant? Don't make me laugh."

Trixie picked Carroll up, turned her over her knee, and swatted her rear end. "Stop teasing people or I'll send you to your room," she said.

"But—"

"No buts." Trixie stood her up again.

"Is this new life all torture and hitting people? I can't stand it. I'll walk off a roof," Carroll said.

"Behave yourself and things will get better," said Trixie.

"Yeah," Maggie said. "Think before you talk. Everybody here is bigger than you now, and some of us are gifted."

"I want to go home," Carroll said.

"I wonder what Arthur and Alex and Gwen and Sarah would do to you," Laura said. "Last I heard, Gwen didn't enjoy spending that week as a hunting dog. The twins weren't happy as bookends. Michael didn't enjoy being a rug. And all those offenses are six years old. I wonder what you've been doing lately?"

Carroll picked at a loose strand of elastic on her sleeve. She bit her lip and looked at Trixie.

Trixie stroked her head. "I'm not asking much, sweetie. Just be civil."

"I'll try," she whispered.

"Good." Trixie got up and fetched cereal and a bowl from the cupboard. "What bothers me most is Bert. He would have tried to get in touch. We've seen each other every day for the last five years. I can't imagine why he isn't here or hasn't at least left a note."

"Is Bert an old, tall man?" Carroll asked after a moment's silence.

Trixie stopped pouring milk and looked at her.

"He is, isn't he? The taxi man."

"Have you seen him?" asked Trixie.

Carroll stared at the floor. "I put him in the basement."

Tom went to the basement door, opened it, and turned on the light. Dasher, who had been cowering under the kitchen table since everyone ran out the back door, barked. A huge yellow cat yowled, flew out of the basement, and clawed its way up onto Tom's shoulders. "Calm down," said Tom. He stroked the cat. It bit his hand, then began to relax, the stiffened ridge of fur on its back settling, and its bottle brush tail beginning to skinny. It mrrowed, ending on a raised note like the inflection of a question. "Bert?" Tom said. "I'll fix this. But I think I should find your clothes first."

"Downstairs," said Carroll. She looked wistful as she stared at the cat, her final handiwork for who knew how long.

Tom headed down the basement steps, closing the door behind him. Bert rode his shoulders to the bottom of the stairs, then leapt onto clothes which lay in a strangely corpse-like formation, empty socks in empty shoes below empty brown pantlegs, which stretched up to an empty shirt inside an empty yellow jacket.

"Come here," Tom said. He sat on the bottom step.

The cat mrrowed and approached.

Tom blinked into Othersight. He could tell Carroll had done good work on this transformation: the cat was knitted into a black cocoon of force, and the ghost shape of Bert's true form above it was very faint. Tom reached out. He noticed his fingertips glowed foxfire green as he touched the webs of Carroll's spell, which fell away. The cat wailed as it changed, a wail that deepened to a moan.

Then Bert sat shivering on top of his pants in the dim cellar light.

"Are you all right?"

"Sprained dignity," said Bert. He got to his feet and dressed, shivering the whole time.

"May I give you warmth?" Tom asked, feeling awkward.

Bert glanced over his shoulder as he pulled on a sock. "Can you?"

"I tried it a couple times today. It works."

"I'm game," said Bert.

Tom sent out a silver net, whispering warmth to each strand. As the net settled around Bert, Tom became conscious again of how tired he felt, how prickly and uncomfortable his skin was. He sighed. Bert straightened, touched one hand with the other, then peered at Tom. "Okay. Thanks. How did you know it was me?"

"Carroll told us she put you in the basement."

" 'She'?" Bert folded his arms. "Where have you been all day? Where was Trixie? What do you mean, 'she'?"

Tom scrubbed his hands over his face and yawned. "Jaimie took us over to see Barney, Annis, and the baby. We stayed all day. When we got back, Carroll was waiting here. Did he look like a werewolf when you got here?"

"What?" Bert touched his upper lip, reached to feel the base of his spine. "You know, I felt weird being a cat. I got here just after lunch. What time is it now? I been a cat ever since. It never got dark to my cat eyes, but now I see it must be night." He glanced toward one of the cellar windows. "I got used to being that size, having those muscles, seeing everything clear but kind of black and white." He glanced at his fingers, then toward the top of the stairs. Tom looked up too and noticed new pale scars on the base of the door, scratches. "It felt great to dig in," Bert said.

"I've got some souvenirs, too," said Tom. He lifted his pantleg, revealing scratches under the dark hair on his calf. They stung.

"I'm sorry about that, but that idiot dog scared me. That was weird too. I had—instincts."

"I'm glad you enjoyed it," Tom said, pulling his pant-leg down again. He felt as if he'd die of itching if he didn't get a shower soon.

Someone knocked on the cellar door. "Hey! You alive down there?" called Trixie.

"Yes," Tom and Bert answered. Tom stood up and they started up the stairs.

"Listen," Tom said, pausing with his hand on the door-knob. "I turned Carroll into a little girl."

"You *what?*"

Tom looked at Bert.

"All right," said Bert, "I guess I heard you, I just didn't believe you. Jeeze, Tom, I never imagined . . ."

"That wasn't part of your master plan?" Tom said.

Bert buried his hands in his pants pockets. "Actually, miles better than anything I could have wished for. You had a reason, right?"

"He was threatening Maggie. And Trixie."

Bert smiled up at him.

"You approve?" Tom said. It suddenly occurred to him that Bert had ethics, albeit slippery ones, half-submerged. Tom's own feeling for Bert was warm, and the fact that Jaimie and Barney trusted Bert when they weren't talking to anybody else meant something too.

"Oh, yeah. Tommy, could you turn me into an animal?"

"Right now?"

"No. This is not a request. I'm asking for information."

"Oh. Probably I could, then."

"I'd like to try . . . being a cat again, and not locked up. Or maybe a big dog. Not right now, though."

"You're a very strange person," Tom said, and opened the cellar door, letting a flood of yellow kitchen light into the cellar's gloom.

"Bert, are you all right? Were you really that cat?" Trixie caught Bert as he emerged and gave him a hug.

"I'm fine," said Bert. He looked embarrassed.

"So you really can unspell," Carroll said to Tom. She sat at the table, her chin propped on her fists, a bowl of soggy cereal in front of her.

"What'd you think?"

"It's a rare talent. How do you do it?"

Tom looked at Laura. She grinned. She stood leaning against the sink, her arms crossed over her chest, her tawny hair coming loose from its coil. She grinned at him, her eyes sparkling. He caught his breath and took a step toward her.

"Answer me!" yelled Carroll, pounding the table with her spoon, one bang per syllable.

"Manners," Trixie said.

"Oh. Sorry. Answer me, please."

"That information won't do you any good now anyway," said Tom without taking his gaze off Laura. "I am going upstairs now. I'm going to take a shower. After that, I'm going to bed. Want to come?"

"Oh, yes," said Laura.

"Make sure you shut that shower door all the way," Trixie said. "If you get water on the floor, it drips into the front bathroom."

"We'll be careful," said Laura.

"Where are the towels, please?" Tom asked.

"Go ahead and know that." Trixie shooed them away.

As Tom and Laura's footsteps faded beyond the top of the stairs, Trixie headed for the stove, and the pot of coffee Tom had started that morning. She turned on a burner under it. Bert went to a drawer in the counter and got out a pack of worn cards, then sat and dealt himself a hand of solitaire at the table across from Carroll. Carroll looked at Maggie, who leaned with her back to the wall.

"Don't," said Maggie.

"Don't what?"

"Don't look at me like you own me. Never again."

Carroll raised an eyebrow, then took another bite of cereal. She spat it out. "It's *mugwa*," she said.

"What is that in real words?" Bert asked.

"Slop," said Maggie. Carroll turned to her again, surprised. "What do you expect, I'm going to hear you people griping all day and night, watch you throw things, boss people around, and not understand you?"

"I wish I'd known you could talk."

"So you could make me scream like the others?"

Carroll's brows slanted up. "No," she said in a small voice.

"Then why? For all the talking fetches get to do at the Hollow, we might as well be rocks."

Carroll stood up, turned to Trixie, who stood by the stove, sipping leftover coffee, grimacing, then taking another sip as though trying to prove to herself it was really bad enough to throw away so she could start another pot. "I don't want this anymore," Carroll said, pointing to her cereal.

"Throw it down the garbage disposal and wash the dish," said Trixie, sitting down with her coffee.

Carroll lifted the bowl. Some milk spilled over the edge. She looked at the splotch of by-now pale pink milk on the table, then at the bowl in her hands as if surprised by the unstable quality of its contents. She glanced wildly around the kitchen. "Please," she said. "How do I—" She pointed to the spill. "What's a garbage disposal?"

Maggie came out of her stiff pose against the wall and grabbed Carroll's arm, dragging her around the counter to the double sink. "There," she said, pointing at the split rubber cover over the drain. "That's a garbage disposal. Real people's houses have them. Pour it in there."

"I can't," said Carroll. "It's all over the floor now." Her voice sounded high and scared.

Maggie looked and saw Carroll had spilled everything out of the bowl on the route between table and sink. "You stupid *tanganar*, you clean that up right now." Maggie turned to the paper towel dispenser and jerked paper towels off the roll. She wadded them up and threw them at Carroll. "Clean it up! Don't leave a drop or something you hate but can't imagine will happen to you. Get to work! *Sti kravna plashtookna, kurovny. Akenar! Kalla!*"

Carroll stood motionless, arms bent, her hands palm outward in front of her face, as Maggie pelted her with wadded paper towels. Furious, Maggie jerked Carroll's hands away from her face. Carroll had tears on her cheeks.

"That's it! Cry, scream. We prefer the screaming method. Three weeks and you'll adjust. We could just enchant you into liking it here, but it makes you stupid, and we like it better if you're smart. You're more fun to play with."

"I never said that to you," Carroll said, her voice wavery.

"Sure! I didn't cry or scream any to begin with! I heard that speech three times. Isn't that what they always say to new fetches?"

Carroll jerked herself free of Maggie's grip and dropped to the floor. She retrieved some paper towels and scrubbed at the spilled milk.

"*Kooshna,*" Maggie said, loathing in her voice.

"Maggie, please," said Trixie.

Carroll glanced up with narrowed eyes. "Oh, she just wants to turn into me," she said.

"*Tashkooly!* Take that back!" yelled Maggie.

Carroll stared at the floor, focusing all her attention on rubbing milk.

Maggie grabbed her shoulder and shook her. "Take it back," she said.

Carroll looked at her, wide-eyed and unresponsive.

Trixie came around the counter. "Leave her alone, Maggie. Haven't you done enough?"

"But—" Maggie let go of Carroll and straightened. She looked down at the smaller girl, scrubbing at the floor, her hair tumbling down, obscuring her face. Maggie felt an aching sadness flood her. She turned and ran up the stairs away from it.

Trixie got a sponge and ran warm water on it, wrung it out, and joined Carroll on the floor. "Look, this way's easier," she said, sliding the sponge along a streak of pink milk and picking it up.

"What is that thing?" Carroll asked in a low voice.

"This is a sponge." Trixie handed it to her.

Carroll held it, turned it over, squeezed it until everything it had just picked up ran out of it. "Oh, no!"

"Wipe it up again."

Carroll tried it. "This is magic," she said. She skated the sponge along the trail of the spill.

"When it gets full, you squeeze it out over the sink and start over, understand?"

Carroll tried it. She smiled, delighted, cleaned up her spill, cleaned the milk splotch off the table, washed a coffee ring left by someone's mug. Bert played solitaire and watched her without expression. Trixie sat on the floor and straightened out crumpled paper towels, piling them in a loose stack. Carroll dropped the sponge in the sink and joined her.

"Are you all right?" Trixie asked.

"I don't know," said Carroll. "All those dark places on me hurt. I'm not used to it."

"I mean what just happened with Maggie. Did that upset you?"

Carroll stared down at the towel between her hands. It was white, with a faint green print of bell peppers, onions, carrots, lettuce, and radish bunches on it. Her hands trembled. Then her arms trembled. Then all of her was shaking, and she couldn't even look up at Trixie, and she despised herself for being small and powerless in this place where she could not escape and everyone was angry with her.

—Maggie, she thought, shaking, the paper towel making a muffled rustle between her hands. She saw an image of Maggie's pale face, three years younger, looking up at Carroll with utter trust and hope.

Trixie picked Carroll up, a vast warm presence she could shiver against, firm hands and arms holding her without judging or demanding. Carroll could not remember being embraced like that before. She put her arms around Trixie's neck and held on tight, smashing her face against Trixie's shoulder. "Time for bed," said Trixie.

Bert watched Trixie carry the little girl away. He finished his solitaire hand, thinking about his first view of Carroll that day, a full-grown man sitting uninvited at Trixie's table, eating pretzels and studying the newspaper. Bert had always kept his distance from Carroll, though he had contacts in Chapel Hollow. "Step into the basement," Carroll had said in a beautiful and persuasive voice. "You're not the one I'm waiting for."

Bert had walked without question into the basement, and spent a long afternoon being a cat.

Now Carroll was a little girl without her full range of powers, but she still had calculation on her side.

Humming the way he did when he was deep in thought, Bert put dirty dishes in the dishpan to soak, then let himself out of the house, locking the door behind him.

Chapter 18

Trixie woke up without the benefit of coffee the next morning, surprised awake by the presence of someone small and warm in her bed. She lay looking at the lamp on the bedside table, a pale ceramic lamp she and Tyke had bought at the Danica outlet on a trip to Portland. It was elegant and didn't go with anything else they owned.

She had last awakened next to someone the morning Tyke died. He had gone in the night, not unexpectedly; he had been twenty years older than she, and his health had been seeping away since a stroke two years earlier.

She had opened her eyes to morning, and reached out her hand to Tyke, touched his shoulder. It was warm, but not blood warm. She had sat up and searched for a pulse at his wrist, staring at his peaceful face, beautiful and pale. Breathing did not disturb his tranquility.

As she dialed Doc Hardesty a sense of loss had crept down her throat and into her chest, where it spread out like thick hot syrup, claiming her as its territory . . .

She reached out under the covers, touched the small shoulder of a child, felt the child stir. The echo of her old loss invaded her, and she hugged the child to her, feeling it press its face to her breast and slip an arm around her as far as it could reach, clutching a fold of her flannel nightgown in its other hand. For a long time they lay unmoving together. She felt her longing for Tyke gentle down to manageable again. She lifted the covers, stroked the child's curly head. It looked up at her, green eyes in a face of innocence, though it had a scrape on its cheek, now nicely scabbed over.

"Hi, sweetie," she said.

It gave her a tiny smile in return, a smile that melted right away as if uncertain of its reception.

"You ready to get up?"

It looked away, its eyebrows rising on the insides. "Do we have to?" it said.

"I don't know about you, but I have company, and I have to see to them. Aren't you hungry?"

"Yes," said the child, and swallowed.

"Come on. Let's go look at what we found in the attic last night, see if you like any of these clothes." She threw off the covers; cold air surrounded them instantly, and the child pressed itself against her.

"You'll warm up with some cocoa in you," Trixie said, sitting up. "Let's go get dressed."

The child rubbed its eyes and followed her over to the dresser and the easy chair. She had draped clothes from her children's youth over furniture.

"Can you cut off my hair?" the child asked, catching sight of itself in the mirror on the vanity.

"Manners."

"What?" The child stared up at her, confused.

"When you're asking someone for a favor, you say please. When someone does you a favor, you say thank you."

The child nodded. "Oh. Yes. Please, can you cut off my hair?"

"Sure."

The scents of coffee and melting butter greeted them, and the kitchen was alive with people.

"Barney wants me to be his best man," Bert was saying as Trixie and the child walked to the table and took seats, Trixie next to Maggie, the child edging its chair close to

Trixie. "Out of everyone in town, he asked me. I've known him since he was little, but doesn't he have any friends his own age?"

"He's got friends," said Laura, and yawned into the back of her hand. "I suppose they don't approve of what he's doing. Or maybe he's just afraid they won't approve."

Maggie, whose black eye had darkened to plum purple, got up and brought Trixie a mug of coffee. "Thanks," said Trixie. "I promised the kid some cocoa. There's instant in the cupboard over the stove, if there's water hot."

"Wish I could do that kettle trick like yesterday," said Maggie, studying Carroll, whose hair was now cut about even with her earlobes. In jeans and a black T-shirt, Carroll looked androgynous, too young for gender to matter. "Never saw you do that."

"What?" said Carroll.

"Just hold a kettle in your hands and warm up water."

"That's a water skill, and I am of earth. Was of earth."

"But couldn't you just transform it from cold water to hot?"

Carroll frowned. "Mm," she said, and gave Maggie a lightning grin. Startled, Maggie grinned back, then thought about it, frowned ferociously, and went into the food prep area, where Tom was operating the stove. He handed her a mug full of steaming water, a spoon, and a packet of Carnation instant cocoa.

"Want some too?" he asked her, but she shook her head. She already had a mug of coffee waiting at her place at the table, between Laura and Trixie. She took the cocoa fixings and set them down in front of Carroll.

"Thanks," said Carroll, picking up the sealed foil packet of mix, turning it over and studying it. After a moment she bit her lower lip and looked up.

"What time is the wedding?" Trixie asked Bert.

Maggie took the packet from Carroll, shook the powder into one end, tore a strip off the other, and dumped the powder into the mug of hot water. She put the spoon in and stirred. "You got to mash the lumps up," she muttered.

"Thanks," Carroll muttered back. Maggie handed her the spoon and she worked on blending.

"Two o'clock this afternoon," said Bert. "Father Wolfe is waiving the license and the blood tests, since it's a Hollow thing. Barney asked me to invite you all."

"Who wants what eggs?" Tom asked over the sizzle of frying butter.

"Two, sunny side up, please," Trixie said.

"Toast?"

"Mmm. It's been years since I had this kind of service at breakfast."

Tom grinned. "Laura, what would you like?"

"A piece of toast. I'm not a big breakfast person."

"Maggie?"

"Uh—oatmeal?"

"It'll take a little while."

"Whatever's easiest, then."

"This is easiest," he said. "Bert? Carroll?"

Bert glanced at Carroll, who was eating cocoa with her spoon. Carroll lifted an eyebrow.

"Two over easy?" Bert said.

Tom cracked two more eggs into the frying pan.

"One, please," Carroll said.

"How do you want it cooked?"

"*Svitly.*"

"Speak English, Uncle," Laura said. "Tom doesn't know *Ilmonish* yet. She means over medium."

" '*Svitly*' means 'over medium'?"

"Uh—no, it means 'no jiggles.' "

"Oh." Tom added another egg, slipped two staring yolk-topped eggs out and onto a plate. Toast popped up. He buttered it and added it to the plate, then brought the plate, silverware, a napkin, and a jar of raspberry preserves to the table for Trixie. "Butter?" he said to Laura, catching another piece of toast as it popped out of the toaster.

"Please," said Laura. He buttered the toast, put it in the center of a plate, and held the plate up.

"Take it?" he said.

The plate drifted through the air to Laura.

Tom went back to coordinating the meal.

"So do you all want to head over to the church together?" Bert asked as Tom handed him a plate with two eggs on it.

"We could all fit in one cab," Tom said. "What if someone else needs a cab, though?"

"We officially take this time off. I'm part of the ceremony, and you're not technically a driver anymore."

"Okay," said Tom. He gave Carroll a plate with an egg on it and a knife and fork, then went back to the stove and dished up two bowls of oatmeal. Taking maple syrup from the fridge, he brought it and the oatmeal over to the table, handed one bowl to Maggie, and sat down between Bert and Laura. He poured milk and syrup on his oatmeal and ate.

"But what do we do with the kid?" Bert said.

Carroll stretched her hand out toward the salt cellar, frowning in concentration. Trixie passed it to her. She sighed and salted her egg.

"She goes too," Trixie said.

"I don't think so," said Bert.

"Why not? We can hardly leave her somewhere."

"Don't you think she'll make a fuss?"

Carroll set the salt down and looked up. "Make a fuss about what?"

"About the wedding," said Bert.

"What wedding?"

"Barney and Annis," Trixie said.

"Annis? You didn't say Annis!" said Carroll. "Who's she marrying? That fetch *akenar* she ran off with? How can she? Tom, you let me go now. I have to stop them."

"No way."

"You don't understand! This is important! Annis has

more potential than Laura. She must come back to the Family. We need her bloodline.''

"No you don't,'' Tom said, though he heard echoes of Peregrine's logic in Carroll's speech.

"Yes we do.'' Carroll opened her mouth to say more, then glanced at Trixie, Bert, and Maggie. "Would you—please—come in the other room with me a minute? Please?''

Tom glanced at Laura, saw her sparkling with inner delight. He ate another spoonful of oatmeal, then said, "Okay.''

Carroll looked at Laura, then decided something and shook her head. She grasped Tom's sleeve and led him into the front parlor.

"Look,'' she said after he sat down on the sofa. "I know you don't think I—you don't understand how I operate. I know I can't figure *you* out. I'm sorry I said things and did things to you when I met you, but how was I to know you'd be—'' She frowned. "It's that Laura. She has never done anything right. So now, when she actually brings us good blood, I have trouble getting used to it.''

"Are you saying you're glad Laura married me, in spite of everything that's happened?''

Carroll paced back and forth, her face set in a frown. "I am and I'm not. I hate being so weak and powerless. I feel like I have no choices in this body; people are telling me what to do all the time, and they can force me to do what they say. You made me like this. But your being able to do that, that's a sign of great hope for the Family, if it's a power you can pass on to your children. There are two halves of me, me alone, and me of the Family. And the Family is in trouble. You'll help the Family.'' She searched his face for signs of comprehension. "Your children . . .''

"I understand.''

"But if Annis goes off and marries this—Barney? Some *tanganar*—that's a waste of bloodline. We don't have any to waste right now. The blood's thin. The talents are dy-

ing. I can't stand it, I can't stand watching my Family
die." She looked at him with tearbright eyes. "I don't
know what you've done to me, but I've been thinking
about it all night. I wonder if I'm really a girl inside, and
if I carry the same bloodline I had before. If I do, maybe
I'd ask you to leave me this way, only if I could be four
years older, so I could have a baby—" She turned away,
and hit the coffee table with a fist. "Because I'm the most
gifted of my generation, but I have sowed my seed and
none of it quickened. My male self has no hope of children." She stared at him with eyes that burned with green
fire, a terrible smoky despair.

Abruptly she paced away, stood facing a wall. "So what
I'm asking—and if you grant me this, you can do whatever
else you like to me—is, if you'd just let me be myself long
enough to hunt Annis and Jaimie up and take them home
where they belong. Please, please, please."

Tom bit his lip.

"Please," Carroll said, turning to stare at him again.

—Is this a weasel ploy? Tom asked Peregrine.

—Perhaps, but he speaks from the same place I speak
from when I talk of Family, and that, I believe, is sincere.
With your leave, I will answer him.

—Go ahead.

"Descendant Carroll Bolte," said Peregrine.

Carroll jumped and straightened, eyes wide. "What?
Presence?"

"Yes. I have taken up residence in this student. I am
training him. I share your concerns, but I wish to tell
you that as far as Annis is concerned, all is accomplished.
I tested her fetch: he is not wholly *tanganar*. I tested their
child: it is a child of power, sign fire. I duly sealed it to
the Family, and sanctioned their union, with the aid of
another Presence summoned for the work. Family will
benefit from this union; be easy in your mind."

Carroll bunched up like a rubber band being twisted
tight. Then she sighed and relaxed. "All right," she said.
"Thank you, Ancient. Which Presence are you?"

"Peregrine Bolte."

"The same that spoke to me after Michael's and Alyssa's Purification?"

"The same."

"Threatened to unleash the deep fire on me?"

"Aye."

"Ancient, could you grow me up a little bit, please? Please? Heal me and strengthen me? I should hate to die before I had a chance to give the Family a child."

Peregrine laughed. "I know it doesn't seem it, but you are safe here."

Carroll gripped one hand in the other, twisted her fingers. "There is a feeling of safety like I have never known," she whispered, "with Trixie. But what if my fetch finds me alone?"

"She is my daughter, and she is finished with you," said Peregrine in a stern voice, "provided you take pains not to provoke her again."

Carroll rubbed her hands over her eyes. "Ancient. She has been my fetch three years, and though at first I cherished her, I have not been kind to her. I have used and neglected her, and kept her a prisoner in her body. How can one screaming and one fight make up for that? Please let me protect myself. I promise never to harm her again, only to protect myself."

"How could you keep a promise like that?"

She blinked. Tears glittered in her lashes. "Perhaps you're right," she murmured.

"Why did you mistreat her? Why do you have this history? Where does this poison come from, descendant? Better not to sire children at all than to sire powerful poisonous ones."

"But that's why," said Carroll, her teeth clenched. "Because no matter how carefully I prepared, no matter what rites I performed, what spells I cast, none of my fetches gave me children. I tested that Magdalen. She was fertile, but she withheld it from me." She hit the table again.

"The fault was not hers."

Carroll glared. "I know! I did not want to know! Ancient, can I breed?"

"I don't know. Tom worked this change on you. I know not how. His power reserves are vast, and his techniques are foreign to me."

"So I'm stuck here?" She looked at her small hands, stretching out her fingers and staring first at the backs of her hands and then at the palms.

"For now," said Peregrine. "Descendant, I leave you now." He seeped away.

"But—"

Tom stood up. "Come on, Carroll. I'll make you another egg."

"But—all right." She rubbed her eyes. She managed a smile and followed him back to the kitchen.

They stopped on the threshold. Michael and Alyssa sat at the table between Laura and Bert. Alyssa stared down into the coffee mug she held. Michael, looking uncomfortable, hugged himself and glanced sideways at Bert, who looked puzzled and apprehensive. Trixie, her mouth a straight line, was clearing dishes off the table. Maggie sat very still. Laura offered Tom a wide grin.

Carroll grabbed Tom's sleeve. "You said I'd be safe here," she whispered.

"You will be. I'll take care of you." He took her hand and led her to the table. "Hi. Is this a stop on your honeymoon?"

"Not exactly," said Michael. He lowered his eyebrows and stared at Carroll, smiled, shook his head, then looked at Tom. "Wait a sec. Why do I think I know her?"

"Family resemblance. Trixie, are these people bothering you?" said Tom. Carroll hid behind him, keeping a firm grip on his shirt.

"Not as much as they would have day before yesterday," she said. "I'm getting used to Boltes in the kitchen. Nuts and Boltes."

Michael's eyes widened. He stared at Trixie and his face lost color. He lifted his hand—

"None of that," said Tom. Laura flicked her fingers at her brother. Tom saw, with Othersight, that she cast a small blue net around Michael's hand, then tugged it tight so his outstretched fingers curled into a loose fist.

Michael stared at her, his mouth open.

"Our house and our hostess," said Laura. "No casting."

"Did you really—" Michael struggled and managed to flex his hand. "Did you do that, Laura?"

Laura looked at Tom, who nodded. "Probably," she said. "Do you get the message? You're visiting. Exercise courtesy."

"All right," said Michael. He glanced at Alyssa.

She licked her lip and ventured a little smile. "We're nervous," she said.

"But curious," said Michael. "Still in white, Tom?"

"I haven't had time to pick up my other clothes. These are great. They stay clean no matter what else happens. Did you do that on purpose?"

"I don't know. I was a little drunk at the time."

"Have you met everyone?"

"I haven't," said Alyssa. "Laura was just going to tell us—" She peeked past Laura at Maggie. "But you look familiar."

"Uncle Carroll's fetch," said Michael.

"Her name is Maggie, and Tom and I have adopted her," said Laura. "This is Trixie Delarue, our hostess. Trixie, my brother Michael and his wife Alyssa."

Alyssa and Trixie nodded at each other. "We've met," said Michael, but he looked puzzled.

"You probably came into my husband's pharmacy, like everybody else," Trixie said.

"Your husband?" Michael looked at Bert.

"Not him. My husband, Tyke Delarue. Tyke's?"

"Oh, yeah," said Michael. He looked at his hand a second, then held it out to her.

Trixie stared at his hand just long enough to raise his hackles, then took it, shook it, and let him go. He glared at her. She burst into peals of laughter. "My, that feels good," she said.

"What?" asked Michael, insulted.

"Not being afraid to offend you." She smiled, radiating cheer. "You Hollow people stomped on enough uneaten candy bars to keep a town full of trick-or-treaters happy, and broke enough toys to give an orphanage a merry Christmas, not to mention what you did to the domestics and drugs. That's one of the reasons I was just as glad we sold the business when Tyke retired. The waste broke my heart. I like getting a little piece of it back."

Carroll peered out at her from under Tom's left arm. Feeling the child's gaze, Trixie glanced at her.

"Manners?" Carroll said.

Trixie's grin was bright as lightning. "Yes! Maybe that's why I'm glad you're here. Somebody didn't raise you right. I know I can do better."

"Who—?" Michael glanced from Trixie to Carroll and back.

"No, we're skipping Bert," Laura said. "Michael, Alyssa, this is Tom's boss, Bert."

"I know Bert," said Michael.

"Like your dad. Interested in cars," Bert said. "But you didn't go ask Pops how they work. Used to open up my cabs and break the engines a new way every week, trying to figure it out on your own."

"I didn't mean to break them," said Michael. "I just wanted to find out about them."

"Did it ever make sense to you?"

"No."

"If you want to know something, asking questions is a good way to find out. What's done is done, though," said Bert.

"Michael, is your whole past like this?" Alyssa asked.

"Like what?"

"Full of people you hurt, people who couldn't protect

themselves from you? I'm amazed we're sitting here in this kitchen.''

"What do you do at Southwater?"

"We never show our powers in public," she said. "That's how we're raised; gifts are family matters. We pass for normal. Only sick people take fetches, out of necessity. I can't remember anyone in my lifetime taking one; it's something I've only read about in history. You have a whole town that knows about you and fears you. I don't understand how it operates.''

"Tradition," said Bert. "Chapel Hollow and Arcadia are locked to each other by ages of tradition. Used to be more positive for both sides, remember, Trix?"

"Mm," she said, nodding.

"Started changing, gradually, about thirty years back. Just been getting worse and worse. Might be changing for the better now, though," said Bert.

"How?" Michael asked.

"Well, look. You're sitting at a table with us."

Michael, hugging himself, with his hands tucked into his armpits, glanced around the table. "Yeah," he said. "It feels really strange, but here we all are." He looked at Carroll. "Only who's the kid?"

Carroll glanced at Laura, who raised an eyebrow. "Your decision," Laura said.

Carroll kept a grip on Tom's sleeve. She stepped up beside him and looked up at him; he looked down at her. "This is how it is?" she said.

"Do you really want to go back?"

She looked at Trixie. Her eyes misted. "No," she said. " 'Cause I could make somebody do it, but it wouldn't be the same.''

"Do what?" asked Michael. "What are you talking about?"

She glared at him, then closed her eyes. Her face smoothed. When she opened her eyes again, she was still, centered. "Quiet, please. Give me a moment." She let go of Tom's sleeve and went to the table, gripping its edge, staring at Trixie. "Can I please stay with you, please?"

Trixie took a deep breath, let it out. "You want me to raise you?"

"Yes, please. I need . . . a teacher."

"Manners and all?"

"Manners. And electric blankets?"

"Oh," said Trixie. "Both?"

"Yes."

"What's going to happen when you turn thirteen? I need rules. And if you stay here, you're going to do your share of the work. Are you going to hate me for that?"

"No," said Carroll.

"Because I'm not going to cherish you if you plan to destroy me or anybody else. I hear you talking about anything like that, I'm going to send you to bed without your supper, understand?"

Carroll frowned at a fork on the table in front of her. After a moment, she looked up. "I understand. But will you *talk* to me?"

"Yes. I'd like that. I've been lonely since the kids left. You'll have to go to school, though, or people will wonder. Hell, they'll wonder no matter what, but I can say you're a grandchild. Can you handle that? Go to school, and behave at home?"

Carroll tapped her lips twice with her index finger. "Yes."

"Things won't be what you want all the time."

Carroll glanced up at Tom. "I'm learning that. I don't like it, but I think I can learn it."

"Bert, what do you think?" Trixie asked.

"I think you're crazy. What do you think's gonna happen when she gifts? Think she'll stay this way? She'll go back to being her old self. You don't keep a cougar as a pet just because it was a cute kitten."

Light flared in Carroll's eyes. She stared at Bert, her lips thinning. He met her gaze unsmiling. At last she looked away. She picked up the fork and felt the tines of it, then looked at Trixie, tearblind.

"Maggie?" Trixie said.

Carroll turned to look at Maggie.

Staring at her, Maggie said, "Last night?"

Carroll waited.

"You were right, and I hate that. I hate what you taught me. I'm going to get rid of it, not live that way."

"Yes," said Carroll

"Klanishti koosh. If I can, you can. Bert's wrong."

Carroll tapped the palm of her left hand with the business end of the fork. She began jabbing herself. "I don't know," she said to Maggie. "I don't know what's wrong or right. I don't know what I can let go of."

Maggie jumped up and grabbed her hand. "Stop that!" She jerked the fork out of Carroll's hand and slammed it onto the table top. "Nobody gets to hurt you but me. Look what you did."

Carroll looked at her left palm and saw it was beaded with blood.

"Laura, will you please fix this?" Maggie said.

"If you let me do your eye."

Maggie stared at Laura; her breathing deepened. Then she turned to Carroll. Each of her breaths held the tag end of a sob. "Oh, I hate you," she said. "I hate you and I love you." She closed her eyes and hugged Carroll . . . and felt small arms return her embrace. For the first time she felt warmth from Carroll. Then gradually something changed—the embrace still felt warm, but different, familiar. She squinched her eyes tight shut, hugging as hard as she could, trying to resist unwanted knowledge.

"Sirella," she heard Michael whisper, and she opened her eyes. The face closest to her was male, and he had his eyes tight shut too. Carroll, restored, knelt with his arms around her.

"Let go," she whispered. "Please let go."

His eyes opened. He released her and stared, appalled,

down at himself. "No," he said, "No, not now. Not now!" He turned to Tom. "Not now."

"I didn't."

"You must have. Please. Change me back, please. Maggie—"

She backed away from him.

Carroll, still on his knees, looked at everyone: Laura, who looked sad; Bert, remote; Alyssa, frightened yet intrigued; Michael, appalled; Maggie, waiting; Tom, puzzled; lastly, he looked at Trixie.

"I slept with you last night," she said, and laughed uproariously.

"That was the nicest thing that ever happened to me," he said, resting his hands on his thighs. "Will you do it again?"

"Hell, I was ready to adopt you."

"Please," he said. Then to Tom, "Change me back? I know I can't do it right myself. I want these rules and these manners and—" He glanced at Trixie. "I don't want to lose everything important." He frowned and looked at Maggie.

"You can do it for yourself," Tom said. "You've been inside of it. You know it from skin to bones."

"If I try and screw it up, will you help me?"

"All right."

"Can we go in the other room?"

"Okay."

Carroll rose to his feet. He pinched the material of his jeans and shirt; they had grown with him, which made him wonder if Tom were lying when he disclaimed responsibility. It took a neat thinker to adjust clothes as well as body. And how else could this have happened?

"Wait a minute," said Maggie

He looked down at her. It felt strange to see her from above again.

She took two steps forward, then a third. "I'm not scared of you anymore," she said.

He smiled.

"Want to try an experiment." She took his left hand and looked at it. It bore fresh scabs from his recent attack with the fork. "Now you can heal it yourself, can't you?"

"Not one of my strong suits."

"You can so heal. I know from experience. Do it."

Eyebrows up, he sent energy into his hand and healed it.

"Okay, good," Maggie said. "Remember what I told you, about getting rid of stuff."

"I remember everything I've heard you say."

She tugged on his shirt. "Come back down here a second."

He went down on his knees in front of her and waited.

She hugged him. He closed his eyes and breathed carefully, afraid anything he did would upset her, not wanting to upset her during the first touching she had ever initiated with him in his own form, but he could feel his body responding to her; without his intending it, his arms went around her. It was not like hugging Trixie; the energy was different, not a vast outflowing of uncomplicated love and acceptance from her to him, but the touch of two bodies who had known each other in many ways, seeking to learn a new way to relate. He felt uncomfortable but excited, uncertain, afraid. She moved one of her arms and he froze, wondering what would happen next. She slid her hand up between them and gripped his chin, then tipped her head and kissed him, surprising him completely. He felt heat flash through him in a way he had never experienced before, but his body's physical response was familiar. He gripped Maggie's shoulders and gently pushed her away. "I don't know how this works for you," he said, and stopped, thinking about that. He had never focused on how his partners felt, beyond a rudimentary concern for their comfort and readiness. "—but I can't take any more."

"Why not?"

"Because I wouldn't stop if we went any further. I don't want to do that to you again. But I do want to—" He touched her black eye, channeled healing at it, stopped when the discoloration and puffiness had vanished. Then he let go of her and put his hands on his thighs again.

"Don't change, Carroll," she said.

"How can I learn when there are no restraints?" Already he could feel the wanting rising in himself. All these people watching them. Simplicity to turn them into stones so he could be alone with Maggie, explore what they might do next. Or he could take Trixie into another room, weave the slenderest of compulsions and lay it tenderly on her, setting in her mind that he was a cherished son who could do no wrong. It wouldn't hurt her, and how wonderful it would be to know that he could always come into town and be welcome into the warmth of this house.

"Put them on yourself. You can."

He thought about that. If he cast a tangle just right, he could give himself a mental straightjacket, reduce his abilities to near nothing, with a secret word to unlock it in case of emergencies. Or he could try to operate from one moment to the next, block all the impulses he had grown accustomed to satisfying. Hard work. He could work hard, and did, in service to the Family. But so much easier to have the restraints be external. He looked at Maggie. "I don't know. And there's two parts to this, anyway. The other part is fertility."

She opened her mouth, closed it. "You were planning to have a baby?" she said.

"Is your head screwed on tight, boy?" Bert asked, apparently against his own will.

Carroll turned terrible smoky green eyes on Bert, who leaned away from him.

"Stop it," said Maggie, snapping her fingers in Carroll's face. He shook his head and smiled at her.

"What do you want with a baby, Uncle Carroll?" Laura asked, laughter in her voice.

"A baby is imperative," he said. "Is that another thing you don't know?"

"Manners," said Trixie.

"Sorry." He shook his head again, focused on Trixie. She returned his look. Their gazes locked; she saw the little girl, remembered sitting her down in the master bathroom early that morning, putting a towel about her shoulders, snipping off her curls—a child who sat preternaturally still, smiling a small smile; who afterward held one of her own curls and marveled at it, so that Trixie knelt and let the child touch her hennaed hair, to feel the difference between coarse and fine. She remembered the sweetness of awakening to someone live curled up against her.

She saw the man, and remembered him stalking around the pharmacy, saying things in that foreign tongue. Tyke made it a policy that both of them retired to the back room when Carroll came in: less seen, less noticed, less acted upon. Trixie remembered going to fetch a light bulb for a customer after a visit from Carroll and finding nothing but naked filaments in sockets and glass dust. She remembered watching him from the pharmacy window one evening as he dropped from the sky in front of Polly Martin, who was fifteen and should have known better than to be out walking after dark. Polly had not even screamed. She had stared at Carroll, leaned closer, until his arms went around her and he lifted her into the sky and she disappeared forever. Trixie had watched. Everything in her had screamed to stop it, but she knew there was nothing she could do but call Polly's mother and tell her to grieve.

"Will you come home with me?" Carroll asked Trixie.

"Is that an order?" said Bert.

Carroll glared at him, then shook his head, put his hand over his eyes. "No," he said.

"No, it's not an order?"

"No, I'm not going to turn you into a cat again. Restraints. You're her friend."

"And no, Carroll," said Trixie. "I won't go home with you, but thanks for asking."

"Will you—" He frowned and stood up. "This is hard," he said to Maggie.

"Yeah," she said, grinning.

"Will *you* come home with me?" he asked her.

"No."

He opened and closed his hands. "I'm going to lose it," he said. "If I go home alone. They all know who they expect me to be, and it will be hard to be someone new without help."

"Don't go home," said Trixie. "Stay here."

"Your room?"

"The couch in the front parlor," she said.

"Okay. Thanks. I'm going to get some food for you now."

"What?"

"I want to help. You need food. I'll be back soon."

"Do you have any money?" Trixie asked.

"No."

"Money's part of manners, Carroll. Only—" She went to the counter, to her purse, and pulled out her wallet. After looking in the currency compartment, she frowned. "Damn!"

"They wouldn't understand at the market anyway, Aunt. I never use money."

"You better start. I know. I'll write a check. Let me make a shopping list." She took a pad of paper and a pen out of one of the drawers and began checking through her cupboards.

"Uncle Carroll?" Michael said.

"What?"

"Have you gone crazy?"

"I don't think so. I don't know. Nor do I care." Trixie brought him her list and a check filled out for everything but amount. He accepted the pieces of paper and touched her hair, his movement slow, as if he expected to be challenged.

"You upset?" she said.

He nodded. She saw the hand that held the papers shake.

"I'll let you out the front door." She headed for the hall, and he followed her.

"Carroll," said Bert.

He paused at the threshold and looked back.

"The wedding's in a couple hours. You want to come, I'll give you a ride."

"Thanks," said Carroll. Closing the door behind him, he followed Trixie down the hall and into the front parlor.

"Talk to me," she said when they arrived.

"You're afraid of me," he said.

She hesitated. "Yes."

"Maggie says she's not, but I could change that with a word. I don't want to. But it feels like—it's so much easier to make mistakes now. I have the power to make big mistakes, and you can't stop me when I'm in this form. I have habits. I don't know if I can catch them in time to stop them. I—don't know if I'll want to enough, if there's no more . . ."

"No more what?"

He stared at the floor. "No more electric blanket," he said, and she saw the muscles in his arms tense and release.

"If I sleep with you, you won't hurt anyone?" Trixie felt pain in her gut. She remembered Polly Martin, and what little she knew from Maggie. "All right," she said.

"No! Not like that," he said. "Not because you're scared or because you want to save somebody else. Not because I force you. I've already done that. I try and try. I know there's something I need. I could never find it—until I was little and weak. Then you cared about me. If that's what I have to do, I'll do it again. But first, I'll get groceries. I won't be able to do that later. They won't know me to be scared of me."

"Do it different. Look, this is a check," she said, showing him what he held. "You take the groceries through the checkout line, and when Verna totals them up, you write the amount in here. Okay?"

"This is money?" He studied it.

She grinned. "Yeah."

"This is your money."

"Yes, Carroll."

"But if I use this, Aunt—it won't be a present."

"Yes, it will. Manners. Every time you use manners I consider it a gift. All right?"

"All right," he said.

She frowned. Then she hugged him, finding it easier than she had thought it might be. He was shaped the same as her boy Ray, tall and thin but wiry, and with her eyes closed she could almost forget she had her arms around the most dangerous person in the county, and was about to send him off to terrorize other people.

"Thanks," he said. He touched her face and left.

"When did he get here? What did you *do* to him?" Michael asked in a whisper as the door closed behind Trixie and Carroll.

"Michael," Laura whispered. He leaned forward. "That's none of your business."

He lifted a hand toward her. Alyssa slapped it down. They looked at each other a long moment; then Michael smiled. "Yeah," he said. He sighed. "Yeah. We really came to see how you were doing," he told Tom. "There were a lot of parties and meet-the-in-laws and spellcasting for fertility and all that *skoonaclah,* and our wedding night—" He glanced at Alyssa, who grinned. "But I've been wondering about you ever since you came. And Laura. I always knew where you were, but I didn't really know—who you were, maybe?"

"You always knew where I was?" said Laura.

"Yes. First Seattle. Four years—college. Then San Francisco. Then L.A. for a little while, then Portland."

She laughed. "You were the person I was hiding from."

"I knew that. That's why I found you, at first. But then, I don't know, you were in school, Outside. I kept thinking of long distance things to do to you, but they stopped being funny. You were just too—too normal or something. It didn't seem fair."

"What you did to me at home was never fair either."

"Yeah, but everybody seemed to *expect* me to—I don't

know—'' He bogged down and looked at Maggie, who had taken her seat beside Laura again and was sipping coffee. ''I thought there was something wrong with you.''

She waggled her eyebrows at him.

Alyssa tapped his shoulder. ''Don't change the subject, Michael. Are you saying you used to persecute Laura as well as all the others?''

''I guess you could call it that,'' he said.

''Why?''

''I had power, and she was wingless.''

Alyssa said to Laura, ''He calls you his favorite sister and says he loves you and that you're coming to our wedding if he has to go get you himself. I don't understand your branch of the Family, Laura.''

''Who is the teacher?''

Everyone turned to Tom, who had retrieved his oatmeal and taken Carroll's seat, and he realized the voice that had just spoken was Peregrine's.

Trixie, subdued, came back from seeing Carroll off. She sat down beside Bert.

''What do you mean, Ancient?'' Laura asked.

—Tommy? May I pursue this?

—Sure.

''Who's teaching you the disciplines these days?'' Peregrine asked.

''Great-aunt Fayella,'' said Michael.

''Small and venomous,'' muttered Peregrine. ''Jaimie mentioned her. We should have paid more attention.''

''What do you mean? What's going on, anyway?'' Michael asked. ''Why are you calling your husband ancient, Laura?''

''The Presence who possessed him after purification—it stayed inside him. Sometimes it talks. Ancient, what does the teacher have to do with this?''

''It is the teacher's job to balance the scales, to subdue the strong and protect the weak, to instruct each into a sense of his own worth. When Jaimie spoke of her schooling, she said the dark disciplines were encouraged, but all the others were slighted. Only, you learned them all, niece?'' He looked at Laura.

She shrugged. ''Book learning, anyway. She rushed through a lot of subjects, but I took good notes and studied them. I spent a lot of time in the library, too. She really rewarded the masters of the dark though. When Michael transformed something—me, half the time—she gave him *tishina*. Same with Gwen and Sarah and Marie and Piron; and who knows about the younger ones. And she rewarded deadwalk, and illspeak, and fetchcasting, and beguilements; she liked ill-eye and all the tangles, and she rewarded us when we practiced these things on each other.''

''Was she Carroll's teacher too?'' Peregrine asked.

''Oh, yes,'' said Laura. ''She's been . . . teaching since . . .'' Her eyes widened. ''Since the late fifties.'' She looked at Peregrine, then across at Bert, whose eyes narrowed.

''There are Fayella stories,'' said Trixie slowly. She frowned, her brows pinching together. ''Hard to remember. The Nightwalker.''

''Oh,'' said Bert, touching his temples with the first and second fingers of both hands. ''Say more.''

''Charlie Campbell,'' Trixie said, and touched her throat.

''Oh, God,'' said Bert.

''Charlie Campbell,'' Trixie whispered, rubbing her throat in little circles. ''That was in the days when the whole upper and lower school was just a couple of rooms— no portables. Charlie was in the seventh grade when I was in third, just before the Second World War. The trains used to stop in town then and we had strangers around; things hadn't boiled down into the kind of isolation we have now. Nor we weren't so frightened then, at least not of people from the Hollow, not until the time Miss Fayella took Charlie, the handsomest boy in the whole school. And she—'' Trixie paused. She pinched the bridge of her nose. ''I forgot this. I forgot it.'' She looked up. ''She

was a right handsome young woman in those days, but
even so, she robbed the cradle. She took him away . . ."

"And she sent him back," said Bert. His face wore no
expression, but his eyes were hot.

Trixie nodded. "She sent him back some months later.
I must have been about eight. I saw Charlie walking the
streets in the twilight. I was just a little kid then, running
around with the boys. We were always running along the
backs of buildings 'cause you never knew what somebody
might throw out. Bert, you were just a baby. Must have
been about four. How can you remember any of this?"

"I was always interested in everything."

"I saw Charlie walking the streets in the twilight. I ran
up to him. I thought he must have gotten away from Miss
Fayella somehow. But he was dead. Parts of him were
gone. Oh, God."

"They put a curfew," said Bert, "and the Everything
Store got in blackout curtains; everybody in town bought
'em. Nobody went out after dark if they could help it. But
it got so bad Lem Hickory went out to the Hollow and
talked to Mr. Jacob about it. Mr. Jacob put a stop to it.
Said they hadn't even known she was doing that. Miss
Scylla went to the Campbells's holdings with apologies
and charms and the rites of grief and comfort, and no one
saw Miss Fayella in town anymore."

"So she stayed home and trained up the young ones?"
said Trixie. "How could they make a decision like that?"

"When was the war?" Peregrine asked.

Everyone looked at him.

"I have been dead a long time," he said in the face of
their shock.

"It started, for our country, in 1941," Bert said.

"And she did not begin to teach until the late nineteen-
fifties, Laura?"

"That's what Jess told me."

"So she was sequestered for a period," Peregrine muttered. "Someone must have tried to give her a deep

cleansing. I hope. But it has not worked. She has put everything out of balance. This must stop.''

"No wonder Carroll is so mixed up," said Trixie.

"Ancient," said Laura, "is that why Michael had so much trouble during Purification? Would Carroll fail?"

"During Purification, deeper presences than I manifest, and their tests measure qualities I cannot sense. You are right, though; character weighs in the balance, and past actions. Your training, and how you have incorporated it. I do not know if Carroll would succeed. There is a solid core in him—but I don't know if he knows it." He felt pain in his left hand, and shook it, then noticed that the wedding ring was glowing again.

"Oh," said Tom. "Eddie. It must be. The rest of us are here. I've got to go."

"What?" Michael asked. "Not now. I'm just finding out—"

"That can wait, and this won't," said Laura. "Michael, you be nice while we're gone." She jumped up and went to Tom, putting her arms around him. He dropped his arm around her shoulders and spun a strand to pull them both to Eddie.

Chapter 19

Gas fumes almost overcame them when Tom got them fixed and focused into the reality of Pops's garage. Eddie was spraying gas everywhere, yelling, "No! No! No!" as he did it. Pops lay on the ground, gas-spattered, his glasses smashed beside his head, his eyes shut. Tom saw his chest rise and fall.

A green-clad woman, young and very beautiful, stood on top of the regular gas pump. "Yes, yes," she said, jabbing her index finger toward Eddie like a radio controller aiming an antenna at a model airplane. "Get it all ready. We'll have a friendly little fire."

Tom slipped out of Laura's arms and ran to Eddie. Sticky tar-black strands webbed around Eddie, but Tom's foxfire touch dissolved them. Eddie flung the gas nozzle away. He screamed and ran for the regular pump, grabbing the woman's ankles and jerking her down so suddenly she had no time to react. Her head hit the pump, and she barely managed to break her fall with her arms. "You bitch!" Eddie yelled, kicking her in the ribs.

"Stop it!" Tom caught his shoulders and dragged him away. The woman pushed herself upright. She spat at them. A shape like a translucent black bat flew from her mouth, landed on Eddie's neck, and tried to creep into his shirt. It refused to dissolve when Tom touched it with

foxfire. Instead, his fingers burned. He could see the bat
eating at Eddie's skin with its under-surface.

—Peregrine! What is it! How do we fight it?

—A power of water. Spit blue at it.

—What?

Eddie jerked and twisted in his grasp, gagging and
choking.

—Spit blue!

Tom hawked and tried to imagine himself spitting a
color. He saw a shape like a blue hand leave his mouth
and smother the bat. The black and blue fluttered against
each other, then dropped off Eddie's neck and fell battling
to the ground.

Eddie curled over, coughing. Tom glanced at the
woman, saw her open her mouth again. He spat first. He
saw a red hand emerge from his mouth; it flew to her face
and gagged her, making her swallow what she was preparing to spit. She started coughing with her mouth closed,
her face going red. While she was incapacitated, he cast
a tight-woven silver net around her, thickening it until he
couldn't even see her. "Helpless but healthy, helpless but
healthy," he whispered to his net, then wondered if that
was too generic a command; it was a condition, not a
shape. He looked around for Laura, saw her carrying Pops
inside the station, with his glasses floating after her.

"Eddie?" He knelt beside Eddie.

Choking and red-faced, Eddie tried to straighten. His
throat was red and peeling, as if eaten by acid.

"What did she do!" —Peregrine, can we heal?

—Try. Summon and harness energy; touch the afflicted
area; concentrate on the golden reweaving. Pour it there;
it asks and aids the body to make repairs whatever way is
best.

Tom remembered the golden glow he had seen Laura
summon when she healed Maggie. Carroll had used it too.
Tom touched Eddie's throat and called. Presently light answered his call, flowing around Eddie's neck and sinking
into his skin. The ravaged tissues restored themselves un-

der the glow's influence. Eddie touched his throat, managed to stand up. After a minute he looked at Tom. "God, that was awful. Thanks for coming." Then his eyes widened. He looked around. "Pops! Where's Pops? She was gonna make me burn up the station and Pops too! What happened to Pops? She made me knock him over and pour gas on him. If I hurt him, I'll kill myself."

"Laura took him inside," Tom said. "If anything's wrong with him, she'll fix it."

"How can you trust one of those murdering bitches!" Eddie ran into the shop with Tom trailing him. "You get away from him, you evil witch!"

Startled, Laura looked up. Pops lay on the couch in the room where people waited for their cars to get fixed. Laura held his head in her hands. Eddie ran toward her, arms outstretched, his hands aimed at her throat.

"Stop!" Tom yelled, and Eddie froze. "Don't ever talk to Laura like that, and don't you hurt her."

Eddie shivered. He opened and closed his mouth. "You're doing it too," he said at last. "Just like them. Pulling my strings."

"I warned you."

Pops's eyes flickered open. Laura let go of his head and smiled down at him. Pops smiled back. "Miss Laura! So nice to see you," he said.

"Thank you." She picked up his glasses from the table and held them. Tom saw a flash of silver around her cupped hands. "This might make it easier," she said, offering the glasses, restored, to Pops. He put them on with trembling hands. He reached up and patted her cheek.

Tom relaxed the strands of the net he had spun around Eddie. Eddie glared at him, then went to Pops. "You okay? Oh, Pops. I'm so sorry."

"I feel fine now," said Pops. He sat up. "I feel good!" He tapped his chest. "Miss Laura, what did you do? I don't have pain here anymore."

Laura looked at Tom, then at her hands. "Gates opening again?" she asked. "Are you doing it, or am I?"

"You are."

Eddie said, "Sorry. Sorry I yelled at you."

She gave him a smile. To Tom, she looked like the most beautiful woman he had ever seen. He blinked and saw her features glowing golden, remembered her talking about addressing her spark, and figured she was doing it now, whether she knew it or not. "You were upset," she said to Eddie. "And you don't know me. It's okay."

Carroll strolled into the station carrying two sacks of groceries. "What is that thing outside?" he asked.

Eddie jumped up, putting himself between Pops and Carroll. Carroll made a half-smile.

"What? What thing?" Tom felt a shiver of apprehension. He ran past Carroll outside. Something lay at the base of one of the gas pumps. At first Tom saw only his silver net. Then he looked without Othersight and saw what appeared to be a person-sized pink potato. "Oh, God. Is she dead?"

It quivered.

Tom glanced back over his shoulder at Carroll. "You take Laura home if she wants you to?"

"All right."

"Help her clean up the mess here?"

Carroll grinned. The green in his eyes silvered. A dimple flashed in his cheek. Tom had never noticed it before. "All right," he said.

"Thanks. I'll be back." Tom spun a strand out to the clearing where he and Carroll-as-raven had had their talk. He pulled himself and the pink blob there.

He sat down, hugging himself, facing the thing he had turned the woman into. Another rash choice, but he had had to think fast. She was Family; she had *sitva;* she was still alive. Was she still herself? He tuned in to his net. "You may speak," he said, hoping she would have something to say.

"Who are you? What did you do to me? Stop it right now, or my whole Family will be after you, and once that happens you're worse than dead."

He felt relieved. "Who are *you*? Are you Gwen?" His voice dropped as Peregrine took over. "Do you think the Family would sanction your harming anyone in town? You mistake, young woman! What is rule one in *tanganar* relationships?"

—What *is* rule one? Tom wondered.

"Never hurt them where they live," Gwen said.

—But Carroll almost took Trixie in her home, Tom thought.

—He had descended below the threshold of reason, into the realm of upper madness; something kicked him over that edge. It was a blessing you could take action, and a blessing you chose the action wisely, Peregrine thought. Aloud, he said, "You are in no position to threaten me. I would like to hear one reason why I should restore you."

"Who are you, please?" Gwen said in a small voice.

"I am two people: Thomas Renfield, husband to Laura Bolte, and Peregrine Bolte, from the thirteenth generation."

She was silent a moment. "One reason you should restore me," she said at last. "I'm fertile."

"That is no longer reason enough. You came close to killing two people in their home."

"One of them my own fetch! And a disobedient fetch, a runaway fetch. Surely that mitigates."

"You acted without knowledge. He was no longer yours."

"How not?"

"I took him from you. I dissolved your bindings and established my own."

She was quiet. "How was I to know?" she said.

"Answer your own question."

"Check," she said. "But I've never heard of anything like this happening. I didn't know to look for it. And— no."

"What?"

"When I tried to re-establish—at first I couldn't control him at all. I see. I see. But when he threatened me—"

"Self-preservation transcended," Peregrine said, "and you misused it."

She waited another moment. "Are you going to leave me like this, blind, unable to move, to care for myself?"

"No." He sighed. Tom murmured, "Gwen. Gwen," to his net, told it to relax around her but stay in place. She took shape again, crouching.

Her dark brown hair veed back from a deep widow's peak, to fall in long, ragged-ended shocks about her shoulders. Her face had an angularity about it that reminded Tom of how he imagined faery folk would look. She had pencil line brows and slanted green eyes, set far apart, above broad, high cheekbones; a narrow nose, and a wide, thin-lipped mouth. She owned a compelling, exotic beauty. Her body was muscular and rounded, graceful as a horse's. Her toes were so long they reminded him of fingers.

She studied him as he studied her. Their gazes caught and held. She widened her eyes, and the tip of her tongue made a full, slow circuit of her mouth.

"Refrain from that, unless you wish to be helpless again," said Peregrine. "We must talk."

She sighed. She squatted, elbows on knees, and hands dangling.

"Do you agree to abandon this pursuit of the fetch?" Peregrine asked.

"What choice do I have? Either your host is very powerful, or you are."

"Answer yes or no."

She looked at the ground. "Yes. I agree."

"And you will not seek reprisals by attacking another person in place of the lost one, or by attacking someone I care about?"

"But, Ancient—"

"Let it go, descendant Gwendolyn."

"I'll lose status."

"The whole system is due for reworking. I have already initiated it."

"What?" She stood up.

"I require your agreement. No reprisals, Gwen."

She stalked away, shaking her hands as if she could shed his words like water drops. But at length she came back. "Or else?"

"Or else," he said.

"I agree," she said.

"You may go home now."

She glared at him. She flew away.

He pulled himself along a silver spider thread to Laura.

"Detergent might do it," Eddie said. He swept at sawdust on the pavement; they had scattered it in an attempt to soak up the gas. "I remember we used detergent to get oil off seabirds after one of those big oil spills in southern California."

"There's an easier way," said Carroll.

Tom went to Laura, who stood by the door to the station's waiting room, with Pops beside her. She looked very calm—calmer than Eddie or Pops, both of whom watched Carroll with guarded expressions.

Carroll held out his hands. He closed his eyes. Tom saw shimmering pulses of amber light rippling from his hands, spreading to touch all the pavement and everything Eddie had splashed with gas, including Pops's clothes. Then Pops's clothes were wet, and the gas fumes were gone.

Eddie stooped, touched the wet ground, and smelled his fingers. "Water! Great!" he said. "Oh, God. I never thought I'd say this. Thanks, Mr. Carroll."

Carroll looked at Tom, one eyebrow up. Feeling awkward, Tom smiled at him, wondering how to relate to Carroll now that Tom wasn't controlling him, and Carroll wasn't trying to get back at Tom. Was Carroll serious about trying to civilize himself? Tom didn't yet know how to do the truth flame; still, on some level he trusted Carroll's new direction. On some other level he worried. Carroll had such a weight of history and habit to fight; Tom wondered how long he would struggle against the tide before lapsing back into his old self.

—If he is determined, he can change everything, Peregrine said. —There are precedents. Not many; but a few.

"We better go home," said Laura. "We have to get ready for the wedding."

"Whose?" asked Pops.

"Barney Vernell's and my cousin Annis's. Two o'clock," Bert said. "Father Wolfe—does that mean the Catholic church, Pops?"

"Episcopal," said Pops.

"Barney and Annis?" said Eddie. He looked at Carroll.

"Sanctioned by a higher authority." Carroll's shoulders slumped. "I want to go home now."

Tom heard exhaustion in his voice, and went inside to pick up the groceries. "Pops, you take care," he said as he came out. "I made Gwen promise she wouldn't come back, but she might try something else. Call me at Trixie's if you need me. Or Eddie can call me without a phone."

"All right, Tommy. Tommy? What happened to you?"

"It's a long story, Pops, and we don't have time now. Excuse me, please."

"Sure, sure." Pops waved his hands in a shooing motion.

"Double excuse me for this," Tom said. He spun Carroll, Laura, and himself back to Trixie's kitchen.

No one was in the kitchen, but sounds upstairs meant someone was home. Carroll let out breath.

"Are you okay?" Tom asked him, setting the sacked groceries on the counter. Laura started unloading the bags.

"I feel tired." Carroll sat down at the table. "The market was harder than I thought it would be. I never really looked at the people before."

"What happened?"

Carroll shook his head, put his elbows on the table and leaned his forehead on the palms of his hands.

"Uh—do you want to go to the wedding, or would you rather rest?" Tom asked.

Carroll took a deep breath, then let it out. A moment later he straightened and looked up. "Which is better? Ancestor? What should I do?"

—Go ahead, Tom thought, then thought he didn't really need to think it. He and Peregrine were meshing tighter all the time, changing places more easily, though they still had their own separate views on everything.

"You are committed to changing?" asked Peregrine.

"Yes. Something—when you asked me to help clean up—no one ever—I've never—that felt like—I want things to be different. I'd like to help. I'm afraid! They'll despise me for weakness at the Hollow. What if you're twisting my brain and these are not my own thoughts? I want them to be my own thoughts. I don't want them to be your beguilements."

"There is a way for you to check." Peregrine went to the front bathroom, found a hand mirror, and brought it back to the kitchen. He handed it to Carroll.

Laura stopped putting things away and came to sit at the table. "Things seen and unseen?" she said.

"A property of air; but earth, which transforms, can handle it too. Sketch the first four signs, descendant, and look into your eyes."

Carroll lifted his hand. He framed the signs slowly, as if dredging them from deep memory. Silver flared around him. *"Sirella!* What is that?" he asked.

"My casting. Search your eyes."

First Carroll lifted his arm and looked at the elegant silver flickerings that sheathed it. "You did this?"

"Tom did it. I forgot it would be revealed."

Carroll looked up. "I am in your hand."

"Your physical form is. Search your eyes before the vision fades."

He studied his face in the mirror. "Nothing gets in or out, but that you will it. My eyes are clear; my thoughts are mine. The casting is very beautiful."

The light around him flickered and faded. Carroll set

the mirror down and looked up at Tom. "You don't trust me."

"With some things I do. Do you want me to trust you with everything?" Tom couldn't tell if he spoke or Peregrine did.

"Not yet," said Carroll.

"Are you serious about becoming small again?"

"I don't know," Carroll said. "Perhaps I can succeed without it. It's harder, because I'm not as frightened. Sometimes I think I need fear. And I wouldn't have understood how Maggie felt if she hadn't been able to hurt me, if I hadn't felt what it was like when there was nothing I could do to protect myself, no escape . . ." His voice sank to a whisper.

Peregrine said, "Tell me when you decide what shape you want to walk in, and I will grant it. For now, though: the wedding. In my mind I have no doubt that things must change here and in the Hollow, and you can aid that change if you come to this wedding in your own shape, watch it, and do nothing to interrupt. It will surprise everyone. If you wish to stay away, that is understandable."

"I'll go." He stood up. "Ancient, what changed me back to this form this morning? Was it you or Tom?"

"We did not make the decision. You did. I suspect Tom laid a condition on the casting that said when you lost the desire to do harm you could return to yourself, but since he worked in ways that elude me, I cannot be sure."

Footsteps sounded in the hall. A moment later Maggie, Michael, Trixie, and Alyssa came into the kitchen, carrying armloads of clothes. "Oh, hi! Welcome back," said Trixie.

Carroll smiled at her.

"Trixie saved every piece of clothing she ever bought or owned," Maggie said. She was wearing a pale green dress with a white lace collar, puffed sleeves, and kick pleats; and a pair of white tights and white maryjanes. She looked like a twelve-year-old on her way to an Easter service. Her brown hair had been pinned at the sides with silver star-shaped barrettes. "Everything anybody outgrew. This was her daughter Pearl's ninth-grade graduation dress."

"You look good," Carroll said. Tom touched his shoulder. He glanced back, wondering if he had done something wrong, then realized Tom was feeding energy into the casting. Carroll felt the fatigue wash out of him. He touched two fingers to his lips, then sketched an old sign for gratitude. Would Tom understand? The Presence could explain it. Tom nodded and smiled, then went around the counter to finish putting away the groceries.

"Found you a coat," Maggie said. "It used to be Mr. Delarue's. It doesn't go with the jeans, but it'll make you look more official." She handed him a black velvet smoking jacket with satin lapels.

"Thank you," he said. He glanced at Trixie, and she nodded. He slipped the jacket on over his T-shirt. The shoulders were a little too wide, but the sleeves were just the right length. He lifted a lapel and sniffed the odor of ancient pipe smoke.

"I like this," said Michael, holding up a dark green jacket that had a shimmer on it.

Alyssa wore a white dress with tiny black hearts and arrows all over it. It hung straight down to her hips, then gathered, with a short pleated skirt below, and a large black bow at the side just below her right hip. She struck a pose.

"My mother's best jazz party dress," Trixie said. She wore a wine-colored tent dress made of some shimmering unnatural fabric. Somehow it did not clash with her hair, perhaps because she also wore a white fox fur. "This is so strange. I can't remember the last time I dressed up, barring Tyke's funeral, and that wasn't colors. But I figure if ever there was a time for it, this qualifies. See anything you like, Tommy? Laura?" Michael, Alyssa, and Trixie draped a variety of clothes over the kitchen chairs.

Tom reached for a fine herring-bone patterned three-piece suit in brown and white with baggy pleated pants and wide lapels. "Hot damn. Other clothes at last."

Laura handed him a white shirt and a wide red silk tie, then lifted a red dress from under a pile of pastels. "Us," she said. "Come on, husband. We'll be right back."

"You'd better," Trixie said. "Bert'll be over in about two minutes to pick us up."

In their room, Tom and Laura changed quickly. The clothes fitted as if made for them. Laura's red dress had a low V-neck, narrow wrist-length sleeves, a tight waist, and a sheath skirt, slit up the side. Tom zipped the back for her, and she tied his tie. As she adjusted it under his collar, he put his hands over hers and looked into her eyes.

She smiled, her eyes glowing golden.

"We don't know each other yet," he said.

"No," she said. Her face sobered.

"I know you go to sleep well and you wake up well, and I love to look at you and to touch you; and when we work together it feels great. I like what I've seen of the way you think. And sometimes I just feel really, really weird."

"I know what you mean," she said. "It's like I stepped out of my real life into this—tornado. But what a ride!"

"But we're not going to get down off it anytime soon."

"Yes, we will," she said. "The real question is where: Oz, or Kansas?"

"Things have changed so much for me in the last three days that I think I'm going to have trouble adjusting to Kansas."

"Me too. Maybe we should go someplace entirely new, where we can be alone among strangers and figure out who we are before we have to deal with other people."

"That sounds great," he said.

"In any case," she said, "I like spending time with you. And I *am* in love with you."

He put his arms around her. "I love you," he said, and wondered what that meant. He remembered how much his mother had loved him, and Aunt Rosemary, and the casual kindnesses along the way of uncles and cousins and aunts who didn't know what to do with him, but sometimes tried to do right.

Laura in his arms was warm and alive, smelling of sage and spice and a hint of jasmine, tied to him with a spectrum of threads, some they had spun themselves, some supplied by others. He knew this was different from everything he had experienced before. Exciting and scary; another challenging new thing to learn. She tipped her head up and he kissed her and stopped thinking about anything else.

"Hey!"

Laura giggled and he felt the faint buzz of her voice against his lips. He lifted his head, turned to see Trixie in the door.

"Bert's here," she said.

"One sec," said Laura, slipping out of his arms and dashing into the bathroom. He followed her, since she didn't close the door, and watched as she lined her eyes with a delicate rim of black, brushed a color onto her lips that matched her dress, and touched the ridges of her cheekbones with gilded peach. "My hair," she said.

"Looks perfect," he said.

She gave herself a concentrated stare in the mirror, grabbed a red and black hair clasp from her toiletries bag, combed and then clubbed her hair at the nape of her neck, then looked at him and wiggled her eyebrows.

"Okay, even more perfect," he said, and they ran downstairs.

Bert had slicked his hair back and was wearing a brown suit a size too small for comfort. "Come on!" he said as they poured out of the house. "We should be there already!"

"Weddings always start late," Trixie said.

"Should I warm up Old Number Two?" Tom said, looking at the eight of them. Old Number One had broad bench seats in the front and back, but—

"What are laps for?" Bert said. "Get in!"

They all managed to fit, Maggie and Trixie in front next
to Bert, Laura on Tom's lap in the back seat, Carroll,
subdued, in the middle, and Alyssa on Michael's lap.
Alyssa giggled. "Mischief," she said. "Mischief."

"What's all this traffic about?" muttered Bert, swerving
to avoid a car pulling out of a driveway.

"Maybe everybody's coming," said Trixie. "Lord!
There's Custis. Wish I had a hat to tip. I wonder if the
kids invited the whole town?"

"Father Wolfe'll have the biggest congregation of his
career, and no chance for a sermon," said Bert. And he
turned out to be right; by the time they reached the church,
there wasn't a space left in the parking lot. "How do you
like that!" Bert said. "And me best man."

"Park illegally, boss," said Tom.

"You learn to fix tickets as well as everything else,
Tommy?" Bert parked in a red zone and everyone piled
out of the car.

Maggie went to Carroll, who looked pale. "Lean over,"
she said. He leaned over and she smoothed his hair. "Now
do your arm like this," she said, crooking her elbow. He
copied her and she linked arms with him. "Scared too,"
she muttered, "so can I hang onto you?"

"I would prefer it."

They all went in together, Michael and Alyssa holding
hands, Carroll and Maggie following them, Tom between
Laura and Trixie, Bert dashing for the front of the church
to ask the priest where he could find the groom. The organ
was already playing, and the pews were full, but as they
came down the aisle voices stilled, and started again in a
hushed tone. People scooted away from them. Carroll
heard his name on the crest of the whispers, but wherever
he looked, people fell silent. Some trembled. Behind them,
some people snuck out.

"Oh, stop it," Trixie yelled. "We're only here to wish
them health, okay?"

"I better go talk to Annis, tell her who's come, and that

it's all right," Laura whispered to Tom. She turned and
went toward the back of the church.

Carroll decided to take advantage of his ability to make
people disappear. He stared grimly at the second pew on
the right until it emptied of people, then tapped Michael
on the shoulder and aimed him in that direction. They sat
down. The mutters near them evaporated.

The organist, who had faltered for a moment, recaptured the strains of the Bach prelude she had been playing.
She cut the volume as the priest came in, followed by Bert
and Barney. Barney was wearing a toast-colored suit and
a silver-blue tie; he looked like an accountant on his way
to work, although the set of his shoulders and a faintly
grim expression gave him the appearance of defiant
strength.

Barney and Father Wolfe looked astonished when they
saw the crowd in the church. "So they didn't invite 'em
all," Trixie whispered to Tom. "I wonder how people
found out?"

"Laura told Pops," Tom said.

Barney and Maggie exchanged a long look; she gripped
Carroll's arm and smiled. Barney looked disturbed, but he
turned back to business.

Laura came back, carrying Rupert, and slid into the pew
next to Tom. Rupert looked out of place in his little yellow
sleeper lying against her red dress. Barney's mother, Jane
Vernell, sat in the front pew. She turned to look at the
baby. Her eyes were full of longing. Laura leaned forward. "Haven't you seen him yet?" she whispered.

"Barney's not speaking to me," Mrs. Vernell whispered back.

Laura turned Rupert around to face his grandmother. He
was fast asleep. "This is Rupert," Laura whispered. She
felt a force to her right and glanced over to see Carroll
leaning forward, his whole being focused on the baby.
Mrs. Vernell touched Rupert's face and smiled, then turned
her smile toward Barney, who looked stern.

Laura sat back, aware of Carroll's concentration. She

nudged Tom with her elbow. "Is he safe?" she murmured, nodding toward Carroll.

"Oh, yes. I don't know about the situation, though. What if everybody thought he was going to hurt the baby? Might be a riot."

"He wants so fiercely."

"He's learning he can't always have what he wants. And this is Barney's and Annis's moment. I wonder, though. Could any message be better?"

Rupert stirred, opened his eyes, and began to squirm. He turned toward Carroll.

Laura handed the baby to Tom, who passed him to Trixie. She hugged him and handed him to Maggie, who placed him in Carroll's arms.

Carroll's eyes silvered. He stroked Rupert's back; Rupert calmed and snuggled against the black velvet of his jacket. Carroll cradled Rupert in his arms.

Barney looked uneasy, but Bert said something to him. The organ swelled with "Here Comes the Bride," everyone rose, and Annis came in, dressed in a plain blue dress, followed by Jaimie in pale green, looking a little out of her element. Annis walked without resorting to the traditional bride's shuffle straight to the front, where she stood beside Barney, Jaimie going around to her left. Everyone sat down.

"Dearly beloved," Father Wolfe said. His voice wobbled. He took a breath and went on. "We have come together in the presence of God to witness and bless the joining together of this man and this woman in Holy Matrimony . . ."

When they had finished their vows and the ensuing prayers, and received blessing and peace, the organist played the bride and groom out with Mendelssohn, and everyone stood up.

Many melted away, though some people stood around talking.

Tom whispered to Laura, "I liked ours better."

"Much shorter," she said.

"But just as important, right? But we haven't done any of the legal work. Blood tests, licenses, like that. Maybe we should do a civil ceremony."

"Yes," she said. "I sure don't want one like this. Though I've seen some weddings that make this look like a short subject with a low budget."

Barney's mother asked Carroll if she could hold the baby. He hesitated, then passed Rupert to her. When Annis came to retrieve Rupert she found Carroll and Mrs. Vernell with their heads bent over the baby, studying him.

"He's sealed," Annis told Carroll. Her nostrils were pinched, her mouth a straight line.

"I know," said Carroll. He held Rupert out to her. She snatched him away; the baby stirred and began crying. Annis turned and walked out of the chapel.

"Well," said Mrs. Vernell, "we're both *persona non,* I guess. I don't think I've met you." She held out her hand. He took it. "The groom's mother. Jane Vernell."

"Carroll Bolte. Why are they mad at *you?*"

She blinked and lost her smile, then glanced around as if searching for help. "I told him not to follow her home. I told him it would be the death of him," she said.

"So we were both wrong." He released her hand and gave her a grin.

"You're going to let them be?"

"Yes. It's a beautiful baby, isn't it?"

"Oh, yes. Looks just like Barney did at that age. . . . I feel very uncomfortable."

"I'll go talk to someone else," said Carroll. "Nice to meet you."

"You too," she said, and covered her mouth with her hand as he turned away.

The marshal cornered Tom. "What's happening now?" he asked. He glanced at Laura, then away. "What's Mr. Carroll gonna do? He came to the market and paid with a check! Trixie's check. He put the fix on her? He going to snatch everybody in town? Is this a good thing, or what? How come Bert and Trixie are in the line of fire?"

"You going somewhere with this, Sam?" Tom asked.

"Yeah! Are things getting better or worse?"

"I think they're getting better. I think the wedding was a good start. Don't you?"

Sam stared at him with narrowed eyes. "I recall the last time I got to talking about Hollow weddings with you, it turned out that you—Tommy, is Barney one of you too? He'd have to be, wouldn't he, or Mr. Carroll and Mr. Michael wouldn't have sat still for it. How can that be? I've known that boy all his life."

Tom frowned. "Sam, let me see your hand a minute."

"What?"

"Whichever hand you write with." —Peregrine?

—Yes, Tom. Couldn't hurt.

Sam held out his left hand. Tom let Peregrine take over. He sketched a sign on Sam's palm. It glowed a dull red-orange.

"What the hell are you doing!" Sam said.

"Sign earth," said Laura, interested.

"At the Hollow, they think they're running out of Family," Tom said. He dropped Sam's hand and laughed.

"Just a darn minute! You explain that, Tommy!"

Tom grinned at him. He linked arms with Laura and they walked away.

Eddie found Maggie. "You okay? I got here late. I saw Mr. Carroll's here. Is Tom protecting you all right?"

"I'm fine," said Maggie. "Better than fine—"

Carroll came to her, touched her arm. He was glancing over his shoulder at Mrs. Vernell's back as she fled up the aisle. "I can't talk to these people," he said.

"You're the bogeyman. What do you expect? Carroll, was Miss Fayella your teacher?"

He stopped glancing around to see how quickly people faded away, and switched his focus to Maggie. "Yes," he said. He raised his eyebrows.

"Oh—so that fits. Tell you later. This is Eddie."

"I know."

"Thought you didn't notice anybody less than a relative out in the Hollow."

"Not true. Noticing everything was part of our training. Anyway, I stopped at the gas station on my way home from the market."

"He turned all our gas to water," said Eddie.

"All?" Carroll asked. "Even the gas in the pumps? I didn't mean to do that."

"That's okay. Better than the mess we had. Pops is expecting a delivery day after tomorrow, anyway."

"I can fix it, though."

"I hate to ask this. But why? Why, Mr. Carroll?"

"I don't like making mistakes," said Carroll, an ominous edge in his voice.

Eddie, conditioned from his time at Chapel Hollow, dropped his gaze and took a couple of shuffling steps away. Maggie grabbed his hand and pulled him back. "Wait a minute, Carroll. How can you expect people to talk to you if you threaten them? If you don't like a question, just say 'no comment.' "

"What does that mean?"

"Means you don't answer. Politicians say it all the time."

"But I *did* answer, Maggie."

"Yes, but—" She dropped Eddie's hand and said, "Urrrh!" at Carroll. "Then I guess you don't really want to talk to people."

"I'm scared of them."

"What?" said Eddie.

"I don't—" Carroll let go of Maggie, turned away a moment, then turned back. "I don't know how—the structures, I haven't built them—if I were fetchcasting, I would know what to say."

Eddie shuddered.

"What do you do when you . . . fetchcast?" Maggie asked, her voice tight.

"Seduce: I charm and persuade you to come with me.

If you say no, I cannot take you. Remove: I take you to my home. Train: you remember that part.''

Maggie's breathing quickened and deepened. She opened and closed her hands. "So it's all . . . planned ahead. Practiced. I hate you.''

His eyes darkened. He curled his hands into fists and crossed his arms at the wrist over his chest. Then he turned away, stumbling a little, and walked off, people melting out of his way, and searched for something to hold onto.

"How could you say that to him?" Eddie whispered. "How come he didn't fry you? God!''

"Oh, I can't help it! Hate how we were! He came down out of the sky when I was in bad trouble, and used magic to save me from this evil guy, and I thought, here it is, my fairytale come true; and at first, he was so gentle and nice to me, like nobody I'd known, and I thought, this is love; and then he just got impatient and careless and mean. And I thought—'' Red washed her cheeks. "Maybe I was doing something wrong? Couldn't figure out the right thing to do. Couldn't get him to change back. Then just started hating him. Hated him most for making me believe real good could happen. . . . Didn't know he had a program! Makes me feel even more like an idiot for believing . . . except he's trying to change now, but how can I trust that?'' An angry tear streaked down her cheek.

Trixie was asking Marcia Pickett how the pharmacy was doing when Carroll found her. He touched Trixie's arm, and she turned and glanced up into his face, which looked haunted. " 'Scuse me, sweetie,'' she turned to say to Marcia, but Marcia was gone. "Let's go home,'' Trixie said to Carroll. She put her arm around him—he seemed frozen into a strange position—and steered him toward the door. After a few steps he breathed normally again, and then his arms came down, one around her shoulders. "What happened?'' she asked.

His face tightened. He shook his head.

"All right. Okay, sweetie. Let's go home. I'll make you some warm milk.''

He smiled a shadow smile and touched her cheek.

The church was surrounded by clumps of talking people. Barney, Annis, and Jaimie, with Rupert, stood by the gate, captured by someone. As Trixie led Carroll up, Barney turned, along with everyone else.

"Oh. Carroll," Barney said. "Thank you for coming."

Carroll stared at Barney a moment, then smiled. "You're welcome. Have more kids. Or am I not supposed to say that?"

Barney took off his glasses and studied Carroll. His naked eyes were intense brown. "Will you be Rupert's godfather?"

"What does it mean?"

Annis said, *"Miksash,* Uncle."

"Do you want that, Niece?" he asked, after a moment's pause.

"Are you—different?" she asked.

"I'm working at it."

"I would claim you. Rupert could hope for no one stronger."

"What about Tom?"

"No one knows him—not to my satisfaction. If you smiled on our baby, the others would have to pay attention; they all know you."

"I accept."

Jaimie held out the baby to him.

Carroll let go of Trixie and took Rupert, who calmed in his hands. He studied the baby's face as if he had not been memorizing it all during the wedding. Finally he kissed Rupert's forehead, leaving his own trace there. He hugged Rupert, thinking he had another reason to learn new ways now, so that he could give the child clean care, not polluted with darkness. He surrendered the baby to Jaimie again. "Thank you. Thank you for asking me. Annis, this is my—*troosh,*" he said, touching Trixie's shoulder. "She is teaching me how to care about children."

"We met. Yesterday? I thank you, Miss Trixie."

"Any time," said Trixie. "I suppose we'll be seeing

you? You folks moving into town or staying out in the wilds?''

"We haven't decided yet," said Barney. "For now, we feel safer out there. But I guess we don't have to be so scared and careful . . .''

"Right. We'll see you." She took Carroll's hand and led him out through the gate. They walked down the street together, leaving the church and all the people behind. After a block, Trixie said, "What *did* happen, sweetie?''

"Maggie hates me again.''

"New reasons or same old?''

"Same old. I want to be little, Aunt. Tom said I could choose. Would you still take care of me?''

"If you'll help around the house like you said. It's a big house for one person. Could you help without magic?''

"Yes. I would like that. I liked that sponge.''

"But it won't stay new very long.''

He looked at her and smiled. "That's all right. I want to—know what it's like to be a fetch. Otherwise Maggie . . .''

"Carroll," said Trixie, when the sentence went unfinished, "whatever happened to Polly Martin?''

"Mostly she does laundry, but she's training with Cousin Nerissa in the mysteries of weaving lately. She has a gift.''

"She's not dead?''

"I haven't killed anyone. I'm usually not nice to them either. I want you to know this.''

"I hear you.''

They came to Pops's garage. "Wait a minute," said Carroll. He detoured toward the building. There were NO GAS signs hanging on the gas pumps.

Pops came along the sidewalk from church behind them. He whistled. His whistle stopped when he saw Carroll, then resumed.

Carroll waited until Pops arrived. "I made a mistake before," he said.

Pops peered at him through his glasses. "What?''

"Eddie said—" He pointed to the pumps. "Did I turn the gas underground into water too?"

"Yes, but that's fine, Mr. Carroll. The tanks were pretty low anyway; we were expecting a delivery. I think we can get the water on out of there without too much trouble, and we'll get some new gas soon."

"I'll turn it back. I need some real gas to sample, though."

Pops looked at him a long moment. "Follow me," he said at last, and led Carroll around the side of the building to his old Frazer Vagabond. He opened the gas tank. "Can you tell from here? This is premium. I don't have any samples of unleaded or regular."

Carroll ran a finger around the opening of the tank, then smelled the gas. "All right," he said. "I'm ready. Where do you want this one?"

Pops opened one of the caps on an underground tank, and Carroll knelt and directed energy down into the hole. After a moment he got up again. "You want this in the other tanks?" he asked.

Pops hesitated. "It would be okay for the regular. Not the unleaded. Can't put it in unleaded engines, it clogs the converter. No, let's just leave it like this. Thanks, Mr. Carroll."

"You're welcome." He went to Trixie.

"What is this all about?" she asked.

Carroll looked at Pops.

"Well," said Pops. "Well, we spilled a lot of gas. It was a fire hazard. Tommy asked the boy to clean up the mess, and he did; he made the gas into water. He just did it too good is all."

"This is where Tom disappeared to?"

"I don't know," said Carroll. "He was here when I walked home."

"Miss Gwen came and tried to get Eddie back," said Pops. "She knocked me on the head. When I woke up, she was gone, but Tommy, Mr. Carroll, and Miss Laura were here."

"That was Gwen Tom was dealing with?" Carroll said, fascinated. Then he said, "Oh, no. Oh, no, Aunt, I can't get small then. What if she comes back?"

"Tommy said she promised she wouldn't," said Pops.

"She's just like I am. If there's a way to get around a promise, she'll find it."

"That's what you're like, eh?" Trixie said.

Carroll looked at her. "Was like. Was like, all right?"

"Okay. Come on, let's go home." She took his hand again. "Bye, Pops."

"Bye. Thanks."

They hadn't gone very far when Maggie showed up. She laced her left arm through Carroll's right and frowned ferociously. "Don't say anything. Not one word. I'm not in the mood," she said, her frown almost a snarl.

He walked down the road with his face tilted toward the sky, Trixie on his left and Maggie on his right. He felt very happy.

Chapter 20

"Is there a reception, or do we all just mill around talking?" Tom asked.

"No reception," said Father Wolfe. "We hadn't planned on this being a big wedding. I had no idea anyone other than the principals would show up."

"Bert invited us," said Laura.

"I'm very glad, Miss Laura. I'm glad to see you at all. The town has missed you."

"Why—thank you," she said.

"Already I see your influence at work. Your uncle and your brother sitting quietly through a whole church service—forgive me, but I never expected to see the day."

"Oh, that wasn't my influence; that was my husband's."

"Tom?" Father Wolfe turned to him.

"No," said Tom. "I think you're missing the point. They came because they wanted to. Annis is a relative. And people in Chapel Hollow take weddings very seriously; that's almost the first thing Laura told me about them."

"I suppose Mr. Carroll and Mr. Michael are older than they were the last time I had anything to do with them . . ." His eyes reflected inward. He frowned.

"And Michael got married," Laura said. "Settled him

right down. Have you met his wife? We'll go find her."
She linked arms with Tom and led him off.

"What?" Tom asked her when they were out of ear-
shot.

"It just fries me. He thinks the Hollow is full of Satan
worshippers and demons, and everybody in town thinks
I'm a saint because I was never strong enough to pester
them. I'm like King Kong's girlfriend or something, the
pure fainting maiden among the beasts. I'm really tired of
it. I don't know Alyssa very well, but I bet she'd make a
better saint than I ever did. I think I'll nominate her."

Before they could find Michael and Alyssa, Laura's high
school English teacher stopped her, wanting to know about
her college career if any, and what had come of it. "I've
been seeing a face that looks a lot like yours on the covers
of fashion magazines, but that seemed so unlikely," said
Miss Finch.

"It was mine."

"What happened to you? Use your mind, girl. Quick,
before you lose your face. Or is that one of those things
you Boltes don't do? Age, I mean. I loaned you *The Picture of Dorian Gray* once, didn't I?"

"That was one of the meaner things you did. Yuck!
Miss Finch, this is my husband, Tom Renfield."

"Do you find yourself in an analogous situation?" asked
Miss Finch.

"Analogous to what?"

"I mean your literary precedent—your name, Renfield—Dracula's insect-eating sidekick. Any truth in
names, or would you smell as sweet with another?"

"Are you casting me as Dracula?" Laura asked.

"It would be an interesting choice, wouldn't it? If you
applied yourself, you could be quite good. Hmm. I see
now I should have loaned you some different books. Your
problem was never the proper use of power, was it?"

"What do you think it was?"

"Claiming power. Look what you've done with yourself! Turned yourself into a flat unspeaking image, inca-

pable of movement. Isn't that what your pestiferous brother was always trying to train you to do? Now you do it for a living!"

"I'm good at what I do, and I make a lot of money. Are you telling me that's wrong?"

"What happened to your acting? You had talent. I've never had another student who could change so completely under the influence of a role; it led me to speculate about what you must have endured at home, to be able to see other viewpoints with such conviction. That's a gift, Laura, not a liability. Why don't you exploit it? Why didn't you at least try to pursue it?"

"I did. That's how I got into modeling. I was in a play at the college theater, some ingénue dewy-eyed part, and an agent saw me and told me to put together a portfolio. She got me a job right away. Most of the actors I know don't work at acting—no eating money in it. How dare you berate me for choosing survival?"

"I just hate to see you betray your muse. Hey, you, Renfield. Why don't you support her until she gets a break acting?"

"Okay," said Tom.

"See? That's the only reason to marry—latch onto someone who'll help you survive until you get a chance to follow your dream."

"No," said Laura. "I'm happy now."

"Wearing things thought up by men with Spanish Inquisition minds to convince women they want to undergo torture to look like you, knowing they'll never succeed in looking like you, only in suffering? I'm sorry!"

"Are you trying to provoke me?"

"Provoke you to do what?" asked Miss Finch.

Laura looked at Tom. Her tawny eyes had gold sparks in them. He grinned. "Provoke me into claiming my power and turning you into a toad," said Laura.

"Is that possible? I had no idea," said Miss Finch.

"It's possible."

"But is it a mature response?"

"Who cares? I'm tired of being grown up all the time. And I'm tired of being the family saint, and I'm tired of taking care of other people's business when I ought to be on my honeymoon. Tom, take me away from all this."

"How? Up through the roof? Just disappear? Or would you rather walk out the front door?"

She gave him an irritated glance, then said, "Let's go through the roof. I'm mad at Father Wolfe."

Tom shook Miss Finch's hand. "A pleasure meeting you," he said. "I'd like to talk with you again sometime."

"I look forward to it."

Tom put an arm around Laura's waist. A lifter pulsed up out of the floor, and he communed with it so that it supported them on up into the air; when they reached the ceiling, he spun a net so quickly they did not even pause but slid through boards, beams, insulation, space, rafters, tarpaper, and shingles.

They stood on the roof. "How did you do that?" Laura asked.

"I don't know." He had an idea that they had stepped sideways into the travel dimension and back out on the roof. But he wasn't sure.

"So ghostly! So perfect. Thank you, my love." She kissed him.

"Where do we go from here? Chuck it all? I've got a new suit. I'm happy. We could fly off to Mexico."

"What about Maggie?"

"Have you looked lately? She can take care of herself."

"What about Carroll?"

"I'm getting the feeling that you don't want to leave town yet."

"Maybe not," she said. They looked down at the people in the churchyard and parking lot; few had driven away. Most of the businesses in town had closed for the wedding. Tom saw a car come down the ramp from the interstate. He wondered what the driver wanted. Probably something that wouldn't be available until talk about the wedding had run out.

Father Wolfe came out of the church and peered up at them, an action that proved contagious. Jaimie waved from the front gate.

"What do you think? Notorious enough for you?" Tom asked.

Laura laughed. "I don't think I've destroyed my good girl image completely, but I don't know if I want to take the next step and grow horns and a tail. Let's go up."

He caught another lifter and they rose until the town dwindled to a dark triangle of cross-hatching nestled in the golden land beside the gray snake of highway and the much wider silver snake of river.

The day was cool and hazy, birdless except for some transient gulls come up the river from the sea, haunting the rest stop to the east and living off tourists' garbage. Tom and Laura stood on air. Far south he saw the trees around Chapel Hollow, a bulge of dark green and black and gold that erupted from the twisty meander of trees along the creek. Peregrine woke inside him and looked at the view, savoring it, telling Tom he had never been a very good flyer, though he was an air power. They watched waves rise from the ground. —This vision of yours opens worlds, said Peregrine. —I wish I knew where you got it. I pray your child has it.

They waited as a cold wind blew past them, fingering their hair and clothes without chilling them.

"This is what Maggie wants?" Laura said at last. "A kite's eye view?"

"I can give it to her now. Peregrine says there's a way. I just have to be more careful, and plan better. I must admit there's real pleasure in making everything tiny and looking down on it."

"Mmm." Another moment. "You think Trixie has any more cocoa?"

"Carroll bought some; I put it away."

"Let's go down there . . . of all the places I've ever

been, Trixie's kitchen feels most like home. Everything in my apartment in Portland is blue and white, the colors of air and distance. I don't even remember the bed being warm. Tom?''

''What, love?'' He guided them down slowly, using the invisibility Peregrine had taught him on their journey crossing the river.

''I don't feel the cold anymore. Is that something you did?''

''No. More gates opening, probably.'' They landed on Trixie's driveway with a faint jar, taking a step to steady themselves. ''How do you feel about that? Would you really want to turn your old teacher into a toad?''

''She was acting like one.''

''Was that typical behavior?'' he asked.

''No.'' Laura stared into a distance that wasn't there. ''She was my real teacher, Tom. When everybody at home kept trying to convince me I was worthless, she snuck me books and told me I had a gift. She taught me how to be curious and search for answers. She encouraged me to act, and she let me stay after school and help her with things. She made life bearable.'' She looked at him. ''I should have said thanks, instead of arguing with her.''

''I think she was having fun with you.''

''She was always tricky. She used to give us simple-sounding homework assignments, like write an essay on our family, and then she'd cull the statistics from the essays and give us a lesson on demographics—number of single parents, siblings, what the birth order was, how the sample in class matched with the community at large. She's a very weird woman.''

''I liked her. Did you really want to turn her into a toad?''

''I really wanted to turn Father Wolfe into a toad.''

''Now that you know you have powers, do you want to use them like Gwen does?''

''No!'' She took a step away from him and glared. ''I

wouldn't, even if I knew how! I just wanted to see what it felt like to act like everyone else in my family."

"How did it feel?"

"Familiar. Like I was someone else, but somebody I know really well. And don't like much." She turned and walked up the driveway. "I still don't see why *I* have to be the one who acts grown up all the time!" she yelled at him over her shoulder as she opened the kitchen door. Then, in a quieter voice, she said, "Oh. Sorry. Didn't know anybody was home."

Coming up behind her, Tom grinned at Michael and Alyssa, who sat at the table playing a card game with a layout he had never seen before. "There you are," he said. "We were looking for you to introduce you to Father Wolfe."

"Wasn't that ceremony torture enough?" asked Michael.

"I've never seen a *tanganar* wedding before," Alyssa said. "It was ugly, except for the flowers. It went on too long, and there weren't enough thanks, and they with a baby already."

"Well, I'm glad you left. We needed an excuse to leave too," said Laura. "And we left through the roof. So there." She stuck her tongue out at Michael.

He stuck his tongue out at her.

"Laura?" said Alyssa. "What was that you were saying about acting grown up?"

"Oh—" She glanced at Tom, who had moved past her and was getting instant cocoa out of a cupboard in the kitchen area. "Oh, I don't know. Maybe I'm just jealous. Tom keeps going off to take care of other people. Or—"

Tom leaned over so he could peer at her through the gap between the counter and the hanging cabinets.

"I wonder where you came from," Laura said to him. She came in and shut the door behind her. "Is this what you always do, Tom? Sweep in and take charge of wherever you are?"

"I never did it before I met you."

"You're saying I had something to do with it?" she asked.

"I don't know," said Tom. "There are a lot of things I never did before I met you. All connected to everything." He straightened, set mugs on the counter, filled the kettle with water, put it on a burner, and turned the burner on high. "I feel—I feel like I was only half alive until you walked into the bar."

"This is so romantic I may vomit," said Michael.

Tom came out of the kitchen alcove and leaned against the wall, his arms crossed over his chest. His gaze met Laura's. "Toad?" he said.

"Toad," she said.

"Why not try something creative, like a kangaroo or something?"

"Toad," she said.

"Will you do it, or shall I?"

"Well, I've never done it before. But—"

"Yes, about time you did your own spinning. Let me help you this first time." He went to her. Standing behind her, he put his arms over hers. "You imagine net spinning out of your fingers to encompass him," he said. "You did it before—spun a net around his hand, when you stopped him from casting at Trixie."

"Oh. Hmm. Net?"

"That's what I see. What did you think?"

"I didn't know."

"Wait a minute," said Michael. "Are you talking about transforming *me?*"

"Yep," said Tom.

"Don't be ridiculous! That's way out of her range. She's only a minor fire power."

"Net," Laura said.

"Uh-huh."

She flicked her fingers, working them back and forth. Tom saw blue threads striking out and clinging to Michael, eeling around him and knotting to each other. It looked different from when he did it—his nets usually spun together in air and then wrapped around people. Michael tried to slap the threads away, but they tightened around him until he couldn't move.

"Not so tight," Tom said. "You don't want to strangle him. Tell your net, 'Michael. Michael.' "

"Michael," she said, still spinning, and the net relaxed. Michael could move, but it clung to him like another skin.

"Enough net," Tom said. To his Othersight, Michael looked like a blue man. Laura stopped spinning. She snapped her fingers, severing the last threads, which wrapped around Michael.

"Now it's your net around him. You speak to it, and it'll turn him into whatever you like."

"Tom? Fayella never gave us any lessons like this. Where did you learn?"

"Part of it is how I see, and part of it is instruction from Peregrine."

"Bless the Presence," said Laura. She hesitated, staring at her younger brother, who looked shaken. Laura glanced at Alyssa. "Your permission, Sister?"

"To turn my husband into a toad?" said Alyssa. "For how long?"

"That depends."

Alyssa frowned. "Oh, very well. But I want him back soon."

"Toad, toad," Laura whispered to her net, and Michael shrank down to toad size. Tom saw a shadow of Michael's human form hovering over the small toad-shaped piece of himself. When Carroll had changed Tom into a jackass, where had the extra come from? Did everyone own bigger selves than they knew, with much of it residing sideways from them along some other axis?

The toad in the kitchen chair thrummed. Laura slid away from Tom and danced around the table. She touched the toad's head and laughed. Then she ran back and embraced Tom. "Okay! I did it! Now I can let go of it. How?"

"Tell your net, 'Michael. Michael.' "

"I don't dissolve my net? Fayella always said to clean up after our spells."

"Well . . . I never dissolve my nets."

"You just leave them there? Oh! 'Things seen and unseen.' Carroll. And he doesn't even hate you for it. But if I leave this on Michael . . ."

"Your choice."

"Take it off, please," said Alyssa.

"All right." Laura whispered "Michael" to her net until the toad changed back to himself, then pulled the net inside her. Tom watched it happen, not understanding: the net slid off Michael, flowed across the floor, enveloped Laura and sank into her.

"Weird," Tom said.

Michael touched his arms and face. "Oog. You did that good, Laura. How? How could a wingless learn to do that? What kind of powers do you have, Tom?"

Tom shook his head.

Laura said, "I was never really sick." She grinned.

A car pulled up outside. The teakettle whistled. "How many cups of cocoa?" Tom asked, and Bert walked in.

"I want one. Cocoa, Bert?" said Laura.

"Yep. Where'd everybody run off to? I saw you two rascals fly away, but when did Mr. Michael and Miss Alyssa leave, let alone Trixie and Maggie and Mr. Carroll?"

Tom stirred cocoa in three mugs and gave one each, still with spoons in them, to Bert and Laura. He kept the third for himself.

"That place made me edgy," Michael said.

"He dragged us off before I even had a chance to meet the bride and groom and admire the baby," said Alyssa.

"It's time for us to go home and report back to the elders," Michael said. "I mean, normally Alyssa and I would be on our Together Quest by now, but . . . I don't know if anyone at the Hollow has any idea of what's going on here, and I think it's important—maybe even as important as World War Two."

"What are you talking about?" asked Bert.

"All this mixing. The marriage—a landmark! We were sort of prepared because at first we all thought Tom and Laura were a mixed—but that's not it. Tom overpowers us, and that's not new. But Barney and Annis and the baby—"

He broke off as Trixie, Carroll, and Maggie came in, all with rosy cheeks, though Maggie's half-bare arms were smooth, un-goosebumped. Laura narrowed her eyes, studying the three people just in from the chill afternoon. Then she glanced at Tom. "Leftover nets?" she asked.

He nodded.

"Fetching," she muttered. He looked at her with wide eyes.

"—and if Carroll's going to stay in town, they should know that," Michael said. "They'll need to get Alex and Arthur to step into the hunting shoes. And we need to tell them we have friends in town so they'll leave you alone."

"Tell who what?" asked Trixie.

"The elders at the Hollow. Alyssa and I should go back home. We have all this news."

"And you don't understand half of it," said Carroll.

"What do you mean, Uncle?"

"You let the wedding proceed without questioning."

"So did you!"

"I questioned it; I knew it was sanctioned. I have a lot more background on these developments than you do, but Tom and Laura have the most information of all. Honored, would you agree to come back to the Hollow and offer news?"

"You talking to me, Carroll?" asked Tom.

Carroll nodded. He wore not a trace of a smile.

Tom looked at Laura. She nodded too. "Ask Peregrine," she said. "I think he plans to change things out there. He's been talking like he has plans. I don't know if we can leave on our own Together Quest without clearing this up, or at least making some attempt."

—Peregrine?

—For the sake of the Family, she is right. But I leave the decision up to you, Tommy. My most important work is your training; I will not force you to do anything.

"I thought you wanted me to take you away from all this," Tom said to Laura.

"I do, but I can wait. Maybe one more day. For—for Family."

"I don't want them doing to my *miksashi* what was done to us," said Carroll. "I don't know what it was; I just know it hurt, until I came here."

"Your *miksashi*, Uncle?" Michael asked.

"The boy Rupert," said Carroll. He grinned. "Barney asked me."

—*Miksashi*. Special guide and guardian. There is wisdom in that, Peregrine told Tom. —The better for our blood.

"All right," Tom said. "I'll go back and talk to them again. I don't promise anything. But this Fayella business . . ."

"Fayella?" Carroll looked at Maggie, who still had her arm through his.

"We talked about it after you left to get groceries this morning," said Michael. "The Presence thinks she may be—what was it you said?" he asked Tom.

"She rewards the dark disciplines and bypasses the light ones," said Laura.

"She unbalances everything. The faults at the Hollow may lie not with the blood, but with the teaching," Peregrine said. "The more I observe, the more I believe this. So many of your generation are cripples."

"But this stuff is not all new," said Trixie. "There's strange stories about the Hollow going back to the founding days. Some of them not so nice."

"Good mixed with bad," Peregrine said. "You speak of Mr. Israel and Mr. Jacob setting things to rights as best they could, and of aid during disasters."

"And Mr. Hal and Miss Laura are good souls, even if Mr. Hal got into mischief," said Bert.

"No," said Peregrine. "Designated cripples. They

made friends in town because they had few friends at home.''

Laura punched his arm. "Ow!" said Tom. "He's not just talking about power cripples, he's talking about emotional cripples too, understand? Carroll and Gwen didn't come out of this any better off than you, my love."

"Sorry. I forgot that if I punched him I'd hurt you."

"Okay, for now. We're going to have to work at this, I guess. Anyway, sure, I'll go out to the Hollow and talk to them. Anyone join me?"

"I will," said Carroll. "Maybe with a proper farewell, I can come back and change in peace."

"I will," said Michael. Alyssa nodded.

"I'll go, and do my own toads this time," Laura said.

"I'll go if you need me," said Maggie.

"No. Oh, no," said Carroll. "Somebody might hurt you."

She opened her hand to show him the silver seal in her palm.

"Oh," he said, taking her hand and touching the brand. "I forgot. Would we need you?"

"Who can tell?" said Tom.

"Hell, we'll all go, and scandalize 'em," said Trixie. "I'm game if Bert is."

"I'd like a chance to see the inside of that place, and this expedition sounds like it might get in and back out again," said Bert. "I've been puzzling over what it must be like out there for years. Those who visited to talk to the *Arkhos* never did come back with a very clear description."

"Now?" asked Tom, looking around the room. Everyone was still dressed up from the wedding.

"Now," Maggie said.

"Just coming up on suppertime," said Laura. "The important people will be in the kitchen great hall, where we met just after Purification, Tom."

"All right," Tom said. He already had loose nets around Carroll, Bert, Maggie, and Trixie. He flexed his hands and sent out sheets of silver net to envelop Michael, Alyssa, Laura, and himself. With Othersight he delighted in the vision of the beautiful silvery net as it settled around all of them, linking them to him. He sent a thought thread ahead to the kitchen, finding enough empty space for them to land, and pulled his whole family there.

"Hi," he said to a startled group of people eating soup. "We've come to talk." Behind him he felt the others gather closer, linking hands.

Chapter 21

With Othersight Tom could see the bright hazes that enveloped each of the people sitting at the kitchen table. More than twenty people sat there, each centered in his or her own net of colored light. The ceiling, too, was full of varied glows, some almost blindingly bright pinpoints of colored light, others diffuse trails of light beads or knots. Below, dimmer lightshadows moved among the seated ones; Tom blinked and saw the Henderson sisters, Chester, and a few other people dishing food onto plates, or clearing dishes. The kitchen cavern was full of the scent of spicy stir-fried meat and vegetables, with an underlay of woodsmoke from the open fireplace. Tom tried to remember his last meal and couldn't. He ignored his hunger and started sorting people out by appearance, remembering some of them only from the festivals.

"Hello," said Aunt Agatha. Candlelight made flickering reflections on her glasses. "Been fetchcasting?"

"Not exactly," said Tom.

"We brought news," Michael said.

Hal stood up, setting aside his napkin and knife and fork. "Beatrice," he said, studying Trixie. "No, I can't allow this. Not Beatrice or Bert as fetches. Who dared? May, stop them."

"Stop what?" asked Bert. Trixie stared at Fayella, who sat hunched in her dark green cape, her deep-set eyes shining. Fayella grinned, showing pointed teeth, and held up her fork with what looked like a child's hand pierced on its tines. Trixie gasped.

"No, Aunt," said Michael. He flicked fingers at Fayella, but she blocked his spell with ease. Alyssa snapped her fingers and the hand vanished, replaced by a carrot. Fayella laughed.

"We don't eat people," Carroll told Trixie. "It was illusion, Aunt."

"I don't know what to believe about the Nightwalker," said Trixie.

"Oh, best of my students, my precious one, whom are you calling Aunt?" Fayella asked Carroll, her voice low and musical.

Carroll's eyes widened. He went toward her, sleepwalking.

"What have they done to my boy?" Fayella asked. "Have they twisted you in the head? Come, let me heal and restore you." She rose, holding out her arms to Carroll.

"Stop it," said Maggie. "Shut up!" She ran and grabbed Carroll's arm. He turned on her, his eyes smoky and green. "Wake up, Carroll." She snapped her fingers in his face. He blinked. His brows drew together.

"So it speaks?" Fayella said. "We can remedy that." She twitched her hands, casting a quick, perfect spell at Maggie. Tom saw it, yellow and glistening, as it shot through the air. He used his still-present silver net to deflect it, but it struck and smoked and sputtered against his shield, eating at it; he felt pain in his hands, as if acid ate his palms.

—Peregrine!

—Change your casting to glass.

Tom imagined his net crystalline and smooth, like the bubble he had encased Carroll in not so long ago. The slime of Fayella's spell slid down it and ate a hole in the rock floor.

"Is this a test of power?" Hal asked in an angry voice. "No one has declared!"

"Cease this strife," said Aunt Agatha. She said it with a doubled edge to her voice that froze them all, reminding Tom of the voice Laura had used on him during the drive out to the Hollow. "Boy, explain the purpose of this visit," Agatha said to Tom.

"We came to offer information," Tom said.

"You brought strangers among us. Now we must own them."

"No," said Michael. "No, Aunt. That's part of our news. Annis married Barney today, a ceremony sanctioned. Sanctioned, Uncle?" He turned to Carroll.

Carroll nodded. "Sanctioned by Presences, and their child sealed to Locke. I am its *miksash*. It is named Rupert Locke, sign fire."

Conversation broke out among people at the table, their words climbing one another and striking echoes out of the stone around them.

"How could she wed filth?" Fayella demanded, her voice a knife that cut through all the others. "How could she pollute her womb with filth?" She spat on the floor, leaving a smoking splatter.

"The child is whole and perfect. I have seen it," said Carroll.

"You are all eroded, eaten from within," Fayella said. "Family, we must slice these limbs from the tree, cut the thread that binds the bones. These are diseased and threaten to infect us." Her voice was beautiful, with a golden undertone that carried absolute conviction. Tom felt sick.

—She uses the gift of mindshift, Peregrine said. —Can you make a shield against it? I have heard of such a shield, but never crafted one. It is called a truth strainer, a power of air. None of those alive in my day had such a strong voice as hers, so I never needed to learn the craft.

Tom put his hands near his ears, imagined he could craft nets that fit just over his ears and sifted out the lies, letting only the truth get through. He felt and sensed something happening. Whether it would work was another question.

Bert gripped Tom's shoulder. Tom glanced at him, saw him staring around the room and up at the ceiling. Tom looked at the Powers and Presences on the ceiling, saw that their numbers had grown, with more arriving every second. The pale Presences of ghosts were silently arriving, too, coming in through walls or emerging like breaths from the floor.

"Thus you pass judgment?" asked Aunt Agatha, her voice still hard-edged and formal.

"I declare it by all that is in me," Fayella said.

"Any seconds?" asked Agatha.

"Hear us, first hear us," said Michael.

Tom touched Laura's hand. "Do 'Seen and Unseen,' " he whispered.

Gwen stood, her chair scraping the floor behind her as she pushed it back. Her gaze met Tom's, and a smile flickered across her face. She opened her mouth.

Laura lifted her hand and made the first four signs with her thumb, the gestures expansive but controlled. The cavern flared with ghost fire, tall beings kindling into sight, glows and suns and lightsnakes scattered across the ceiling like stars and comets fallen too close to earth.

Maggie saw a ghost woman beside her, a compact silver-blue person in the garments of a long-gone age. "Sister, thy permission?" said the ghost. Maggie released Carroll's elbow and held her arms out, and Ianthe walked into her.

"I am Ianthe Bolte," said Ianthe, through Maggie, "of the fourteenth generation. I counsel you, descendants: let none of you act in haste, for you know not who or what stands trial tonight." She smoked free of Maggie and all the Presences began to wink out as Laura's spell wore off.

"Laura, when did you learn to cast like that?" May asked, her voice warm and laughing.

"May," said Aunt Agatha, "that's hardly the issue."

"It's the heart of the issue," Tom said.

"Stop his mouth," cried Fayella, "block his words. He is cancer."

"Whatever hurt you so badly?" Tom asked her.

"I was blind! I did not see it soon enough. I should have killed or confused you when I had the chance. You are destruction. You are corrosion. You are death to order. Family, cast him out before he infects the rest of us as he has these."

"You may speak in your own defense, Tom," said Aunt Agatha.

"She's right, though; I embody those things." He held out his hands, open. "I bring you change."

Hal hit the table with his open hand, making a slapping sound. "I charge that these proceedings have not been formalized."

"*Skaloosh plakna,*" said Michael. "I call the Powers and Presences to witness that I grant salt privilege to Bert Noone and Trixie Delarue."

"Thank the Powers that somebody in this family has sense," said May. "Never suspected it would be you, Michael!"

"It's a start," said Hal.

"We haven't finished supper yet," Perry said.

"Do not eat, do not drink," said Fayella. "Not while they are still here, unstratified. Do nothing to bind them to us when they are in this state of betrayal."

Jess stood. He looked at Fayella, then picked up his cup and plate and walked toward Laura. "I extend welcome, sister," he said, offering his dishes, which still held food and drink. Laura smiled at him and reached for the proffered plate and cup, but Fayella cast, and this time Tom wasn't prepared. Acid dropped down in a shower from the air, devoured plate, cup, and contents, then started on Jess's fingers. He cried out. Laura bridged the gap between them, taking his hands in hers and summoning healing energy.

When Jess's raw flesh had been repaired and glowed with new pink skin, Laura released Jess and stepped past him. Her eyes blazed. She said, "Aunt, you have no right to interdict me! I have not been cast out." She gestured toward the laden table and a bowl of stew flew to her outstretched hand. She dipped fingers in it and licked them. Then she walked to Maggie. "Take, eat: this is the life of our household and a covenant between us as equals and friends."

Maggie glanced at Carroll, who looked remote and sad. She turned to Laura. She dipped two fingers into the bowl and licked them. "Salt between us. Salt for peace. Salt for memory," she said.

"No!" Fayella screamed. "Ash and earth, no!" She gestured with both hands, her fingers performing an eerie and intricate dance, smooth as the cadence of a grandmother knitting. Tom saw streamers of yellow-green slime emerge from her fingertips; he stepped forward, glassing his shield, but in case that didn't work, he stepped in front of Laura and Maggie.

"Stop," said Agatha, her voice focused and tangible. Fayella's casting retracted into her hands, which she plunged into her cider mug. Steam rose. "Order," said Agatha. "Wait for recognition hereafter. This chaos cannot continue."

Carroll lifted a hand to shoulder height, index and middle fingers extended, the other two bent. Agatha nodded to him. "Status, Aunt. All are now shielded, by word and custom if not by casting. We come to tell you that things have changed in town. Annis married her fetch, the union sanctioned by Peregrine Bolte of the thirteenth generation, the issue *Ilmonish*. If salt is not enough, I declare these three people, Bert, Trixie, and Maggie, mine by right of combat. No one of you touches them or harms anything belonging to them unless you challenge and defeat me first. Furthermore, Maggie is sealed to Tom, and he is the only one here who *could* defeat me. Let there be no more breaking of bindings."

"I witness it," said Michael.

"Do any challenge?" Agatha asked.

Fayella hissed. Agatha stared at her and she subsided. "Carroll's information stands unchallenged," said Agatha. "Thank you, Carroll. Is that all?"

"No. I am living in town now, and I pass my service to Family to Perry, Alex, and Arthur, if they are willing."

"How can you separate from Family and live in town?" asked Agatha, her voice thawing into her normal tone. She sounded worried and sad.

"I have lessons to learn and little to offer."

"But we have contracted for Talitha Keye—"

"No," said Carroll. "Send her my regrets."

"But Carroll—"

"Miksash is the highest status I can aspire to, and I have achieved it, Aunt."

Perry stopped chewing on a sneaked heel of bread. Everyone sat silent, all motion suspended.

Agatha pushed back her chair and stood up. "I call conference," she said. Everyone, including the fetches, cleared dishes and utensils off the table. People stood up and retreated, fanning out around the edges of the kitchen. Carroll and Laura shooed the rest of Tom's contingent toward the kitchen area; Tom found himself standing beside the Henderson sisters, Delia, and Chester, with Maggie next to him. "Hi," he said, but they shook their heads and stared at the plates and bowls they held.

Agatha crooned and struck the rock floor with a stick, sang, and gestured. The regular table and benches sank level with the floor, which moved in low waves like a slow-motion sea. In place of the previous furniture, a round table with a hollow center appeared, ringed with rock stools.

"Presences, Powers, I call you, entreat you," she said in the other tongue; Peregrine translated for Tom. "Powers and Presences, bless us and aid us to see, hear, and think, to decide and to choose; give us the clarity to choose the right way; make clear the winding ways buried in hearts; help us to heal what is ailing or ill; help us to strengthen the good in our Family; and help us to listen to each with respect. By earth and by air, by fire and flood, by all force and objects, seen and unseen. By blood and by ties that bind us together, help us to seek for the truth and the right.'' People repeated the words with her. Then they all stood silent, feeling a strange thickening of air that was almost a sound, a pressure on the skin and in the ears. It touched and then lessened.

''All right,'' said Agatha in English. ''Thank you. All come and join me.'' She sat on one of the stools she had created, and people came to join her around the table, bringing the remnants of their meals with them. Tom waited, glancing at Delia, who touched Maggie's shoulder.

Maggie looked at her.

''Did you get away? Are you your own, or has Mr. Carroll recaptured you?'' whispered Delia.

''Mine,'' Maggie said. ''Mostly. You ready to leave yet?''

''No,'' said Delia softly. ''I've been here nearly sixty years; I was sixteen when Miss Leah took me, her so sick in childbirth with Miss May, and I helped raise the babies ever since. They're more real to me than my own family. I'm sure my mother is dead by now.''

Maggie touched her hand, then followed Carroll to the table, Tom trailing after. ''Have you eaten?'' Agatha asked the newcomers, and they shook their heads. ''Well, no harm in it now.'' She glanced at the business end of the kitchen. Chester came and handed out plates, napkins, and silver. ''Float whatever you want,'' said Agatha, gesturing toward stewpots, bowls of steaming vegetables, and plates of buttered bread people had brought back to the table.

''But Aunt,'' said Jess, ''not during conference! Never in the past three hundred years—''

''Thank you, Jess. I'm *Arkhos* now, and I've just changed that rule. First question. Why have these Presences gathered without our summoning them? Tom?''

—Peregrine?

—How did Bert perceive them?

—Don't confuse me with that just now. Help me, please. Why so many ghosts tonight?

—Ianthe and I summoned them to conference. It is time for an updwelling, a face-to-face confrontation with history . . .

"It is time for an updwelling," Peregrine said aloud.

"What?" said Agatha.

"An updwelling!" said Jess. "Spirits taking a hand in our affairs, an interest in us, teaching us. We haven't had an updwelling since the Old World." He blinked. "Spiritspeak. I need spiritspeak. Think of the treasures of history they hold. Damn!" He banged his fists on the table, then looked at his hands.

"Ancient? Please explain," said Agatha to Peregrine.

"We have slept too deeply, and let things slip too far out of balance. We have let this generation be poisoned. We must work toward a remedy before the Family frays any further."

"Have you traced the source of this poison, Honored? We have all noticed its effects, I think," said Agatha.

Carroll, Laura, Michael, Alyssa, Bert, Trixie, Maggie, and Tom looked at Fayella. "She spoke the truth about me," said Tom, "but she was describing herself."

"But—" Agatha began.

"How can you people take a woman too dangerous to let come into town, where we know you, and put her in charge of your children?" asked Trixie.

"Wait for recognition, Beatrice," said Agatha. "I recognize you."

"Miz Agatha, you remember what she did in 1940."

"No, Beatrice. I was in Southwater then, married to Charlie, and I lived down there till he died in '69. When I came back, Fayella was our teacher, and had been for more than a decade. Cousin Israel said she had a better command of the disciplines and forms than any other living member of the Family, and when the children passed *plakanesh* and she taught them, they were very capable.

Fayella is the only master of more than one sign in this generation, and she was eager to teach as her service.''

Trixie said, ''She taught 'em, Miz A. She taught 'em how to hurt each other and themselves. Tommy's ghost calls it crippling.''

''Ah ha,'' said May, in a ''Eureka'' voice.

Fayella sat thin-lipped, motionless. Her eyes could have started fires.

''How do you answer these accusations, Fayella?'' Agatha asked.

''I do not speak to trash. I do not listen to trash. I have heard nothing since conference was called.''

''Descendant!'' Peregrine said, his voice ringing against the rock walls, floor, and ceiling.

''I do not recognize you. I see only a hateful poisonous stranger who has deceived all the weaker members of my Family and will corrupt the fabric of the Way if allowed a voice. I alone resist. I expect to perish for it, but I will be vindicated in death.''

''Fayella!'' said Agatha.

—How can we answer that? Tom asked.

—Grant me the use of you and I will speak to her in the language of the Root.

—What? Wait, her hands—

Tom blinked, staring at the glow growing around Fayella's hands. She worked her fingers in her lap. No one else seemed to notice the searing light she was generating beneath the table except Bert, who squinted, then shielded his eyes with his hands.

—Oh, Thomas, let me—no, you must do it, I haven't the control—but you don't understand what she's doing— grant me the voice—

—Yours.

Peregrine cried, ''House! She spins the Great Unbinding!''

Everyone leapt up; many ran for the doors. Agatha turned on Fayella, grasped her arms, tugged at her, but Fayella only laughed and wept and worked her fingers.

"Before I let corruption take us, I will cleanse and purify you all," she whispered, her whisper strong as a desert wind.

—Stop her, Tom!

—How? What is it?

—She unknits the forces that hold together our shared reality, the castings that let us exist. Stop her or she will destroy the hall and everyone in it, and who knows what beyond.

—How!

Peregrine had no answers. Tom saw Presences gathering around Fayella, reaching out intangible limbs in an attempt to smother the searing light she was making. It pulled them apart and absorbed the pieces and grew brighter, a bright beyond white, a bright so strong it could melt the back walls of one's eyes. Tom closed his eyes and still saw it.

Laura. Maggie. Trixie, he thought, and then he cast aside all thought of them and went to work.

He wove the best, strongest net he had ever made, weaving steel and glass amongst the silver, reaching for everything he had learned since he met Laura: how to change another's shape so the other retained identity; how to slide past things without disrupting them or self; how to ride earth waves into the sky; how to spin threads to connect with a person or place and pull oneself there; how to speak with people from the past; how to perceive the lights of Presences and selves; but most of all, how all the world was bound to all the rest of the world, brothers to sisters, parents to children, children to parents, friends to friends, friends and enemies to each other, the healer and the hurt, the wanter and the desired, teacher and taught, victim and persecutor, lover and lover, observer and observed. Ties everywhere. He wove it all into his casting and sent his casting out to encompass Fayella.

From the core between her dancing fingers, light leaked out, curves and squiggles, colors and darkness, and wherever it touched, it melted and dissolved. Presences pressed against it, trying to block it, but it changed them instead, their light scattering and fading, their shapes dissipating. The air tasted thinner. Pencils of light strobed out to Tom's great tapestry of casting, and everywhere they touched, the threads frayed and untwisted. With a tearing pain that shook him, the net he had woven ripped to shreds and vanished in splinters of thread down into the vortex between her hands.

"No!" he said. "No!"

In the eerie destructive silence, Fayella sang as she untied the knots in the fabric of reality. Her voice sounded like a young girl's. "The water is wide, and I cannot get o'er," she sang. "Neither have I wings to fly . . ."

Tom walked toward her, eyes shut, pressing against a tide of heat that pulsed from the center of her casting. He felt sweat seeping out of his skin, only to evaporate immediately, leaving a kiss of cold that vanished in the onslaught of more heat. He smelled scorched rock and the sizzling of human hair. The rock table and chairs had melted into pooling puddles around Fayella, so that the floor he walked was liquid. Everyone else had gone beyond the range of his senses, except Laura and Maggie; when he glanced over his shoulder, opening his eyes a slit, he saw them wading blind after him into the rage of light. Their hair and clothes caught fire. "Go back," he screamed, surprised that his voice emerged at all, its loudness startling, though Fayella's spellcasting was silent. "Go back! Have a future! Save the child!"

At his words, Laura turned back, pulling Maggie with her.

Tom faced the heat of the sun and felt his brows and eyelashes flare, burn, and ash. His skin blistered.

Then he was close enough to embrace her, and he did, hugging her with the core of the unbinding pressed against his stomach; at least he stilled her busy fingers, though he could smell his own body cooking. The pain was a scream in his head that attacked his thoughts. Then the heat grew so strong that after a moment, he felt nothing at all. He reached for threads to tie the world back together with, and felt a sluggish response in the part of him that spun. Slender silver threads—he sent them out to snag whatever he could before the unbinding devoured them. He felt them take root in some of the presences, which still pressed in around them like a cocoon made of moths, fighting to press their hearts to the light.

And in the terrible silence of a world about to dissolve, he touched something else: Fayella still sang, though she had stopped spinning. "Build me a boat that can carry two, and both shall cross, my true love and I."

The unbinding ate its way up between them until it spun between his face and hers. Its light no longer burned so bright he could see the shadow of his skull with his eyes closed. He wondered if it were dying down, having unbound so much of the room and of their bodies.

Then it tugged at the fragile threads of thoughts and pulled his mind apart.

Tatters of Tom's and Fayella's memories unspun:

After midnight, he stood beside his cardboard suitcase at the bus station, with the cracked, fading picture of his mother, his last memento of her, in his shirt pocket where he always kept it. He felt as if his life before age nine would cease to exist when the picture turned to dust. The air was full of exhaust fumes and the scent of deep-fried food cooked hours earlier. As usual, he was waiting for new relatives to come pick him up. The last new relatives; he had worn all the others out somehow, though they never seemed to be able to tell him what he had done wrong. He knew it was his fault, but what was it? He had tried to stop doing everything he could think of that had bothered anyone before. Would he figure out what not to do before he upset Aunt Rosemary and Cousin Rafe? If he didn't, where would he go from here?

Fayella lay on her bed and stared at Cousin Alexander. His face was gold and peaches, his dark hair curled like a cherub's, and his eyes shone bluer than the sky after sunrise. He smiled at her and his smile raised shivers in her. He was coming closer to the age of the wall test. She imagined him breaking free of the rock, scattering it everywhere in an acclaim of his power and joy, stepping out ready to father children as beautiful as he was, turning to her, though she was only eight, saying he would save his precious seed for her; of course, she would pass the wall test when her time came. At eight, she had already passed the little *plakanesh,* and gifts had started to manifest themselves, granting her the earliest passage in Family history. Mistress of water and earth, two signs: nobody had been able to do that in three hundred and fifty years. Together she and beautiful Alexander would found a new dynasty.

"Of course you didn't mean to hurt him, Tommy." His mother touched his hair, then pulled him into her embrace, stroking his head and rocking. He rubbed his tears off on her sweater, smelling her perfume, which was like flowers that bloomed after dark. "Nobody ever means to hurt anything," she whispered, her hand patting his back again and again. He cried because he felt scared, and he felt scared because he knew she was, she had that gray color around her she got when something scared her. The color was in her eyes and in her voice. He cried because he could still feel the sting of the red scratches on his arms. And he cried because the cat wouldn't move or purr anymore, ever.

"No," said Fayella, but only to herself. Adults didn't like it when children said no. She watched the white sky-light descend to bathe Alexander and his promised bride, Gwenda Bolte. Presences and Powers blessed the union. Fayella had cleaned and purified herself before the ritual, like everyone else, but she knew a dark spot stained her unseen self no matter how hard she scrubbed, which prayers she prayed. This was wrong, wrong; how could the Presences and Powers betray her this way? Alexander was hers, and no *tanganar* Southwater Clan girl could claim him. He belonged to Fayella; hadn't they lain together in the grass on long spring nights, sipping Gramma Betsy's cinnamon wine, exploring each other's bodies and spinning their futures out of moonlight and mist? He was precious and perfect and promised to her.

She did not join in the thanksgiving casting that followed. She stood silent and blocked all the praise and joy from invading her; she cut the thread that binds the bones and set herself apart.

"What I want you to remember, honey," said Aunt Rosemary, waving her half-empty wine glass at Tom, "what I want you to remember is the best thing you can do is get forgotten. You want to work on that, Tommy, because once people start remembering you, they won't let you alone. You're too special. I used to be special too—not the same way you are; I was going to be an artist, a good one. I was so special I shone, and Jim found me, and he wanted me because I was special, and he locked me up in this house like treasure, and I haven't touched my paints since. Now, Rafe—well, he's special, but it's another kind of special. He's what everybody asks Santa for. He'll be all right. But nobody asked Santa for you, Tommy. You be careful."

Alexander's sister Cousin Scylla was spiteful and mean. And bossy? She wanted to tell everybody how to hold their forks, even adults. Curious? She went around ferreting out everybody's point of conception so she could do a figurement on them. She did starcasting and consulted auguries no one had addressed in ages. She had a pet Presence that answered her questions sometimes if she fed it crystallized ginger. She found out things about you you didn't know yourself, and certainly didn't want anyone else to know.

When Fayella woke to see drifts of silver and blue sparkles in the air above her, she knew she would find Scylla beside the bed when she rolled over. Only Scylla had mastered krifting; she was a whiz-bang at testing people to see where their potential lay. Fayella basked in a nest of her own warmth and stared up at the dancing points of light, charmed at first because of the strength and number of the sparkles, then slowly alarmed as she realized what the colors revealed.

No orange of earth or green of growing. No babies, ever. That most important part of her was dead.

She screamed. When her voice gave out, the scream went on and on in her head.

Uncle Jim's ghost showed up on Thanksgiving, when the house was warm from baking and smelled of turkey, fresh bread, and pumpkin pie. Tom watched Uncle Jim's ghost walk in through the closed kitchen door, sit at the head of the table, and reach for the ghost of the electric carving knife. Rafe came in then, carrying the turkey, and went to the head of the table. He sat on the ghost; neither seemed to notice the other. Rafe reached for the carving knife. In a weird ballet, the ghost's hand carved the turkey, Rafe's hand following each slice with unnerving precision, as if he had studied his father's every move in years past, memorized the classic turkey attack. Tom watched the hands follow one another. He felt dizzy. "I think I'm going to be sick," he told Aunt Rosemary, and ran from the room.

"Bad stuff in that boy," Tom heard Rafe say as the door closed behind him.

* * *

Had she killed Alexander? She must have. No one in the Family could die in such a stupid way; it must be her fault, even though she hadn't been present when he slipped down the cliffside and broke himself open. He was an earth power! How could a cliff hurt him?

Fayella hadn't been present, but she had been thinking curses at Gwenda ever since the wedding—wishing that the worst possible thing would happen to her, and earthing the curses in a mudball she had made with earth Gwenda had stepped on, mixed with Fayella's own spit and a few strands of Gwenda's hair. She had even put a splinter of crystal from one of the old hoard of Family snow crystals in the center of the ball, to add the stored power of the past to her curses.

It hadn't occurred to Fayella until too late that maybe the worst thing that could happen to Gwenda was Alexander's death.

Gwenda and Alexander had gone on their Together Quest into the wilderness, seeking conversation with spirits who could tell them a map of their lives. Gwenda returned weeping and alone, and some of the air sign people flew out to retrieve Alexander's remains so the Family could perform the proper blessings, praise, and unbindings on them, releasing his spirit so it could travel on or earth itself unhindered.

Uncle Matthew, sign earth, did the earth-shifting out in the forest to open a grave for Alexander, and asked the trees for feathery branches to lay him on.

Fayella stood beside the grave as Grampa Samuel summoned Presences to guide Alexander, and told the air everyone would miss him and had been blessed by his presence. Everyone joined in the closing song, thanks and grief and letting go.

Fayella's mouth made the words, but she did not listen to them. She smelled the raw, open earth, the blood-sap of fresh branches, the start of decay in Alexander. She stared at his beautiful face. It wore se-

renity like a mask. He must know something now she
had no notion of, something calm. As the others sang
a song to release him, she sang a binding song, silently, but putting all her power into it, tying a knot
in his still-present soul so it could not escape.

That night, long after the affirmation meal, when
all the house was asleep, she crept back out to the
forest and shifted aside the earth under which Uncle
Matthew had buried Alexander.

Dead, his body, too, was earth, and responded to
her gifts, rising from its resting place in a semblance
of life. She stared at it. She touched it. She hugged
it, and made it hug her back. She ignored what it
smelled like, summoning instead her memories of
Alexander, his touch, his movements, his warmth.
And she tugged on the knot she had tied to his soul,
inviting it to return to its vessel.

It fought her.

At first it was gentle, consoling; it whispered love
to her, and comfort.

She slapped it. "No," she said. "You betrayed
me. You chose her."

It pleaded with her, tried to reason with her, to tell
her that defying the decisions of the Presences and
Powers would have led to a miserable life for both of
them.

She pulled it down and locked it back in its body.
"Dead love to dead love," she whispered, pressing
herself against the length of his flesh, thinking warmth
into it, though it did not warm as much as it had
alive. "You're mine now," she whispered.

She kept it caged for almost two years, hidden out
in the forest. It fought and struggled, but she always
bested it. She only let it go when the last of its flesh
was gone; bones did not anchor it strongly enough.

When he had been successfully spirit-blind for so
long that he had come to believe it would be forever,

Tom found the boy in the janitor's closet at Arthur High. It was the end of a long day for Tom; the cafeteria basement had flooded, and he had spent several hours trying to fix it and finally resorting to a plumber, who came two hours after the time he said he'd come.

And still there were floors to mop, rest rooms to clean, wastebaskets to empty, windows to wash, walls to scrub.

When he had finished with that night's circuit, he kicked open the door into the janitor's closet on the third floor, and there was the boy, sitting in the enormous sink, shivering. Tom had turned down the thermostats in the buildings, leaving just enough heat in the chill, early winter night to keep the pipes from freezing again. After a shiver when he switched on the lights and realized his personal preserve had been invaded, Tom pushed the wheeled mop bucket ahead of him into the closet, annoyed at having to evict the boy from the sink before he could dump filthy mop water; how long would this take? He and Althea, his next-door neighbor, had planned an evening around take-out Chinese and the umpteenth run of *Casablanca* on television. He had already called her once to warn her he would be late. Now this.

"Who are you, and what do you want?" Tom asked.

The boy stared at him, eyes wide and unfocused. His dark hair was wet; strings of it twisted over his pale forehead and draggled down into his eyes. Tom took two steps closer. The boy wore a white shirt, so wet it was translucent, slicked against his thin arms and chest. Must be some kind of bully's victim, Tom decided.

"You must be freezing. Let me help you out of there." Tom advanced on the sink. The boy cowered.

"No, come on. You can't stay here. You might need to go to the hospital. How long have you been here?'' He looked at his watch. It was approaching ten o'clock. Tom reached out, and his hands closed on empty air where the boy's arms should have been.

''Oh, God,'' Tom said, staring at the boy who was not there. ''Oh, God.'' He had shut his eyes so carefully after that time at Mother Denver's, when he was fifteen and he realized the world was layered with ghosts, ages on ages of them, an atmosphere: when he had opened his eyes and seen them, clustered so thickly everywhere, clutching their fragments of personal history, he could not breathe for fear of inhaling them. To survive, he had closed his eyes again and prayed, breathing (was that an ancient hand slipping down his throat? did the hair of a long-dead woman brush against his nose? that musty smell—) and whispering, ''Don't let me see, don't let me see, don't let me see.'' He had drummed it into his head.

When he opened his eyes again, the ghosts had vanished, leaving Mother Denver's living room the same haven of plastic-covered furniture and plastic runners protecting the rug it had always been. He had hoped the ghosts were gone forever.

It had taken three more years of constant work to drum them out, though, and his school work had suffered, but he had gotten rid of them.

Until now, ten years later.

The boy's teeth chattered like the muffled click of chess pieces shaken in a locked box.

''Can you tell me what you need?'' Tom said to the boy in the sink.

The boy's wide eyes stared through him.

''If you can't tell me—'' Tom said, and waited, hearing the rattle of teeth.

''If you can't tell me—'' Tom lifted the mop bucket, a heavy galvanized steel receptacle with a lever-operated wringer on top and wheels underneath. One of the wheels swung on its caster, a frictiony metal-on-metal squeak. ''—I'm going to dump this and go home." He felt dizzy. These fragments of dead people always seemed to want something, and he had never been able to find out what and give it to them. His survival had depended on his ability to figure out what live people wanted, though he had never been very good at that, either.

The boy did nothing but shiver and stare. Tom closed his eyes and dumped the mop water into the sink. He imagined he heard a long, agonized scream. He opened his eyes. The boy had vanished.

Surfing on this tide of melting memories, Tom tried to slow down. He reached for anything, searching for anchors.

—Ring calls to ring.

He had thought he might never feel anything physical again, that the pain of burning from the unbinding had overloaded his receptors so they would never unblock—no future he could imagine had him lasting long enough for his nerves to heal, if nerves ever did heal. But in his left hand, shielded from the unbinding because he held it in the small of Fayella's back, he felt a fire that did not burn. The heat of a heart, necessary to life. He focused what rags of consciousness remained on that heat, leaving the memories behind.

Laura was there. Gold and blue, a lifeline, cool strength reaching out to link with him. An anchor. A stronghold.

—Spin.

He no longer knew who whispered to him, but he thought about spiders, twisting thread into beautiful symmetry, taming chaos with ordered nets that greeted the dawn, hung with globes of dew that caught and held cores of sunlight, and tiny images of the world. He spun, inviting Laura to spin with him. They cast threads out to each other, silver and gold, green and blue, twining together like the souls of mother and child. We bridge the gap. We are the bridge, and there is no gap.

Before his face, he sensed a slowing in what whirled in air.

—More.

From Laura's end he felt another color of thread coming, lavender and green, riding the back of one of Laura's golden weavings. Maggie. And then a vivid red-yellow presence cast silky lines to him. Carroll. Strong, fiery flickers of gray and yellow. Agatha. Tom took the ends and wove with them, a tapestry like the one he had fashioned earlier, but this time much stronger, augmented by the wills of others. From within him Peregrine offered threads of indigo and powder blue. More colored threads came to him and he meshed them in, Bert's deep grass green, Trixie's orange and pink, Michael's thick strong red, Alyssa's sky blue, others; colors he connected to people and others he did not recognize, some cast to him from living presences and some from dead ones, some from creatures of other species living in the nooks and crannies of the kitchen, some from the *tanganar,* but no time to stop for greetings. Time only to weave. He sensed the unbinding slowing in its manic counterclockwise spin, foiled by this tapestry of ties.

In the end even the rock of the kitchen walls, ordered from years of being shaped by minds, added its lava-orange strength to their work. The unbinding slowed, stopped, died within the compass of their binding-together.

He could hear his own ragged breathing, and Fayella's. His eyes seemed fused shut; either that, or they were already wide open and he could see nothing anyway. He thought perhaps he could let Fayella go now, but his arms did not respond to him. He remembered the air pockets in the lava that had covered Pompeii, shaped like the people molten rock had covered before heat turned them to ash. He and Fayella were frozen statues of disaster victims, and their breathing was just an illusion.

Hands reached into his nightmare and touched him,

familiar hands. He felt cool healing spread across his back.

After the work of trying to hold everything together, he decided it was time for him to fall apart. He let go of everything.

Chapter 22

—Maggie? May I come in?

Maggie lay on her back and looked up at another new ceiling, this one with a skylight somewhere way up through rock. Daylight came down the shaft, scrubbing a square of blanket white down near her feet. Beside her she heard sleeping breathing. Her cheeks were still sticky with dried tears she had been too tired last night to wash away, and she could smell her own sweat. Rank. The scent of smoke and fire was strong too. Suddenly a great choking flood of sadness swamped her, and she felt new tears form and head out for her ears. She turned her head enough to look toward the other person in the bed, and saw the back of someone's head, bristly with smudged, burned hair. After a moment she decided that it must be Laura's head.

—Maggie? May I come in?

—What? Who—Ianthe! Huh? How can you talk to me unless you're already in?

—I know I have trespassed, but it was the only way I could speak with you. May I stay?

Maggie rubbed her eyes with her fists. —As long as it's safe for me, she thought. Then she thought, *Must be the first time I've ever said* that *to someone who wants to use me.*

—Thank you. You are generous. Maggie, just now you

are our only conduit to those living, and we must speak to them. Will you be our voice?

—*Me?*

—Without Tom and Peregrine, you are the only one experienced enough.

Maggie lay back and laughed at being a voice for a whole tribe in a place where she had been voiceless.

—When you are ready, my question still begs an answer. Ianthe's thought was tinged with dry humor.

Beside Maggie, Laura groaned and sat up.

—Okay, Maggie thought. —What do we do first?

She felt strange strokings inside her, as if a feather brushed along her bones. —Food, my poor child! Do you know how few reserves remain here?

—I don't feel hungry.

—You are too far past hunger to feel it. I cannot remain in you when you are this depleted; you have no protection. Go, fetch food and force yourself to eat it. I will stay beside you.

Maggie sat up. Her clothes were scorched and flaking, some of the material burnt into her skin. It was the death of Pearl's graduation dress. Moaning, she pried fibers away. Whole patches of her skin burned and throbbed. When she couldn't stand the task anymore she got up on shaky legs and headed into the bathroom, pulling off everything she could, and went to stand under the shower's warm rain until she was pretty sure she was wearing her skin and nothing else. Most of her hair was burnt down to bristle. Her head itched and so did the places where her eyebrows used to be, and her skin hurt, even though the rain was gentle. She opened her mouth to the rain and swallowed water, which soothed her throat as it went down.

Laura was waiting when Maggie finally stepped out of the shower. She had brushed the ash off her head; she actually looked good with the equivalent of a crew cut. She held out her hands. "I've still got a little healing in me,'' she said. "I'm sorry I didn't give it to you last night.''

"Had other things on our minds.'' Maggie walked to her and closed her eyes, feeling the cool strength coming from Laura's hands, warming as it spread through her, taking away the burning. "Thanks,'' she said. "Gotta eat. Get strong.''

"Yes,'' said Laura. "I'll be right down. There are clothes in my wardrobe. Help yourself to any of them.'' She stepped into the shower.

The kitchen floor had sunk down about two feet, and its surface was pitted, ridged, cratered, and pooled, a picture of what the top of boiling water would look like if you could freeze it. The food preparation area was devastated, wood cupboards singed, metals smoke-darkened, all the hanging herbs crisped to shadows.

Maggie stood on the kitchen threshold, wearing a ceremonial white robe that must have fitted Laura when she was a head shorter, and now fitted Maggie. All Laura's shoes had been an inch too long for her. She didn't know if she wanted to chance bare feet on the ruptured floor, even though her feet were tough and calloused. The entry to the pantry looked relatively untouched; maybe there was still food there, but it was across the frozen cauldron of stone.

"*Wish* I could fly,'' she muttered. A hand touched her shoulder and she jumped as if shot.

"Sorry,'' said Carroll, looking down at her with his head tilted. He had all his hair. "Here.'' He held his arms out.

She bit her lip, remembering her first vision of him, just like this, holding out his arms, asking her if he could take her away, a light of appreciation in his green eyes. She had stepped into his arms unspeaking, and he had lifted her up into the air, a flight toward a new life, away from the old one, and for a moment she had believed dreams could come true.

She went to him and he picked her up. They drifted a couple feet above the floor across to the pantry's entrance. He set her down there and snapped glows and they looked around.

She went to the smoker and opened it, found jerked beef on the top rack, nibbled an edge of a piece and decided it was done. With the first salty vinegar taste, she discovered her hunger and sat down and ate, gnawing meat and swallowing without chewing much.

Carroll poked through containers, lifting lids and sniffing. "Apples," he said. "Want one?"

"Uh-huh," she said.

He fished a couple out of a barrel and came to sit down beside her. She handed him some jerky. After they had taken the edge off their hunger, Maggie said, "I'm on a mission from a ghost."

"What?" he said, and laughed.

"Laugh now," she said, "before she comes inside me and bosses you around. Ha!"

"What are you talking about?"

"You'll see." She grinned at him and went to the bread box. She pulled a heel off a loaf and dipped it into the butter crock, smearing it against the butter's surface, then went to one of the water barrels and scooped up a pitcher full of water. She rejoined Carroll on the floor, broke the bread, and handed him half. "Salt between us," she said.

"Thanks," he said.

Boot heels slapped on the floor outside, and then Laura came in. She was dressed in a white blouse, jeans, and cowboy boots. "Where's the licorice, Maggie, do you know?"

"In a box on the top shelf," Maggie said, pointing into the upper reaches of the room.

Laura held up her hands and the box came down to her. "Can't explain it, but I have this craving—"

"My ma used to say the body always knows what it wants when you're expecting, and that's when you learn to listen." Maggie ate about half her bread, sipped water, and felt she had had enough.

Laura lifted the top off the box and grabbed a handful of black licorice twists, then sent the box back. Carroll stared at her with narrowed eyes as she came over and perched on a barrel near them, pulling her legs up and sitting cross-legged.

"Expecting?" he said.

"Has it occurred to you yet that Fayella may have been twisting a lot more than our minds?" Laura asked him before she savagely bit the ends off six licorice twists at once.

"What do you mean?"

"Earth and water, Carroll. Know how many body systems that covers? Powers of generation, and . . ." She demolished licorice, then looked up, and sudden tears streaked down her cheeks. "The babies," she said. "The dead babies. Thank Powers Mom warded us all when we were little."

She jumped down. "I'm going to check on Tom."

"I'll come with you." Maggie got up, wishing the robe had pockets so she could stash some food. She joined Laura on the threshold of the pantry and stared at the floor again.

Laura stooped. "Climb on my back," she said.

"You sure? I—"

—Maggie?

—Ianthe! Come on in.

She felt the Presence settling into her. Under the nudge of Ianthe's explorations, she curled her toes and wiggled her fingers. "Rise," said Ianthe to Laura, who stood and stared at her with wide eyes.

"Maggie, do you still have your safeguards?" Laura said.

Ianthe gave her back her voice. "Uh-huh," she said. "She says I'm the only one who can spiritspeak right now, but she says she'll only stay as long as it's safe."

"Maggie?" said Carroll from behind her.

—Say hi, Maggie thought to Ianthe.

Ianthe turned and studied Carroll. "You are an earth power? Have you healing skill? Look to this wounded ground," she said, pointing to the floor.

"What?"

"Is it not a good servant, who has given years of service to the Family? The time has come to give back."

He stared at her with narrowed eyes for a long moment, then looked at the floor, frowning.

"That is my message," she said quietly. "The time has come for healing."

He sighed and went out to the center of the floor, kneeling in a clear spot and putting his hands against the ground.

After the Great Unbinding had been tamed to nothing the night before, Miranda Locke, eighty-two and still the best healer in the Hollow, had consulted with Michael, who was sign earth and had more energy left than Carroll. Under her direction he had built two incubators in the large cavern, bubbles in the rock that could hold a person each and would remain a constant temperature and tend as best they could to body needs. Weavers brought the softest cloth they had; one of the gardeners supplied cotton for softening the surface. Everybody who could heal had done what they could.

Laura looked into Tom's bubble, stared for a while at him, naked, pink, hairless, curled half under a sheet, lashless eyes closed, breathing sleep-slow. She reached into the warmth of his safeplace, touched his head. She sensed no response, not physically, and not in the new spectrum of the nonphysical she had been learning to perceive.

—Tom?

In the midst of weaving the night before she had realized that of course she could talk underneath. It was strange, as if she suddenly realized she had had two arms all along, when she'd been using only one.

—Tom? You in there somewhere?

After a long time, the thinnest thread of whisper responded: —Is it morning yet?

A laugh bubbled out of her, shocking her. —No! No. Go back to sleep, and get better.

First came the scents, sun-baked rock and clean sheets. Tom's stomach hurt; he felt like he had been kicked several times in the gut. He opened his eyes. The world swam in a haze. Everywhere he looked all he saw was a yellow-orange blur, until he glanced toward his hand, a pink blur, and saw he was half enmeshed with something else, a pale lavender blur. He blinked. Nothing got clearer, and Othersight did not kick in. He touched the lavender with hypersensitive fingertips, felt linen, fine rough texture like the lightest lick of a cat's tongue. Reaching out to the orange, he felt the rough grit of warm rock. He lay and listened to his own breathing; it was the only thing he could hear. It sounded soothing. He fell asleep again.

Somebody smelled like violets. He opened his eyes and looked up at what was probably a face, though it was too blurry for him to be certain. It was a tan-pink blur, with gray above it, and two dark spots where eyes should be. "Aunt Rose?" he asked, and the deep voice of a stranger came out of his mouth.

"Tom? Are you awake?"

"You're not Aunt Rosemary," he said. Listening to himself, he realized he was no longer thirteen, and the stranger's voice in his mouth was his own. "Is this a really weird dream?"

"No. Are you all right?"

"I can't . . . see very clearly. Aunt Agatha?"

"Yes."

"Wait." He lay and thought his way down to the tips of his toes, working upward along the arched bones of his feet. For a moment he contemplated his ankles, then moved on to consider the rest of his body piece by piece, rebuilding it in his mind, touching himself to assure himself that he existed. His stomach and his gut were still very tender, the muscles slack. He touched the top of his head and felt stubble, and found more on his chin.

"We did what we could to heal you, but that doesn't seem to include hair," said Agatha. "And we can tell eyes to heal, but we can't tell them what to see." Then she said, in a gentler voice, "How old are you?"

"Thirtee—thirty."

"Do you know where you are?"

He glanced up at the orange above him and realized he didn't have a clue. "Nope."

"What's the last thing you remember?"

He closed his eyes and took inventory. While he was trying to figure it out, though, a young voice answered. "I'm only eight but I can fly already, and I'm going into town! We're going to steal newspapers from Tycho's Pharmacy and find out about the war. A German submarine sank the *Lusitania*. Alexander says we have to care about what happens in the world beyond, but I'm not too sure. It doesn't have anything to do with us, does it?"

Silence answered the voice. After a moment, Agatha said, "Tom?"

"Yeah," he said.

"What was that?"

"Probably a ghost." Ghosts sometimes spoke through him, though he usually didn't admit it to people. He closed his eyes.

"Whose?"

"Fayella's," he whispered, then sat up, galvanized. His head brushed the ceiling but didn't bump it. "Aunt! The Unbinding?"

"Stopped. It's over. Do you remember?"

He pressed his hands to his chest, where his heart was hammering.

"We owe you a debt we probably can't repay," Agatha said. "We'll give you whatever we can. Is there anything you want right now?"

"Information," he said. "What happened to her?"

"She's asleep, and we're not letting her wake up. We haven't figured out what to do with her yet. Jess has been ferreting out information for us. Tommy, this thing went a lot deeper than any of us realized."

"What do you mean?"

"Are you ready for an extended discussion? This is the first time I've been sure your mind is still in there, though Laura told us two weeks ago you could think."

"Two weeks ago?" He blinked, frustrated by the blurry vision. "Aunt, where am I?"

"In the Hollow."

"Not a part I've seen before."

"Michael crafted this for you. It's a recovery room."

"Oh." He leaned back against the wall. It was warm and sandy against his back, and it gave a little. "Nice."

"Are you hungry?"

"No. Laura. You said Laura. Is she all right? Is Maggie all right? Are Bert and Trixie?"

"The living all survived. Ianthe says we have lost many Presences to the Unbinding."

"I remember," he whispered. They had pressed what little self they had into the light, trying to stop its spin, and instead it had splintered and fractured them.

"One Presence I'm worried about."

"Who?" asked Tom, then wondered what had become of Peregrine.

"Fayella. How can her ghost speak through you when she's still alive?"

"At the end, her memories got mixed up in mine. I don't think it's really a ghost."

"Oh, good. Wait. Does that mean you might act like her?"

He could hear the fear edging her voice, and it worried him. —Peregrine!

No response.

—Peregrine? Peregrine, please wake up.

"Tom?" said Agatha.

"What? Oh, no, no. Nothing like that. You said before

this went a lot deeper than you thought. What did you mean?''

''Jess found some diaries Scylla must have hidden, dating way back to when she and Fayella were girls. Scylla was worried about Fayella. She wrote a lot about her.''

''Fayella was in love with Scylla's brother Alexander.''

''What? How did you know?''

''More of the memory mix. Go on.''

''Scylla cast klish stones for Fayella and got skulls and snakesheads, sure portent of something gone wrong. But she doesn't seem to have warned anyone else about it. Scylla said Fayella did abominable things, and that she was trying to contain them, but then, all of a sudden, the diaries stopped talking about Fayella altogether. Jess reminded me of an old discipline, a minor unbinding, one of the tangles, which makes people forget you. We've been wondering how much Fayella practiced that one on all of us. Nobody alive in the Hollow remembered the Nightwalker story until Beatrice told it to us, and there's evidence that Beatrice is tangled about it, too.''

''There's things in my head that support what you say.''

''About what's in your head, Tom.''

''Yes?''

''Is Peregrine there?''

''I don't know. I haven't found him yet, but I haven't been awake long.''

''Are you tired?'' Her voice was instantly soothing.

''No. I need to see Laura soon, though.''

''Of course. I'll go get her. You look for Peregrine, all right?''

''Why?''

''His daughter is driving us crazy.''

When she was gone, Tom lay back down on soft floor and pulled the sheet up around him, closing his eyes. He realized he was tired after all. He focused all the energy he could dig up, and sent out a summons. —Peregrine?

For a long time he felt no response. He wondered if

Peregrine was one of the Presences who had been swallowed in the vortex of the Unbinding. Then came a faint stirring in his bones. —Tom? Are you alive?

—Yes. Are you?

Peregrine's laughter felt like the gentle skim of butterfly's wings on skin. —Not really. Not for a long time.

—Peregrine, if I die, what happens to you?

—I don't know. Just now I'm glad we don't have to worry yet.

—I guess we almost did. I've been asleep two weeks. And watch this.

Tom opened his eyes and looked around, at blurs.

—Hmm, said Peregrine. —Maybe we can heal it. Or perhaps you need spectacles. At least we have some vision, which is surprising, since we have stared into the heart of Oblivion.

—Tom?

—Huh? he thought. It was a new voice in his head. For a moment he was afraid it might be Fayella.

—You awake now? Is it morning?

No. Not Fayella. He had heard that voice before, but not since the day he drove Laura to the Hollow in the cab.

—I think I'm awake.

He looked toward the opening in the orange egg and saw a head-shaped blur. A moment later it was coming closer, followed by a blur that had to be a body. He pulled the sheet up over his head.

—What are you doing? she asked, lying down beside him and tugging at the sheet.

—I don't have any hair.

—Neither do I. It better not matter to you.

—It doesn't, since I can't see.

—That better be a joke.

She pulled the sheet down and put her arms around him. He hugged her tight, eyes closed, and wondered if he had finally found someone who wouldn't leave him when he got too strange.

After a long moment, he figured he couldn't get any

stranger than he was right now, and here she was, her arms warm around him, her mind snuggled beside his, her scent wild and enticing and familiar. The last guardian of his heart put down its shield, and he let Laura all the way in.

She laughed against his chest. —Anyway, she thought,— hiding in a sheet won't protect you from me. It's impossible to escape this Family. I know. I've tried.

RETURN TO AMBER...
THE ONE *REAL* WORLD, OF WHICH ALL OTHERS, INCLUDING EARTH, ARE BUT SHADOWS

ROGER ZELAZNY

The Triumphant conclusion of the Amber novels

PRINCE OF CHAOS   75502-5/$4.99 US/$5.99 Can

The Classic Amber Series

NINE PRINCES IN AMBER	01430-0/$4.50 US/$5.50 Can
THE GUNS OF AVALON	00083-0/$4.99 US/$5.99 Can
SIGN OF THE UNICORN	00031-9/$4.99 US/$5.99 Can
THE HAND OF OBERON	01664-8/$4.50 US/$5.50 Can
THE COURTS OF CHAOS	47175-2/$4.50 US/$5.50 Can
BLOOD OF AMBER	89636-2/$3.95 US/$4.95 Can
TRUMPS OF DOOM	89635-4/$3.95 US/$4.95 Can
SIGN OF CHAOS	89637-0/$3.95 US/$4.95 Can
KNIGHT OF SHADOWS	75501-7/$3.95 US/$4.95 Can